First Do No Harm

A Benjamin Davis Novel

A. TURK

Copyright © 2013 by Alan Turk

ISBN: 978-0-9892663-0-7

All rights reserved. No portion of this book may be reproduced, stored in a retrieval system, or transmitted in any form or by any means—electronic, mechanical, photocopy, recording, scanning, or other—except for brief quotations in critical reviews or articles, without the prior written permission of the publisher.

First Do No Harm is the first novel in the Benjamin Davis Series by author A. Turk. The story is a work of fiction, based upon and inspired by actual cases prepared and tried by Alan Turk, a prominent Nashville attorney. For the purposes of dramatic effect and to protect those involved in the underlying cases, the names of the parties have been changed, as have certain incidents, characters, and timelines. Certain characters may be composites, while others are entirely fictitious.

Cover design by Dan Swanson and book design by Elaine Lanmon. Cover photographs by Steve Lefkovitz.

Printed in the United States of America.

Special Edition

To Lisa,
I love you with all my heart;
you are my partner in life.

I am not I; thou art not he or she;
they are not they.

—Evelyn Waugh, *Brideshead Revisited* Author's Note

CHAPTER ONE

MESSAGE SENT

WEDNESDAY, SEPTEMBER 22, 1993

Benjamin Davis, like Nashville's historic Printer's Alley, was feeling and looking beaten down. At only thirty-eight, he was much younger than the Alley, a landmark for almost two hundred years. During the late nineteenth and early twentieth centuries, it formed the respectable center of the Christian publishing world, producing Bibles, pamphlets, and the classics. But during Prohibition, a dozen speakeasies sprang up, offering bathtub gin and illegal gambling.

Today the Alley houses the city's sleaziest clubs, where stripper poles have replaced the printing presses. Yet the same turquoise iron archway marks its entrance, and tourists still snap photos of loved ones standing under it. The mouth of the Alley is adjacent to the rear of old Steine's Department Store and the law office of Benjamin Abraham Davis Esquire.

The brick building housing his office was the only respectable edifice left on the Alley. The sign etched in stone above his entrance read "Steine's Department Store: Employees' Entrance Only." Most buildings bore neon signs of naked women, poker hands, or whisky bottles.

The building was empty at 6:00 a.m., and Davis relished the solitude. His daily morning routine afforded him a solid two hours of uninterrupted work. With neither the phones nor his staff to distract him, he could complete his daily dictation, thus freeing the rest of his day for meetings with clients, answering telephone calls, and going to court.

His office occupied the entire eighth floor, which had previously been the shoe department. Oak-framed, calf-high mirrors ran along the bottoms of the corridor walls, and as he glanced down, he noted that his black loafers could use a shine.

Just as he entered his office, the phone rang. When he picked up, he heard heavy breathing and then a click. He was glad it was a wrong number. He needed his morning cup of coffee before having to deal with anyone.

Davis placed his new calfskin briefcase on his secretary Bella's desk. Running his hand over the ultra-soft leather, he admired his gold-embossed initials, BAD. The briefcase was a recent gift from his brother for serving as his best man. It was beautiful, but even better it contained a check for $50,000 payable to Benjamin Davis.

On his way down the hall, he glanced in the mirror on the back of the kitchen door and frowned at his reflection. He'd gained twenty pounds in the last six months, and his potbelly was becoming more noticeable, despite his tailor's best efforts. Davis shook his head in disgust and wondered what he was doing to himself. The job was stressful, and he coped by eating.

Coffee cup in hand, he sat down at his desk covered with several piles of files. He had to get back to the Plainview cases. He glanced at a draft response in the Rosie Malone case and made notes in the margin. Rosie

Malone died unnecessarily at Plainview Community Hospital.

A firm knock at the door startled him. The knocking got louder and more persistent as he walked toward the door. "I'm coming. I'm coming." Annoyed by his visitor's impatience and the interruption of his morning's privacy, Davis was prepared to give the visitor a piece of his mind. But he didn't have the chance.

As he opened the door, the butt of a shotgun struck him square in the nose. He heard his nose break, and he felt blood spew from his nostrils. The blow staggered him, and it was all he could do to remain upright.

"What the fuck?" Davis yelled as he tasted blood.

Two men dressed in blue overalls burst in, and Davis knew he would never forget their faces. They looked like a modern-day Laurel and Hardy. Davis couldn't see but sensed the presence of a third man.

The thinner assailant didn't waste time. He smacked Davis across the face with the stock of his gun. The hammers of the shotgun caught flesh, cutting Davis's lips. The flow of blood increased to a spurting gusher. This blow knocked Davis off his feet, and he fell backward over an end table, shattering the new Waterford lamp his parents had given him for his birthday.

For a big man Hardy moved quickly, straddled Davis, and placed two-inch black electrical tape across Davis's mouth. Having his mouth taped and his nose broken made breathing difficult, and Davis slipped to the edge of consciousness. His sandy hair was a bit long for the 1990s, a throwback to the 1970s, and for good measure Hardy grabbed Davis's hair and banged his head on the floor.

Davis's thoughts drifted to the television westerns of

his childhood. John Wayne and Clint Eastwood knew how to take a punch. They would have fought back. Davis knew he wasn't the Duke or even Dirty Harry.

He lay on the carpet as Hardy began to kick him. Like a possum, Davis curled into a fetal position, praying for some respite. Out of the corner of his eye, he saw the third man leaning against Bella's desk, watching. He couldn't focus on the uninvolved observer because both Laurel and Hardy were now kicking him with their steel-toed boots, cracking his ribs. Then the fat Hardy thug used his heel to stomp on and dislocate Davis's left shoulder.

The thugs began to laugh, taking joy in the pain they were inflicting. Their laughs were the first sounds the bastards made. Davis was entirely at their mercy, and he was well aware that if they wanted him dead, he could do nothing to stop them. The thought of being completely helpless made Davis dizzy and nauseous at the same time. His mind drifted to his beautiful wife and his two adorable children. He desperately wanted to see them again.

Laurel and Hardy then turned to Bella's desk, grabbed papers, and scattered them around the room. Hardy picked up the calfskin briefcase and used it to strike Davis in the head. On the third blow, the brass lock cut Davis's cheek. As Hardy lifted the case to take another swing, Davis could see his own blood staining his new gift.

I'm no victim of a robbery, thought Davis.

The clang of Bella's file cabinet drawers opening and closing told him that they weren't searching for anything. Davis then understood the reason for this attack. These bastards were sending him a message: get out of Plainview. *Could I have avoided this if I had not met Dr. Laura Patel?*

Davis concentrated on staying alert. He heard something hit the floor next to him. It was his favorite family photo. His wife, Liza, and his two children, eight-year-old Caroline and five-year-old Jake, dressed in ski clothing were smiling up at him. Davis's twelve-year marriage was a solid one, and his wife had gotten used to his long hours and absences from the family—which of course didn't mean that she was happy for him to be gone so much.

The third man strode over and ground his heel onto the picture. As Davis heard the glass and picture frame shatter, he started to cry.

"Life's a very fragile thing," the third man muttered.

The third man bent down, lifting the briefcase. Davis noticed a T-rex dinosaur tattoo with fiery yellow eyes on the man's right forearm. T-rex brought the briefcase down hard, and Davis descended into darkness.

CHAPTER TWO

WRONGFUL DEATH

SUNDAY, FEBRUARY 2, 1992

(ABOUT NINETEEN MONTHS EARLIER)

On a raw February night, Dr. Laura Patel paused at the water fountain just outside the entrance to the critical care unit and took a long drink. She rubbed her eyes. It was almost midnight, and she was sixteen hours into a twenty-four-hour shift. Tomorrow was about to begin.

She missed her family and Saint Francis Hospital, where she did her residency in Saint Paul, Minnesota. She regretted moving to Tennessee and hated the administration of her new employer, Plainview Community Hospital.

Although Saint Francis was a Catholic institution, run by Sisters, Laura, who was a Hindu, had not felt alienated by the staff or the clergy. But here at Plainview Community Hospital she was an outcast. Her dark brown skin set her apart from Plainview's southern white medical staff, and her education and professional training only emphasized her differences.

Her specialty was in osteopathic medicine, while all the other physicians on staff were medical doctors. Her degree lent itself to conflict with medical doctors. Historically, there had always been a divide between DOs and MDs because the MDs felt superior. The American Medical Association for many years ran a very successful negative ad campaign against DOs targeting both the general public and its MD membership. In the United States the DOs image was tarnished and denigrated.

The ignorance of her colleagues didn't upset her, though. Laura thought the controversy made her strive to be a more holistic and better physician.

Laura started making her rounds in the critical care unit. No one was at the nurses' station. It was unheard of for the nurse and two techs to be away from their post at the same time. According to hospital policy, at least one medical professional was supposed to monitor patients at all times, with the only exception being a Code Blue.

She continued down the corridor, wondering where they'd gone. As she walked, she asked herself again why she had ever come to Plainview. She'd first been attracted to Tennessee by the hospital's generous compensation package. The hospital's two-year employment contract guaranteed a minimum salary of $5,000 a month and allowed her to generate additional income by developing her own private practice. The hospital also agreed to pay her office rent for the first two years. The medical staff of the hospital, after the bankruptcy, left town in disgrace, and Woody Douglas, the hospital's administrator, was on a mission to replenish the staff through attractive offers of employment.

Plainview not only offered a slower pace, allowing her to focus on her instantaneous family, but it was also close to Nashville, where Maggie, Laura's life partner, grew up. Maggie's family supported their same-sex relationship and loved the little girls. Laura and Maggie recently adopted two Chinese orphans, Kim and Lee.

I'm so glad that Maggie's parents and sisters embrace our family, Laura thought. *Our daughters need to be surrounded by loved ones.*

Laura's immigrant father was less understanding, and her American mother was embarrassed. Neither the Indian nor Hindu cultures tolerated homosexuality. Her father had come to this country during India's nonviolent, yet bloody, revolution for independence. Laura's father and his brother worked for their uncle, who managed a hotel in Minneapolis. Eventually, the brothers owned a Howard Johnson's franchise in West Fargo, North Dakota.

Growing up, Laura had been a source of great pride to her parents. She excelled academically and displayed a strong work ethic. However, her deeply religious family did not understand Laura's chosen lifestyle. Her parents had met Maggie only once, at Laura's graduation from A. T. Still University, the oldest DO program in the country. Her parents had not yet met her children, which saddened but didn't surprise her. *Maybe if I keep sending pictures of the girls, they'll ask to see them in person.*

A faint cry from down the hall broke into her thoughts: "Help, please help me."

Again, moments later, she heard moans for help and determined that the sounds were coming from room 303. She grabbed the chart off the desk at the nurses' station and walked to the ailing patient's room. The patient, an elderly woman, was obviously in pain.

Laura quickly read the admission notes in the chart:

> Rosemary "Rosie" Malone, age 67, admitted January 29th at 9:00 a.m. Diagnosis: multiple

gallstones and severe abdominal pain. Admitting physician: Dr. Lars Herman; Surgeon: Dr. Charles English.

The next page had the patient's physician orders. Gentamicin was a pretty powerful antibiotic, and it was being given in large doses. Dr. Herman must have suspected a severe infection. As she continued reading, her suspicions were confirmed. On February 1st at 9:00 a.m., Rosie Malone's temperature was 102.4. By 2:30 p.m. that day her temp had risen to 103.8.

Mrs. Malone's last recorded temp, at 9:30 that evening, had been 104.2. Clearly, the gentamicin wasn't working. During the January 31st procedure, the surgeon, Dr. English, had to have nicked the bowel. A third-year resident would have reached the same conclusion. Within a day after the surgery, Mrs. Malone had developed an infection that was currently traveling through her bloodstream. The patient was slowly but surely dying from septicemia as the infection was shutting down vital organs.

Laura checked the patient's drips and temperature. Mrs. Malone was getting a high dose of antibiotics and morphine, and the thermometer read 104.8. Sweating profusely, she was literally lying in a puddle of sweat.

"Help me, I'm burning up. I want my doctor. I need Dr. Herman, please," the patient whispered weakly.

Laura left the room and went directly to the nurses' station. Carole Black, RN, had returned to her post while Laura was with Mrs. Malone.

Wasting no time with pleasantries, Laura asked, "Where were you?"

Nurse Black looked annoyed. "Ladies' room. When nature calls, it must be answered."

Laura accepted the response but pushed forward. "What's the story on Rosie Malone?"

"Miss Rosie has been a regular around here. She was admitted in February 1990 for a heart attack. We almost lost her then. This is her third hospitalization since that time. Last week Dr. Herman diagnosed her with gallstones after she presented with abdominal pain. This was all confirmed by an ultrasound at Dr. Herman's office. On the 31st, Dr. English performed a laser procedure removing her gallbladder, but it appears he nicked something. Her white count is off the chart. I was about to retake her temp."

"Don't bother. I just took it—104.8. The gentamicin isn't working. We should try vancomycin or maybe alternate gentamicin and vancomycin. This patient is septic, and without a change in course, she'll die. You need to call Dr. Herman and get him here immediately. His patient is deteriorating quickly."

Without another word, Laura returned to room 303. Mrs. Malone had both cardiac and pulmonary history and needed to be referred to a cardiologist and a pulmonologist. She also needed an infectious disease specialist to address her septicemia. However, none of those specialists was on the hospital staff. Rosie Malone needed to be transferred to Nashville where she could get the care from the subspecialists she required.

Without warning, a hand was placed on Laura's shoulder, and she was spun around. She was face-to-face with Dr. Herman, who did not look at all happy.

"What the hell are you doing to my patient? Everything is under control."

Herman's antagonistic demeanor took her by surprise, but Laura immediately explained the situation: "I heard this patient calling for help, and there was no one at the nurses' station. Her temperature is over 104. It needs to be addressed, and at the very least, she needs her bedding changed. Despite the high dose of morphine, she's still in pain. It appears she's septic, and her systems are in distress—"

Herman cut her off. "Look, Doctor, this is *not* your concern. She's my patient. Thank you for your interest, but this is a complex case, and I don't need you second-guessing Dr. English and me. Now get out of my way so I can treat my patient."

She was astonished by Herman's words and attitude. One of her responsibilities as the physician on call was to check on all patients in the critical care unit and to provide treatment as needed. It was not unusual for the on-call physician to write orders for other doctors' patients.

"Doctor, I was just trying to care for your patient. She was in obvious distress and needed treatment."

"Well, I'm here now, so move on. I will not be second-guessed by a DO."

Laura realized she was getting nowhere with Herman. Whether it was the fact she was a woman or a doctor of osteopathic medicine, she couldn't be sure. All she knew is that he never liked her, and he certainly didn't respect her. She wondered if her sexual orientation created resentment as well or just made Herman feel threatened. She left the doctor with his patient and continued her rounds.

An hour later, she returned to the CCU. Nurse Black was seated at her desk, but Dr. Herman was nowhere in sight. Laura was somewhat concerned that Nurse Black would report patient follow-up to Herman. Nevertheless, she grabbed the Malone chart and walked into an empty room to read it undisturbed.

A more careful review of the surgical report confirmed what she and Nurse Black suspected. Dr. English had nicked the patient's bowel three days earlier during a laparoscopic gall-bladder surgery. Two days post-op, Mrs. Malone's fever spiked and continued to rise. Twelve minutes prior to Laura's return, Dr. Herman had taken the patient's temperature, and it was up to 105.1. Herman's physician note and order were illegible, but Laura made an educated guess about his intended course of treatment.

He increased her antibiotic dosage and her morphine, read Laura. *But this patient is at serious risk of cardiac arrest and is in severe pulmonary distress.* Although the morphine was helping to manage the pain, it was also shutting down the patient's systems. *To receive the necessary standard of care, Mrs. Malone should be transferred to either Vanderbilt Hospital or Saint Thomas Hospital in Nashville where specialists can treat her. What is Dr. Herman thinking? This patient will die if she remains at Plainview.*

Laura suddenly understood the real reason Mrs. Malone was not going anywhere: those bastards were trying to cover up their mistakes. By keeping Mrs. Malone at Plainview, Drs. Herman and English would be able to control and maintain the medical records, thus concealing their breach of the standard of care. *Those assholes!* She almost yelled out loud.

Laura felt ethically obligated to advocate for the transfer of Mrs. Malone, even though she was not the treating physician. She couldn't just let a human being die, nor could she let Herman get away with his deception.

She approached Nurse Black, who was checking the monitor of the patient in room 301. "Carole, I just looked in on Mrs. Malone in room 303. When are you scheduled to take her vitals again?"

"Dr. Herman ordered that they be taken every half hour, and if there is any deterioration of her condition, I'm to call him at his home. He's very concerned about her."

Laura decided to continue monitoring the situation. An hour and a half later she returned to the CCU and checked in with Nurse Black. Mrs. Malone's temp was at a constant 104.8, and her vitals were about the same. At least the temp had gone down slightly.

She went back to the critical care unit at 6:00 a.m. The patient's temp, taken just minutes before, was still 104.8. Laura decided to report Mrs. Malone's condition to Woody Douglas, the hospital administrator.

At 7:10, Laura walked into Douglas's office and asked his secretary if she could see him immediately. Douglas's secretary knocked and led Laura into his private office.

Woody Douglas was seen as a hero, taking Plainview Community Hospital from red to black under his leadership. This turnaround was quite an achievement. It had been difficult for Douglas to recruit doctors after the bankruptcy four years earlier, so the thirty-seven-year-old had definitely earned the huge golden trophy, prominently displayed on the corner of his desk, from an appreciative board.

"Hello, Dr. Patel. What can I do for you?" Douglas asked.

"Woody, we've got a serious situation in critical care. Rosie Malone has a temperature of almost 105, and there's no indication that it's going anywhere but up. She's septic and needs an infectious disease specialist. In addition, she has a cardiac and pulmonary history. She needs to be transferred to Nashville."

"Since you're here and reporting these concerns, I assume she's not your patient." Sitting back in his chair, he folded his hands on the giant desk. "Whose patient is she?"

"She's Dr. Herman's and Dr. English's patient."

"Have you discussed your concerns with either of them?"

"I tried to talk to Dr. Herman last night, but he abruptly told me to mind my own business."

"I suggest you let the treating physician handle the care."

"Woody, this patient is going to die if she's not transferred to Nashville. You've got to intervene," Laura insisted.

Douglas quickly responded, "I'm not a physician. I can't second-guess two members of our medical staff. You did what you could. You expressed your opinion to Herman, but he's the one who has to make the final medical call. It's hospital policy."

"Then I want to make a formal complaint."

"That's your prerogative, but it's against my advice. A formal complaint will go to committee at the next scheduled meeting. What will that accomplish, considering that it's two weeks from now? If she dies, you can file an incident report with the Morbidity Committee."

What a cold-hearted jerk! Laura seethed.

"It will be a little late, Woody. Mrs. Malone will be dead and buried by then. Is Dr. Kelly here? I want to bring this to his attention. Dr. Kelly, as the medical director of the hospital, can call an emergency meeting of the Executive Medical Committee. I have no alternative if you're going to sit on your hands and let this patient die."

"Dr. Kelly is on vacation out of town and won't be back until Thursday. You can take it up with him then."

"Rosie Malone will be dead by Thursday."

"Then Dr. Kelly won't need to call an emergency meeting, and the transfer of Mrs. Malone will be a moot point."

"I'll bring my formal complaint to you by tomorrow morning."

Laura was off all day Monday and could think of nothing but Mrs. Malone. She called the CCU nurses' station twice, learning that the poor woman's temperature was 105.1. Laura sat at her desk in her office and prepared the formal complaint against Drs. Herman and English for failing to transfer Rosie Malone to a better-equipped hospital. She kept her report simple, never questioning the surgery or its incompetent execution. She focused on the problem she could solve: getting the patient transferred. When she finished and reviewed it twice, she let Maggie read it. Both anticipated a huge backlash from the complaint.

First thing Tuesday morning Laura dropped off her formal complaint in Douglas's office. She planned on visiting Mrs. Malone in the CCU but made a quick U-turn when she saw Dr. Herman at the bedside. At 10:30 a.m. Laura returned to the CCU; the coast was clear. She went to the nurses' station and questioned the nurse on duty.

"How's Miss Rosie doing?"

"Not good at all. Her systems are shutting down."

Laura could barely keep from yelling. "Why in the world hasn't she been transferred to Vanderbilt or Saint Thomas?"

The nurse shook her head. "That's a question for Dr. Herman. He's calling the shots."

Laura looked in on the patient, now comatose. The more she thought about what was happening, the more pissed she got. Rosie Malone was about to die, and good medicine easily could have prevented her death. The system failed Rosie Malone. The system needed to be fixed.

The next evening, Laura learned that Rosie Malone, at the insistence of her daughter, Lorraine Burke, had finally been transferred to Saint Thomas by ambulance and had died on the table during emergency surgery. The Saint Thomas surgeon could not have done anything to save her at that point.

Dr. Lars Herman signed the death certificate on February 6th. He listed the cause of death as "cardiac arrest."

Laura wondered how many other patients would meet the same unhappy ending within the walls of Plainview.

CHAPTER THREE

VALENTINE'S DAY

FRIDAY, FEBRUARY 14, 1992

Dr. Herman pulled into his office parking lot just before 7:00 a.m. He loved everything German; he drove a German car and even looked Aryan. He had cropped blond hair and blue eyes. His skin was a pasty white. He was stockier and shorter than one would expect, at five feet seven inches, for a self-appointed German superman.

Getting out of the car, he removed a wrapped box from the backseat. When he entered the office reception area, three patients were already waiting. He smiled and said good morning to his first scheduled patient, Mrs. O'Malley. His receptionist, Sheila, was behind her desk drinking her second cup of coffee. Herman nodded to the other patients as Sheila gave him his morning charts.

He accepted the charts and handed Sheila the heart-shaped box of chocolates he had concealed behind his back. He then pulled a white envelope from his pocket and placed it on her desk.

In a deep voice that had a hint of a South American accent, he said, "Happy Valentine's Day, my dear. Thank you for all your good work. Please take your husband out to dinner, on me."

Sheila tore open the envelope to reveal a gift card

from Ruby Tuesday. She thanked him for the thoughtful gift and tucked the card in her purse before she ripped into the box of chocolates. Sheila was a large woman, weighing more than two hundred pounds. Herman doubted she would share the chocolates with waiting patients, let alone have leftovers to take home.

Herman grabbed a cup of coffee and entered his private office. He sat behind his mahogany desk and stared at the photos of his mother and his wife, Alice, before he got to work. He studied his appointment calendar and smiled. This would be a very busy and profitable day.

Sheila knocked on the door and waited for a response before leading Patricia O'Malley into the office. Dr. Herman oozed charm and confidence as his patient took a seat.

He reached into the glass candy canister on his desk, pulled out a pink heart candy with "Be Mine" written in faded red letters, and placed it in Mrs. O'Malley's palm.

Mrs. O'Malley chuckled nervously but kept her eyes glued on the manila folder sitting on the desk. Herman's lame attempt at humor had only marginally broken the ice.

"I have gone over your ultrasound results, and I'm afraid I have bad news."

He moved from behind his desk and pulled a chair next to hers. He put his arm around her shoulder and held her ultrasound film up to the light.

"Can you see those dark spots?"

Mrs. O'Malley nodded her head as tears formed in the corners of her eyes. Her body began to shake under his arm.

"Those dark shadows are gallstones. I'm afraid your gall-bladder is diseased and has produced these calcified foreign bodies. These objects in your abdomen are the culprits of your pain and indigestion. We're lucky we caught this in time. Left untreated, these could cause serious damage. One of these gallstones could get caught in your bile duct and your gallbladder could rupture. If we don't intervene now, it could lead to a life-threatening situation. I recommend the immediate removal of the gallstones and your gallbladder."

She wiped her eyes, and he could see the fear on her face.

"Am I going to die, Doctor? How can I live without my gallbladder? I thought my indigestion was getting better when I started drinking the pink stuff after every meal. The nerve medicine you gave me also seemed to help."

He patted her hand reassuringly. "Don't worry, Mrs. O'Malley. The gallbladder assists in digestion, but you can live a long and productive life without it. The Valium I prescribed will relax you, but that medicine can't cure your gallstones. That will require surgery."

"How much is this going to cost, Doctor? The county doesn't pay me much to drive a school bus."

"That's not a problem, dear. Your insurance company will pay for everything except your deductible. Sheila checked, and since it's still early in the year, you have $350 left of your $500 deductible. I'll waive that portion of my fee as a courtesy to you."

"Thank you, Doctor. That's very generous. Bless you."

"Here's a renewal prescription for your Valium. Remember, I only want you taking them after work. The label specifically warns you not to take them and operate heavy equipment. We don't want you taking them and driving your school bus. You need to be alert, not relaxed, when you're driving those kids around."

She let out a deep breath and gave Dr. Herman a hug. She was glad he renewed her nerve medicine. It made her feel so much better.

"Will the surgery hurt? You know I don't tolerate pain real good."

"You won't feel a thing. After the surgery, I'll prescribe a powerful pain medicine that will keep you comfortable."

He knew Mrs. O'Malley was sold. She would follow his advice unquestionably.

"I took the liberty of scheduling an appointment for you with Dr. Charles English. He's the general surgeon upstairs and will confirm my diagnosis that surgery is your best option. Please take your ultrasound upstairs to him for review."

"I don't want another doctor. Why can't you perform the surgery?"

"I'm not a general surgeon. But I'll be there to oversee your recovery at the hospital. Don't worry. Dr. English is an excellent surgeon. I send all my patients to him."

"Can this wait until summer? I can't afford to miss much work."

"I wouldn't recommend that. However, you won't be off your feet very long. Dr. English is the only doctor in Plains County who can perform the surgery laparoscopically. Any other doctor would need to make an eight-inch incision across your belly to remove the gallbladder. Under those circumstances, you would be out of work for two, almost three, weeks. Dr. English will make only two small holes, each about the size of a dime. In one hole, he will insert a small camera, which will let him see inside you. In the other hole, he'll use a tiny laser to blast the stones and gallbladder into small pieces that your body will then absorb. With Dr. English's method, you'll be in the hospital one day, and you'll be back to work within three."

She was obviously relieved. Three weeks off work was more than she could financially handle. She thanked him and went upstairs to see Dr. English.

Herman owned the office building in which he practiced. He purchased the three-story building in 1990, when he first arrived in Plainview. Unlike most doctors, he was an exceptional businessman, capitalizing on all possible revenue sources. He knew it was smarter to own rather than to lease. His modest $20,000 down payment more than paid for itself. He borrowed the balance from the local bank, and the hospital guaranteed the loan. Herman was proud of the sharp deal he brokered.

His office occupied the first floor and operated virtually rent-free. His mortgage payment was covered by the rent generated from his tenants, Dr. Charles English, the general surgeon on the second floor, and an OB-GYN on the third floor. The hospital cosigned for those two doctors' lease payments, minimizing Herman's risk.

Putting a call in to Woody Douglas, Herman wanted to review the terms of the lease renewals for his tenants.

Woody himself answered the phone. "Lars, how are you doing? How's business?"

"Couldn't be better. This ultrasound machine is a cash cow. I'm thinking of getting another machine and hiring an operator, business is so good." He only had two hands, and he didn't like leaving money on the table. "I just had a consult with a patient and diagnosed her with gallstones. I just sent her upstairs for a consult with Charlie. He'll probably be scheduling her for surgery next week. It's the perfect assembly line. I diagnose them, he cuts them, and we all make money."

The conversation turned to the leases. Woody was unhappy about the terms, especially the rent increases. "I'm the one who set you up with both doctors. I know you're getting a referral fee from them, Lars."

My business relationships are none of your business. The hospital is benefiting financially from this arrangement, as are you personally, thought Herman. He replied, "I'm the reason your income's doubled. My ultrasound makes a lot of money for your hospital. It's your job to make sure your pathology department keeps backing up my diagnoses of stones. Now just sign the goddamned leases, and let's move on."

Next he asked Douglas about Patel's formal complaint concerning Herman's care of Rosie Malone. The report had just come in, and the charges had been dismissed with no criticism of Dr. Herman or Dr. English. The findings concluded that during surgery, Dr. English had "inadvertently injured the patient's bowel," but that the "informed consent signed by Mrs. Malone had acknowledged that surgical problems, including puncture of the bowels and internal bleeding, were known risks of the procedure." The Executive Committee report further stated that "the failure to transfer the patient to Saint Thomas until February 5th at 6:00 p.m. was within the standard of care because the patient was not stable and transport in an unstable condition had inherent risks." The report concluded that

Dr. Herman, the treating physician, was "in the best position to evaluate whether to transfer the patient and that Dr. Herman used his best medical judgment."

The rest of the day went like clockwork. Herman performed seven ultrasounds, at $1,500 a pop. He ended the day at six o'clock, earlier than usual, and hurried home to take his beautiful wife, Alice, out for a Valentine's Day dinner.

Alice was waiting by the door when her tired husband walked in. She threw her arms around him before he could even take his coat off. She could feel the exhaustion in his body but knew his weariness was not the result of a long day at the office. Valentine's Day was always a difficult holiday, but usually Lars masked the sadness.

Valentine's Day was an annual reminder of Lars's mother, Margot. It was the day she was horribly disfigured during the firebombing of Dresden in 1945. It was also the day of his father's death. He was one of the many German soldiers killed in that horrific air raid. Valentine's Day was never a celebration in the Herman household; it was a day of remembrance. Every year of his childhood, his mother took him to the beautiful Iguazu Falls near their home in Misiones, Argentina.

After a few minutes of chitchat about the day, Lars turned to Alice and asked, "Will you be my valentine?"

"Who else would be, Sheila?"

They laughed at the thought.

"Seriously, you're the only woman who's ever loved me, other than my mother," Lars said.

"I wish I had met her. From what you've told me she was an incredible person and a great doctor. She would be very proud of you, Lars."

"I wish she had seen me pass the FLEX exam and seen our dream came true. All she got to see was how hard I struggled."

He started up the stairs and noticed a rectangular-shaped shipping crate on the landing. "What's this?"

"It's from Argentina. The return address is Uncle Wilhelm's."

Lars got a hammer and carefully opened the crate. As he suspected, it was a painting. He read the note out loud:

Dearest Nephew,

I hope my note finds both you and Alice doing well on this Valentine's Day. It has been forty-seven years since that tragic day when you lost your father, and your mother's hospital was destroyed and she was injured. She's gone but not forgotten by either of us.

I have enclosed a Renoir titled *La Femme au Puits*. I picked it up from an old Parisian Jew in 1942. It was one of the first pieces I acquired for my private collection. He's been dead for almost fifty years, so he won't mind my gifting it to you. If you decide to sell it, be careful. Use the sources I previously provided you.

I will love and remember your mother, my dear sister, until the day I die.

Love,

Uncle Wilhelm

Lars began to cry. Although Alice made dinner reservations at their favorite Italian restaurant in Nashville, she went to the kitchen to take two steaks out of the refrigerator. There would be no restaurant visit tonight.

CHAPTER FOUR

THE HOOK

FRIDAY, MARCH 6, 1992

Benjamin Abraham Davis was not a native Nashvillian. He was a nice Jewish boy, born in Brooklyn, New York, who grew up on Long Island, but he left New York when he was eighteen years old. Nashville had been his home for almost twenty years now. He had come to the city to get his law degree and a master's degree in business from Vanderbilt University but stayed after meeting his wife and his boss, Morty Steine. He was a Yankee, proud of his distinct New York accent. Davis used the cachet of his accent to his advantage by charming his clients. His charm first won over Morty.

Davis was a second-semester punk law student when he applied for a clerkship at Morty Steine's office. To that point, the cigar-smoking Steine was a lone wolf, practicing solo, with the help of his middle-aged secretary, Bella Rosario. Despite its size, the Steine law firm had achieved national prominence, with Morty representing many celebrities, specifically country music artists and songwriters.

Davis worked diligently with Morty, learning from him, benefiting from his guidance, and ultimately earning his respect and a partnership. Davis became the son that Morty and his wife, Goldie, never had.

However, he was smothered professionally by Morty. Despite Davis's hard work and dedication, Morty got the credit, not only in the eyes of the clients but in Davis's eyes as well. Davis felt a twinge of jealousy enhanced by his strong need for recognition.

After working together for almost twenty years, as he explained to his protégé, seventy-two-year-old Morty was retiring to spend as much time as possible with his beloved Goldie, who was dying from stage IV ovarian cancer. Whatever time she had left, he wanted to be by her side. She needed him, Morty confided to Davis, and he knew his clients would be in good hands. He would, however, work a few hours a couple of days a week until he finished up two pending cases.

Davis was confident that the clients would get excellent service from him, but he was concerned that because of Morty's charisma and dominance, the clients might elect to go elsewhere for their confidential and personal legal advice. Davis felt he needed Morty's unconditional endorsement so that the firm's business would transfer effortlessly. The clients knew Davis and were familiar with his work, but they loved Morty.

Yesterday was Morty's last full day at the firm, and tonight Davis and others would honor him for his contribution to the law and to the community. Davis was throwing Morty a retirement party at Hillwood Country Club, where Davis was a member. The club was within walking distance of Davis's house, although he never had time to play golf. Living in Hillwood, in West Nashville, was not as prestigious as living in Belle Meade, but it was a well-respected neighborhood.

Davis had invited almost three hundred clients, politicians, and members of the Bar and judiciary.

Beyond honoring Morty, it was also Davis's coming out party from under the shadow of his friend and mentor. He needed to impress the firm's clientele.

Davis had flown in a very special toastmaster, retired United States Supreme Court Justice Thurgood Marshall. Morty and Marshall fought shoulder-to-shoulder for equality and civil rights in the fifties when Marshall was the general counsel for the NAACP.

Liza and Davis picked up the Steines at their farm, Squeeze Bottom, and drove them to the party. Liza, a registered nurse, volunteered to keep an eye on Goldie, who was very frail. As Davis glanced in the rearview mirror, he saw her wince in pain. Tonight was going to be difficult for this extremely sick and brave woman, but Goldie insisted on being there to join others in honoring her husband of forty-four years.

As they entered the club, Liza took Goldie to one side and found her a place to sit so she wouldn't be trampled by the dozens of well-wishers who converged on Morty. Morty acknowledged the accolades of his guests but made a beeline to shake hands with his old friend Justice Marshall, who was standing in the corner, drink in hand.

The open bar flowed, and all enjoyed the food. About an hour into the party, Justice Marshall made a short speech and described Morty as "not only a great lawyer, but one of the greatest men I've ever known. Morty didn't use his God-given talent to just make money and benefit his clients. Rather, he made a significant difference in this world." Marshall actually got a little emotional and thanked Morty for their fifty-year friendship.

Even Davis was impressed by how much Marshall

recognized the old man. Davis thought, *It has been an honor to be a part of Morty's legal career, even a small part.*

After Marshall spoke, Dolly Parton, whom Morty had represented for more than thirty years, climbed onto his lap and sang "I Will Always Love You." It brought the house down.

After Miss Dolly kissed the top of Morty's balding head, the old orator stood and addressed the crowd. He thanked Justice Marshall for his kind words and Miss Dolly for her beautiful song: "I've enjoyed my legal career, representing some of you and doing battle with others."

Morty specifically recognized several prominent politicians, including two United States congressmen and two Tennessee Supreme Court justices. The room was filled with a who's who of the state of Tennessee for the last fifty years.

"I've loved one woman my entire life, the still beautiful Goldie. We married in 1948, and she's been my partner in life ever since."

He regaled the crowd with their story. Morty stared only at Goldie as he recounted the day they met at Steine's Department Store, she a salesclerk and Morty a young lawyer, a World War II veteran, and the owner's son to boot. People could almost picture the tall, handsome man with curly black hair as he stood before them. Now slightly stooped, Morty had only a fringe of gray.

The guests laughed as Morty told them all about what a good team he and Goldie made. "But I knew who the boss was," Morty added with a grin. "If you corner her, she'll tell you that I like to think I'm calling the shots in our partnership, but that's not the truth. She just lets me think I'm in control," he said.

Looking at the tears streaming down Goldie's face, Morty blew her a kiss before turning to Davis.

"Well, in my professional life, I've only had one partner: Ben Davis. He and I have been together since 1975, and like Goldie, he's figured out that it's easier to plant one of his ideas in my head, let me call it my own, and let me take credit for it. He's been doing that for years, and I've let him because I enjoy taking the bow. But it's time to give credit where credit is due. I toast my friend, my partner, and a great lawyer, Ben Davis. Thank you for this memorable evening."

The open bar remained open, but the evening began to wind down as judges and politicians left the club severely under the influence.

Liza informed her husband that she would be giving Morty and Goldie a ride home and that Sammie Davis, their niece, was his ride. Davis and Sammie needed to remain until the forty or so diehards at the bar and at tables decided to leave.

As Davis watched Liza rounding up Morty and Goldie, Bradley Littleton approached him. With urgency in his voice, Littleton said, "Ben, I've got to talk to you immediately."

"I can't now, Brad, I'm busy. I'm about to sit down with the manager to go over the bill. Call me at the office on Monday."

"This can't wait. Pay the bill. I'll wait over there, and then we can talk." Littleton pointed to a table in the corner.

"Brad, I'm sure Bella can fit you in sometime on Monday afternoon."

"This can't wait. Take care of the bill, and we'll talk."

What a pain in the ass, Davis thought. *Why the hell was Littleton even invited to the party?* Davis couldn't remember Littleton's name on the guest list, and he wondered if the son of a bitch crashed the party. He decided to ask Bella about it.

Davis walked over to his niece, who was dressed in a midnight blue strapless evening gown that complemented her blue eyes. Normally, she wore her hair in a long ponytail, but for this special occasion, it was up, showing off her exquisite tanned neck and shoulders. She was the most beautiful woman in the room, but that didn't prevent Davis from feeling a little burdened by her. Sammie was in Nashville, working for him out of pure nepotism. If it wasn't for her grandmother's influence with her son, Sammie would be unemployed. A Jewish mother's guilt was a powerful thing.

"Brad, this is my niece and paralegal, Sammie Davis." Davis then moved closer to the manager as he finished giving orders to his staff.

While they waited on Davis to return, Sammie told Littleton that she had been working in Nashville for only three weeks. She was living in the loft above Davis's office. Her father, George, was Mr. Davis's older brother, and her parents divorced when she was five. She had grown up with her mother in Miami, and she spent summers with Davis's parents in Woodbury, Long Island.

She also told him that she was a graduate of the University of Florida and a recent graduate of a paralegal program. But these qualifications didn't impress her uncle, who thought she had no practical or life experience.

"Sammie Davis, are you a Jr.?" Littleton asked with a smile.

She shrugged. "My mother has a twisted sense of humor; she loved the Rat Pack."

After Davis wrote a check for just under $10,000 to the club manager, he strode over to the table where Sammie and Littleton were waiting. *It was an expensive night, but well worth it,* he thought.

He sat down and couldn't help noticing Littleton's straight-forward gaze at his twenty-four-year-old niece. "Brad, do you mind if my paralegal sits in on this meeting? Sammie is shadowing me to gain experience."

"It will be a pleasure. She obviously got the looks in the family."

Davis didn't like the way that Littleton was almost leering at Sammie, but that reaction was typical. He had seen how men looked at her, almost smacking their lips. He didn't care for Littleton before this display, and now he just wanted to get the conversation over with.

Bradley Littleton was about fifty, more than ten years Davis's senior. Littleton was short and weighed about two hundred and fifty pounds. Davis was about the same weight, but at six foot two with the broad frame of a football player, he towered over Littleton and carried his weight better. Davis met Littleton four years earlier when they represented co-defendants in a contract dispute. Davis defended the case to trial and received a defendant's verdict, while Littleton settled with the plaintiff immediately prior to trial. Davis's client got off with paying only legal fees while Littleton's client paid a significant settlement and even greater legal fees.

Littleton seemed to attract profitable clients. He had a network of stooges who directed family, friends, and innocent strangers to him for representation and legal advice. Davis wondered whether Littleton compensated his bird dogs because any payments to non-lawyers would be unethical fee splitting. Littleton had a good bedside manner and appeared more competent than he really was.

Davis sighed. "Brad, it's late and I'm tired. What can't wait till Monday?"

"I need your help. I've stumbled onto a great opportunity. There are these two incompetent doctors in Plains County. One's a family practitioner, and the other's a surgeon. They've been terrorizing an entire community. Do you know where Plainview is?"

"Yes. It's about thirty miles south of Hewes City. Plainview is the county seat of Plains County."

Littleton described a string of potential medical malpractice cases that occurred over the last year at Plainview Community Hospital. He said that a conspiracy involved unnecessary laparoscopic gallbladder surgeries. According to him the co-conspirators, Dr. Lars Herman and Dr. Charles English, were corroborating each other's false diagnoses and removing healthy gall-bladders. Littleton was very critical of the hospital for allowing Herman and English to continue to admit patients and perform surgeries, even after receiving multiple incident reports. He also blamed the hospital for ignoring this clear pattern of unnecessary surgeries. According to Littleton, the hospital remained silent because the doctors were the hospital's highest earners.

Davis listened carefully. He knew how to try a medical malpractice lawsuit, boasting that he'd tried twelve but never lost one yet.

After hearing Davis's track record, Littleton could no longer remain silent. "Ben, that's why you're the man for this job. The defendants will be scared shitless when they hear you're representing the other side."

Davis was not taken in by Littleton's flattery. "Brad, how do you know all this? Have you met with any of the clients? Have you gotten signed medical authorizations? Have you reviewed medical records?"

Littleton shook his head. "There's been a recent death at the hospital. The patient died unnecessarily. The nursing staff is upset, and a physician on staff, Dr. Laura Patel, even made a formal complaint. She got sideways with the administration for reporting English and Herman for malpractice and unnecessary surgeries. The Executive Medical Committee took her information but didn't investigate."

Davis was skeptical. "This doctor on staff probably won't amount to much. She'll never testify against her employer and fellow doctors. Patel might be a start, but you're going to have to find an out-of-state family doctor and a general surgeon to testify."

Apparently Littleton hadn't anticipated that problem because he rarely graced the inside of a courtroom. He didn't consider that Patel's testimony was tainted. It was equally obvious to Davis that Littleton had never prepared a medical malpractice case for trial, much less actually tried one.

Littleton confirmed Davis's suspicions with his next question: "Why do you need expert witnesses from out of state?"

Davis looked over at Sammie, who was listening intently since none of this was covered in paralegal school.

"You should know why. It will be impossible to get a Tennessee doctor to testify against another Tennessee doctor."

"Why's that?"

It was unbelievable to Davis that he had to explain this basic idea to a fellow attorney. *At least an explanation will be a teaching moment for Sammie.*

"Brad, there's about an eighty percent chance that both English and Herman are insured by Tennessee Mutual Insurance Company. Tennessee Mutual insures about eighty percent of all doctors practicing in Tennessee. These doctors are shareholders of the company. That's what makes it a mutual insurance company. They're not going to testify against fellow shareholders. It doesn't matter how egregious Herman's and English's actions are. No Tennessee doctor will help get a judgment against his own company. Any verdict would be paid from the doctors' profits and would increase their premiums. No Tennessee Mutual doctor will agree to testify. You're dreaming. This Dr. Patel won't testify against her colleagues. She would have to be suicidal."

Littleton slapped the table. "That's why I need you, Ben. I'll get the cases, and you get them ready for trial. We'll make the perfect team, and we'll split the fee fifty-fifty."

Davis laughed and shook his head. "You've got to be kidding. I'm not going to do all the work and get fifty percent of the fee. If I'm doing all of the work, ethically I could give you a five percent finder's fee. If you want a greater fee, you'll have to work for it. Quite frankly, you don't know much about this area of the law. Have you ever tried a malpractice case?"

"No, but I have been practicing law for twenty-five years. I've taken plenty of depositions. They may not have been medical in nature, but not all the depositions will be medical. I can do legal research and write briefs.

I can argue motions and help you at trial if it comes to that."

The next point had to be made. "If you accept a case, you've got to be willing to try it. That's my rule of thumb. If you do twenty percent of the work and pay twenty percent of the expenses, you can have twenty percent of the fee. Do we have a deal?" Davis asked.

After pausing a moment, Littleton countered, "I'll do a third of the work and advance a third of the expenses, for a third of the fee. You'll be lead counsel. We may sign up as many as twenty cases. Imagine twenty cases against two doctors and the hospital. That sounds like a pretty good deal to me."

Davis admitted to himself that twenty cases against the same three defendants would be interesting *and* profitable. And they would never try all twenty. After a trial or two, the balance of the cases would settle. The defendants would be unwilling to risk twenty juries.

Davis never really believed that Littleton would or could do a third of the work. Maybe he would do twenty percent, and that was probably worth a third of the fee. At least Davis would have help with a third of the expenses. He was sure that the Plainview clients didn't have the expense money to fund the cases. He knew it was going to be expensive.

"If we get retained in only ten cases, your share of the expenses could amount to $70,000 over the next two years. If it's twenty cases, you can double that amount. Are you prepared to make that financial commitment?"

"Ben, you have my word."

"Forget your word. I'll draw up a contract. It will commit you to a third of the hours and a third of the expenses. The fee will be divided two-thirds/one-third.

It will also provide that I'm lead counsel and primary contact with the clients. I will control the cases and make all legal decisions, including settlement recommendations. That's the deal. Take it or leave it. We'll use Dr. Patel as an advisory expert to review the medical records, and based on her recommendations, I'll select the best cases to file suit. Do we have a deal?"

With a nod, Littleton accepted the deal. "Ben, after Bella types it up, fax it over, and I'll sign it. This will be an incredible opportunity for both of us. Maybe the cases will settle quickly, and we won't have to do much work."

Davis's statements hadn't registered with Littleton. All he could see were dollar signs. Davis should have stopped right there, but greed is a terrible thing and clouds one's judgment.

CHAPTER FIVE

CONFRONTATION

WEDNESDAY, APRIL 8, 1992

It was a long day and an even longer night. Dr. Laura Patel had been at Plainview Community Hospital for twenty hours of a twenty-four-hour shift that began at 9:00 a.m. She felt grimy and sweaty and probably smelled a little ripe. There were large sweat stains under each armpit. Being on call was both physically and emotionally exhausting, and she longed for a shower.

The emergency room had certainly lived up to its name and reputation. Laura had just stitched up a redneck who had been cracked over the head with a beer bottle in a bar fight. A barroom brawl was a dime a dozen on a Saturday night, but unusual for Wednesday. As she finished, she commented to the patient: "You're lucky. An inch lower, and you would have lost your eye."

She turned to the ER nurse, excused herself, and headed for the doctors' lounge. Only one other doctor was on call. Dr. Lars Herman had recently come off break and was standing in the hall, reading a chart.

She walked over to him. "Lars, it looks like it's quieted down. I think I'll try to shut my eyes for a few minutes in the doctors' lounge."

Herman grunted an acknowledgment without looking up from his chart. Before he could change his mind, Laura hurried to the lounge. In the back room of the doctors' lounge were three cots and a La-Z-Boy. She fell into the La-Z-Boy and pushed the chair to its fully reclined position. She was only five foot one, and her legs didn't reach the end of the footrest. Her long black hair was in a ponytail, which she placed over the headrest. At thirty, Laura had an athletic body with small, firm breasts.

Just as her black eyes shut, she heard screaming from the ER. After taking a few seconds to process the situation, she jumped from the chair and ran to the emergency room. Dr. Herman was struggling with and screaming at a patient.

"Get out of my hospital, you foul-mouthed animal."

A crowd of people was standing around the nurses' station watching the dramatic events unfold. Laura grabbed the elbow of an ER nurse and asked for an explanation. The nurse said that the patient had driven his car off the road and had arrived by ambulance. The man was intoxicated and belligerent. When Dr. Herman tried to treat him, the man told Herman to "keep his fucking hands to himself." The nurse recounted that Herman then pushed the patient, who tried to take a swing at Herman but missed. Both men fell to the ground with Herman on top. The drunk cried out in pain.

"Get the fuck off me, you douche bag. You've broken my ribs, you asshole."

Laura thought, *I better step in. It's getting ugly, and the patient is injured*. She felt that she had an ethical duty to do so. The patient reeked from alcohol, and it was obvious that his intoxication had caused the confrontation. She really didn't want to get involved, but despite her trepidation, she interjected herself into the deteriorating situation.

"Dr. Herman, please let the patient up. I'll treat him. Why don't you retire to the doctors' lounge?"

Both men jumped to their feet. She was amazed at the agility of the drunk. The inebriated man spat in Herman's face. Herman quickly wiped the greenish saliva from his cheek and lunged at the man while yelling, "You goddamned asshole! Get the hell out of my hospital!"

Laura stepped between them, and because of the sheer momentum of Herman's body, all three fell to the tiled floor. The drunk screamed again, as if in horrific pain. All three got up quickly, and the drunk vomited on the floor, right next to her feet. Laura, as a doctor, had a strong constitution, but the smell was overpowering.

Herman turned to her and began shouting, "How dare you put your hands on me? I could have you charged with assault and battery. I was defending myself, and you interfered. Who the hell do you think you are? You're nobody. That's who. You're not even a real doctor. I want both you and this asshole out of my hospital immediately!" Herman was red in the face, and the veins in his neck were bulging.

Laura thought he was about to have a stroke. She and Herman had never gotten along, but this confrontation was serious and very public. Laura looked around the room for support. All of the ER staff witnessed his behavior and heard him voice his utter disrespect for her.

"Look here, Dr. Herman, you obviously mishandled this problem. A doctor should never get physical with his patient. Even in the worst circumstances, you call security."

He became even angrier, as if that were possible. "Don't tell me how to practice medicine. If I wanted advice from some dyke, I'd ask for it. Keep your opinions to yourself, you Indian bitch."

She was almost speechless as he outed her in front of a room full of people. She had to respond, but she tried to compose herself before she did. In a calm, steady voice she said, "I intend to submit an incident report to the ER Committee today."

Dr. Herman glowered at her, but she didn't back down.

"I remind you of your Hippocratic Oath and your professional obligation to first do no harm. You've certainly strayed from that principle this evening. If you'll excuse me—"

He tried to block her, but Laura darted around him and took charge of the drunken man. "This patient needs to be taken to radiology for an X-ray."

She looked at the faces of several of the ER staff and felt confident that they would back her up. She was actually proud that she managed to respond to Herman. He had gone way too far. *The nerve of that quack,* thought Laura. *How dare he question my competency? How dare he call me a dyke? My sexual orientation is none of his business.*

As she was helping the patient into a wheelchair, Herman took his parting shot: "We'll see who gets reprimanded. This isn't the first time you've questioned my treatment of a patient. But let me assure you, it will be the last. I'd start packing my bags if I were you."

She couldn't let the threat just sit there. "Don't threaten me. I have a contract, and I'm here to stay, despite your best efforts," she stated evenly.

He retorted, "You just don't know who you're

dealing with, but you'll find out soon enough."

She decided it was best to end the conversation. The patient came first. She waited in radiology until the X-ray was taken. The patient was diagnosed as having three fractured ribs.

Laura worked the remaining hours of her shift. She was tired and just wanted to get home for a hearty breakfast with Maggie and the kids and then take a hot shower.

Within fifteen minutes of the end of her shift, Laura heard her name over the intercom system. She was to come to the administration office. She wished she had prepared her report and gathered the witness statements, but she had been working since the incident with Herman. Obviously, Herman had run to Woody Douglas and told his twisted version of the facts. It would be Herman's word against hers.

At the administration office, Woody Douglas, Dr. Herman, and Dr. Robert Kelly, the medical director of the hospital, were waiting for her. There was also an older, stately gentleman, whom Laura didn't know, seated next to Herman. *This group looks like trouble,* she said to herself.

Bracing herself for what was to come, Laura held out her hand to the unknown person and introduced herself, "Dr. Laura Patel, family medicine."

The man responded, "Grayson Stevenson III. I represent Plainview Community Hospital."

She was taken aback. She was not expecting the hospital's attorney to be there. She nervously turned to Douglas and Dr. Kelly and asked, "Why is there a lawyer at this medical meeting? I haven't filed my formal complaint against Dr. Herman for his unforgivable conduct this morning yet. At this point, this is an internal hospital matter—"

Dr. Kelly, who was senior of the group, broke in and said, "You're mistaken about why you're here. Dr. Herman is not the focus of this investigation. You are, Dr. Patel. Dr. Herman has leveled very serious charges against you."

Dr. Kelly handed her the formal complaint signed by Herman, Douglas, and himself. Douglas and Kelly represented two-thirds of the Executive Medical Committee. The investigation was over before it began; a majority of the committee had already found her guilty.

Laura felt sick to her stomach. The document alleged that she had struck Herman, interfered with his treatment of patients, acted unprofessionally, and brought dishonor to the hospital.

She reread the document. Herman had stacked the deck against her. He even had the hospital's lawyer at the meeting. *How did they get Mr. Stevenson here so fast? Could my confrontation with Herman have been some sort of setup?*

Dr. Kelly interrupted her thoughts. "What do you have to say for yourself, Doctor?"

She started to respond, "Sir, I would really—"

Grayson Stevenson III pulled from his inside coat pocket a small tape recorder. "Let's keep a record of what's said here today." Stevenson turned the recorder on.

Laura heard the click and hiss of the tape. She was a little intimidated by Stevenson and his tape recorder but pressed forward: "I'll agree to this meeting being recorded as long as you'll give me a copy of the tape."

Douglas agreed.

Laura described what happened between Herman and the drunken patient in the ER: "The patient was intoxicated and belligerent, but he was an admitted patient. That patient was entitled to full patient rights under the hospital's Code of Conduct and the Declaration of Patients' Rights. Dr. Herman threw the patient to the ground and broke his ribs."

"I had a right to defend myself," interjected Herman.

"You were totally unprofessional and abusive. You called me an 'Indian bitch' and a 'dyke.' I find those remarks very degrading," she fired back at him.

This time, Douglas interrupted, "Well, are you?"

She was shocked by Douglas's question but managed a quick comeback: "My father was born in India. I was born in West Fargo, North Dakota. I'm sure we can all agree that I'm not a female dog, although that's not what he meant. My sexual orientation is my own business."

Herman chirped in, "So you're not denying that you're a lesbian?"

Stevenson whispered something in Herman's ear.

Seeing this angered Laura, and she lost her cool. "I thought we were putting this meeting on the record. Why is Dr. Herman whispering? Mr. Stevenson, what is the good doctor hiding?"

It was Stevenson's turn to be aggressive. "Dr. Patel, your last statement was a misrepresentation of the events and distorted the record. Dr. Herman didn't whisper in my ear. Rather I whispered in his. I have no personal knowledge of any of the facts being investigated, so the only thing I could have told him was legal advice. My legal advice to him is protected by the attorney-client privilege."

She was shaken. If she wasn't, she might have pointed out that Stevenson represented the hospital, not Dr. Herman.

The office felt small and hot, but she managed to regain her composure. "Before I move on from what happened this morning, I want to state for the record that almost every member of the ER staff can verify what I've said and can confirm the inappropriate behavior of Dr. Herman. I intend to collect written statements—"

Dr. Kelly jumped in hard and barked at her, "You'll do no such thing. No one other than the Executive Medical Committee will investigate these charges. If our investigation is interfered with or hampered by you in any way, there will be serious consequences. Do you understand, Dr. Patel? Do you have anything more to say?"

She decided that since a record was being made, she might as well be sure it was complete. She decided not to hold anything back and started to give her statement.

Dr. Kelly immediately interrupted, "If that's all, Dr. Patel, we'll adjourn this meeting."

The hospital's investigation is going to be a whitewash. This might be my last opportunity to say my piece. "No, I'm not done, sir. There's a scam going on, and this hospital is a part of it. Mr. Douglas knows about it. I've reported it to him twice and made a formal complaint. A woman died unnecessarily two months ago because of it."

Glancing at Dr. Herman, she watched his bright blue eyes turn to steel. "This scheme has to do with laparoscopic gallbladder surgeries recommended by Dr. Herman and performed by Dr. English. In the last two years, the number of gallbladder surgeries at this hospital has increased six-fold. I sat down and reviewed the surgical logs from before and after Dr. Herman and Dr. English arrived at this hospital. Dr. Herman's purchasing an ultrasound machine and Dr. English's training in the use of the laparoscope should be obvious evidence of their involvement with the dramatic increase in the number of procedures. Who proctored Dr. English in laparoscopic gallbladder surgery?"

Dr. Kelly looked at Douglas, and Douglas, back at him. They didn't have an answer because there was no good answer to the question.

Laura took their silence as her opportunity to continue: "He took a three-day course, and then he showed up at Plainview Community Hospital and started performing laparoscopic gallbladder surgeries. There are some weeks English removes a gallbladder every day. Who at the hospital made sure that he knew what the hell he was doing? I'll tell you. No one."

Grayson Stevenson broke in, "Those are slanderous allegations, Doctor. You could get sued for such statements."

Stevenson's threat didn't unnerve her. She was on a roll and was committed to telling the whole story to Dr. Kelly and Stevenson, whether they wanted to hear it or not. She knew Herman and Douglas hadn't revealed the facts and wouldn't do so.

"Bottom line, unnecessary tests, procedures, and surgeries are performed at this hospital for profit. The hospital administration knows about the dramatic increase in tests and procedures and remains silent because the hospital is making big money."

She took a breath; it felt good to get some air deep into her lungs and to get her accusations off her chest.

She added, "What makes matters worse is the total incompetence of both Dr. Herman and Dr. English."

Herman almost came out of his chair; he looked as if he was ready to strangle her.

Next, Laura described the death of Rosie Malone in detail and how the older woman's medical condition deteriorated right before her eyes. Everyone in the room knew the story, except Stevenson. She described how Dr. Herman blindsided her and in a very accusatory way ordered her to "mind her own business."

She couldn't contain herself any longer and jumped to her feet to make her most serious accusation. She had sweated through her scrubs and white coat and knew that in the confines of the small office she gave off an unpleasant odor, differently from Stevenson, whose cologne gave off a sickly sweet odor.

She pointed at Herman. "He let her die. He wouldn't transfer Rosie Malone because he didn't want the physicians at Saint Thomas to see what English and he had done to that poor woman. He didn't want to be second-guessed because she didn't need the surgery in the first place, Dr. English nicked her bowel, and the postoperative care was horrendous."

Herman jumped to his feet and shouted at her, "Who do you think you're talking to, bitch?"

Laura and Herman were standing about three inches apart then. She could smell his hot breath. He desperately needed a breath mint. "It was your reckless failure to transfer Mrs. Malone that killed her."

She turned to Douglas. "I begged you to transfer her, but you ignored me. And three days later she was dead. She never would have been transferred if her daughter hadn't pressed for it. He wanted Rosie Malone to die so his malpractice would die with her."

Kelly had enough. He took charge of the meeting and stated sternly, "Your hospital privileges are suspended pending further investigation, Dr. Patel. You're not to communicate with Mr. Douglas, Dr. Herman, or Dr. English. If one of your patients requires hospitalization, refer him or her to another physician, one with privileges. Your suspension is immediate and without pay—"

Now she interrupted Dr. Kelly: "I have a contract. The hospital is obligated to pay my rent and $5,000 a month in salary through July. That was our deal."

Kelly responded, "Well, *you* broke our deal. *You* interfered in another physician's treatment of his patient. I'll be calling your landlord this afternoon to inform him that *you'll* be making next month's payment."

"You'll be hearing from my lawyer," she replied.

Dr. Kelly stood up, followed by Douglas and Stevenson.

Stevenson fielded the hollow threat, saying, "Here's my card. You can have him or her call me."

With nothing left to say, Laura walked out of the room. Her head was pounding as she headed toward the doctors' lounge.

After a few minutes, a security guard approached her and said, "Excuse me, Doctor, but Mr. Douglas says you have to leave the hospital right now. I was told to escort you off the property. I'm sorry."

The security guard followed Laura to her car. It was so humiliating that she completely forgot about her personal effects in her locker.

While she drove home, she tried to think of what to

tell Maggie. Laura was the breadwinner, and the family depended on her. Maggie, five-year-old Kim, and almost one-year-old Lee would be waiting for her at the breakfast table. But she found the kitchen empty.

She'd forgotten that the meeting made her more than an hour late. Maggie and the kids had eaten pancakes without her. As she walked toward the den, she could hear *Sesame Street* on television.

Maggie came up from behind Laura and put her arms around her. Laura began to shake all over and made a strange humming sound. Maggie looked surprised when Laura broke down, sobbing. It took fifteen minutes for her to tell Maggie what happened. Maggie just listened, interrupting only to ask, "Did you get a copy of the audiotape?"

Laura was angry at herself for her stupidity at leaving without a copy. Maggie kissed her hard and assured her that they were going to be all right. Then Maggie stated the obvious, "You're going to need a damn good lawyer."

Maggie's words were prophetic. Two days later, Plainview Community Hospital sued Dr. Laura Patel in Plains County Circuit Court for breach of contract. A sheriff's deputy served Laura at her office in front of a waiting room full of patients.

Things went from bad to worse. The following Monday night, as she was leaving her office, Laura found a pink flyer with bold red lettering on her windshield. She removed it and started to wad it up but stopped and uncrumpled the document.

The flyer was about her. It accused her of being homosexual and wrongfully accused her of having illicit affairs with two married female patients, causing their marriages to end in divorce. The flyer correctly stated that Dr. Patel was currently having a lesbian relationship and had adopted two Chinese daughters. The flyer concluded by questioning, "Do you want your wives and daughters treated by this person?"

Only two other cars were in the parking lot, and each windshield had a pink flyer. Laura gripped the steering wheel tightly. She was pissed and wanted to lash out in revenge but didn't know where to start. *It could have been any one of those bastards, but which one?*

She started driving home but remembered that Maggie wanted her to pick up milk for the girls. She pulled into a busy convenience mart. Almost every car had a flyer on its windshield. She must have just missed the bastards spreading the lies.

While she waited to pay for the milk, Laura noticed two women whispering in the corner. She knew they were talking about her. The word was out in Plainview: Dr. Laura Patel was a home-wrecking lesbian.

Obviously, the distributor of the flyer wanted to destroy her office practice. Plainview was a pretty conservative town, and very few patients would be willing to be treated by a lesbian doctor.

She made an appointment with Bradley Littleton Esquire, a business acquaintance of Maggie's father, in Nashville. She didn't trust the local lawyers. She was certain that they could be influenced, if not controlled, by the hospital. Laura knew she was in for the fight of her life. *Am I ready for this?*

CHAPTER SIX

A NEW CONSPIRACY

FRIDAY, MAY 15, 1992

Friday was usually Dr. Herman's slowest day at the office but not today. He had made a small fortune by seeing more than forty patients. It was almost 7:00 p.m. but still light out when he left his office. He had to make rounds with sixteen of his patients admitted to the hospital. Although it was his duty, he made each patient feel special.

He drove his black Mercedes to the hospital and parked in his reserved space. He removed his Ray Ban sunglasses and flipped the visor down. Taped to the bottom of the visor was a photo of his mother, Margot. He touched his fingers to his lips and then placed them on the photo. This was part of his daily ritual before making his hospital rounds. Dr. Margot Herman was his inspiration, and he knew his mother would be proud that her only son chose to follow in her footsteps.

As he entered the hospital, he decided he needed a cup of black coffee to help him through his rounds. Coffee was his drink of choice, he never drank alcohol, and he was critical of those who overindulged. It was suppertime, and the cafeteria was two-thirds full. Most patrons were concerned family members biding their time, as their loved ones lay upstairs. He walked over to several tables and casually chatted with his patients' spouses and siblings.

Dan Cooke stopped eating his potpie and rose to shake Dr. Herman's hand. "Bobby seems to be doing much better. Thanks, Doc."

His son had fallen off a merry-go-round and fractured his collarbone. All Herman did was consult an orthopedic surgeon, but he was the contact to the family and was happy to take the credit.

Another woman bear-hugged him, almost spilling his coffee. This scene was not unusual. What Herman lacked in skill, he more than made up for in bedside manner. His patients and their families loved and respected him as their family doctor.

On his way to the elevator, he walked past the open door of the doctors' lounge. Herman spied Charlie English sitting alone with his head in his hands and mumbling to himself. Herman couldn't quite make it out, but at the end of the diatribe, he understood, "When hell freezes over."

Seeing Herman walk in, English jumped to his feet. A wild, glazed expression was on his face. After a moment, his confusion changed to a stupid grin, and he sat back down. "Hey there, Lars."

Herman looked him up and down, noting his unshaved face and wrinkled clothes. "Are you all right?"

English laughed oddly. "You caught me by surprise. That's all."

Herman had given English a prescription for Klonopin to help him cope with the stress of his divorce and legal problems, but the man's red blotchy skin suggested he might be overusing or self-prescribing.

English was in his late forties. Slightly older than Herman, he once sported a full head of ginger hair, but now the top of his head was bald. In the last few years, he had developed a paunch around his midsection. A robust Herman encouraged English to exercise to manage his stress. Herman even invited English on his 5:00 a.m. jogs, but English refused. Herman, as his treating physician, would have preferred exercise to medication, but English was a difficult patient, in part because he was a fellow physician. He treated English as a courtesy. Herman reluctantly prescribed sleeping pills and Valium to help English cope with the pressures of his life.

Herman approached his friend cautiously. "What's the matter, Charlie?"

English looked up from his hands. His eyes were red from crying. He cleared his throat and said hoarsely, "Women, Lars, fucking women. They're driving me crazy. I'm paying alimony to one ex-wife, Charlotte, and child support for my two children and alimony to the other one, Susan. The children and Susan live in Hewes City. They're bleeding me dry. The lawyers' fees are killing me. I have to pay my lawyer and theirs. These bastards charge $300 an hour. I'm broke. And what's worse, their hounding me is affecting my marriage to Joan."

Herman didn't know much about English's personal life, but he had heard the rumors. Although Herman regarded English as a friend, their relationship was more or less professional. Herman had heard bits and pieces of the English marital drama through his gossiping receptionist, Sheila. He knew that English's most recent divorce transpired after his second wife,

Susan, found him in bed with the third and current Mrs. English, Joan. Herman wouldn't be surprised if the first Mrs. English left under similar circumstances or if it was Susan who had been caught in the compromised position.

Herman was in sensitive territory, but that didn't prevent him from making his sales pitch. Organizing his thoughts, he responded deliberately: "Lawyers and your ex-wives aren't your problem. You need more money. Alimony, child support, and legal fees are the reality of your life. These are the costs of ten years' worth of bad decisions. I think I have a solution to your problem. I've been doing some research. Gallbladders aren't the only organ that can be removed laparoscopically. In California and New York, doctors have been removing appendixes laparoscopically for years. It will be just like removing gallbladders. The appendix is a useless organ and won't be missed. I'll screen and diagnose the patients, and you'll perform the surgeries. The real beauty of an appendectomy is that it's fully covered by insurance."

His proposal would be a win-win for both parties. The more procedures English offered, the more referrals Herman could make. He made money from every surgery English performed. The plan was perfect.

Herman pressed English further. "We'll send you down to Atlanta to take another three-day course to get your certification. When you come back, you'll be the only general surgeon in Plains County who can perform a laparoscopic appendectomy. I'm thinking about buying a second ultrasound machine. Between gallbladders, appendixes, and the OB-GYN's practice, I think we can support a second machine. The quicker we get the ultrasounds done, the quicker you can get them into surgery and we get paid. We'll make money hand over fist, and your financial problems will soon be over."

"A new machine isn't cheap. Where are you going to get the hundred grand to pay for it?" asked English.

"I've sold some art that was gifted to me by a relative."

"That must have been some piece of art if you can buy another machine."

Herman wasn't about to tell English about Uncle Wilhelm and his Nazi background and stolen art treasures. English was too unstable. "Charlie, don't worry about how I get the money. All you need to know is that you'll be doing twice as many surgeries and making twice the money."

English jumped up and squeezed him so tightly that Herman couldn't breathe. When he let go, Herman choked out, "I guess that means we have a deal."

CHAPTER SEVEN

THE LIBRARY

MONDAY, JUNE 22, 1992

Sammie drove separately from her uncle to the Plains County Library in Davis's convertible. She listened to a tape of Frank Sinatra and his daughter, Nancy, singing "Something Stupid," while her long blonde ponytail flapped in the wind. She sang along, ". . . something stupid like I love you." Like her mother, she fancied the Rat Pack singers: Sinatra, Martin, and her namesake, Sammy Davis Jr.

She arrived fifteen minutes before Littleton and her uncle and slipped into the back of the library. Her job was to observe the crowd during the presentation and later report the crowd's reaction. Afterward, she was to help Bella collect the names, addresses, and telephone numbers of prospective clients. She was very excited about getting out of the office. She was sick of making copies and typing letters. This meeting and getting into the trenches with her uncle were not topics covered during her undergraduate study at the University of Florida or in paralegal school.

The local library looked dated, like something out of the 1960s or 1970s. There weren't any computers in sight. Behind the circulation desk were small wooden file drawers, which housed the Dewey Decimal index cards.

The library reading room was set up with plastic chairs in neat rows, and it was almost filled to capacity. More than eighty people attended the meeting. Sammie took a seat and tried to blend in, which was easier said than done for her. Every male there was staring at the beautiful, well-built stranger.

The attendees began to grow restless as the clock chimed seven o'clock. Sammie looked around the room; there were a few people her age, but most of them were over forty. Overall, the group had a beaten-down look.

Bradley Littleton was seated next to her uncle on a small platform by the podium. Littleton acknowledged her with a wink, which made her skin crawl.

Davis had explained to her that because of Littleton's connection to Patel and several other persons he met in the community, there was no choice but to keep Littleton involved in the malpractice cases. Littleton represented Dr. Patel, she was the advising expert for about two months, and she knew most of the people in the room and could help secure them as clients.

Littleton had filed an answer to the hospital's complaint, a counterclaim for breach of contract, and claims of libel, slander, and discrimination against the hospital, Dr. Herman, and Dr. English in the Circuit Court of Plains County. Dr. Patel was his client, and she had access to and could obtain the malpractice cases, whether Davis liked it or not.

Sammie noticed an Indian woman in the back row and suspected that she was Dr. Patel. She made a mental note to introduce herself to the doctor at the conclusion of the meeting.

Littleton moved to the microphone, took a deep

breath, and addressed the crowd. He seemed nervous as he introduced himself and Davis as lawyers from Nashville.

"Mr. Davis and I are here tonight to discuss a very serious problem in your community, which is directly affecting the lives of you and your loved ones.

"For the past two years, there have been two doctors practicing medicine without regard for the welfare of their patients. These incompetent doctors are motivated by greed rather than by the principles of their Hippocratic Oath. They are profiting from their mis-diagnoses and unnecessary tests, procedures, and surgeries.

"How many of you have been treated by Dr. Lars Herman? Let me see a show of hands."

Approximately two-thirds of the people raised their hands.

"How many of you have had surgery performed by Dr. Charles English?"

Almost all of Dr. Herman's patients raised their hands.

"Approximately two years ago, Dr. Herman and Dr. English came to Plainview. The hospital never verified their credentials. They applied for privileges at the hospital and were given whatever privileges they requested. The hospital was desperate for new doctors, and it cut corners. I'm sure you all remember when your community hospital went bankrupt. Most of the doctors who once treated this community disappeared over-night. For decades, the hospital had been owned and run by the local doctors who genuinely cared about this community. Now a faceless corporate outsider owns it."

Sammie was not familiar with the story of how

Plainview Community Hospital went bankrupt, but she figured everybody else there knew how their community hospital went down the drain.

"When the hospital was sold, the new board cut the nursing staff in half. These discharged registered nurses were replaced with techs, most of whom did not have high school diplomas and were far less experienced. But they were cheap. With the less-qualified staff came less-qualified care. The board was concerned only with cutting costs in order to increase profits."

The crowd reacted to the reference to "profits." An obese woman stood and yelled loudly, "They kept operating on my mother until there was nothing left of her. Dr. Herman kept insisting he could make her better, but all he did was make it better for him and the hospital."

Sammie thought the woman hit a nerve with the crowd, and several others made loud grumbling noises. The atmosphere changed drastically to one more like a revival meeting.

As Littleton continued his presentation, he stumbled a bit over his words: "Two years ago, the hospital was marginally profitable. Today, Plainview Community Hospital is flush with profits, through Dr. Herman's and Dr. English's unethical practices. What are these unethical practices? They perform unnecessary medical tests, procedures, and surgeries. This is how the hospital has dramatically increased its revenue. Profit was gained as Dr. Herman and Dr. English risked the lives of you and your families. Profits are why the hospital has turned a blind eye to Dr. Herman's and Dr. English's wrongful actions."

People in the audience forgot about Littleton and

started chatting among themselves.

A young woman about twenty moved to stand in front of Littleton. Tears were running down both cheeks. "You all knew my sister, Irene. Dr. English lost her last March. She was just twenty-six and left behind a husband and two small children."

An older man came up from the second row, put his arm around the young woman, and ushered her to the back of the room.

Littleton had lost control, so he sat down.

Sammie was concerned that the crowd was about to turn ugly; someone needed to gain control—fast.

Davis jumped to his feet, cupped his hands to his mouth, and produced a rebel yell. The crowd was familiar with that battle cry.

It may not have been the most professional thing to do, Sammie thought, *but it got everybody's attention and they stopped talking.*

Davis said, "I apologize for my weak Yankee attempt at your battle cry, but on behalf of Mr. Littleton and myself, I would like to thank you for attending this information session."

Sammie noted that her uncle's voice was deeper and more authoritative than Littleton's; he sounded like a radio announcer and projected loudly enough to reach the back of the room. He was much taller, stood more erect, and generally carried himself better. She could tell that he immediately gained the trust of the crowd, the same way he secured the trust and confidence of a jury.

"The health and well-being of your community are at stake. Without health, you have nothing. We live in a dangerous world. With every breath we take, there are microbes and countless other foreign bodies that could affect our health. If you farm, as I know many of you do, your hard work places you at risk every day for accidents, both minor ones and life-threatening ones. Heck, anytime you get in your car you're at some risk that a fool not paying attention will run a red light or even worse that a drunk driver will cross the yellow line and plow right into you."

Davis continued, "These are problems we have come to expect, and they're part of life. But it's different when men you've placed your trust in betray you. These physicians took an oath to protect this community, and they placed themselves and their wallets ahead of you. Unlike the drunk who crosses the yellow line, they weren't all liquored up. They knew exactly what they were doing. They were stone-cold sober and stone-cold-hearted."

Davis stopped and looked directly at Sammie, or at least she thought he did. She suspected that everyone there felt the same way: he was speaking directly to him or her. Her uncle cleared his throat, took a sip of water from a bottle hidden under the podium, loosened his tie, and unbuttoned his top button. He was establishing a relationship with the audience, becoming one of them. His piercing blue eyes scanned the crowd. Sammie did the same with her even deeper blue eyes and saw that he mesmerized the patients and their kin.

"Earlier, Mr. Littleton mentioned the hospital's lax attitude when checking the backgrounds of new physicians. Dr. Herman went to medical school in Mexico, at the University of Mexico City. By law, because he was a foreign-trained physician, in order to practice medicine in the United States, Dr. Herman was required to pass a qualifying examination known as the

FLEX exam. This test certifies that foreign-trained doctors possess the minimal skills and knowledge to treat patients in the United States. The American Medical Association doesn't want unsuspecting Americans to be treated by foreign-trained quacks. Dr. Herman, amazingly, failed the FLEX exam eight times before finally passing."

Davis paused for effect. "Now everything I've just told you about Dr. Herman's education, training, and FLEX exam results is a matter of public record. Why didn't the hospital call and get those test results? And if they did, why did they grant privileges to Dr. Herman?"

After another pause, Davis turned his attention to English. "Dr. English attended Peterson University in the Dominican Republic. In 1985, Peterson University lost its accreditation as a medical school. The American Medical Association, after a thorough investigation, determined that Peterson had been issuing fraudulent medical degrees. This finding has been widely publicized throughout the general media and was also widely known throughout the medical community. I have here an article from the *New York Times* on August 31, 1985. It explains why Peterson was forced to close its medical school. Today, seven years later, Peterson University's medical school remains closed. Dr. English graduated in 1982. His education and training were stated on his application for privileges at your hospital."

Davis held up the application and told the audience that the document was a matter of public record, filed with the state. "Plainview Community Hospital should have conducted a serious investigation of Dr. English's qualifications. It didn't. The mere reference to Peterson on English's application should have been a red flag."

A tall redheaded gentleman stood and addressed the

audience, "I lost my job of ten years because of Dr. English's botched surgery last year. Dr. Herman told me I had stones, and I needed my gallbladder out. They told me I'd be out of commission three days, but I couldn't go back to work for almost a month. After three weeks my boss replaced me with a younger guy who'd take a lot less money. I'm still on unemployment, and the insurance company has paid English for the botched surgery but not for all the additional medical expenses I ran up after the surgery. It ain't right."

"Ladies and gentlemen, I only took the Bar exam once," said Davis. "Each time I walk into court, I represent that I am qualified to practice law. It was the hospital's job to question and investigate Dr. Herman and Dr. English before it let them loose on this community. You and your families are the victims. Greed, rather than good medicine, controlled your care. That's the truth."

Sammie noticed the Indian woman in the back row smile in response to Davis's last remark.

"Mr. Littleton and I are here to offer you an opportunity to set things right. You may or may not have a valid lawsuit. That question can only be answered after a qualified doctor reviews your medical records. At no expense to you, we are willing to investigate. If you or a family member was damaged by sub-standard care, you are entitled to be compensated under the law. My assistant has a legal pad at the circulation desk. If you are interested in having your medical records reviewed, please give her your name and contact information. One of my paralegals will be calling you. Thank you again for coming here this evening." Then Davis sat down.

The room filled with angry voices. The meeting lasted less than thirty minutes, but Sammie could feel the tension in the room. Her uncle and Littleton had raised the awareness of these confused and desperate people. A line of people formed next to the circulation desk, where Bella was waiting.

Sammie approached the Indian woman. "Dr. Patel?" Sammie shook hands with the doctor, and after a brief conversation, she joined Bella to help record contact information.

They ended up with twenty-six names. The first three were Thomas Malone, Wendy Jones, and Edith Easter.

CHAPTER EIGHT

THE FISHING HOLE

SUNDAY, AUGUST 23, 1992

The Davis family was running about an hour late. Davis knew that Morty had already gone through his tackle box in anticipation of an afternoon of fishing, drinking beer, smoking cigars, and bullshitting. As usual, Morty would make his ham and cheese sandwiches with spicy German mustard. The two had been fishing together since 1975, and Morty always made the same type of sandwich and made the same bad joke about "two Jews eating ham in a row boat."

This time Davis brought along Liza, their children, and Sammie. Bringing the family was an extra bonus. The whole family loved Morty, and he got a kick out of being with the children. They were the grandchildren he never had. Davis wanted Jake to learn how to fish with him and Morty. Liza, Sammie, and Caroline would play Frisbee and have a picnic lunch while they waited for the main course of the evening's catfish dinner to be caught by the men. After they pulled into Morty's driveway, Ben sent the three females to the pond in one of the golf carts so they could set up their picnic lunch.

Since Goldie's death from cancer on July 4th, Morty had been living like a recluse, never leaving his farm, Squeeze Bottom. He had aged in the last month and now looked used up. Davis invited the old man to his house for a home-cooked meal at least a couple times each week, but he politely refused.

On May 8th, Morty retired completely in order to spend more time with Goldie. He hoped that they would share more than a few weeks together, but God had other plans.

The younger man tried to stay in touch via the telephone. However, his family and a busy law practice preoccupied him. He tried to go fishing with Morty as often as possible because he knew that those trips were the highlights of Morty's weeks.

Davis and Jake walked in the house without knocking; Davis had been there more than a hundred times. "Sorry we're late. Let's not keep those catfish waiting."

Morty's grandfather Abe had purchased Squeeze Bottom, a house and 288 acres, in 1914. Despite its age, the main house appeared almost new due to a fresh paint job.

As they left the house, Davis held the screen door open and took the fishing rods and tackle box from his older friend's hands. It was a glorious day. The sun was shining, the sky was dotted with cotton ball–looking clouds, and the birds were singing.

The trio stepped into the other golf cart parked in the circular gravel driveway, and Jake drove, sitting on Davis's lap, to Dear's Pond, which had been named in honor of Morty's mother, Deidra. Morty took great pride in his private fishing hole.

As Davis and Jake unloaded the gear, Morty took a seat on his usual stump and began peppering Davis with questions. "How's the practice since I left? How's my girl Bella doing? How's Sammie working out? Is she as smart as you thought she'd be?"

Davis laughed. "Everybody's doing fine. You know Bella is the one who keeps things moving along and on track. Sammie's got some skills. She can work the computer and she knows how to research, but she's raw and inexperienced. She also has an annoying habit of listening to music while wearing headphones. It's very unprofessional."

"Don't sell her short just because you're related by blood. Give her a chance. She's smart. She needs to be taught," Morty reminded him. "And with hard work and guidance, she could be a real asset."

Morty baited Jake's rod while the five-year-old squirmed almost as much as the worm on the hook. Jake asked Morty if the worm felt any pain. The old man looked grandfatherly, lied, and assured the child that the worm was more than happy to cooperate so they could catch a catfish dinner.

After Jake was settled down in the small bass boat, waiting for his first fish, Davis explained to Morty how hectic things had been. "You know how busy it can get. There aren't enough hours in the day."

He could tell that his old friend missed the excitement of the practice of law. Davis worked his way into the primary purpose of his visit. "I took those medical malpractice cases Littleton referred out of Plains County. It's ten cases, and I'm a little overwhelmed by the thought of drafting ten separate complaints."

Davis took the oars and repositioned the boat about twenty feet from the shore.

Morty baited his hook and cast his line with authority. "That shouldn't be too difficult. The cases involve the same three defendants and revolve around almost identical negligent acts. You'll draft a template and then vary the document to fit the particular facts of each case."

Davis cast his line and pretended to concentrate on his floater, but in reality he was listening intently to the old man.

"In each case you'll have to at least prove negligence. Recklessness will be a harder sell to a jury. You'll have to establish recklessness by clear and convincing evidence rather than by a mere preponderance of the evidence. I don't know that you can prove that these doctors and the hospital disregarded the consequences of their actions." Morty stopped talking a minute to light his cigar with his gold Dunhill lighter, which Davis always admired. It was a gift from Willie Nelson.

Davis had reached the same conclusion about the probability of a jury verdict of recklessness and an award of punitive damages.

"If the court allows you to introduce evidence of a pattern of either negligence or recklessness, the hospital can be held liable." Morty dropped an ash from his cigar in the lake and continued, "Another issue that you'll have to address is that Tennessee Mutual will insure at least one of those doctors. You can forget about retaining a Tennessee expert witness." Morty shook his head. "I think you're making a big mistake. These cases will preoccupy you and take away from the rest of your practice. You'll also dump a ton of money in these cases. You should just let Littleton keep the cases and drown on his own."

Morty stopped to respond to his bending pole, but

despite being an experienced fisherman, he over-corrected and lost the fish. Jake was so disappointed.

Morty sighed and turned to Davis. "When was the last time you were in Plains County?"

"Last month."

"And before that?"

Davis thought a few moments. "Never."

"Bingo. You're trying these cases in Plains County, the defendants' backyard, and you're a New York Jew."

Davis had to agree with Morty. He made a good practical point.

Morty continued, "That hospital is the largest employer in the county. How are you going to get an impartial jury? Do you know how difficult it is to change venue in a civil case? During my forty years I changed venue a half dozen times in criminal cases, but I never changed venue in a civil case. In a criminal case you can always argue to the court in a rape or murder trial that the county jury pool is too prejudiced. In those cases, it's one of their own raped or murdered. But in a malpractice case, you'll need at least three affidavits from disinterested persons. You couldn't even get one of the local barbers to give an affidavit. Everyone knows everyone else in these small towns, and nobody's disinterested. You can't get a fair trial in Plains County.

"You also better start thinking about who you're going to get as local co-counsel to help you pick the jury. You'll need someone with good connections with the judge. Jack Barnes is the man for the job. I'd give him a call right away and get him on your team. He's an experienced trial lawyer who knows his people. Give him a piece of the action. Better yet, give him Littleton's piece of the action. Is Judge Robert E. Lee Boxer still on the bench in Plains County?"

Davis hung his head and looked despondent.

"What's wrong?"

"I waited too long."

"What do you mean?"

"I wanted to retain Barnes in June, right after the meeting at the library. I knew we'd need his local political pull with the judge and his experience for the jury selection. Littleton talked me into waiting. He was convinced there'd be a quick settlement. He didn't want to give up a percentage of the fee to Barnes. While we waited, Dr. Herman hired Barnes as his personal lawyer."

"Lesson number one, don't listen to Littleton. He's an idiot."

Davis nodded and told Morty that Boxer had two years left on his term and served three county circuits: Plains, Hewes, and Briar. He had been on the bench almost six years, and he was only in his late thirties. Davis had never appeared in front of Judge Boxer before. Davis didn't get to Plains, Hewes, or Briar often. His practice was primarily in Nashville, Davidson County. He knew to keep his New York Jew ass in Nashville and hire a lawyer when he went to adjacent rural counties.

Morty emphasized the point: "I knew Boxer's Uncle John pretty well. He was a great judge and held his bench for three terms, twenty-four years. He was scholarly and always prepared. John wouldn't let a lawyer get away with anything. If a lawyer was avoiding a question with a witness, John would ask that question for the lawyer. I hated when he did that. I've been before his nephew. To his friends, he's Bobby Lee.

But you'll be calling him Judge Boxer. Bobby Lee's half the man that his uncle was, but that just makes him your average county judge, more politician than scholar."

Both Morty and Davis understood courtroom politics. Morty was usually the beneficiary of such political favoritism.

"I know how you can get Boxer to move these cases. As a circuit judge, he presides in three county seats. The cases must be filed in Plains County because the alleged negligence and acts of malpractice occurred in Plainview. So you file there, but then move for a change of venue to Hewes County. I predict it will probably be granted."

Davis looked at Morty with astonishment.

Morty had more to share: "These ten cases are going to tax any county court system. This is going to be a handful for any judge. Each trial will last at least two weeks, with endless motions and required court appearances. The entire process, if all ten cases are tried, will last at least five years, won't it?"

"Absolutely."

"So, if you were the judge faced with these cases and all this extra work, would you want to travel ninety minutes, forty-five each way, to court to preside over these trials? Or would you prefer to roll out of bed and walk to your courtroom? What does human nature tell you? And where do you think Judge Boxer lives?"

Davis smiled and said, "Hewes City, the seat of Hewes County."

Davis's tone turned serious. "Morty, I need your help. These Plainview cases are overwhelming. I'm ignoring my other clients."

Before Davis could even ask the question, Morty reached his hand across the boat to shake Davis's hand

and said, "Give me a dollar, Ben."

Davis reached for his wallet and pulled out a one-dollar bill. He handed it to Morty.

Morty put the dollar in his pocket and said, "Say hello to your new senior associate. I want to mentor Sammie, and unlike when I taught you, I'll have the time to do it right."

"I don't think you did such a bad job."

"There's always room for improvement," Morty said with a grin.

Davis was forced to give Jake a dollar too and agreed he could be his new "junior associate."

The disappointed fishermen decided to call it a day, and Davis rowed them to the bank. They rarely ended their outing without bringing in at least a couple of good-sized fish. Jake was the most disappointed of all.

Looking confused, Caroline met them and asked, "Dad, where are the fish?"

He replied, "Well, Morty decided he wanted to take us to the Loveless Café for supper tonight. What do you think?"

Excited, she ran to tell her mother and Sammie.

At the café about an hour later, the family had their favorite dishes, including the house specialty: fried chicken, biscuits, and jam. They talked about everyday family things, not a word about law or legal cases. Jake told silly jokes that kept everyone laughing. It had been a good family day for all of them.

Davis decided to wait to tell Liza and Sammie the good news about his "new" senior and junior associates until they got in the car for the ride home. He knew they would be pleased; he certainly was.

CHAPTER NINE

A SISTER'S HELP

FRIDAY, SEPTEMBER 11, 1992

Laura arrived at Davis's office ten minutes early. She had made arrangements for him to contact her mentor, Sister Leslie Carson. Davis was to place a conference call and interview Sister Carson as a potential expert witness. Sister Carson's testimony would criticize the hospital's credentialing of Herman and English. She would also speak to the failure of the Plainview committee system to stop the repeated acts of malpractice by Herman and English.

Laura had worked closely with Sister Carson during her residency at Saint Francis Hospital in Saint Paul, Minnesota. Carson was the president and administrator of Saint Francis and reported directly to the Board of Trustees as to hospital matters and to Mother Superior Paula Nash as to spiritual matters.

Saint Francis was a 250-bed, not-for-profit hospital. Because Sister Carson also sat on each of the medical committees that supervised the various functions of the hospital, she worked very closely with the medical staff. She was also responsible for the credentialing of all new physicians. She was an active member of the American Association of Hospital Administrators and the American Association of Healthcare Executives. With her background, Sister Carson's testimony would be very damaging against Plainview Community Hospital for its part in the conspiracy.

When Laura arrived at Davis's office, Bella greeted her with a Diet Coke and sat across from her in reception. Bella was almost six feet tall and had an ample bosom. Laura guessed she was in her early sixties.

"Are you a native Nashvillian, Ms. Rosario?"

"Please, call me Bella. No, I'm originally from New Jersey. I moved to Nashville in fifty-nine with my husband, Tony, and our three children. It has been a great place to raise a family.

"I've been Mr. Steine's secretary for thirty-three years, long before Mr. Davis joined us in 1975. I suppose you know that Mr. Steine is a legend in his own time. He has a marvelous reputation as a lawyer, not the least for his leadership in the civil rights movement and in helping singers gain power from the recording companies by becoming their own publishers. But even before he started the practice of law, he made his mark as a fighter pilot, first for the RAF and, then after Pearl Harbor, for the US Army Air Corps. He still flies today."

Changing the subject, Bella asked, "Where are you from, Doctor?"

Laura felt right at home with this woman who was everyone's mother personified. She took a sip of her Diet Coke and explained her background and heritage.

"I'm from West Fargo, North Dakota. My father emigrated from India with his brother in 1948. My mother is American. My parents, with my uncle and aunt, own a Howard Johnson motel and restaurant. My dad and uncle run the motel, and my mother and aunt run the HoJo's restaurant. My three cousins and I took turns as waitresses, maids, and laundresses. I didn't think I'd miss home when I moved to Tennessee, but I do."

Laura was surprised by how much she opened up to this stranger. It was not in her nature to openly discuss her life with such a new acquaintance, but it felt right.

"Did you move here with any family, Doctor?"

Laura hesitated only a moment. "I moved here with my life partner, Maggie. We have two daughters, Kim and Lee. Maggie's from Nashville. Her parents and two sisters are the reasons we moved to Plainview. It's only fifty-nine miles away."

"Bella, please bring Dr. Patel back," Davis's voice boomed from the intercom.

Davis extended his hand and gestured for Laura to take a seat. Although she had only met him briefly at the library meeting, she had been working with him closely via phone for the past six weeks. Laura had assisted Davis and Littleton in selecting the ten cases that best demonstrated a pattern of malpractice. Most were gallbladder cases, but Davis insisted that they pick a couple of other acts of malpractice to prove to the jury that the negligence wasn't limited to gallbladder surgery. She was impressed by his dedication; Ben Davis was a serious man on a mission. Laura couldn't testify as an expert witness because her litigation with the hospital rendered her far too biased.

After she completed her evaluations, the selected patients' charts were sent to Dr. Harlan Swanson and Dr. Ralph Adams. Davis retained these physicians to testify against Herman and English. Dr. Swanson was a board-certified family practitioner with an active medical practice in Connors, Georgia. Dr. Adams was a board-certified general surgeon who also worked out of

Connors and had performed more than one hundred laparoscopic gallbladder surgeries in the last seven years.

These expert witnesses were ideal because Connors' demographics were very similar to those of Plainview. Tennessee law required that expert witnesses practice medicine in a same or similar community as the defendant doctors, and the experts had to be from Tennessee or from a contiguous state. Within four weeks of receiving the ten patients' charts, Drs. Adams and Swanson generated detailed reports in each of the ten cases. In their professional opinions, Drs. English and Herman had been not only negligent but also reckless.

Laura felt that the reports were very comprehensive and detailed. On more than one occasion, she expressed that opinion to Davis. He assured Laura that he would be able to draft the complaints based on those reports.

Davis picked up the phone and dialed the number for Sister Carson. He hoped the Sister was able to at least skim the twenty reports he faxed to Saint Francis six days ago. Once the phone started to ring, Davis hit the speakerphone button.

"Sister, this is Ben Davis. Dr. Patel is here with me on speakerphone."

"Hello, Laura. So this is the famous Ben Davis that you've been raving about."

"It's a pleasure to meet you by telephone, Sister. Have you read Dr. Adams's and Dr. Swanson's reports?"

"I'm about halfway through them. It's a lot to digest. I've read ten reports on five of the cases. I was particularly impressed with Dr. Adams's criticism of the surgical proctoring procedure at Plainview. I'm amazed at how lax the hospital was in its credentialing."

Laura spoke up, "There's no real credentialing procedure. It's a matter of what the physician applies for. I could have requested procedures that I was unqualified to perform, but that would have violated my Osteopathic Oath. Herman and English clearly violated their Hippocratic Oath and took on procedures and surgeries that they were not qualified to perform."

Carson got right to the point: "Why didn't the Surgical or Pathology Committee expose these scoundrels?"

Laura almost flew out of her seat to answer the question: "The Executive Committee is composed of Dr. Kelly, the medical director; Woody Douglas, the hospital administrator; and the chairman of the pathology department. The Executive Committee controls the whole process. The individual committees rubber-stamp whatever the Executive Committee finds."

Davis broke in: "Is that the standard of care, Sister?"

Carson explained that at Plainview, the roles of the Executive Committee and the department committees were reversed; the departments, not the Executive Committee, should investigate.

"Plainview Community Hospital isn't following the standard of care set by its internal bylaws and regulations or by the standardized rules of the Joint Commission on Accreditation of Healthcare Organizations."

"Sister, I must ask you if you are willing to testify to that."

"I'm inclined to testify, but I must get permission from Mother Superior. What exactly would I be agreeing to do, Mr. Davis?"

Davis replied, "I will need a report in each of the ten

cases. Ninety percent of the reports would be identical because they all generally address the hospital's same breach of the standard of care."

He wanted Sister Carson to know what she was getting into. "The defense counsel will want to take your deposition after they've had an opportunity to read your reports. The deposition will probably take place in Nashville. They'll fly you down and put you up in a hotel room. The defendants will pay you an expert witness fee to take your deposition. I will also pay you for your time, reviewing the records, writing the reports, and testifying in court. The whole process will take maybe forty to sixty hours of your time. How much do you charge?"

"I've never been asked to be an expert witness before. What's the customary charge?"

"Experts charge by the hour. The dollar amount is based on your profession and level of experience. How much is your time worth?"

"Mr. Davis, my time is God's time. My salary as president and administrator of Saint Francis Hospital is nominal. I live with my order and have very little need for cash."

"Sister, you've got to charge for your services. You can donate your fees to the church if you want, but I can't let you work for nothing. How about $100 an hour? You can do with the fees as you see fit."

"All right by me, but I'll still have to get permission from Mother Superior. I have your contact information, and I'll get back to you. You're doing important work, Mr. Davis. God is looking down on you and wants justice to prevail."

"Thank you, Sister. I look forward to working with you."

When the line went dead, Davis turned to Laura. "She'll be great. She's got no ulterior motive. She simply wants justice to be served. The jury will love her. The fact that she's donating her fee to charity removes the prevailing bias of all experts. She has no financial gain."

Laura took a deep breath and changed the subject. "Ben, I need your help. Will you join my defense team and take the lead from Littleton?" It was apparent to Laura that Davis was the much better lawyer. He was personable and poised.

"Laura, I can't. If I became your attorney, it would reduce my credibility as the attorney in the Plainview malpractice cases. It's a matter of conflict of interest. It would be ethically improper to damage the interests of my clients. I'm sorry."

Laura got up without another word and left Davis's office. She wasn't mad at Davis. She understood, but she didn't like being stuck with Littleton. As she walked past Bella's desk, she was crying.

CHAPTER TEN

COUNTRY GIRL

WEDNESDAY, SEPTEMBER 16, 1992

Sammie was responsible for scheduling the appointments with the Plainview plaintiffs to go over the draft lawsuits that her uncle prepared. She was the firm's contact person with the clients during this initial stage.

Morty worked his magic with the press; he was very well connected. He played poker twice a month with two television station managers and for the last twenty years had a regular golf game with the editor of the *Banner*, Nashville's afternoon paper. As soon as the lawsuits were filed, he'd have no problem getting press coverage.

Edith Easter and her children, Allie and Howard, had a ten o'clock appointment. They were about fifteen minutes early, and Sammie led them to the conference room. She offered them Cokes or coffee.

Sammie had read the draft complaint, so she had a good idea of what happened to Edith Easter at Plainview Community Hospital. Her gallbladder surgery was unnecessary, and she suffered complications.

"How are you feeling, Mrs. Easter?"

"I'm feeling much better, thank you. I'm here 'cause Allie signed me up at your library meeting."

Allie broke in, "Dr. Herman urged Momma to have surgery, and then Dr. English screwed it up. She was sick for months because they wanted to make some insurance money."

At that moment Davis entered the conference room. He exchanged pleasantries but soon got down to business.

"Ms. Easter, based on your interview with Sammie, you executed a medical authorization, and I got copies of your mother's medical records. A medical doctor and I have reviewed them. These are the records." Davis pointed to a stack of documents six or seven inches thick.

"Based on my review of those medical records and an in-depth discussion with the medical doctor who reviewed your charts, I've prepared the draft complaint that I sent to you last week. Did you read it and make notes in the margin like I asked?"

Allie replied, "Mr. Davis, we don't understand it."

"Well, that's why we're meeting today. This document must be accurate, and you need to understand as best you can what it alleges. Do you know what the complaint is?"

"Not really," responded Allie.

"Well, let's start with that," Davis said.

Sammie was impressed with how at ease and patient her uncle was with these country folk. Davis, despite his Yankee background, had learned to communicate with his southern clients quite well. With Morty's help, he learned to talk slower and to enunciate his words. He was comfortable dealing with all types of persons, from Edith Easter to a client who was the president of a company.

He explained what a complaint was and how it functioned in the legal system. Then he said, "The law requires a person who brings a lawsuit, known as the plaintiff, to put in writing what you claim the hospital and the doctors did wrong. The doctors and the hospital, the parties being sued, are known as the defendants.

"This is a medical malpractice case. We are claiming that the hospital and the doctors made wrong decisions. We are claiming that the hospital and the doctors acted unreasonably and that the medical care you received was substandard, below what you were entitled to. That's called negligence. When a doctor and a hospital are negligent, that's called malpractice."

Sammie didn't think the Easters would ever understand the intricacies of the lawsuit, but she knew her uncle had to at least try to explain. Sammie pointed to the medical records on the table. "You don't understand those medical records, do you, Mrs. Easter?" she asked.

Edith Easter hesitated, choosing her words carefully, "Well, Miss, I dropped out of school in the sixth grade, so I don't read real good."

Sammie handed Mrs. Easter her copy of the complaint and pointed to a paragraph. "Can you read this?"

"I broke my glasses several months ago, and I can't read very good even with them."

Sammie pointed to Edith Easter's name in the third paragraph. "Do you recognize your name, Mrs. Easter?"

"Yes, but the rest of the paragraph don't mean nothing to me."

Davis turned to Allie and asked, "Do you read better than your mother?"

"Yes, sir, I can read, but I don't understand much."

"Well, we've got our work cut out for us today, but I have plenty of coffee and plenty more Cokes. So, we better get started."

Davis explained in the most basic terms what Mrs. Easter's medical records showed, interjecting the opinions of the experts he hired to review them. He explained that her surgery was unnecessary and that Dr. English messed up the surgery.

"The hospital's radiologist, Dr. Gerald, agrees with our expert that your gallbladder should not have been removed and that Dr. English perforated your bowel when he performed surgery."

Davis spent the next two hours reading the complaint and explaining each paragraph to the Easters. Allie asked a few questions, but basically Davis read and explained the document with little interruption.

"Mrs. Easter, if a jury finds that those tests and surgeries ordered by Dr. Herman and Dr. English were unnecessary and that the hospital knew or should have known that, the jury could award not only compensatory damages but also punitive damages. Compensatory damages are to compensate you for your injuries, while punitive damages are to punish the hospital and the doctors."

Finally, for the first time, Howard spoke up: "How much will the jury give Momma?"

Davis replied, "No one knows the answer to that question. It depends on how much a jury determines that your mother has lost as a result of negligence of the defendants. She's retired, so she has no lost wages. The amount of the award would vary from one jury to another. Juries are unpredictable. That's why most cases settle, because of the uncertainty."

The Easters spent more than four hours with Davis. Sammie wondered whether all of the Plainview meetings would be as exhausting and time consuming. When the Easters left, Sammie ushered in the next scheduled Plainview plaintiff. It was going to be a long day.

CHAPTER ELEVEN

SERVED

TUESDAY, OCTOBER 20, 1992

Dr. Herman was at his office at 6:30 a.m. Sheila got there a few minutes earlier. The patients began arriving at 7:00 sharp. Herman had scheduled several early-morning ultrasounds.

While Herman was mentally counting his money, Sheila walked in and said, "A Plains County deputy sheriff is here to see you."

When the deputy entered Herman's private office, he handed the doctor the legal documents. Herman was angry and embarrassed but tried to compose himself. Begrudgingly, he choked out a "thank you."

The deputy turned and left.

Herman sat down behind his desk and flipped through the complaint. The title of the document was Wendy and David Jones vs. Plainview Community Hospital, Dr. Lars Herman, and Dr. Charles English. The complaint was sixteen pages long, and Herman debated whether to read it all now or treat his patients. He put it aside for the moment and decided to read it at lunch. It was too important to skim through, and patients were waiting. He left his office upset, but there was money to be made.

By one o'clock he had seen more than ten patients. Eight of them required an ultrasound. Herman broke for lunch to eat his sandwich and read the complaint. With each word, he could feel his blood pressure rise:

> On November 5th, 1991, Wendy Jones, a twenty-five-year-old married person presented herself at Dr. Herman's office complaining of throbbing pain above the right eye and temple. She had experienced several episodes of dizziness and blurred vision. Dr. Herman admitted the patient to Plainview Community Hospital for tests and evaluation.

He tried to remember what Wendy Jones looked like, but he couldn't. He read further. The complaint alleged that he was negligent and reckless in failing to obtain a sedimentation rate. The complaint also alleged that he permitted Dr. English to perform unnecessary brain surgery on his patient and that Mrs. Jones should have never been admitted to the hospital for her symptoms.

Herman couldn't believe what he was reading. He could feel his blood pressure hit the roof. *Who are these lawyers to question me a year after the fact? My patient was in pain, and I was trying to diagnose the problem. How could that be negligence? How could that possibly be reckless?*

The document claimed that despite Herman's efforts and English's surgery, Wendy Jones continued to experience headaches for the next six months. Eventually, Mrs. Jones sought a second opinion and was prescribed medication, which ended her headaches after only two weeks.

Not only was Wendy Jones suing him, but also her husband, David, was suing him. How could the husband sue him when he'd never been a patient?

In the last section of the complaint, Wendy Jones claimed she was entitled to damages in the amount of $100,000. David Jones was seeking damages in the amount of $35,000 for disruption the surgery and his wife's recovery had on his marriage. It asserted loss of consortium, a disruption to their normal marital life, including the intimacy of their relationship. The complaint demanded that a jury try the issues. It was signed "Benjamin Davis, Attorney at Law."

He hated Benjamin Davis, even though he had never met the man. He threw the document to the floor in disgust but then bent down and picked it up, realizing that he needed to take action rather than pout.

He called Woody Douglas, who answered on the first ring. The hospital had also been served. Douglas told him not to worry but call his medical malpractice insurance carrier, Tennessee Mutual Insurance Company. Douglas assured Herman that his carrier would protect his interests and hire him the best defense lawyer. Feeling a little better, Herman hung up.

Next Herman called the insurance company and eventually got through to a vice president named Larry Pinsly. Pinsly was very calm. He asked Herman to fax the complaint so he could read it.

Before Pinsly hung up, he tried to settle the doctor's uneasiness. "Don't worry, Dr. Herman. I deal with this every day, and you shouldn't make a mountain out of a molehill. Tomorrow I'll call Sean McCoy, an excellent malpractice lawyer we keep on retainer. He'll be defending you. I'll also call the hospital's attorney, Grayson Stevenson. I know him very well, and we'll begin coordinating our defense. I don't think the company will have any trouble getting expert witnesses to testify that you didn't breach the standard of care."

Herman agreed and felt much better. He decided to return to work to take his mind off the problem. His next patient was the ninth ultrasound of the day. He referred six ultrasound patients to Dr. English for a surgical consult. For two years, Herman and English had had a profitable business relationship. However, English's personal life was starting to interfere. Charlie was falling apart. *I wonder whether Charlie is becoming mentally unstable? Legal fees, child support, and alimony have placed incredible financial stress on him. His appearance has deteriorated, and he looks disheveled and unprofessional most of the time now. Will patients start to doubt his ability?*

With these thoughts racing through his mind, Herman was moving the ultrasound wand over a young woman's abdomen when he heard a knock at the door. It was Sheila, and she seemed upset.

He came to the door, even though he didn't like to be disturbed. "Sheila, what is it? I'm kind of busy here!"

Sheila sheepishly responded, "Doctor, the postman's here, and he has a certified letter from the Board of Medical Examiners. He insists only you can sign for it."

He asked Sheila to bring the postman to his office. Herman signed the certified letter, and the postman left. The top left-hand corner of the envelope was embossed with the Board of Medical Examiners' logo.

The board's main function is to issue, suspend, and revoke medical licenses. *The lawsuit is a pain in the ass and a tremendous inconvenience. However, the insurance coverage will pay out any judgment against me. But if my license is suspended or revoked, I could lose everything,* thought Herman.

The title of the document was Notice of Charges. It identified the authority and responsibilities of the Tennessee Board of Medical Examiners. The notice was divided into sections, each identifying a separate accusation of a patient. Herman read the allegations: thirty counts of overmedicating and prescribing improper medications; twenty-six counts of performing unnecessary ultrasounds; eighteen counts of unnecessary surgical recommendations; and one count of issuing a false death certificate. Herman faced a total of seventy-five separate charges. If he was found guilty of the charges, the Board of Medical Examiners threatened the revocation of his medical license and a civil assessment of $150,000. The notice recommended that Herman retain counsel. It added that a hearing would be scheduled in accordance with due process.

While he read the state's claims against him, the room grew hotter and hotter as the sunlight blazed through the window. He could hear the traffic outside. Suddenly, Herman had a blistering headache. He opened his desk drawer, pulled out a bottle of aspirin, and took three.

He faxed the Notice of Charges to Pinsly of Tennessee Mutual. He wouldn't call Woody Douglas. He knew that English would be calling him after he saw the postman. Herman sighed. Charlie was already half crazy, and this problem might push him over the edge. He decided to wait for Charlie's call.

CHAPTER TWELVE

A NEW CLIENT

THURSDAY, OCTOBER 29, 1992

Amy Pierce's day began with the sounds of Bruce Springsteen's "Born to Run." She reached across her empty bed to turn off the alarm. She sat up quickly and walked into the bathroom to splash water on her face to wake up. She had a full day ahead.

Looking into her vanity mirror, she felt old. She had dark rings under her eyes, and the black roots at the crown of her red hair were starting to show. Although she was only thirty-six years old, her youth was slipping away while she worked seventy hours a week. She had no time for exercise, and her once-supple body had lost its firmness and ached.

She stretched her arms over her head and bent first to the right and then to the left. As she moved from side to side, she was an imposing figure at five feet nine and a half inches. She had been an All-State center for her local high school. She had a scholarship to Harpeth Hall, a girls' school in Nashville. The school had high academic standards, so Amy had to work hard there. Her aunt, the school's librarian, raised her after the deaths of her parents in a car accident.

Turning sideways in the mirror, she puffed out her stomach. Despite her lack of physical activity, she still had firm, supple breasts and no belly, and she weighed in at only 120 pounds. *Things could be worse.*

Amy walked into her son's bedroom. Carter was still fast asleep under his dinosaur quilt. She switched on the bedside lamp and gently nudged Carter awake.

"Morning, sweetheart. Happy birthday!"

"Morning, Mommy. Can I have my presents now?"

Amy brushed his matted hair off his forehead and planted a kiss.

"Why don't we have breakfast first? What would you like? You can have whatever you want since it's your birthday."

Carter gleefully responded to his mother's question with one of his own: "Birthday cake?"

Amy tried to formulate a diplomatic response: "If we eat the birthday cake now, what will we serve your friends tonight at Chuck E. Cheese's?"

Carter understood the predicament and shrugged his shoulders. "I guess I'll have a Pop-Tart in the car. I'll save the cake for later."

By 6:00 a.m., Amy and Carter were in the car on the way to school. She was thankful that Carter's school had a morning care program. It meant that she could get an earlier start to her day at the law firm.

She was a senior associate with the Nashville law firm of Dunn, Moore and Thomas, also known as DMT. The firm specialized in the defense of insurance companies. For four years, Amy had labored long hours at DMT, as was expected of associates. Working the twelve-hour days, five days a week, and at least eight hours on Saturday, she was expected to get her work done, and if there weren't enough hours in a six-day week, then her Sundays with Carter had to be sacrificed. DMT didn't worry about whether its associates attended church; the work came first.

Rather than give up her family day, she chose to bring work home during the week and work long after Carter had gone to bed. Most nights, Amy didn't fall asleep until two, and she was up before six. Long ago, she learned to get by on less than four hours of sleep.

Amy desperately hoped her hard work would be rewarded with a partnership. The promise of that achievement was the very reason she returned home following her divorce. She knew achieving partnership in New York would be arduous. She also recognized that back home Carter would have a good environment in which to grow up near the aunt who raised her and her younger cousins. Amy's decision to return to her hometown of Franklin, Tennessee, and work in Nashville was not the path she originally intended, however.

In 1983, Amy Pierce graduated second in her class from the University of Virginia Law School. Her ex-husband, Daniel Smith, was the valedictorian. After graduation, Dan and Amy, Mr. and Mrs., one and two, had accepted positions with large law firms in New York City. But their jobs were very demanding, with each working eighty hours a week. They barely saw each other. While Amy loved the work and the pace, Dan crumbled under the pressure. Their marriage was always under stress, and the birth of Carter added to their existing problems. Even Amy had difficulty balancing motherhood and career.

Dan was no help when it came to Carter. He was no more ready for fatherhood than he was for a high-intensity career and marriage. Dan became an alcoholic and, despite trying AA, eventually got fired because of his drinking. At twenty-nine, he was washed up and spiraling downward. Amy had no intent of being pulled down with him, so she divorced Dan and moved to Franklin.

She took the I-65 exit ramp toward downtown Nashville. Amy was in a particular rush this morning because before she left last night, the firm's managing partner, Lowell Thomas, requested an 8:00 a.m. meeting to discuss Amy's assignment of a new client. Amy wanted to review the background of the client, Planter's Insurance Company, or PIC, before sitting down with Thomas. She had been given a great opportunity, and she intended to make the most of it. The information in the file on her desk told her that Planter's was going to be a substantial and lucrative client. This assignment would raise Amy's visibility at the firm above the other associates and might increase her status with the Partnership Committee.

As she was thinking of her new client and trying cases on its behalf, Thomas stuck his head in her office. "Amy, change of plans. I need to cancel our meeting. Last night, Jim Davenport of PIC called and said he'd be in Nashville for lunch. He requested a noon lunch meeting with the two of us, so rearrange your schedule."

Because she was unsure of the meeting's length, Amy rescheduled two appointments.

At 11:40, Thomas walked back into her office. "Let's go. I don't want to keep Davenport waiting."

Amy and Thomas rode the elevator to the twenty-seventh floor to the Capitol City Club. Despite Thomas's best efforts to be early, Davenport was waiting in the entry hall. Thomas introduced Amy to Davenport, and they were led to their table. The trio exchanged greetings and chitchatted for a few minutes.

Davenport proceeded to cross-examine Amy about her education, employment, and experience, even though he already knew the answers from her bio in the firm's brochure. He wanted to hear it from her.

Davenport then guided the conversation to PIC. He described the company's history and business philosophy. Two families, one from Birmingham and the other from New Orleans, had founded PIC in 1954. Previously, the company had limited its coverage to medical malpractice insurance in Alabama and Louisiana. After seeing an opportunity in new markets, PIC decided to expand to Tennessee and Arkansas, and Davenport was the newly appointed regional manager for the state of Tennessee.

He looked directly at Amy. "You'll be dealing with doctors. They're used to calling all the shots, and surgeons are by far the worst. Nobody in their office or at the hospital ever stands up to them. The doctors just run roughshod over everyone who comes in contact with them. Handling a lawsuit is not like being in charge of a medical team in an operating room. In an operating room everybody is working toward a common goal, to help the patient. Doctors are simply not equipped to deal with the adversarial nature of a lawsuit, so you need to take firm control over the litigation."

Amy was well aware that doctors were difficult clients. Probably the only thing worse was representing another lawyer.

This was Davenport's meeting, and he continued, "A lawsuit is a business transaction. You've got to weigh the risk and the monetary cost of a judgment against the cost of defense. Luckily, here in Tennessee, you've got a natural impetus against large awards, the jury system. Tennesseans are naturally conservative and suspicious. They don't give large judgments, and they especially don't award punitive damages. PIC has been doing business in Alabama and Louisiana for almost forty years. Jury verdicts in Alabama are out of control. The city of Huntsville is a fourth the size of Nashville, yet our research shows that on average Huntsville's juries give verdicts three and four times greater than those of Nashville."

Amy followed the dollar amount of jury awards throughout the United States; the sizes of those awards were directly related to the geographic location of the trial. Certain states were actually competing to see which local community gave the largest verdict. For example, in last month's *New York Bar Journal,* an attorney in a closing statement argued that Brooklyn, and not the Bronx, had the largest award of compensatory damages in a medical malpractice case. No wonder the tort reform movement was picking up steam throughout the country.

Tennesseans were just the opposite of New Yorkers. They prided themselves on their conservative nature. It was no fluke that people in Tennessee were simply less willing to compensate plaintiffs. Amy knew that was the draw for PIC to Tennessee.

"There are almost three times as many defendants' verdicts in Tennessee than in Alabama. The statistics are similar for Arkansas. That's why PIC is moving into those markets."

Thomas responded to Davenport: "Jim, PIC has made the right decision. The Tennessee malpractice insurance market is wide open. Your competitor, Tennessee Mutual, insures more than eighty percent of the doctors in the state, and it has become lazy. Its premiums have steadily risen despite the fact that the doctors own it. Everybody knows doctors are not good businessmen. There's a real opportunity here for PIC, and I'm confident DMT is the right firm for PIC's litigation needs. We'll make damn sure that PIC doesn't have to pay out any large verdicts."

Davenport got down to specifics: "I've got your first case. Well, your first five anyway. Our insured is a general surgeon by the name of Charles English. There have been at least five lawsuits filed against him in Plains County Circuit Court by Benjamin Davis and Bradley Littleton. Do you know either of them?"

Amy responded, "I don't know Littleton, but I've seen Davis in court. He's good. I've never had a case against him, but I'm sure several of our partners have. He's well thought of as a trial attorney by the Bar. Davis used to be partnered with Morty Steine, who retired this year. Steine was a master in the courtroom, and we're fortunate he's gone. How many lawsuits did you say have been filed?"

"As of yesterday, there were five," Davenport replied. "I've got a call in to the clerk to see if any additional complaints have been filed today. The state's also brought charges against English, threatening to revoke his medical license and assess civil penalties. I'm convinced Davis or Steine instigated the state charges."

Amy was excited. Getting five lawsuits was a great first day with a new client.

Davenport said, "I spoke with English, and as you might expect, he's a basket case. Each case also names

Dr. Lars Herman, a family practitioner. It appears that the two doctors hold privileges at Plainview Community Hospital. Herman is also English's landlord. The hospital has also been sued."

Amy was taking copious notes, and Davenport gave her English's telephone number.

Davenport wrapped up the meeting. He had to be in Knoxville for a dinner meeting with PIC's newly appointed East Tennessee counsel. Davenport promised Thomas and Amy that the lawsuits would be faxed to their office by the end of the day.

After Davenport left, Thomas turned to Amy: "You need to deliver, not just talk a good game. That means winning lawsuits and, when necessary, settling them on the cheap. Davenport is right about one thing. You'd better control these doctors. This surgeon English sounds like he'll be a good test."

Assuring Thomas that she could handle whatever these doctors could throw at her, Amy returned to the sixteenth floor and got back to work.

It took all afternoon for the five lawsuits to be faxed. Each lawsuit was almost twenty pages long, and Amy placed each lawsuit in a separate file. She wouldn't be able to read through them before she would have to leave early for Carter's birthday party. She decided to return the phone calls she missed when she was at lunch. She would jump into the cases first thing tomorrow morning.

CHAPTER THIRTEEN

OPPORTUNITY KNOCKS

FRIDAY, OCTOBER 30, 1992

Carter's birthday party at Chuck E. Cheese's was a resounding success, complete with twenty of his friends. Amy let him stay up past nine playing with his new Nintendo game.

It had been such a hectic week that she neglected to get him a Halloween costume for the school Halloween party. She meant to stop at Toys "R" Us to pick up a Ninja Turtle costume but kept forgetting because she was in a constant rush. She was panicked this morning, rushing around, pulling random clothes together to create a hobo costume. She made a rucksack out of a branch from the yard and attached a handkerchief stuffed with newspaper to the end.

When Carter got up, she furiously applied makeup to his cheeks to further enhance the hobo image. When she was finished, he looked like Emmett Kelly of Ringling Brothers fame.

"But I wanted to be Raphael from the Ninja Turtles," the boy whined.

"I'm sorry, Carter. I'll pick up a Ninja Turtle costume tomorrow. You can be Raphael when we go trick-or-treating tomorrow night."

Carter was not pleased, and he got into the car without saying another word.

Amy arrived at the office just before eight o'clock and dug right into the English lawsuits. She decided to start by reading the notice of charges brought by the state's Medical Licensing Board. The charges were quite detailed, and it took an hour to read them carefully. The state asserted that English and Herman entered into a conspiracy to perform unnecessary procedures and surgeries. The state claimed a pattern of negligent medical care and treatment of patients at Plainview Community Hospital. The charges concluded by claiming that this pattern constituted recklessness.

As Amy wrote down the charges, a messenger brought two banker boxes into her office.

"Mr. Thomas told me to deliver these medical records."

Amy looked at the summary sheet that Thomas's secretary prepared, identifying each of the five Plainview cases. She decided to start with the Rosie Malone death case. She retrieved Malone's medical records from one of the boxes. They included a three-inch-thick hospital chart, Dr. Herman's office records, more than two inches thick, and Dr. English's incredibly thin office records. Knowing this would take some time, she relished the fact that she billed by the hour.

The Malone complaint was sixteen pages long and well written. Davis knew how to draft a pleading. Amy read the complaint and made notes on a legal pad.

The complaints were divided into four distinct parts: "The Parties," "The Facts," "The Allegations," and "The Damages." Amy's answers filed on behalf of English would deny each of the parties' claims. Generally, the strategy of the defense was to initially deny all of the facts, the allegations, and the nature and extent of damages.

Other times, Amy would assert she had insufficient information to either admit or deny a specific allegation and would deal with responsive answers another day. She needed to thoroughly read through each case and digest it before formulating the answers.

She opened Dr. English's office record for Rosie Malone. It contained an admission history, a physical, an operative report, a surgical report, and one physician note. "Not much of a file," Amy said out loud. English's records reflected treatment from January 29th through 6:00 p.m. on the 30th.

Next were Herman's office records. Rosie Malone had been Dr. Herman's patient from January 1990 until her death in February 1992. During that period Herman had seen the patient at least a dozen times in his office. Herman had provided a lot of care and treatment to this patient. No question that Herman, not English, was Rosie Malone's primary care physician.

The handwriting in the file was illegible, however. Amy could read only about every fourth word. The handwritten notes would be a nightmare, particularly for Davis. She presumed English and Herman could read them.

The typed records revealed that Rosie Malone was a sick person long before she met Amy's client. She had been hospitalized at Plainview Community in 1990 and again in 1991 with heart problems, pulmonary problems, and a long history of stomach pain. Mrs. Malone had smoked two packs a day for more than forty years, and according to Dr. Herman's records, she was an alcoholic and a drug seeker.

Amy thought, *Mrs. Malone is far from an ideal plaintiff.* Then she grinned. Rosie Malone's prior conditions would significantly lower any award of compensatory damages.

As she went through the January-February hospital records, it was apparent how quickly Rosie Malone deteriorated after her surgery. Fortunately, English left for vacation the day after the Malone surgery, transferring the responsibility of postoperative care to Dr. Herman. That explained why English had written only one postoperative note. The patient should have been transferred long before February 5th.

The death certificate signed by Herman cited "cardiac arrest." Her heart stopped. *Well, everyone's heart stops when he or she dies.* Even from her brief reading of the Malone file, Amy recognized that Mrs. Malone died of septicemia, not cardiac arrest. Herman had to be kidding.

She was glad that her client hadn't falsified the death certificate. At some point during the case, her strategy would be to shift the comparative fault to Herman. She would try to hold off accusing Herman as long as possible to secure and maintain the cooperation of McCoy, Herman's lawyer. Davis needed to be the common enemy of the defendants.

Just as Amy was strategizing, Thomas buzzed her on the phone: "Morning, Amy. Have you begun work on the answers?"

"I'm about two hours into it."

"How does it look?"

"I don't want to jump to conclusions, but based upon the Malone case, Davis could argue that the surgery was unnecessary. The postoperative care was negligent, but English left town the next day. We can push the responsibility of postoperative care on Dr.

Herman. He treated her for years. He'll take the fall, not English. The compensatory damages should be minimal as the plaintiff had no income and poor health."

Amy could tell even over the phone that Thomas was processing what she just told him.

He responded, "Have you read the Supreme Court decision of Hodges vs. Toof?"

"Of course I have. But I can't give you a definitive answer on recklessness or punitive damages. What I can tell you is that we're going to make a fortune trying to figure it out. We need to coordinate with McCoy on these cases. The longer we can maintain a common front, the better. If we stand together, Davis's job will be much more difficult. There will be plenty of time to shift blame onto Herman and the hospital."

"You're on track. Keep focused, and make us big money."

"Don't worry, Lowell. I've got everything under control."

"Keep me in the loop."

Thomas hung up, and Amy returned to the Malone case. After she finished reading the other four complaints, she decided she needed to introduce herself to her client.

She dialed the number Davenport had given her the day before. The receptionist put her through to English.

"Dr. Charles English, can I help you?"

"Dr. English, my name is Amy Pierce, and I'm with Dunn, Moore and Thomas, a law firm in Nashville. I'm your attorney. I believe Mr. Davenport of PIC told you that you'd be hearing from me. I've read the five complaints—"

English interrupted and in a loud voice proclaimed,

"What a bunch of bullshit! Dr. Herman and I gave the best possible care. Medicine is an art, not a science. There is no guarantee in life. Every one of those patients signed a consent form, and each consent form identified the known risks of surgery. Did you say you read the five lawsuits? I was served with another one today. The total now is six."

Amy asked him to fax over the sixth lawsuit. She then tried to take charge of the situation: "Doctor, I don't want you discussing these lawsuits with anyone other than Mr. Davenport and me. Anything you say to anyone else is admissible in court. I particularly don't want you discussing these lawsuits with Dr. Herman or any other hospital employee. If Dr. Herman tries to discuss them, just blame me. For now, all your communications need to come through me—"

He interrupted again and began a tirade about Ben Davis and the unfounded lawsuits.

She let him rant. He needed to vent, and Amy was the only one who could listen without English injuring his defense. But after fifteen minutes, even though she was billing PIC $200 an hour, she heard enough.

Amy politely interrupted. "I apologize, Doctor. I have a four o'clock appointment," she lied. "My secretary tells me they are waiting in reception. Can I call you tomorrow? What would be a good time?"

"I have a laser gallbladder surgery in the morning. I should be back in the office before noon."

She looked at her calendar. "Why don't I call you at twelve thirty, and we can pick up where we left off?"

They said their good-byes, and Amy hung up. Thinking about what just transpired, she picked up the phone and punched in Lowell Thomas's extension: "Do you have ten minutes?"

"If we can both bill for it, I've got thirty minutes till my next appointment. Come on by."

Within two minutes, Amy was knocking on Thomas's door. As she walked in, he asked, "What can I do for you? More important, who are we billing for the next half hour?"

Amy gave Thomas the twenty-minute version of the English lawsuits. She brought in one of the complaints and quoted from the pleading. Thomas silently took in his associate's words until she paused for a breath.

Thomas jumped in: "Six lawsuits and counting. This could be a gold mine. You'll never try all six, but if you try one or two, the fees will be close to half a million. PIC will become one of our biggest clients. Thank you, Dr. English."

Despite the fact that Thomas was her boss and a named partner, Amy interrupted, "That's why I'm here. This is my big opportunity. And I want some guarantees before I bust my ass and make this firm and its partnership wealthier. Lowell, I've worked hard, and I've turned in results. If I deliver in these Plainview cases, I want your promise of partnership."

"Now, don't be too effective and resolve this matter quickly. We want to milk this situation awhile. You bill, say, at least six hundred hours and then settle them cheap. The new Supreme Court comparative fault and punitive damage opinions should be good for at least a hundred hours of research and briefing alone in these cases," he told her.

"Lowell, stop seeing dollar signs for a second and answer my question. If I deliver on these Plainview cases, do I get my partnership?"

Thomas again avoided the question and mentioned that she'd be working with Grayson Stevenson's firm, which would be representing the hospital. He then said, "We need to feel out the other defense counsel. It's important we present a united front. Eventually the hospital will turn on the doctors and their insurance companies. These two doctors are pretty much attached at the hip, at least until trial. It sounds like Herman should take the brunt of the fall. In that death case, it was Herman's patient, and our client smartly left on vacation immediately after surgery. It's hard to blame English for the postoperative care if he was more than nine hundred miles away."

Amy was becoming annoyed at Thomas for avoiding the most important question of her life. She needed his commitment, or she would quit right here and now. Why do all the work and just let Thomas and his partners make the money? She wanted a partnership from this opportunity. If not, then she had no doubt that she could easily get a job at another Nashville firm. She was a real asset wherever she went and knew she could eventually earn a partnership anywhere. However, it might be years before she was handed another opportunity like the Plainview cases. Most associates never were offered a partnership on a silver platter, but Plainview was most definitely silver.

She needed to be somewhat diplomatic with Thomas and not blow her opportunity. It was still his firm and his firm's client. Davenport and PIC would stay with DMT if she decided to leave. So she took a slightly different approach: "In each case the plaintiff is seeking punitive damages based on recklessness. The Tennessee

Supreme Court opinion in Hodges vs. Toof will, as you say, guarantee a hundred hours of research and briefing. I suspect the six cases will require at least a hundred depositions. The depositions, for the most part, must be taken in Plains County, and I'll charge $200 an hour to travel back and forth for each deposition and court appearance. I'll be billing a fortune over the next eighteen months. I can stretch these cases out for at least three years."

Thomas was getting more excited by the moment, as if he was watching a pole dancer at a strip club. However, his available half hour was up, and his secretary buzzed to say that his appointment was waiting.

Amy stood her ground. "I need an answer right now. I'm not leaving your office without your promise of a partnership."

She folded her arms across her chest and waited for Thomas's next move. He clearly didn't like her ultimatum. But the single mother was convinced that the best move was to press the issue.

Thomas stared at her hard; she'd cornered him and was insisting on an answer.

Amy was both excited and scared by what he might say next.

"You deliver on these Plainview cases, and you get your partnership."

"That's two points, Lowell. I'll send you a confirming memo when I get back to my office."

CHAPTER FOURTEEN

FLIP OF A COIN

THURSDAY, NOVEMBER 12, 1992

Davis was tired. He had slept only two hours the previous night, worrying about the scheduling conference before Judge Boxer.

Morty had always told Davis that the judicial system was supposed to have a predetermined order, but it was flawed and almost never worked the right way. The goal of the scheduling conference was to set deadlines. Deadlines meant that the cases were moving toward trial. Plaintiffs wanted cases to get to trial while defendants rarely wanted to see the inside of a courtroom. A trial carried the risk of a jury verdict. Generally, delay was a defendant's friend. In the case of the Plainview lawsuits, Davis needed the order of the trials to be set so he knew on which case to focus his time and money.

It was a beautiful November morning in Middle Tennessee, and the temperature was mild. Davis and Morty were in Davis's black Eldorado convertible. Davis didn't let Sammie attend the meeting with defense attorneys, held the day before. She spent the day at the office with Bella, while Morty and Davis met with Stevenson, Pierce, McCoy, and Barnes.

Morty scolded Davis that not including Sammie was a bad decision. "How do you expect her to learn if she doesn't observe what happens in the real world and how we handle it? You're a schmuck. She's my responsibility. I'm making the call next time."

Davis was forced to be defensive: "Look, she's got skills, but she's a distraction. She takes up my time and energy."

"It's no longer your problem," Morty shot back.

Davis changed the subject. "How long do you think this damn hearing will take?" he yelled over the howling wind.

Morty hated that the top was down in November. Davis also had annoying habits, which included playing music too loud, without the courtesy of headphones.

Morty expected the hearing to last a few hours. That is, he said, "unless Boxer takes immediate and absolute control of his courtroom. I doubt he will. There are a lot of strong personalities, and they'll be long-winded."

Davis didn't like that answer. He figured that Morty included himself as one of those strong personalities and, jokingly he thought, long-winded. There were at least four defense lawyers for four defendants, and he represented only one party in each case. The process could easily turn into a free-for-all, which would not be in his clients' best interest.

Davis decided to put in his two cents. "I don't think it will take that long. The parties' counsel got a lot of hard work done yesterday. We spent four hours together. We just haven't agreed on the order of the cases. It's our choice. We filed the lawsuits, so we get to decide the order. I wish we had found case law to support that position."

Morty said, "We can assume the defendants didn't find anything favorable on the point either, or they would have argued it yesterday and included those citations in their brief. The judge should be pleased with all that was accomplished by the parties before this hearing."

The four hours of hard work resulted in ten draft-scheduling orders, which set deadlines over the next five and a half years. The trials were scheduled about five months apart with the first case being set sometime in January 1994. The attorneys were in general agreement on the order of the deadlines. The group was able to agree that in the ten cases there were at least eighty-eight specific individuals who had to be deposed, including twenty-three plaintiffs. These witnesses included the injured plaintiffs, their spouses, and the ten Malone children.

The parties agreed that certain depositions, known as common depositions, would be taken only once and then used in all ten cases, which would save both time and money. There were at least forty-eight common depositions; the cost would be shared among Davis's ten clients.

Apart from the common depositions, Davis would have deposed at least seventeen witnesses whose testimony would pertain only to a single case. Everyone agreed that it was impossible at that point to set specific depositions until the order of the cases was determined. The attorneys brought their calendars and set aside seventy-six days between Thanksgiving 1992 and July 4th, 1993, to take depositions in the Plainview cases. Coordinating seventy-six dates for depositions among at least four lawyers' calendars was a monumental feat. The lawyers would later determine which depositions would be taken on which dates. The order of depositions would be determined based upon the availability of the witnesses.

It was a delicate balance for the plaintiffs. Davis and Morty wanted to push the cases to trial, yet they had to give themselves sufficient time to prepare each case.

Despite the general agreement among counsel, the previous night's meeting ended badly. Without any intent, Davis happened to glance over at Stevenson's open folder and discovered that Stevenson had a generic letter that Davis sent to all ten of his own clients. Like Morty, Davis could read upside down. Davis was outraged that Stevenson had the document. The letter notified Davis's clients of the upcoming scheduling conference and had no strategic value, but Davis's concern was that Stevenson had the letter. There was a leak, and eventually that leak would provide critical information to the defense. The leak had to be plugged or used to the plaintiffs' advantage.

Before leaving Stevenson's office, Davis took Morty aside and revealed what Stevenson had. Morty pointed out that only their clients, their clients' families, or someone with access to the ten mailboxes could have taken and provided the letter to adversary counsel. Morty convinced Davis not to confront Stevenson and instead figure out a way to use the theft of their communications to their advantage.

Davis took Morty's advice but could not control his emotions. His attitude changed during the last part of the meeting when he accused Grayson Stevenson of trying to manipulate the jury and the outcome of the trial. The parties could not agree on trial venues or the order the cases would be tried. Davis argued that his clients could not get a fair and unbiased trial in Plains

County. The hospital was the largest employer in the county, and people not working at the hospital were related to or friends with someone employed there.

Stevenson argued that the defendants had a right to try the cases before the citizens of Plains County, not by strangers. Stevenson's position was generally correct under Tennessee law. Therefore, the burden was on Davis to prove that a fair trial was impossible. Under the law, Davis would have to present at least three affidavits of disinterested citizens that a fair trial was impossible in Plains County. The final decision about where the trials would be held would be within the discretion of Judge Boxer.

After the meeting, Morty suggested that their plan should be to isolate those persons whom they suspected had fed the defendants the letter and feed them harmless false information. If they could reduce the number of suspects to five or six, they could vary the false information to isolate the traitor. If they could discover the identity of the source, the defendants and their counsel would be in trouble.

Morty and Davis had no problem with defense counsel trying to manipulate the verdict by who sat on the jury. An attempt to manipulate the order of the cases was a legitimate goal of defense counsel. That was their job, but using stolen letters crossed the line.

The order in which the cases were tried was critical. Whether the defendants were negligent was an important question. The more important question, however, was whether the first jury found recklessness and awarded punitive damages, and the dollar amount awarded to the first plaintiff was most important. The dollar amount of compensatory damages depended on the specific circumstances of each case and the extent of the plaintiff injuries. Another factor in the amount of the award was just how likable the plaintiff was. Whether punitive damages were awarded was a matter of how upset Davis could get the jury. The jury needed to want to punish the defendants.

In contrast, the defense wanted to try the cases where the patient suffered the least damages first, thereby burning up Davis's limited resources. The outcome of this scheduling conference and its resulting order were critical to the cases.

At nine o'clock sharp, Judge Boxer entered the courtroom. Everyone stood in deference. Boxer's clerk recited the traditional opening of court, and Boxer started the proceeding.

"Where are we on an agreed scheduling order? I would prefer that you gentlemen and lady work this out without my intervention."

Stevenson rose and advised the court that counsel for the parties had worked diligently and cooperatively on the scheduling orders. He admitted to the court that some issues were not yet resolved that required the court's guidance. Stevenson noted the issues of trial venue and the order of the cases. Stevenson's presentation was evenhanded. Davis stood and confirmed that Mr. Stevenson correctly identified the remaining issues to be resolved by the court.

Boxer instructed Stevenson to hand the draft scheduling orders to his clerk, who promptly delivered it to Boxer. Boxer spent several minutes scanning the documents. Davis could tell from Boxer's face that the judge did not expect as much progress from these adversaries.

The judge decided to praise them: "I'm pleased. These draft orders show hard work, cooperation, and reasonableness on everyone's part. As to the venue of these trials, I agree with Mr. Davis that a change of venue motion is appropriate. Please file that motion by next Friday, with the supporting affidavits. Despite the heavy burden the plaintiffs must carry, I'm inclined to grant that motion. Mr. Davis, in your motion, please identify where the plaintiffs suggest these cases be tried. If changed, all of the remaining motions in these cases will be held at this venue. I would prefer Hawaii, but the statute provides that the cases must be moved to the closest courthouse where the alleged bias would not prevent a fair trial."

Davis thought he would try a joke to loosen the mood: "What about Bermuda, Your Honor?"

"That's a foreign territory, Mr. Davis. Just identify the proper venue in your motion."

Davis was pleased with the court's remarks and the predetermined granting of his motion. Boxer was inviting Davis to move the lawsuits to Hewes City. At least, it didn't appear that these cases would be tried in Plains County.

The next issue was the order of the cases. This ruling was even more important than the venue question. Davis waited for the judge to address the issue. It was his courtroom. A moment later, Davis got the answer to his question.

"As to the order these cases will be tried, I'm not going to let Mr. Davis determine the order. I will, however, let him call heads or tails."

Judge Boxer pulled a quarter from his pants pocket under his robe and placed it on the back of his hand near his thumb. Both Davis and Steine were astonished by the unique way to resolve a legal issue.

Davis spoke up: "You're kidding, right?"

When the judge neither smiled nor indicated he was joking, Davis continued, "Judge, the flip of a coin is arbitrary. I object to this method of selection. The plaintiffs should select which case is tried first."

"Can you cite a Tennessee case or statute, Mr. Davis?"

Davis decided not to give up so easily. "There's no Tennessee case right on point, Your Honor, but—"

The judge interrupted, "There's no controlling precedent. It's my discretion, Mr. Davis. Call it in the air."

Judge Boxer sent the quarter up in the air, and Davis yelled out, "Heads."

"Sorry, Mr. Davis, it's tails. Mr. Stevenson, please confer with your co-counsel and select the first case to be tried."

Stevenson, McCoy, Barnes, and Pierce huddled and conferred for less than two minutes. Stevenson, as the appointed spokesperson for the defense, walked back to the podium and said, "The defendants select the Jones case."

Davis groaned inwardly. That choice was a nightmare for him. The surgery was clearly unnecessary, but there were no substantial damages. The twenty-five-year-old patient had a small scar on the side of her head where Dr. English performed an unnecessary temporal artery biopsy. The scar was covered by Mrs. Jones's hair.

Davis rose and walked to the podium. He felt anger start to surface, but he controlled his emotions. He was not afraid of Judge Boxer, but he needed to show respect. Morty had warned him, "First impressions are important, and you'll be appearing before Boxer over the next few years, so remain poised and reasonable. Don't show anger."

Davis chose his words carefully: "With all due respect, the court is committing reversible error. The flip of a coin is arbitrary and cannot be a fair and impartial way to select the order of these cases."

The judge was getting angry with Davis and asked, "What's unfair about gravity, Mr. Davis? The plaintiffs had a fifty percent chance, and they lost. Fifty-fifty seems pretty fair to me."

"Your Honor, because this was a scheduling conference, I did not have a court reporter present to record what was said and the court's ruling. In the court's order, I would ask that the court include the method the court relied upon, a flip of a coin, and the plaintiff's objection to method."

"I'll include it in the order, Mr. Davis. Please select the second case to be tried."

"I'd rather not, Your Honor. Why do we need to select the second case at this time?"

"Because I say so, Mr. Davis, and I'm the judge."

Davis felt sick to his stomach. His argument was going badly, close to disastrous. Davis looked at Morty and shook his head in disgust. Davis looked back up at Judge Boxer. "If I have to, sir, the Malone case."

"Mr. Davis, you've lost this argument. You can appeal my decision to the Court of Appeals two years from now, after we try the Jones case."

Davis decided he better stop arguing with the judge. He was sure that Morty would scold him later.

Judge Boxer knew who was in charge. Without a

motion from either side, he pronounced, "I'm also imposing a gag order. Neither side will encourage further publicity of these cases. We've had three articles in the Nashville papers, and over the last two months more than an hour of airtime on the Nashville stations. I assume the hospital is the party that kept these suits out of the local paper, the *Plains County Gazette.* No interviews. All I want to hear is 'no comment.'"

Boxer informed all concerned that if his gag order was violated, the guilty party would be held in contempt. The punishment, depending on the act, would involve both fine and imprisonment.

"Do we understand each other, Mr. Davis?"

"Absolutely, Your Honor." Davis didn't like being singled out.

Davis and Stevenson alternately selected the order of all ten cases. When it was over, almost like kids in a schoolyard choosing teams, Boxer announced that court was adjourned and left the courtroom.

Davis was not happy with the outcome of the hearing or with Judge Boxer. Although Morty taught him never to show emotion in front of his adversary counsel, Davis lost his cool and slammed his fist on the table. After he did it, he knew that he made a serious tactical mistake. Morty would certainly chastise him.

CHAPTER FIFTEEN

THE LEAK HAD TO BE PLUGGED

TUESDAY, DECEMBER 22, 1992

Over the last few months Davis came to respect his niece. She not only had potential, but she jumped right in and made it happen. Her greatest fan was the old man, whom she admired and respected without question. She'd also impressed her uncle and Bella, who'd been around for more than thirty years.

After the scheduling conference, Sammie questioned Morty and her uncle about the legality of the coin flip. After much debate and further research, they decided not to appeal Judge Boxer's ruling. It was a matter of his discretion, and Boxer had spoken. The Court of Appeals would not intervene.

In August Sammie gave up the ninth-floor loft and moved into Davis's guest room when Morty decided to take up residence in the loft to be closer to the office. He could come and go as he pleased, and he had access to the office at night when he couldn't sleep. Since Goldie's death, Morty hadn't been sleeping very well.

Sammie was glad that the old man was happy to be back downtown and at work. She was saving money by staying in her uncle's guest room, but she missed the complete independence she had downtown. Her new living space cost only an occasional babysitting gig, and she had to admit that she enjoyed getting to know her young cousins, Caroline and Jake.

Working on the Plainview cases invigorated Morty. Davis confided in Sammie that Morty would more than earn his one-dollar retainer. Sammie was amazed at the old man's penchant for detail. Each morning, he met with her, and while chewing on a cigar, he'd give her a list of things to do. At the end of the day, hopefully with a different cigar in Morty's mouth, they reviewed her work product. He was patient and explained why he assigned certain tasks. It was the education of a lifetime for her, and he was an exceptional teacher.

Morty helped Davis frame the legal issues of the Plainview cases, and he then worked with Sammie, preparing discovery in each case, propounding questions and requests for documents. Morty taught Sammie the ropes, and Sammie brought to the table her computer research skills. Morty had written more than a thousand briefs in his career, but he still relied on the traditional method of research—books. The closest he came to a computer was three feet.

Sammie walked into the office library, a twenty-by-twenty-foot room lined with ten-foot-high walnut bookcases. It cost thousands each year to maintain the library with new volumes and updates. On the other hand, the computer relied on a single database, Westlaw, which automatically updated weekly.

Davis and Morty were seated next to each other at the walnut conference table. They were smoking cigars. No one would complain, though. Morty owned the building. Sammie walked into the smoky, hazy library, coughed, and sat down next to Morty. She and Morty worked all morning on a list of legal issues. She handed both men a copy of the list, which was several pages long. Davis scanned the document.

Just as the team was about to jump into the outstanding issues, Bella buzzed on the intercom, and Davis picked up.

Bella began: "I've got Allie Easter on the line. She seems real upset. Can you take her call?"

"Sure. There's no point in delaying the inevitable."

"Ms. Easter, Ben Davis. I guess you got my letter?"

"We don't understand. Are you dropping my mother's lawsuit?"

"No, but I am insisting that you be appointed her conservator and replace her as my client. Look, Allie, your mom can't read. There's no point in my sending letters to her house. I suspect that your brother, Howard, is stealing my letters and giving them to one of the defendants, probably Herman. Your brother still does odd jobs for Herman, doesn't he? That gives him access and motive."

"Yes, but Howard wouldn't steal Momma's mail. What evidence do you have to accuse my brother of such a terrible thing? He wouldn't hurt Momma."

Sammie learned from her contacts in Plainview, and reported to her uncle, that Howard had done odd jobs for Dr. Herman at his farm. None of the Easters volunteered this information. That made the Davis team suspicious, and by the process of elimination, they unanimously agreed that Howard was the leak and that he was stealing his mother's mail.

"I have no solid proof, but I'm not comfortable sending mail to your mother. If you become my client, I'll send all my correspondence to you, and you can represent your mother's interests and explain to her how her case is going. Edith won't be excluded from the process, but you'd be the actual client and help me make decisions. Your mother is not capable of prosecuting her lawsuit. Your substitution for your mother is a reasonable request in light of my suspicions about your brother and because of your mother's illiteracy."

"Mr. Davis, you're no better than us. Momma's not a child who needs someone to hold her hand. She's a grown woman who's raised two children. We resent what you put in your letter, and even though she can't read, she's got just as much right to go to court as anybody else."

"Look, Allie, I've got to protect my other clients. I strongly suspect that your brother is feeding information to the other side. He's stealing it, or your mother is giving it to him. Either way, I can't represent your mother anymore. Either you become her conservator and my client, or I must withdraw from her case. I've got no choice. What will it be?"

"Go to hell."

"I'll send you and your mother a copy of my motion to with-draw. Howard can get his copy out of your mother's mailbox."

"Go to hell." Allie hung up.

Morty shook his head. "You really handled that well."

Davis turned to Morty and said, "I know. I screwed up. She's pissed."

Morty smiled slightly and said, "You'd better file a motion to withdraw in Easter, ASAP."

CHAPTER SIXTEEN

ATTEMPTED DIVISION OF LABOR

FRIDAY, JANUARY 29, 1993

Throughout the holidays, the Davis team worked their asses off and accomplished a lot. Despite this progress, Davis was angry not only at Littleton but also at himself. He reached the conclusion that Littleton was a useless piece of shit. Morty warned him, but Davis never thought Littleton would be such dead weight.

Amazingly, Littleton was worse than useless. He'd failed to show up at the scheduled deposition of Thomas Nelson, the paramedic in the Rosie Malone case. It was one of his few assigned tasks and the only deposition Davis actually asked him to attend, and he blew it. The deposition couldn't proceed without him present, and the defense counsel wrote a nasty letter threatening to file a motion for the cost of the deposition.

Littleton delayed moving the cases forward. He refused to reimburse Davis his fair share of the advanced expenses, and he would not raise a finger to prepare the Plainview cases for trial. Ethically, according to the Code of Professional Responsibility, Littleton could not be paid one-third of the fee if he did not do one-third of the work. Davis, in correspondence, documented Littleton's lack of participation and failure to pay his portion of the expenses.

In late December, Davis wrote Littleton a lengthy letter that identified seventy-six tasks that needed to be completed. Davis suggested that they divide the work in the Jones case and the other Plainview cases. Davis's letter also identified more than two dozen motions and legal issues that needed to be researched. After each task, Davis placed either BAD or Littleton's initials, BL, assigning the task. The letter was his effort to divide the labor between the two lawyers.

Davis also needed to raise the issue of expenses. He could not continue to advance Littleton's share. Davis needed to be reimbursed, in full, $35,000. Davis would also demand that Littleton deposit another $10,000 in Davis's escrow account for future expenses. Davis was more than willing to provide Littleton with a monthly accounting.

Davis dialed Littleton, who had been ducking his calls all week.

"Brad, it's Ben. Just checking in on Plainview. How are you doing with the list I sent you?"

"What list?"

"In my letter from December 27th, I created a punch list in Jones and the other Plainview cases."

"I don't remember any list."

"Brad, I'm looking at the fax confirmation sheet. Bella stapled it to the letter. It was received in your office on December 27th at nine fifteen. I'll resend it to you now and call you right back."

Davis slammed the receiver in the telephone base. He hit the intercom and asked Bella to come in: "Please fax this December 27th letter to the same idiot it was sent to on that date."

Waiting fifteen minutes, trying his best to calm

down, he picked up the phone again. "Brad, did you get the letter?"

"I'm looking at it right now. This seems like a lot of work, Ben."

"No shit. That's how you win lawsuits. You prepare them, and then you settle them or bring them to trial. What did you think we were going to do? Did you think they were going to simply write us a check? Brad, we've got to get to work."

Littleton didn't answer.

Davis crumpled the letter and threw it across the room. "Are you really this stupid and lazy?"

"I've got to go. I've got a meeting. I'll look at your list and tell you which items I can get done."

"We've wasted a month. We need to address this problem *now*!"

"I'll get back in touch with you after I've reviewed the list and have had time to think about it."

"What's there to think about? These things need to get done, and you're co-counsel on these cases. You'll either do them or not."

"Who died and made you king?"

"Listen, you prick, I'm lead counsel, and I've advanced every fucking penny in these cases. I need you to write me a check for $35,000 to cover your share of expenses that have already been incurred. Then, I want you to write me a second check for $10,000 to be deposited in my escrow account for your share of future expenses. I'll provide a monthly accounting to you."

"Got to go. We'll talk soon."

Littleton hung up before Davis could respond. Davis wanted to hit something or, better yet, someone.

My home life and practice would be much more pleasant if

I had never heard of these cases from Littleton and then trusted him. Liza is making sure that I don't forget how hard our savings have been hit, and some of my oldest clients are becoming testy about my lack of availability. I'm pretty tired of Plainview and especially Littleton.

As Davis was thinking about these issues, Bella buzzed in.

"What?" Davis asked much too loudly. He immediately apologized: "Sorry, that bastard Littleton hung up on me. I have no right to take it out on you. What's up?"

"Ben, we just got a certified letter from McCoy and another from Pierce. I signed for them. Do you want me to open them or bring them back?"

Hoping that they were settlement offers in the Plainview cases, Davis asked her to bring them back. Davis could not have been more surprised by the contents of McCoy's letter. The envelope contained three documents. The first was a letter from McCoy to the Board of Professional Responsibility of the Tennessee Supreme Court charging Davis with filing the Easter complaint against his client without the permission of Mrs. Easter and misleading her about the lawsuit. Attached to the complaining letter was an affidavit of Edith Easter. The second document was a letter to Judge Robert E. Lee Boxer making identical charges that the Easter case had been wrongfully filed in Plains County Circuit Court, and the Easter affidavit was also attached to the letter to the judge. The third document was a motion for costs against Davis personally for the costs incurred by Dr. Herman in the Easter case; once again the Easter affidavit was attached. Pierce's envelope held identical letters to the board and

Boxer and an almost identical motion by English for his costs incurred in the Easter case.

Davis buzzed Morty, who was resting in the loft. He also asked Sammie and Bella to come into his office. In more than fifteen years of practicing law, no one had ever made a complaint about Davis to the Board of Professional Responsibility.

Davis had each of them read one of the complaining letters and one of the motions. Morty served eight years as the president of the Board of Professional Responsibility; he knew how the system worked. The board moved slowly for good reason: an attorney's license and reputation were at stake. Morty insisted that the best course of action was to file a response to the motions and get in front of Boxer as soon as possible. Boxer knew the cases and would act more quickly than the board to quash these frivolous charges.

Morty suggested that, prior to the motions being heard, they take the depositions of the Easters and possibly Dr. Herman. Davis thought that was a great idea. Davis was convinced that the Easter affidavit was prepared by either McCoy or Pierce and was an attempt to derail the progress that had been made in the Plainview cases.

Davis handed Morty a dollar and said, "I guess I need a lawyer for these board charges. Will this cover it?"

Morty looked at Davis seriously and responded, "Don't expect change."

Davis drove home, obviously not in a good mood. He wanted to see his kids and just forget about Plainview for a while. He'd have a home-cooked meal and then maybe smoke a cigar in his office. The old man had taught him to appreciate a good cigar, and they both smoked them out of nervous habit and to relax.

As soon as he walked in the door, though, Liza was all over him. "Hi, honey, did you see Littleton today?"

Davis didn't want to get into this discussion until after his meal and cigar. "Can we talk about this later?"

"It's a simple question. Did he pay you what he owes you?"

"It's not that simple, and I've got bigger concerns."

Davis was about to explain the Easter board complaint when Liza turned red with anger and burst out, "What could be more important than your family? You need to get that bull-shitter to pay up. We need those reimbursed expenses to pay bills."

She was right. But the Easter charges, although without merit, threatened to suspend his law license and his ability to provide for his family. Davis held his temper and decided not to be drawn further into a fight. He cowardly waited till the next day to tell Liza about the Easter charges.

CHAPTER SEVENTEEN

PROVING A FALSE AFFIDAVIT

THURSDAY, MARCH 11, 1993

Davis hired the best man possible when he retained Morty. Morty scheduled four depositions for today, the three Easters and Dr. Herman, to get to the bottom of the Easter affidavit. The transcription of the testimony would be a rush job because the hearing before Judge Boxer on the Rule 11 motion was set for Monday. Rule 11 of the Tennessee Rules of Civil Procedure provided that an attorney promised the court that the pleadings signed were accurate and correct.

After much discussion, they agreed he would start with questioning Edith Easter and get to the heart of the problem: her false affidavit. That document constituted the basis for the Rule 11 motion and disciplinary charges filed by McCoy and Pierce against Davis.

The depositions were scheduled at McCoy's office because his client, Dr. Herman, was one of the deponents. The Easters weren't represented by counsel. They couldn't afford one, nor did they understand they needed one, and none of the defense counsel warned them. Sammie was surprised that both Barnes and Stevenson sent letters indicating that they would not attend. She figured that neither of them wanted any part of this debacle, since neither signed the motion or brought the charges against Davis.

Morty, Davis, and Sammie were escorted into a conference room and were soon joined by McCoy, wearing a bright yellow bow tie, and his client, Dr. Herman. Pierce arrived separately, and Sammie admired her beautifully tailored midnight blue suit. Pierce had taste, but no class as far as Sammie was concerned. A few moments later, the Easters joined them.

Morty was all business. "We'll start with Edith Easter. Dr. Herman can remain in the room because he's a party to the lawsuit, but the Easter children must wait in your reception area. They can't stay and hear their mother's testimony."

"I'm not leaving," Allie Easter said defiantly.

"You'll leave, and you'll leave right now, young lady," Morty quickly retorted.

McCoy explained to Allie and Howard that under the Tennessee Rules of Civil Procedure, they were not entitled to remain because they were witnesses, and their testimonies could be affected if they heard their mother's testimony. After they left, Edith Easter was sworn in, and Morty handed her a copy of her affidavit.

"Is that your signature, Mrs. Easter?"

"Yes, sir."

"Did you sign this document on February 6th, 1993, as is shown on the document?"

"I guess so. I don't remember the date. It was around then."

Sammie watched the master in action. Morty got Mrs. Easter to admit that Howard, Allie, McCoy, and Pierce were there when she signed the document, and he established that Pierce typed the affidavit. She denied that Dr. Herman was present when she signed it. He introduced them to his lawyers and left.

"Would you read into the record your affidavit, please?"

McCoy objected, "The document speaks for itself. This is a waste of time."

Morty looked over at McCoy. "Your objection is noted, Mr. McCoy. I'll remind you later that you made it and tried to prevent her from reading the document. Mrs. Easter, read your affidavit to us, please." It was not a question; it was a command.

Three minutes went by, and the woman remained quiet. Sammie knew why she didn't start reading, and so did Morty.

McCoy broke the silence. "Just read it to us, Mrs. Easter, so we can get this over with."

Edith Easter started to cry. The court reporter continued to preserve what was said and indicated that the witness started to cry in response to Mr. McCoy's urging to read the affidavit.

Morty was about to lower the boom. Sammie was watching McCoy and Pierce, not the witness. Neither McCoy nor Pierce knew exactly what was about to happen. They looked concerned but were apparently in the dark about Mrs. Easter's illiteracy.

"Can you read?"

"Not real good, and I broke my glasses a few months ago and never replaced them."

Mrs. Easter couldn't identify the name of her eye doctor.

"Can you read any part of that document?"

"My name."

"Anything else?" Morty asked.

"I can make out a few little words like 'is' and 'the,' but that's about it."

"You don't know what this document says, do you?"

"No, sir."

"It says that Mr. Davis filed a lawsuit without your permission; that you never intended to sue Dr. Herman; that he never kept you advised of the progress of your lawsuit; and that he promised you at least $1 million. Did you realize you made those claims against Mr. Davis?"

"He dropped me because he says I was stupid."

"That's not what I asked you. Before you signed the document, did anybody read it to you?"

What Mrs. Easter said next was critical to the outcome of the Rule 11 motion and the disciplinary charges against Davis. It would also put McCoy and Pierce in hot water.

"I don't remember. We talked about Mr. Davis and the lawsuit, and then that lady came back with that piece of paper and I signed it."

"The lady you're referring to is Ms. Amy Pierce, who is seated at this table?"

"Yes, sir."

"So she didn't read it to you?"

"I guess not."

"So you had no idea what it said at the time you signed it, did you?"

Mrs. Easter looked blankly at Morty. He read the affidavit out loud and got her to admit that Mr. Davis, unlike Ms. Pierce with the affidavit, did read the complaint to her, word for word. Sammie was prepared to testify to that fact at the hearing, if necessary. When he read the allegation that Mr. Davis promised her $1 million, she claimed it was the other fat man, Mr. Littleton, who made that promise.

"But this document claims Mr. Davis made that promise."

"I guess I was confused."

"Did your son, Howard, steal your mail?"

"I let him read it. He's my son. He didn't steal nothing."

"Did he give your mail to Dr. Herman?"

"I don't know. You'll have to ask him."

By the end of the deposition, Sammie felt sorry for Edith Easter. The deposition of Dr. Herman was a waste of time. He claimed all he did was make the introduction and then played no part in securing the affidavit. He admitted that Howard did odd jobs for him at his farm but denied receiving mail from him.

Both Allie and Howard Easter lied. They testified that Ms. Pierce did read the affidavit to their mother. They also claimed that Mr. Davis didn't read the complaint to them and did promise $1 million.

Sammie knew that they were lying. She was there, and she would file her own affidavit with the court. If necessary, Morty would put her on the stand at the hearing. She was a much more credible witness than either Howard or Allie, whose testimonies had already been contradicted by their mother's.

Sammie was surprised when Morty turned to the court reporter. "I'd like to ask on the record, Mr. McCoy, did you know before today that Edith Easter couldn't read this affidavit?"

"I'm not a witness in this case. I represent Dr. Herman. My actions are protected by the attorney work product doctrine. I don't have to answer that question."

"Did you read the affidavit to her before she signed it?"

"That's none of your business. My work product is protected."

"You signed a Rule 11 motion and brought disciplinary charges against Mr. Davis. You made it my business, and I'm sure Judge Boxer will agree. I'm sure he'll rule that there is no attorney work product protection if those actions constituted a fraud on the court. You tried to use this false affidavit to win a motion, and even worse, you made unfounded disciplinary charges against another member of the Bar. You're toast. I'm sure Judge Boxer will ask you these same questions at the hearing on Monday, and you'd better have answers then."

Sammie could actually see McCoy's bow tie get tighter around his neck, and he turned red in the face. He didn't respond.

Turning, Morty glared at Pierce. "What about you, Ms. Pierce? You created this pack of lies. They're your words, not Mrs. Easter's. What do you have to say for yourself? Do you think your action of typing this false affidavit is protected by the attorney work product doctrine?" It was one of those rare "got you" moments.

For the first time, Sammie was amazed that Amy Pierce had nothing to say. Pierce always had a sharp comeback or sarcastic remark. She figured that Pierce concluded that silence was better than saying something stupid on the record.

Morty rubbed it in. "Cat got your tongue, Ms. Pierce?"

Morty, Davis, and Sammie left the room with smiles on their faces. Morty turned a bad situation to their advantage and proved, once again, that he knew how to turn shit into apple butter.

CHAPTER EIGHTEEN

THE DISCIPLINARY HEARING

MONDAY, MARCH 15, 1993

That Monday was an important day for Davis, but Sammie wasn't worried. All the defense attorneys and their clients were present, except Barnes. He told Morty that he had a prior commitment and would be unavailable. It was a three-ring circus, and Davis was unfortunately standing in the center ring. Davis was on trial, not English, not Herman, and not the hospital.

These charges were brought by the Tennessee Supreme Court through the office of the Chief Disciplinary Counsel, instigated by Pierce and McCoy.

The motions for costs were based on Rule 11 of the Tennessee Rules of Civil Procedure. The rule was rarely used to challenge an attorney's pleading. But the motion filed by McCoy and Pierce had certainly gotten Davis's attention.

The four depositions, taken the previous Thursday, had been filed with the court, and it was presumed that Boxer had read them. Davis and Sammie had each filed affidavits about their meeting with the Easters. Davis's affidavit attached eight letters from him to Mrs. Easter, which established that he kept her abreast of her lawsuit. His affidavit also singled out the letter that Davis knew had been stolen and ended up in Stevenson's possession.

Stevenson, on behalf of the hospital, had not sought costs and had not participated in the charges brought before the board. Neither had Barnes, even though his co-counsel, McCoy, had. Neither McCoy nor Pierce had filed a pleading in reply to Davis's response to their motion. They took no position that addressed whether they knew Mrs. Easter couldn't read or if they read the affidavit to her.

They were in the Hewes County Courthouse. The judge entered the courtroom, and everybody rose. A court officer identified the judge and recited a canned presentation that concluded with "under God and the laws of the State of Tennessee."

Davis took in the sight, staring at the judge sitting at least ten feet above everybody else. The American flag joined the flag of Tennessee, hanging on the wall behind him, symbols that spoke of justice for all men and women. Along the side walls were photographs of previous judges who sat at the very same bench in the same courtroom.

The county was named for Joseph Hewes of North Carolina, an owner of a shipping business who signed the Declaration of Independence and served in the Continental Congress as secretary of the Naval Affairs Committee. The Hewes County Courthouse was one of the pre-Civil War Tennessee courthouses that survived the war. It had a major renovation around the turn of the twentieth century, then again in the late 1940s, and the last time five years ago. The bench, the witness box, the jury box, and the counsel tables were made of thick polished oak. The room had a very solid look, like something substantial happened here.

Boxer immediately took control of the hearing. "I

take these motions and the allegations brought against Mr. Davis very seriously. The first matter is the defendants' motion to continue, to postpone this hearing, so they can take Mr. Davis's deposition and other additional depositions as to the allegations of these motions. Mr. Steine, what is your position?"

"Your Honor, Mr. McCoy and Ms. Pierce had set out on an expedition to defame and impugn Mr. Davis's character. We insist that the court go forward today so that this matter and these serious allegations can be put to rest and the malpractice cases can proceed. They have Mr. Davis's affidavit, which is sworn to as an officer of this court. I encourage the court to question Mr. Davis at this hearing about what that document says, or his paralegal, Ms. Davis, who was present when Mr. Davis read the complaint to Mrs. Easter. I also encourage the court to question Mr. McCoy and Ms. Pierce about how the Easter affidavit was created and their lack of knowledge of her illiteracy when they filed their motions and the charges against Mr. Davis. If you order Mr. Davis's deposition, I insist that you also order the depositions of Mr. McCoy and Ms. Pierce."

The judge denied the defendants' motion for a continuance. Sammie was certain that he didn't want any of the lawyers deposed; that would have gotten messy. Someone was lying. She could tell by the constipated expression on Judge Boxer's face that he was uncomfortable with the issues raised at this hearing. These were supposed to be medical malpractice cases, not about the lawyers.

Judge Boxer asked Morty to address the allegations of the motions.

He rose and slowly walked to the podium. "I've

known Ben Davis about twenty years. He was my law clerk beginning in 1975, and then he worked with me as a lawyer. Eventually, I thought enough of him to ask him to be my first and only law partner. The things that are important to Ben Davis are the things that are important to the people who matter in this world, such as family and one's reputation. This court can inquire among the Tennessee Bar, and especially the Nashville legal community, and will find that Ben Davis's reputation is unsullied. There's not a blemish on his good name. Even his adversaries respect him and would attest to his honesty. These two desperate lawyers, who represent two desperate doctors, are seeking to divert attention from their own misconduct and focus your attention instead on this exceptional attorney. They have alleged that Mr. Davis has acted 'illegally, immorally, and dishonestly.'"

Morty insisted that if the court believed Mrs. Easter, he should find Davis guilty of violating Rule 11 and throw the book at him. "But this court knows that Mrs. Easter is a liar. You read her deposition. That affidavit was false when given, and these lawyers knew it was false when they got it. If anyone has violated Rule 11, it's Mr. McCoy and Ms. Pierce by filing these motions. I note for the record that neither Mr. Barnes nor Mr. Stevenson has joined in this fiasco. I've known both of them for almost fifty years, and both of them are too reputable to be involved in this tragedy. We know the court will deny the motion, contact the board, and exonerate Mr. Davis. Thank you for your attention."

Boxer looked directly at Davis. "Edith Easter is a liar and/or she's stupid. Her absence today supports those opinions. She couldn't face Mr. Davis with her accusations.

These motions are denied, and I will be contacting the Board of Professional Responsibility and urging it to dismiss Mr. McCoy and Ms. Pierce's complaint."

Sammie was relieved even though she was confident of the outcome before the hearing began.

"Ms. Pierce, did you know Mrs. Easter couldn't read?"

"No, sir, but we did review the affidavit with her. The accusations against Mr. Davis were hers and those of her children. I simply typed up what she said."

"Did you know she couldn't read, Mr. McCoy?"

McCoy's face was as green as his bow tie. "No, sir, she made the claims, and we felt compelled to bring such serious allegations to your attention."

The judge was critical of Pierce and McCoy for not recognizing that the old woman could not read and not conducting an investigation before filing their motion and charges. He didn't go as far as to hold Pierce and McCoy guilty of violating Rule 11 but gave them a stern reprimand: "I want these games to stop, and I want them to stop right now."

Sammie assumed that the judge didn't go further because the Plainview cases could be around for years and he needed to tone down the hostility.

"This was an unfortunate matter, and I question the motives of Mr. McCoy and Ms. Pierce. I hope we can move forward. There are nine other cases that must be prepared. This will require counsel to work together. I don't care if you like each other, but you'd better play by the rules. And it would be nice if you respected each other. I don't want to hear a similar matter in these cases again. Understand?"

With that warning, Boxer left the bench and exited.

CHAPTER NINETEEN

THE QUIET ROOM

FRIDAY, JUNE 4, 1993

Over the last several days, Sammie and Morty worked Plainview day and night as Davis requested. Since Davis's letter of December 27th, the Davis team, despite the distraction of the disciplinary charges, completed sixty-one of the seventy-six tasks listed in the letter. Littleton made no contribution; he didn't complete even one task. Then one day, he called to announce that he was taking on a new criminal case, so he wouldn't have much time for the Plainview cases. Unfortunately, the remaining uncompleted dozen tasks had, because of new developments, grown to thirty-four. A lawsuit was a moving target, and new problems arose based on the changing circumstances.

More important, Littleton had not reimbursed Davis one penny for expenses advanced. Davis was spending too much time on the Plainview cases, almost to the exclusion of his other clients. In the course of one week, three clients quit because of his failure to complete legal work on time. That had never happened to Davis before. His clients had always been satisfied with the timeliness of his work and almost always satisfied with the results. Several other clients voiced their concerns about the status of their legal work, but they liked Davis and gave him leeway to get the job done. But their patience was running thin, and work was piling up.

The humidity could be brutal in Tennessee, even in early June. It was only ten o'clock in the morning, but it was already ninety degrees and almost at ninety percent humidity. Morty made Davis stop twenty-five miles outside Plainview and put the convertible top up because the sun was beating down on them so hard that he could feel the sun burning his bald head. The stop wasn't a problem; they had plenty of time. The deposition of the custodian of records of Plainview Community Hospital didn't begin until eleven.

Under the Tennessee Rules of Civil Procedure, a defendant's deposition must be taken in the county in which the lawsuit was filed or where the defendant resides. Often, for convenience, Nashville lawyers would agree to take depositions in downtown Nashville rather than where the rules required. It was practical. Why have three or four lawyers travel seventy miles round trip when they were all in walking distance of each other's offices? Nevertheless, Stevenson insisted that, because all hospital employees were agents of the hospital, they were technically considered defendants and had to be deposed in Plains County. Accordingly, the deposition of the custodian of records of the hospital, Ms. Lee Johnston, had to be taken in Plains County.

Davis would have preferred to take the deposition anywhere but the hospital. However, he didn't have access to any other place in Plains County that could accommodate all of the lawyers, the witnesses, and the court reporter. When he took depositions of other employees at the hospital, Davis was relegated to the hospital cafeteria. Conveniently, the hospital conference room was always unavailable.

The PA system in the cafeteria was very disruptive to the proceedings, with announcements every five minutes or so. It was so distracting that Davis filed a motion with the court, objecting to take any further depositions in the cafeteria.

Judge Boxer ruled that if the hospital's conference room were not available, Davis didn't have to take the depositions in the cafeteria. The hospital had to provide a suitable alternative location.

Mr. Stevenson offered the quiet room as a possible alternative. It was the hospital's designated zone where grieving families met with clergy or physicians. It was where patients' families were told bad news. The room was used much too often at Plainview Community Hospital. Davis agreed to use it if the conference room were not available.

Grayson Stevenson, the hospital's counsel, met them in the lobby and led them to the quiet room. Morty and Stevenson were contemporaries; both attended Vanderbilt but were as different as two people could be. Morty thought of Stevenson as a pretentious asshole. During the car ride, Morty warned Sammie that Stevenson was arrogant and not to be trusted.

When Morty and Davis stepped over the threshold of the quiet room, they were shocked. The space was no bigger than a large walk-in closet. With the addition of Stevenson, Davis, Sammie, and Steine, ten people were in the room. Davis thought, *Stevenson's suggestion to Judge Boxer to use the quiet room was just another attempt to screw with me. Stevenson misled me and the court into believing that it was an appropriate place for the depositions.*

Being designed to hold no more than six people at a time, the room was crowded and uncomfortable. Adding to the discomfort, there was no window, and the cooling system was inadequate. Davis planned to file another motion with the court as soon as he returned to his office. This would be the last deposition taken in the quiet room.

Morty took the Johnston deposition. He made a few notes and brought Ms. Johnston's subpoena. He knew most of the questions he was going to ask. However, he always professed that he got his best questions from the witness's answers.

Morty began slowly, asking the witness her name, address, employer, job description, and so forth. He then asked the types of records the hospital maintained: "Does the hospital maintain pathology slides of every gallbladder surgery performed?"

"Yes."

"I direct your attention to item five of the subpoena. It requests that the hospital produce its pathology slides for every gallbladder surgery performed from 1989 through 1992. Are they here in the room?"

"No."

"Why not?"

"We destroy them two months into the next year."

"Is Plainview Community Hospital a licensed health care facility?"

"Yes, sir."

"The Joint Commission on Accreditation of Healthcare Organizations, or JCAHO, issues and monitors the hospital's license, doesn't it?"

"Yes, sir." Johnston remained calm. "JCAHO visits the hospital at least once every two years. The visit lasts several days." She went on to say that JCAHO's Rule 301 required that pathology slides be maintained for at least three years. She had no explanation for why Plainview Community Hospital's pathology slides didn't exist. She just sat there silent, and Morty let the liar sit there.

After another hour of difficult questions with no good answers, Morty wiped his face with a linen handkerchief and rested a moment. The old man's skin looked pale, and beads of sweat dotted his forehead.

Davis laid a hand on Morty's arm and addressed Stevenson: "It's hot in here. Can you turn up the air conditioning?"

"There's no thermostat in this room," Stevenson responded.

"Let's get this done so we can leave," Morty insisted.

As Morty stood to remove his jacket, he swayed and clutched the table to steady himself.

"Are you all right?" Davis asked quietly.

Morty fell back into the swivel chair and almost fell over. He loosened his tie. "I'm fine. Let's proceed."

Davis wasn't so sure.

"Can I have a glass of water?" Morty asked.

Stevenson drummed his fingers on the table. "There's a water fountain in the hall."

Davis didn't like the clammy color of the old man's skin. "Let's take a break."

"No." Morty rubbed his chest. "We'll complete this current line of questioning first."

But a moment later, he squeezed his left arm.

Davis sprang to his feet. "Morty, you're sick. We're stopping right now."

Morty clenched his teeth and looked up at Davis,

who was really worried. In a hoarse whisper he insisted, "Get me out of here. I'm having another heart attack."

"We're in a hospital," Davis said.

"I wouldn't let my dogs be treated in this hospital. You've got to be kidding me, Ben."

Davis turned to Stevenson. "Get some help. Now!"

Stevenson moved toward the door, but Morty kept shaking his head and saying, "Drive me to Saint Thomas."

"Stay calm. We'll get a doctor. Stevenson, move your ass. He needs a doctor *right now*!"

"Call my cardiologist," Morty pleaded. "He'll meet us at Saint Thomas."

"Morty, you're crazy. That's a fifty-minute—"

But before Davis finished his sentence, Morty passed out.

CHAPTER TWENTY

A RELUCTANT PATIENT

FRIDAY, JUNE 4, 1993

Morty was admitted to Plainview Community Hospital through its emergency room. Davis decided to call Dr. Laura Patel, who lived only five minutes away.

"Ben, good to hear from you. How are the cases—"

Davis broke in, "Laura, Morty needs your help. He's been admitted to Plainview Community Hospital. He's had another heart attack."

"Oh, my God, Ben. I can't do much. I don't have any privileges. They won't even let me in the front door."

"I want you to assess Morty to see if we can move him safely by ambulance to Saint Thomas. This is America. You have a right to visit anyone you damn well please in the hospital. I'll make sure we've got privacy and his chart is available. Just bring your stethoscope and blood pressure cup."

"What are his vitals?"

"I don't know, but we're going to find out when you get here. Hurry, please."

Laura could hear in Davis's voice that he was near frantic about the old man. She jumped in her car and was at the hospital in record time. Davis met her at the ER entrance. He was talking incredibly fast. The adrenaline had kicked in.

Laura looked around the ER. It was like coming home.

God, I've missed this place. Then she caught herself. *How could I miss Plainview Community Hospital and its schemes and unethical practices?* She momentarily confused the place for her love of medicine and her desire to help people. That's what she longed for.

After a few minutes, Nurse Richie walked past them, and Laura pulled her aside to find out about Morty's diagnosis and treatment plan. Laura and Nurse Richie always had a strong professional relationship, and the RN wouldn't rat Laura out to Douglas or the head nurse.

"What's Mr. Steine's condition?"

"He's had a heart attack. We're uncertain if there's been any permanent damage to the heart. His blood pressure is low, seventy over fifty-five, but stable."

Laura turned to Davis and said, "I don't recommend you move him right now. Let's see how he looks after he's admitted to a room and I get a chance to examine him. We can always discharge him against medical advice and have him transported by private ambulance to Nashville."

She turned back to Nurse Richie. "How long before he's in a private room?"

"About twenty minutes."

Davis and Laura agreed that they would wait in the cafeteria. On the way they ran right into Woody Douglas.

"What the hell are you doing in my hospital?" he nearly yelled at Laura.

Davis answered, "She's visiting Mr. Steine, at my request. Look, Douglas, I'm not going to have any trouble with you. This hospital is open to the family and friends of anyone admitted, and Morty Steine unfortunately falls into that category. I'm in no mood for you.

If you interfere with Dr. Patel's right to be here, I'll slap a lawsuit against the hospital and you personally so fast your head will spin. Now get out of our way. We're going to get a cup of coffee."

Laura was impressed by Davis's confrontation with Douglas. She hated the little weasel, who was part of the conspiracy that cost her job and livelihood. She was now a stay-at-home mom.

Once they got their coffee, Davis explained what happened at the deposition of Ms. Johnston, the custodian of records.

"She's lying through her teeth. I know for a fact that the pathology lab keeps those slides in chronological order. I've seen where they're stored, in a refrigerator in the lab. Each year has its own metal case with the year noted with masking tape on the front."

"Would you testify to that?"

"Without hesitation."

Davis explained that Morty rattled the defense counsel's cage at Ms. Johnston's deposition. The hospital's claim that it destroyed the slides placed the hospital in a difficult position. Maintaining the slides was required by JCAHO, which accredited the hospital. The last thing the hospital wanted was a JCAHO investigation and a possible loss of its accreditation.

Davis continued, "Judge Boxer is likely to instruct the jury that the slides were destroyed to cover up the hospital's knowledge of unnecessary surgeries. That isn't as good as having the slides, which would have proved that English had removed healthy gallbladders, but at least it's something that the jury could rely on to hang the bastards.

"Doc, Morty and I need a favor. Can you spend the

night here at the hospital? Morty was supposed to take two depositions here in the morning, and I don't want to postpone them if at all possible. I can stop by around seven to check in and relieve you before noon. I'll spend the rest of the day with him and, if necessary, tomorrow night as well."

Laura didn't hesitate to agree. She loved the old man too. More than once she talked to Maggie about him and his record as a legal legend and a wonderful human being.

At ten o'clock Laura left Morty's room to stretch her legs. She got into the elevator and went to the basement. The only two departments on that level were the morgue and the pathology lab. At this hour the lab was empty, and only a single tech staffed the morgue. The hallway lights were off to save energy. Laura walked past the morgue. A television was tuned to a *Seinfeld* rerun. She ducked down as she slipped by the morgue's half glass door. She knew the episode; it was the one where Elaine's horrible dancing ability was disclosed at an office party.

At the pathology lab, Laura was surprised to find the door open, yet another JCAHO violation. She made a beeline for the refrigerator and crouched as she opened it. There were the pathology slides, which Ms. Johnston testified had been destroyed. She could carry only two years' worth of slides, so she selected 1991 and 1992. When she left the lab, she debated whether to lock the door but elected to leave things as she found them.

The next morning Laura jumped to her feet when Davis entered Morty's room. She was excited and pulled him into the bathroom to keep from waking Morty.

"What's up? And why are we talking in the bathroom?"

"Look what I've got."

Laura reached into her bag and pulled out the two metal boxes.

In a very low voice, almost a whisper, Davis asked, "How the hell did you get these?"

"I went down to the lab last night and there they were, right where I said they'd be. Johnston lied yesterday, Ben, and now you can prove it."

"But you committed a felony to get them. You've stolen hospital property."

"But she lied—"

"That doesn't matter. You stole. Give me a dollar!"

Laura looked at Davis with a puzzled expression.

"Give me a dollar!"

After she did, Davis smiled and said, "You've just retained me as your attorney in connection with your theft of hospital property. If I reported you, I'd be violating my oath to you and attorney-client privilege."

Laura smiled back. "I've been trying to get you to represent me, and all I had to do was commit a crime. Don't you find that ironic?"

Laura had not thought through how Davis would actually use the slides. She was just excited that he had them.

Davis explained how he would introduce the slides into evidence even though they were stolen. He was convinced that under the Tennessee Rules of Evidence, Judge Boxer would allow him to impeach the hospital custodian of records after she testified in open court that the slides had been destroyed. The judge would not be overly concerned with how Davis got the slides after

Davis proved the hospital's dishonesty in his court.

Laura figured that her motives were pure, although her methods might have been criminal. She thought, *Sometimes the ends justify the means.*

CHAPTER TWENTY-ONE

THE WEDDING

SATURDAY, SEPTEMBER 18, 1993

Following Morty's heart attack, Davis insisted that the old man recuperate at the Davis home with Liza nursing him back to health. Dr. Caldwell, Liza's father, even made house calls to monitor his condition. Fortunately no permanent damage was done to his heart. Sammie moved back into the ninth-floor loft, and within six weeks, Morty was ready to go back to work. He still lived with the Davises, however.

Just like Sammie, Morty was part of the family, and when the family boarded a plane for New York in September so they could attend the wedding of Sammie's father, Morty was right there with them.

The out-of-town trip was also an opportunity to have a few days away from the cases and have fun. They would be staying at the home of Davis's parents, Larry and Shelly Davis of Woodbury, Long Island, New York. Davis always enjoyed being with his parents, and Sammie loved seeing her grandparents. The Davises' son and granddaughter had a close relationship with them, despite being separated by the distance from New York to Nashville.

Davis was the best man for his brother, and Sammie was the maid of honor. Davis's children also took part, with Caroline as junior bridesmaid and Jake as ring bearer. The bride's parents came from modest means, so Larry graciously offered to pay for the reception.

The wedding took place in a predominantly Italian wedding hall as a compromise between the Catholic bride's family and the Jewish groom's family with both a rabbi and a priest presiding. The three hundred guests enjoyed a sit-down dinner of roast beef or salmon. The festivities lasted until the early morning, with the bride and groom leaving about 1:00 a.m.

Following a few hours of sleep and a breakfast of bagels and lox, Davis asked his father if he could speak with him privately.

His father agreed, and when they sat down in comfortable leather chairs in the den, Davis said, "Dad, there's no easy way to say this. I'm overextended."

"What happened?"

"I made a couple of bad decisions. I told you I had taken on those ten malpractice cases on contingency. My co-counsel, Brad Littleton, refuses to put up his share of the expenses. I also miscalculated my cash flow. These cases have taken up so much more of my time than I envisioned. I've pissed off some clients because I can't spend more time on their cases, and my practice has dwindled because of it."

His father, who owned three dry cleaners in Woodbury and two adjoining towns, understood how a businessman could get overextended. His father had done the very same thing when he opened his third location to give George a livelihood.

"How much have you sunk in these cases?"

"I've already spent more than $200,000, and I owe another $25,000. I must have spent well over a thousand hours of my time."

"How much has Littleton given you?"

"Not a penny." Davis shook his head. "He was supposed to put up a third. I've made demands, but he claims he doesn't have it."

Larry thought a moment. "Let him go to his father."

"I don't think that's an option. I could notify the clients, but I don't want to get into a public dispute. The hospital and the other defendants would probably find out. It's a very small town, and the defendants have spies everywhere."

"What does Morty think?" Larry knew that Morty had always given the younger Davis good, solid advice.

"Morty warned me not to involve the clients in my dispute with Littleton."

Davis told his father about the plaintiffs' cases but never shared specifics. He spoke nonstop for an hour, and his father listened with little comment. Larry now understood his son's passion and commitment to the cases.

"Son, this is the worst time. I just paid for your brother's wedding. Business hasn't been good, and I'd like to retire."

"I know, Dad. I just need a loan. I'll pay you back as soon as I can."

"When will these cases turn into money?"

"I wish I knew. The first one is scheduled to go to trial next year. But if I win big, I suspect the defendants will appeal. An appeal would take at least eighteen months, probably more like two years."

"How will you survive? How much will you have to put into the other cases? How will you keep your practice alive for the next three years?"

"Those are all good questions. For a start, I'm going to sit down with Liza, and we'll have to decide how to cut expenses. There is a real possibility that she'll have to go back into nursing. She could earn almost $50,000 a year working at Saint Thomas or one of the other hospitals."

Larry interrupted, "That decision will change your lives and the lives of your children."

"Both kids are in school, Dad. Liza's folks will help after school if we need them."

"Can Morty help?"

"He already has. He's put in more than a thousand hours of his time for a one-dollar retainer. He's agreed to abate my rent for a year and is paying Bella's salary."

The elder Davis shook his head. "You're digging yourself quite a hole, Ben. But I just spent $50,000 on this wedding. It's only fair that I loan you the same amount."

"Dad, I can't tell you how much that will help. I'll pay my bills and use the rest to fund the lawsuits for the next few months. I promise I'll pay you back."

"I know you're no quitter. Just keep pushing forward and work it hard. I have absolute confidence in you, son."

"I won't let you or my clients down, Dad. These people deserve to recover. They deserve justice."

Larry gave his son a hug and kissed his cheek, making Davis feel better. Larry crossed the room to his desk, pulled out his checkbook, and wrote the check. Then he reached under his desk and pulled out a wrapped box. "Your brother wanted me to give you this for serving as his best man. He meant to give it to you last night, but I forgot to bring it. He called me this morning to remind me about it."

Davis ripped open the box and removed a calfskin briefcase with his initials, BAD, embossed on it. With a feeling of relief, though it might have been only temporary, he put his father's check in his handsome new briefcase.

CHAPTER TWENTY-TWO

MESSAGE RECEIVED

WEDNESDAY, SEPTEMBER 22, 1993

Four days after his brother's wedding, Davis opened his eyes and saw his bloody briefcase lying next to him on the carpet of his office. No matter what one used as a measuring stick, it had been a lousy morning. The encounter lasted only ten minutes, but when his attackers left, Davis had a broken nose, cut lips, and a dislocated shoulder, and he was pretty certain he had at least two fractured ribs. He was in a lot of pain.

His office was a wreck. The assailants had taken everything off Bella's desk and had thrown it around the room. They had dumped eight file cabinet drawers all over the lobby. He was covered in paper. He could see glass from the broken lamp strewn about the floor. He lay still on the carpet and gritted his teeth against the pain, trying to decide what to do next.

He was convinced that it was no robbery. The goons weren't looking for a document. Plainview wanted to send a message, a brutal one at that.

Davis tried to get up slowly. The pain, particularly from his shoulder, was unbearable. He worked his way to his knees and scooted the few feet to Bella's desk. He grabbed the phone and dialed home.

Liza answered on the third ring; she had been asleep.

"Listen, sweetheart. Don't interrupt. Just listen," he said, his breath coming in short bursts and blood still running from his nose and lips.

"I need to get up anyway—"

"Stop! Let me talk. Take the kids and get out of the house *now*! Don't dress. Just put on coats. Don't stop to pick up anything. Go to your sister's. I've been beaten up. I'm calling 911."

Before they hung up, Liza told him that she received a phone call thirty minutes earlier from an unidentified caller. "He asked to speak with you, but I told him that you were already at the office. The call lasted no more than ten seconds."

Davis told Liza that he loved her, and in as commanding a voice as he could muster under the circumstances, he ordered her to leave. Her sister Barbara lived only five minutes away.

After he hung up, Davis called Littleton. Littleton was in bed when he received the call, but Davis's sobering story got him on his feet quickly.

"Do you think they're going to come after me next?"

Davis could hear the fear in Littleton's voice as he squeaked out the question.

"Listen, Bradley, just call 911, and I'll do the same."

Davis pushed the line on the phone and then dialed 911. Despite his severe pain, he described in detail what happened and gave his office address. He specifically told the dispatcher that he wanted to go to Saint Thomas Hospital.

After the phone call, Davis lay down, pain searing through his body. His shoulder was the most pressing injury. He knew that it would need to be yanked back into the socket, and he both dreaded and hoped for it to be done so that he could have some relief.

ust then, Bella opened the door and walked in. She took one look at her boss's face and began to scream hysterically. The horrific scream pierced the silence that had fallen over the office.

The paramedics arrived to hear that terrifying sound. They quickly determined that the wailing woman was not injured and turned their attention to Davis. Davis began to cry; he didn't care what the paramedics thought.

They put him on a gurney and took him down the elevator to the lobby. Bella went with him. She didn't take the time to leave a note for Sammie or Morty. One look at the office, and they would know that neither she nor Davis was there. She would call them from the hospital.

The ride from downtown Nashville to Saint Thomas took less than ten minutes, but the blaring sirens and the throbbing of his shoulder made the trip seem endless. When they arrived at the emergency room, Liza and her father, John Caldwell, were waiting. John, a heart surgeon, quickly determined that Davis's left shoulder was dislocated. John paged his nephew, Dr. Robert Caldwell, an orthopedic surgeon, to the ER. John ordered an X-ray, which revealed cracked ribs but no internal bleeding.

Unfortunately, Davis's left shoulder went unattended. He had been at the hospital for more than forty minutes, and the shoulder had not been realigned. He hadn't received a painkiller either.

Trying to ignore the pain from the cuts on his lips, Davis managed to plead with his father-in-law: "John, why hasn't something been done about my shoulder? It hurts like hell. Please do something."

"I want it done right. Robert should be here any minute. Just hold on a few minutes longer, Ben. I would prefer that it be done by family."

Davis was furious. *Dozens of doctors and nurses in the ER could fix my shoulder, but John, in some twisted sense of loyalty, wants it done by family.* He turned to John and Liza. "You're both family. One of you set my fucking shoulder. I beg you."

Reluctantly, his father-in-law pulled his shoulder back into place. The severe pain went away almost immediately and was replaced by a dull throb. Dr. Robert Caldwell arrived about two minutes after the shoulder was set.

Davis remained in the hospital overnight for observation. His ribs were taped, his swollen lips had a couple of stitches, and his shoulder was immobilized. He had a plastic surgery consult for the gash on his left cheek but decided it wouldn't leave much of a scar. After all, he wasn't some twenty-year-old model; a small scar on his face just added a little character.

That night, Liza the nurse arranged for the kids to stay with her parents so she could spend the night with her hospitalized husband.

"Are you awake, you stubborn son of a bitch?"

Davis was enjoying the morphine. It seemed to make his troubles go away. "Why do you put up with me?" he asked.

"Right now, that's a pretty good question. Maybe it's because you're durable."

"I'm so sorry. I know this has gotten out of hand, but there's nothing I can do." His speech sounded a bit odd because of the stitches in his lips.

"That's bullshit, Ben. You can quit. It won't be easy, but you back down and file a motion to withdraw from all of these fucking Plainview cases."

"I can't do that. It wouldn't be the right thing."

Liza resigned herself to the reality of the situation. She knew not to push him. She'd love him, support him, and bury him if need be.

CHAPTER TWENTY-THREE

THE SECRET DIES ON BROADWAY

FRIDAY, SEPTEMBER 24, 1993

Sammie and Bella were just sitting around the office worrying about Davis. They had seen him at the hospital and could do nothing, so Morty sent them back to the office to worry there and answer calls.

The next day, Davis went home; he had his own private nurse. Sammie and Bella fielded the inquiries from the curious and concerned well-wishers. The story was all over the news and was the talk of the town. The Nashville Bar was like its own telegraph system, with lawyers calling lawyers and judges, judges telling court officers, the courtroom officer whispering to clerks, and clerks passing it on to more lawyers. It didn't take long to become common knowledge: it was a good story about a lawyer getting the shit kicked out of him, even though Davis was a respected member of the Bar.

In her office, Sammie was listening to the news on her clock radio when the announcer reported excitedly: "According to police band radio, the assailants of prominent attorney Benjamin Davis have been spotted in downtown Nashville and are under surveillance by police. These men are believed to be armed and dangerous, and police have evacuated two blocks of downtown Broadway as a precaution."

Sammie grabbed her sneakers from her desk drawer and put them on, jumped from her chair, and without offering an explanation to Bella, bolted out the door. She didn't want the older woman to try to talk her out of watching the arrest firsthand.

It was a short jog from the office down Fifth Avenue to Broadway. She hurried past the red brick Ryman Auditorium, a country music shrine, on her left. It was bedlam on Broadway. TV crews were set up in the street, behind the police barricades at Seventh on Broadway, and then around the corner of Fifth on Broadway.

All of the stores and bars, between Fourth and Seventh, on both sides of Broadway, had been evacuated by the police. The merchants would complain fiercely, but public safety was paramount. The Metro police were in charge of crowd control. There were eighteen officers, six plainclothes detectives, and a police captain assigned to the stakeout.

In the middle of the two barricades was Tootsie's Orchid Lounge. It had been located on Broadway, close to Fifth, since the 1930s. It was and still is a Nashville landmark, with its distinctive purple signage. In the thirties and forties it was a honky-tonk famous for bluegrass music. In the fifties, the music venue distinctly changed and moved forward to country music and what came to be known as the Nashville sound. In the sixties, country and country rock, also known as rockabilly, became the lounge's meat and potatoes. At that time, it was the hangout for songwriters such as Johnny Cash, Waylon Jennings, Willie Nelson, and Kris Kristofferson. These unknown songsters, while heavily drinking at a table, would write a song and jump up on stage and sing. Sammie heard the stories, and Morty knew them all. He represented those songwriters. He helped them publish their songs and form their own publishing companies, and he represented them when they got busted for drugs, public intoxication, or barroom brawls.

Sammie, from Morty, knew that this stakeout was a direct result of his phone calls to news outlets. From one of the doctor's offices at the hospital, Morty had called the editor in chief of the *Nashville Banner*. The prominent editor and Morty had worked together in the civil rights movement. The Davis beating story was front page and included the artist's rendering of the two assailants.

Morty also called all three local television stations and spoke directly with their news directors. At five o'clock, on all three major networks, the lead story was the Davis beating. Quite frankly, the attack of a lawyer didn't warrant that much sympathy. To the average citizen, the beating of a lawyer wasn't news; it was cause for celebration.

Sammie couldn't take her eyes off the front door of Tootsie's. Its bright purple sign was vibrant, and there was a strange reflection from the midday sun. Even though it was late September, it was quite warm. The armpits of all of the officers were stained dark blue from perspiration and nerves. She could feel the tension in the air.

She looked at the crowd behind the barricades. Most were staring at the bar's front door, just like her, in anticipation of conflict and possible violence. They couldn't help themselves.

Suddenly, two men emerged from the doorway and walked onto the street. Sammie recognized them as

Laurel and Hardy from the artist's rendering and from their 1930s movie *Babes in Toyland*. The pair moved about six feet forward, away from the front door of the bar.

Someone shouted, "You're under arrest! Hands behind your heads! No sudden moves or you're dead men!"

Even from her distance, Sammie could see the eyes of both men widen and then narrow.

"Fuck off!" Laurel yelled back.

In total defiance, both men reached behind their backs in an exaggerated jerky motion. Their shirts pulled up, and Sammie and the entire TV audience saw a pistol sticking out from each man's right hand.

The police captain in charge, in a shaky voice, began to address them on a bullhorn: "Stop right now! This is your last chance. You're surrounded and—" The police officer never got to finish his threat.

Someone else yelled, "They've got guns!"

Hardy shot in the direction of the bullhorn. Everyone instinctively ducked at the crack of the gunshot. The discharge was all the excuse police needed. More than a dozen officers opened fire at the two gunmen.

Several spectators cried out. A young man who was next to Sammie yelled, "Holy shit," and fell on top of her in a protective maneuver. His hands brushed against her firm breasts, and the man blushed.

She appreciated his effort, but he kneed her in the stomach, knocking the wind out of her. She worked her way up to her elbows so she could see, her new best friend still on top of her.

Sammie was shocked by how fast and how loud the automatic weapons were. Hardy was riddled with bullets, and immediately, a pattern of red blotches, like paint, splattered across his white shirt. She turned away and felt sick, catching her vomit in her mouth, and she breathed through her nose and choked it down.

She needed to get Dudley Do-Right off her. "Move! I can't breathe."

The man rolled off her. A woman next to her fell to the ground hard, and the Good Samaritan jumped into action.

Sammie turned her attention back to Hardy, who was falling backward in, what seemed to her, slow motion. Hardy finally hit the ground, striking his head on the pavement.

Laurel was hit square in the chest with the blast from both barrels of a shotgun. The force of the blast threw him right through the purple plate glass window of Tootsie's. He landed inside the bar with several shards of purple glass sticking out of his back.

There was an audible grumble from the crowd, like that at the end of a football game. Police officers were running frantically everywhere, once again very much like on the field at the end of a big game.

Sammie was shaken. She had never seen anyone shot and killed before. She knew she would remember the scene the rest of her life.

The excitement was over. She turned and started walking up Fifth back to the office. She was in no hurry. There was nothing but more phone calls and more explaining to do back at the office. She wasn't looking forward to recounting the shootout again and again. She just shook her head and mumbled, "Unbelievable! We'll never find out who sent those assholes. The secret dies on Broadway."

She knew that the third man, T-rex, was still out there, but the odds of finding him were slim to none. Davis saw only his tattoo, not his face. Laurel and Hardy weren't lying low and decided to show their faces at a Nashville landmark while the publicity of their actions was still hot.

Sammie was relieved that they didn't have to worry about Laurel and Hardy any longer, but she wondered whether they would have any future dealings with T-rex.

CHAPTER TWENTY-FOUR

FACE-OFF

MONDAY, SEPTEMBER 27, 1993

Davis was glad that Littleton planned to attend Dr. English's deposition that morning. Littleton attended only four of the more than sixty-three depositions but never asked a question or suggested one. Despite his lack of participation, he insisted on a copy of every deposition. What a waste of money and paper. Davis wondered what he did with them. Based on their conversations, Davis knew he didn't read them. He was so removed from the cases that the defense counsel had stopped copying Littleton on all correspondence, and Littleton had complained.

The financial burden on Davis was wearing him down. Despite assistance from Morty and his father, he saw no light at the end of the financial tunnel. In addition his concern about his and his family's safety had intensified, and he was now carrying a revolver in his briefcase and keeping another pistol strategically located at home. Liza insisted, for his own safety, that he take shooting lessons.

Davis had been snapping a lot at Sammie and Bella since he got out of the hospital. It was totally unlike him, and Bella, who had wet nursed him as a clerk, had to bring him back to reality by pointing out what he was doing: "Ben, back off! We know you're under stress, but *we* are the ones trying to help you in every way we can."

Littleton arrived ten minutes early, so Davis decided it was a good time to address the expense problem. They had a written contract, and Littleton was required to advance one-third of the expenses. Davis sent Littleton the document and three letters demanding reimbursement, but Littleton chose to ignore them.

Davis said, "Brad, I need to talk to you before the deposition begins."

"What's up?"

"The rent is up, my friend. I have $15,000 of Plainview bills to pay, and I need you to pay them. I then need you to pay the balance of your one-third. All I'm asking you to do is to live up to your obligations."

"I'm broke, Ben. I just don't have it, and I can't get it either."

Littleton tried to change the subject by shifting to Davis's injuries. "How are you doing? Does the shoulder still hurt?"

"Let's just say I'll never play the piano again. If you had been front man, you could have been the one in the hospital. Remember, after my family, even before 911, I called and warned you. I deserve some loyalty, Bradley. I'm broke also. Morty has waived my rent, I've exhausted my savings, and I've sold my stocks. I'll have to refinance my house just to pay my personal expenses. I can't carry my load as well as yours."

He handed Littleton a document and pointed at it: "Here's the accounting. At this moment you owe $70,000, but by Monday when I pay the next round of bills, you'll owe just over $75,000."

Davis pulled an additional document from his briefcase and continued, "These are all due in the next thirty days and will require $24,000 more. Your share is $8,000. I need a check for at least $50,000 right now."

"I simply don't have it. You can ask all you want, but I can't get it," Littleton repeated sternly.

Davis pulled another document from his briefcase. It was a new contract between Littleton and Davis dividing the fees and expenses twenty-five and seventy-five, respectively, increasing Davis's portion of the fee by eight and a third percent. Littleton signed the document without further argument, but Davis reminded him: "Even under the new deal you still owe more than $60,000. I'll expect your check by the end of the week. I'm not kidding, Brad. Sell something or borrow it."

Littleton snorted, "Don't tell me what the hell to do."

Now Davis was angry. He was very controlled until that point. "Look, you worthless piece of shit, you haven't lifted a finger to do any of the heavy lifting. Unlike me, you haven't worked more than forty hours a week on Plainview while ignoring the rest of your practice. You haven't invested your life's savings, and nobody has beaten you up either. You need to get involved, or you need to get out."

"My name is on all the contracts, right next to yours, in the same size print. You can't get rid of me without risking your relationship with our clients. Remember I represent Dr. Patel—"

"Brad, you're a fool. She's as sick of you as I am."

"I've also got a contract with her. She's not going anywhere. I keep in touch with the Plainview clients."

Littleton was getting on Davis's nerves. This clown didn't even appreciate the weakness of his position.

"They know who's done all the work," shot back

Davis. "It won't be hard to convince them that you're dead weight."

"Ben, don't threaten me. I warn you, if you try to steal my cases, we'll both lose them, which hurts not only us but also the clients. Don't fuck with me!"

Davis didn't like Littleton's last remark. As the argument between co-counsels was about to escalate, Pierce, McCoy, Stevenson, and English walked into the room, and the subject was immediately dropped. Davis knew this was not the end of the matter, though.

It was time for him to take English's deposition in the Jones case. The court reporter came in and set up. She swore the witness, and Davis began his examination.

"Dr. English, on Wednesday, September 22nd, I was attacked in my office. Did you have anything to do with my attack?"

English growled at him and smirked. "I thought you slipped in the bathtub," referring to Davis's still obvious bruises, red areas where his lips were healing, and arm in a sling. He moved deliberately, too, to avoid stressing his still painful ribs.

"No, some thugs came to my office and cowardly sucker punched me."

"That's too bad. You should be more careful. My guess is that in your line of business, you piss off a lot of people."

"You don't like me, Doctor, do you?"

"You're not one of my favorite people. I won't be sending you a get-well card."

Davis decided to move on with the deposition. He questioned English thoroughly about the Jones chart. English could not explain why he performed surgery without first obtaining a sedimentation rate. English agreed that the patient's diagnosis was generally applied to a much older person. After four hours, Davis adjourned the deposition.

CHAPTER TWENTY-FIVE

CALLING ALL SURGEONS

THURSDAY, SEPTEMBER 30, 1993

Dr. Herman woke up and started the day by having a huge fight with his wife. The argument was about nothing. The pressure was getting to him. He realized the fight was his fault, but he couldn't bring himself to apologize.

At the office, Herman was also short with his secretary. "I have to get control of myself. I can't let Davis get to me and win," he muttered under his breath while he waited for his first patient.

His office practice was still doing better than most but not what it once was. Most of his patients remained loyal, although several left at the urging of family members. Many patients stayed with him because they needed their medicine. Many of them depended on the controlled drugs he prescribed. That was one surefire way to buy loyalty.

His hospital practice had been decimated. There was no question that the lawsuits and negative publicity affected him financially. The Nashville papers were constantly running articles about the lawsuits, but the hospital managed to control the local paper. The *Plainview Gazette* ran several letters to the editor, which described the hospital as a vital part of the community. But local support wasn't enough. His attorney, McCoy, warned him that his conduct was "under the microscope" and that he "needed to watch his p's and q's." How dare McCoy question his medical judgment? First, his medical judgment was questioned by that asshole, Davis, now by his own lawyer.

He wasn't just being paranoid. Herman and English were the center of discussion at every committee meeting at the hospital. They had once been heroes, the fair-haired boys; now they were villains and incompetents who practiced bad medicine.

How quickly those ingrates forget that Charlie and I turned their bankrupt hospital around. Douglas didn't return his calls. The hospital communicated with him through his lawyers. There was no question that he made enemies on the staff, including Dr. Gerald. Gerald, the hospital's radiologist, had been jealous of his office ultrasound practice and was now jumping on the bandwagon and kicking him while he was down.

He also recently received a letter from Blue Star of Tennessee. He was being audited for the years 1990 through 1992. Blue Star was focusing its audit on ultrasounds. During that period, he charged that one insurance company more than $700,000 for the various types of ultrasounds. This audit could be a financial disaster.

Compared to the board charges, however, the audit was insignificant. Keeping his medical license was critical. As long as he had the license, he could survive. He could always move to another state and another small rural community that was desperate for a family doctor. It was a license to steal, and he knew how to do that.

He started out with good intentions, trying to follow in the footsteps of his mother, Dr. Margot Herman. In

1945, she was pregnant with Lars and on staff at a small hospital outside Dresden until it was destroyed in the Valentine's Day firebombing. Over the next year, she and her infant son fought their way to join her brother, Wilhelm, in Argentina, where Margot opened a clinic for German ex-pats. Throughout his life Herman watched his mother care for her patients.

Herman struggled in medical school but graduated. Having to repeatedly take the FLEX exam changed him. He studied and failed year after year. He hated that damn exam because it delayed his becoming a doctor. His mother died, never knowing he had passed it and gotten his license, and that left a bad taste in his mouth.

He forced himself to see patients, trying to remain calm and professional. Treating patients actually allowed him to forget his troubles. He was contemplating performing an ultrasound on a patient when Sheila knocked on the door.

"Excuse me, Dr. Herman, but Mr. Douglas is on the phone, and he says it's urgent."

He excused himself from his patient and went directly to his office. "Hello, Woody, what can I do for you? I'm seeing patients right now."

Douglas didn't return his hello. He jumped to the topic on his mind: "We've got a big problem, Lars. Your friend Dr. English didn't show up this morning for surgery. Your patient DeeAnn Bell was prepped and ready to go, but there was no surgeon. The patient's family is asking questions, and I don't have any answers. You made the referral to English. I need you to get down here so we can avoid another lawsuit. That jerk Davis is watching us like a hawk. We shouldn't make it easy for him."

This was the last thing Herman wanted to deal with, but Douglas made a good point. "Let me finish with this patient and I'll be right over. Please stay with the family and tell them I'm on my way."

Herman hung up the phone and cursed Charlie English. He was upset but not surprised. He knew Charlie had been cracking for some time.

Just then, Sheila buzzed him on the intercom. In a much too loud voice, he announced that he didn't want to be disturbed.

Sheila equally raised her voice and said, "You'll want to take this call. It's Dr. English, and he sounds drunk."

Herman hated drunks. He picked up the phone and said, "Charlie, where the hell are you? You missed the Bell surgery this morning. You better be dead or lying in the street run over by a car and paralyzed. You really fucked up this time."

Herman could hear English crying on the other end of the line. Rolling his eyes, he changed tactics. He tried his best to get information: "Where are you, Charlie?"

"I've lost my way."

"Do you have a car? Can you drive? Can I come get you? Tell me where you are."

English was so drunk that he was slurring his words and speaking very loudly.

Herman was livid. The last thing he needed was an incoherent surgeon.

"You can't help me. Nobody can. My life's turned to shit. I'm better off dead."

"Don't give in. Don't give up."

The pressure had been too much for poor Charlie. The lawsuits, the notice of charges, and Benjamin Davis ruined his life and Charlie's.

"Don't let that bastard Davis win. If you don't come back and fight these cases, he wins by default."

Herman tried to calm English down, trying desperately to get the distraught man to talk. "What's the matter, friend? I want to help. Tell me how."

By then, English was crying uncontrollably. He wailed, "I'm being held in contempt of court, and my lawyer insists that the judge is going to throw the book at me. Judge Robert Lewis hates me. He thinks I'm a deadbeat. He has held me in civil contempt for failing to pay eight months of alimony and eight months of child support to Susan. My lawyer told me that civil contempt is far worse than criminal contempt. The judge can hold me indefinitely in jail until I pay the past due alimony and child support, which could be never."

English was still blubbering but started to regain some control. "I can't go to jail for even a day, Lars. So, I ran because I'm not going to stick around to be crucified. Fuck that no good bitch. Let her burn in hell."

Herman wasn't sure that this drunk would listen to reason, but he had to try: "But what about your children? They're only six and eight years old. What did they ever do wrong?"

After thirty seconds, English responded, "They're casualties of war. They are collateral damage. They shouldn't have been standing so close to their good-for-nothing mother when the bomb went off."

Herman made small talk in the hope of putting English off guard. In a soft, comforting voice he asked, "Tell me where you are so we will know that you're safe."

English replied, "You're better off not knowing, or

that maniac judge may hold you as an accessory after the fact."

Twenty minutes of conversation later, Herman didn't want to know where Charlie was. He had enough trouble of his own without the additional headache of Charlie's domestic problems and fugitive status. He decided to end the conversation: "Good-bye, Charlie, and good luck. You're going to need it."

English seemed to be relieved that the conversation was concluding. He ended by saying, "I know you can't come along, Lars. I wish you could. I'd like the company. But I'll send you a postcard when I get settled down and stop running. I think I'll send Davis a postcard too. I'm sure he'd like to hear from me."

He promised Herman that Davis had not heard the last from Charlie English yet.

Herman was not exactly sure how to take English's last comment. But he believed that nothing too bad could happen to Davis to suit his purposes.

After he hung up, Herman rushed over to the hospital to talk to the Bell family, who had been waiting more than an hour for an explanation. Entering the room, he worked his magic. He told them that Dr. English had a family emergency and was forced to leave town unexpectedly. This story was more or less truthful. Herman just neglected to mention that English fled.

The family was satisfied with Dr. Herman's smooth double-talk. Herman manipulated and managed this problem. Benjamin Davis wouldn't get his grubby little hands on this potential case, which was a small victory in the grand scheme of things.

CHAPTER TWENTY-SIX

THE GODDESS ATHENA

SATURDAY, OCTOBER 2, 1993

As she waited in the dark, Amy Pierce knew that contact with English was unethical. He was a fugitive. Judge Robert Lewis, who presided over English's divorce from Susan, issued a warrant for his arrest. Sheriff Buford Dudley of Hewes County asked Amy if she heard from English. At that time, she could honestly respond that she hadn't. That was no longer true.

That's why at 10:00 p.m. she was standing not far from the Parthenon, Nashville's exact replica of the ancient Greek building situated in the popular Centennial Park. She fondly remembered the Saturday that she and Carter went to see the inside of the Parthenon and its magnificent forty-two-foot gilded statue of the goddess Athena. Both of them were impressed. English selected the location of their clandestine meeting, and she thought that the selection was a little melodramatic.

As Amy waited, she replayed her conversation with Lowell Thomas in her head. Thomas would not come right out and tell her not to meet English. PIC, Dr. English's malpractice insurance company, was too important a client to simply ignore English's contact. It was in PIC's best interest and, therefore, also in her firm's best interest for English to stop running.

Thomas told her that if Judge Lewis learned about her meeting with English, at the very least he would turn her over to the Board of Professional Responsibility. He might even charge her with contempt of court. If the board found her guilty, Thomas predicted that Amy's law license would be suspended, possibly for a year. If that happened, Thomas promised that he and the firm would use their influence, but there was no guarantee that her firm could control the board.

Lewis, Boxer, Steine, and particularly Davis would be after her scalp, and all four had influence with the board. Steine served as president of the board for more than eight years and still carried a great deal of weight. Amy had to worry about criminal concerns as well as ethical ones.

Thomas also warned that both Judge Lewis and Judge Boxer could criminally charge her as an accessory after the fact. Both judges had the power to do so, and either or both could convince an assistant district attorney to prosecute. If convicted of a crime, Amy would lose her law license forever. English was putting her and her son at risk. She had worked hard and didn't deserve the position that English put her in.

Lowell Thomas just wanted results. Davenport, the insurance executive, called him directly and insisted that Thomas get English to come in from the cold.

Thomas instructed Pierce: "Amy, English is mocking the system. Judges don't like to be mocked. English is in contempt of court in Hewes County. He's scheduled to give his deposition in the Malone case. If he fails to show, Davis will run to Boxer and ask that the court hold English in contempt. My guess is that Boxer will judicially reset English's deposition in a week or so, and

English better show up. If he doesn't, Boxer will hold him in contempt."

"Do you think it will be civil or criminal?"

"What difference does it make which type of contempt? Either way, English winds up in jail, and our case is prejudiced beyond repair."

Amy felt that she had to make an obvious point: "English is going to jail regardless. Lewis has already found English in civil contempt in the case filed by the second Mrs. English's lawyer. He'll stay in jail for the duration of the Plainview cases. English will have to cure the contempt by paying his arreared alimony and child support, $36,000 and increasing every day."

Thomas was growing angry, not necessarily with Amy, but she was the only one in harm's way. "Look, Davenport is ready to pull the plug on English. If he's not going to attend depositions or participate in the discovery process, he's in breach of contract, and PIC can walk away from the defense. If English, as the insured, doesn't cooperate, PIC doesn't owe him a defense. If PIC walks away from the Plainview cases, we lose hundreds of thousands of dollars in fees. Based on my last conversation with Davenport, DMT could lose the client because of this English bastard."

Amy didn't like the sound of that. She had worked hard on the Plainview cases and had personally billed over seventeen hundred hours in fourteen months. The firm had made more than $250,000 for her time alone. Amy had supervised two other associates who had done much of the legal research. The firm had charged another $110,000 for their time. The firm also made a profit on ancillary charges such as copies, faxes, messengers, and so forth.

Amy estimated the firm's profit at $50,000. All in all, DMT had been paid more than $400,000, either directly or indirectly, through Amy's efforts. There had been no trial. There had been no appeal. Those charges were incurred through discovery. More than eighty depositions were taken, as Amy predicted. The research and briefing on comparative fault and recklessness/ punitive damages had been exhaustive. The Plainview cases had been a pure gravy train. But if PIC pulled the plug, the gravy train would pull out of the station, never to return.

Thomas continued, "This turn of events will not help your chance of partnership, you know."

Amy exploded, "Lowell, that's unfair, and you know it. We agreed on the criteria for my partnership. I've billed twice the amount our deal required, and there has been additional billing to boot. English is a problem but not of my making. In light of his lack of cooperation, I've done an exceptional job, and I'm not going to stand here and take the blame for his actions."

Thomas took an obvious different tactic with her. "You're absolutely right. It's not your fault, but you've got to fix it. You've got to bring the bastard back to face the music. The firm is counting on you. We need to keep these cases going and keep PIC as a client."

With that remark, Amy's meeting with Thomas ended.

English has to be brought back under control. PIC is tired of English's disappearance act. His shenanigans are costing PIC money through unnecessary legal fees and through jeopardizing the defense of nine lawsuits. It's my responsibility to bring English in. The problem is that direct contact with him jeopardizes my career and future.

Waiting in the dark for English, Amy realized she had been daydreaming.

English was late, but he wasted no time in verbally assaulting Amy: "Are you alone, Pierce? You're my lawyer. It's your job to protect me. If you turn me over to that fucking judge, I'll report you to your Board of Professional Responsibility. Then you'll know how I feel, and you'll have to defend yourself." English was nervous, and he kept looking around.

His paranoia was contagious. Amy also started looking around. No one was anywhere near them. She took a deep breath and said, "Doctor, this has to stop right now. You must turn yourself in to Judge Lewis, or your trouble will only get worse."

English interrupted: "How could it get any worse? If I turn myself in to Lewis, he'll lock me up and throw away the key. The Medical Licensing Board is after my license. The board's suspension or revocation of my professional license is much more serious than your malpractice lawsuits. Davis has nine lawsuits pending, and I'll have to sit through nine trials. Life on the run is bad, but my time is my own, and you get used to looking over your shoulder."

"Then why did you call me and agree to meet?"

"It's hard to explain. I could've just disappeared. I wanted to explain to someone why I was getting out of Dodge and why I wasn't coming back."

"You could've done that over the telephone."

"I guess I wanted to say good-bye in person to someone."

Amy thought that was a stupid reason to risk this meeting and put them in jeopardy. She was trying to decide what she needed to say next. Convincing English that it was in his best interest to turn himself in was going to be a hard sell.

"Look, Doctor, the Medical Licensing Board isn't going to take your license away. After this is over, you'll be practicing medicine again. If you cooperate with PIC, it will pay for your defense, and your coverage will pay any judgments awarded. The trials will be in Hewes County. The largest jury award in the history of that county is less than $200,000. Some of these patients weren't even hurt. Davis will have to prove damages.

"Now, Judge Lewis is another story. He will probably throw you in jail, but you're a professional, and after a week or two, he'll probably let you out, particularly if you set up a payment plan on back alimony and child support."

English thought about it a few seconds and then looked Pierce in the eyes and said, "You go to jail. You put your trust and future in that crazy bastard judge. I'm not counting on any compassion from him. I'll be in jail through all nine trials. Don't bullshit me. You're my lawyer, and I don't give a shit if PIC drops me. Those lawsuits are the least of my worries. Your concern is your fee, not me. I'm not going to jail. I'm out of here." With that, English ran into the night.

Still standing outside the Parthenon, Amy spoke to the mighty Athena housed within its walls: "You're the goddess of wisdom. Do you have any good ideas?"

CHAPTER TWENTY-SEVEN

THANKSGIVING

THURSDAY, NOVEMBER 25, 1993

Thanksgiving had always been Davis's favorite holiday. It was not surprising since he loved to eat. Liza and her mother worked for the last two days preparing the meal at the Davis home. Several of Liza's sisters and their families had traveled home for the holiday.

After the meal, the kids went to the playroom to watch television and play video games. The brothers-in-law went into the study to shoot a game of pool, and the women began to clear the table and address the dishes. John Caldwell, Liza's father and Morty's heart surgeon, asked Morty and Davis if he could see them in private.

Davis led them to his home office and sat behind his desk. They left the others under the pretext that he and Morty wanted to smoke cigars. Liza knew this was a ruse because Morty would never smoke in front of her father. After settling in, Morty did pull out a cigar and light it up. He smiled at Caldwell. "I wouldn't want to make your son-in-law a liar."

Davis waited for his father-in-law to get to the business at hand. He looked uncharacteristically nervous.

"I've heard about these Plainview cases. You sued the hospital also."

Davis knew that Caldwell had only the best intentions, but the comment still pissed him off. Despite his anger, Davis tried to soften his words: "John, there's no question in my mind that the hospital knew exactly what was going on. In one year, Plainview Community Hospital went from $2 million in the red to $2 million in the black. Any board would want to know why and how a small community hospital improved by $4 million, if not just to replicate that success next year."

The expression on his father-in-law's face told Davis that he had something else on his mind. "You didn't bring us in here to talk about poor, poor Plainview Community Hospital. What's really bothering you?"

His father-in-law sat back on the couch and hesitated before responding. "I had a very disturbing conversation yesterday, Ben. One of my partners got a call from an executive vice president at Tennessee Mutual. There's nothing surprising about that. Ralph is the contact person for the partnership and has served on the insurance company's board. Based upon our premiums, we own one-fourth of a percent of the company, which makes us the third largest shareholders. According to my partner, this prick came right out and said that because of the two of you, our partnership's premiums will go sky-high as a result of the judgments in the Plainview cases. Apparently, Tennessee Mutual insures Dr. Herman, one of the defendants. He even suggested that we would bear a greater percentage of the loss because you're my son-in-law."

Both Morty and Davis were shocked by such a blatant attempt to wrongfully influence the outcome of the Plainview cases. Tennessee Mutual had balls or, as Morty would say, "chutzpah." Davis was also upset for Caldwell. Davis had known Caldwell for more than fifteen years, and he respected and loved him. Even though Davis was a lawyer who sued doctors and hospitals for a living, his father-in-law had always been supportive.

Caldwell even contributed $500 to the reward fund that Morty created through the Nashville Bar to reward those who had any information that would possibly lead to the arrest of Davis's attackers. Morty drafted the announcement that appeared in an issue of the *Nashville Bar Journal*. He also wrote a personal letter to more than one hundred members of the Bar seeking their support and contribution. Morty got the ball rolling with an initial contribution of $5,000. Davis and Morty raised an additional $15,000, Davis added his own $5,000, and the reward rose to $25,000. The bartender from Tootsie's got the money for calling the police to report Laurel and Hardy's presence in the bar.

Davis almost apologetically asked Caldwell, "How did your partner respond?"

"I was very proud of him. He told the insurance company, and I quote, to 'fuck off.' He spoke to me yesterday, and he scheduled a partnership meeting on Saturday at three. We have a total of ten partners, and our insurance premium covers an additional six associates. Our current premium is more than $1 million per year. An increase in premium affects our bottom line. Ralph and I agreed that our partners have a right to know."

Davis put out his cigar. The room was smoky, but Morty continued to puff away and cherish the smoke in his lungs. Davis was sorry his father-in-law was in this position, but it really wasn't his fault. Tennessee Mutual elected to insure Herman. The company should have known that he failed the FLEX exam eight times; it should have reviewed Herman's privileges at Plainview

Community Hospital since it was insuring his competency to perform those procedures.

"John, this is an obvious problem with mutual insurance companies. Good doctors have to pay for the mistakes of bad ones. You're asking the wrong questions. Your group should question your company, as shareholders, how the underwriting department ever insured this incompetent in the first place. Rather than be on the defensive, your partnership should confront the company."

Caldwell was not an aggressive person, except in the operating room. He would never confront Tennessee Mutual as Davis suggested, but maybe one of his partners would. Caldwell agreed with Davis it was the right thing to do, but it carried a significant financial risk, and he expressed concern over the reaction of the entire partnership.

"John, I'm sorry for any trouble my Plainview cases are causing you with your partners."

"Forget it. Just keep doing the right thing, and follow your heart."

The three men joined Caroline, Jake, and Sammie in the den. They were watching the *Wizard of Oz*. The movie had just changed to color, and Dorothy was in Munchkinland. The rest of the family was scattered throughout the house. Davis and Caldwell sat next to each other on the love seat, and Morty got comfortable in the easy chair.

When the phone rang, Davis asked Caroline to answer it.

She picked it up on the third ring. "Caroline Davis, Davis residence, may I help you?"

"You can help me by sucking my dick."

Caroline turned white and froze.

Seeing the horrified expression on his daughter's face, Davis jumped up to grab the phone from her. He supported her weight in one arm and held the receiver with the other.

"Who the hell is this?"

"It's not a friend wishing you a Happy Thanksgiving, that's for fucking sure. You're a stubborn fool. What do I have to do, kill you? Cut your losses while you still have that beautiful family. Why would you risk everything for Plainview?"

The question was a good one. The answer was complex, and in part, the answer was that Davis was a stubborn son of a bitch.

"Look, you tattooed bastard! If you don't stay away from my family, you'll be extinct just like that T-rex on your fucking forearm. I'll shoot you dead, and that's a fucking promise. I will make it my mission in life to hunt you down and put a bullet in your fucking brain. Tell those assholes that you work for that I'm not backing down, no matter what shit you try to pull. Don't underestimate me, or you're a dead man."

All hell broke loose when Liza heard what transpired. She quizzed Caroline, who repeated verbatim what the caller said.

Liza screamed at Davis, "It's Plainview or us! What's more important? Your family or those damn cases? You've got to choose. Now!"

At Liza's outburst, Caroline ran from her father's side into Sammie's arms, and she was crying hysterically. Jake, in tears, was sitting on Morty's lap while the old man stroked his head. Davis just stood there trying to decide how to answer.

Surprisingly John Caldwell spoke up: "That's an unfair question, sweetheart. Ben's done nothing wrong. I'm proud of him and what he's trying to do. These doctors are nothing more than criminals with medical licenses. They've hurt people; they've even killed people. There's no question in my mind that the hospital's also at fault because it created the atmosphere for this lunacy. Ben, I'd call the police and report this call."

Morty jumped in. "We should also subpoena your phone records. I'm sure this call was made from the hospital. This guy is brazen. He wants us to know he's calling from the hospital."

Davis went over to Liza and tried to kiss her, but she pulled away from him. He wasn't going to answer her question. His father-in-law answered it for him. Davis could not and would not give in. He was taking the Plainview cases to trial, no matter what.

That morning, about three thirty, Davis woke up in a cold sweat. He looked over at Liza, who at the moment was calm because she was asleep. But he knew the storm was not over with her.

After family members left, Liza erupted again and vehemently attacked her husband: "You're not only putting yourself at risk, but this entire family is at risk. Don't you care about your children?"

"You know damn well I care about our children. Don't be absurd."

"I'm sorry, it's hard to tell. I suspect that a casual observer would think these Plainview lawsuits are more important than your family."

Ben shot back, "They are important to my professional reputation but not more important than you and the kids."

"Well, they're more important than me staying home with the children. Plainview is forcing me to go back to work. I'd rather stay home than go back to the hospital."

"Both kids are in school."

"What about Christmas break and the summer?"

"Your mother would be more than happy to help out."

"We borrowed $50,000 from your parents. Let's borrow the same amount from mine."

"No way!" Davis was adamant.

"You're awfully proud, and because of your pride, I have to go back to work." Liza rolled away from him in the bed.

After recalling the exchange, Davis slipped out of bed and walked downstairs to his home office. He sat at his desk and put his face in the palms of his hands. *How did I get into this mess?* He couldn't blame Morty, who warned against taking the cases. He could blame that worthless piece of shit Littleton, but what good would that do? *No, this is my fault, and I'll have to figure out how to fix it.*

The most dangerous problem out there was T-rex. Davis rubbed his shoulder as a reminder of his beating. That scumbag called his home this evening, probably from a pay phone. Davis didn't agree with Morty that it was made from the hospital.

Davis banged his right fist on the desk, disregarding the pain. He would subpoena his own phone records, but unless T-rex called from Herman's or English's office, it wouldn't make a difference. He knew that the two calls on the morning of the beating, first to his home and then to the office, came from the hospital. That information didn't impress the police. There were dozens of phones at the hospital, and almost anyone had access to make the calls. It did prove, however, that his beating was connected to the Plainview cases. But Davis didn't need the phone records to know that.

He pulled open the middle drawer of his desk and retrieved his .357, a gun he'd gotten from his friend Brian Bubi, who took Davis to a gun-training course. An identical gun was in his bedside table. He had shown the weapons to Jake and Caroline and warned them that the guns were Daddy's and that they were not to touch them under any circumstances.

He opened the chamber and took out a bullet. He held it between his thumb and his middle finger and thought about the yellow eyes of the T-rex that stared him down on the morning of his beating. A shiver went up and down Davis's spine, and he said out loud, "If that son of a bitch comes near my family, I'll put this bullet right between his eyes."

Davis chambered the bullet and put the gun back in his desk drawer. After he showered and dressed, he opened the drawer, put the gun in his briefcase, and left for the day. It was just before five.

CHAPTER TWENTY-EIGHT

I'LL CALL THE POPE

THURSDAY, DECEMBER 9, 1993

Laura Patel had requested a meeting with Davis two weeks earlier, but because of the Thanksgiving holiday and his work commitments, he had to put it off until now. Bella explained to Laura that his schedule was a mad house.

When Laura arrived, Davis was already in his office with a client, so she visited with Bella. She found her easy to talk to.

"How's it going, Doc?"

In response, Laura began to cry.

Bella came from behind her desk and gave her a big hug. "It's going to be all right, darling. Tell Bella what's wrong."

Laura immediately opened up: "I had a good practice. I was close to my patients. I had a loving relationship with Maggie and my children. In a matter of days, those bastards turned my life upside down. I lost my practice. They smeared my good name professionally and personally. My life with Maggie also changed, and I'm not sure how I feel about it. I'm unemployed, and Maggie took a job at Vanderbilt Children's Hospital in her chosen profession as a child psychologist. Our roles have reversed. She's become the breadwinner, while I'm the stay-at-home mom."

Bella just listened. Then choosing her words carefully, she said, "You're a doctor. That's a big part of who you are, but you're also a mom. You're torn between the two things you love. Both you and Maggie have a desire to serve others, particularly children. So, the right solution is for you to take turns. Last year, it was Maggie's turn to be with your children; now, it's your turn. Enjoy this time. Focus on your children. Besides, you need to concentrate on your lawsuit against the hospital. What's the status of your case?"

When Laura started crying again, Bella wondered what she said to turn the water works back on. "Doctor, what did I say?"

"Nothing. You're as sweet as can be. But my lawsuit isn't going that well. Brad Littleton is no Ben Davis. He doesn't return my phone calls, and there's no question he's outmatched by the hospital's attorneys. My deposition was a disaster. I don't think Littleton properly prepared me. Right after my deposition, the hospital filed a motion for summary judgment, seeking to dismiss my counterclaim, and our response is due Monday. I've tried calling Littleton, but he hasn't returned my calls. That's what I'm here to see Mr. Davis about. I need his help."

Davis greeted Laura warmly, and that encouraged her. They sat at the conference table in his office while Laura expressed her concerns about Littleton and the status of her case. Davis shook his head in disgust. He didn't interrupt her. It felt good just to speak her mind. He was a good listener.

After she finished, Davis began, "Laura, you've been not only a friend but also a valuable resource to me throughout these Plainview cases. You helped me understand the medical aspects of the cases and introduced me to Sister Carson. Her testimony will prove that the hospital knew or should have known about the unnecessary tests and surgeries that those criminal doctors were performing on unsuspecting patients. What you've done will help Plainview and its citizens. You should be proud, and so should Maggie."

He paused a moment, letting his words sink in. "But I can't represent you. Brad and I are already sideways in the Plainview cases. If I accept your case, I could injure the rights of my other clients. I can't risk that. Brad would go berserk. He's threatened to blow up the Plainview cases if I try to remove him as my co-counsel. He'd rather see everybody get nothing than be excluded from the process. He's dead weight, but I've got no choice. I've got a contract with him. More important, his name's on the contracts with each of my clients. I don't trust him. I'd love to get him out of the cases, but we're tied to each other like two guys in a three-legged race.

"I'll give Littleton a call and try to light a fire under his ass. I'll review their motion and casually make suggested arguments to counter the motion. He'll piss and moan, but in the end, because he's lazy, he'll take my recommendations. I'm sorry, but that's the best I can do. I wish I could do more, but I can't."

"I wish you could take control of my case, but I do understand. Any help you can give Littleton will be greatly appreciated," Laura told him.

"Laura, remember that all the response must do is raise a material fact in dispute to defeat their motion. I promise that both Morty and I will examine the facts and try to identify at least one material fact in dispute.

"Doc, I have a telephone message from Sister

Carson. She called earlier today. Would you like to sit in on the callback?"

"I'd love to be included. We spoke last week about the Malone case. Anytime I get to talk to her is a treat. She's been very supportive in helping me deal with my unemployment. She's inspirational."

Davis dialed Sister Carson's number. The phone rang twice, and an unfamiliar voice answered.

"Mr. Davis, thank God you called back. Sister Carson is with Mother Superior Nash. I know they want to speak with you. I'll transfer the call."

The Sister put Davis on hold, and the next thing that Davis heard was the Mother. "Mr. Davis, Mother Superior Nash here. Sister Carson is with me. I have you on speakerphone."

"Good morning, ladies. I have Dr. Patel with me. May I put you on speakerphone as well?"

When both lines were on speaker, Mother Superior Nash took control. "This morning at about eight I was in a meeting, and my secretary took a message from Dr. Charles English, requesting that I call him back. I was not familiar with the name, so I called back immediately. I was concerned that one of my Sisters was either sick or injured."

Davis asked, "What did Dr. English have to say?"

"The conversation was about you and Dr. Patel. Dr. English was very angry, and he sounded like he was either drunk or on medication because he slurred his words. He was very loud and quite obnoxious. His tone was so unusual and aggressive that I decided to make notes of our conversation. Let me read them to you."

Laura felt tension sweep through her body. She never expected any of the defendants to contact Sister

Carson or her order directly. Dr. English was out of control.

Mother Superior Nash began to read: "'Did I know Sister Carson?' I informed him that she was a beloved member of my order and the administrator and president of Saint Francis Hospital. 'Did I know Dr. Laura Patel?' I said I did. She had been a resident at Saint Francis several years ago, and Sister Carson had introduced us. He asked me if Sister Carson had anything to do with Dr. Patel's adoption of two 'Chink babies.'"

Laura couldn't take it any longer: "He's a very sick man. He needs psychiatric help."

"I couldn't agree more, my dear. I told him that I found that term offensive. I asked him why he was asking these questions. He accused Sister Carson of judging him without all the facts. He mentioned a Jew by the name of Ben Davis. He said that this Jew was trying to destroy his life and livelihood, just like the Jews killed Christ."

Davis hadn't spoken since the introduction. "Did he threaten you in any way?"

"He very loudly stated that he could not believe that a Catholic Sister could be a party to this. He claimed that Sister Carson was unwittingly being duped by Ben Davis and that, as her superior, I should intervene and prevent this injustice.

"Furthermore, he threatened to go to the bishop and, if necessary, the pope to prevent Sister Carson from threatening his livelihood. He said he would 'pull out all guns,' and he wouldn't rest until this injustice was righted."

Sister Carson broke in, "Mr. Davis, Mother has known about my involvement in the Plainview cases since the beginning. I spoke to her immediately after our first conversation in 1992. I had her permission to testify as an expert witness."

Laura could hear the two clergywomen talking on their end of the line.

"If you recall, you notarized my affidavit. My testimony is directed against the liability of the hospital, but clearly my opinion is that Dr. English and Dr. Herman were guilty of not only negligence but also recklessness. The hospital and doctors were all about the money. They cared nothing about their patients."

Mother Superior Nash added, "He scared me, and I don't scare easily. What do you think we should do?"

Laura felt compelled to answer, "These men are dangerous. Mr. Davis was recently beaten up in his office. He has not outright blamed the defendants in the Plainview cases, but God forgive me, I suspect Dr. English and his cohorts."

Mother Superior Nash's tone was even more concerned: "How badly was Mr. Davis injured?"

In a low voice, Laura answered for Davis: "God was protecting him."

Davis supplied details: "My face was bruised and cut pretty badly. I had a couple of broken ribs and a dislocated shoulder."

Laura knew that the seventy-four-year-old Mother Superior was a fighter and wouldn't be scared off by English.

She proved it by her concluding remarks: "God will provide, and with the Lord's help and a little bit of help from Mr. Davis, we'll teach Dr. English about justice. I refuse to let this doctor intimidate us. We can risk a fight if it's for a good cause."

"Do you have a fax machine at the sanctuary?"

Sister Carson responded in the negative. There was a short pause before Davis continued: "Sister will drive back to the hospital and fax me the Mother's notes so I can prepare an affidavit for her signature. Tomorrow, I'll file a faxed copy of the affidavit with the court and ask for a protective order preventing Dr. English from contacting either of you two again. Sister, have you explained to the Mother that Dr. English is on the run and a criminal with a medical license?"

"No, I haven't."

Davis then gave Mother Superior the five-minute version of Dr. English's legal problems with one ex-wife and his current status as a fugitive. Davis reported that he disappeared about seventy days ago and that the only person who possibly knew his whereabouts was his attorney, Ms. Pierce.

Sister Carson hesitated. "Ben, I'm willing to go forward and testify, but I can't allow any of the defendants to injure the church or my order. I should also give an affidavit that Dr. English's call was taken by me as a serious threat and that it was clear his purpose was to intimidate me and that now I am apprehensive. He clearly threatened to try to damage my reputation with the church, which is my most sacred possession. I told the Mother that if Dr. English in any way jeopardizes the order, I would withdraw my testimony."

Davis assured them that Judge Boxer, within a day or so, would issue an order preventing Dr. English from further contacting them.

Sister Carson asked a relevant question: "Ben, if neither you nor Judge Boxer knows where Dr. English is, how are you going to prevent him from coming here? He could travel to Saint Paul, either by plane or by car. He could be on our doorstep tomorrow. We need your help and the court's protection."

"You have my word, Sister, and my word is my bond."

CHAPTER TWENTY-NINE

WITHDRAWAL OF DEFENSE

MONDAY, DECEMBER 13, 1993

Sammie and Davis waited for twenty minutes in the conference room of Dunn, Moore and Thomas, Pierce's firm. They timed their arrival perfectly, five minutes before the deposition was scheduled to begin. It was supposed to start at nine, and according to the subpoena, English was already fifteen minutes late. It was the first deposition in the Plainview cases scheduled by subpoena. All of the other ninety-nine depositions had been set by agreement of the attorneys as to time and date.

Dr. English failed to appear for his December 1st deposition in the Malone case. Earlier, Pierce warned Davis that English might not appear because he was afraid to enter the state for fear of arrest by order of Judge Lewis.

On the run for almost three months Dr. English requested a leave of absence from the hospital that, in light of the circumstances, the hospital was more than happy to grant. As far as Davis knew, Dr. English stayed out of Plains County and the rest of the state.

English owed a substantial amount of alimony and child support for his two children to his ex-wife, Susan. Judge Lewis was a mean son of a bitch. When he found English in civil contempt, Lewis knew exactly what he was doing. Unlike criminal contempt where the judge must issue a sentence for a specific length of time, under civil contempt the sentence lasts until the offending party cures the contempt. In one case in Tennessee, a woman was held in contempt for more than six years because she refused to let her ex-husband see their son since she alleged he was a child molester. She hid the child while she served her unending sentence in prison. She was a very sympathetic figure. Even the other prisoners treated her with respect and did not bother the middle-class mother. Eventually, the United States Supreme Court ordered her released on the grounds that serving six years for contempt was cruel and inhumane punishment under the Eighth Amendment.

Davis was growing restless. Besides Sammie, only the court reporter was present. The court reporter had preserved the testimony of more than half the witnesses, so she was well aware of the particulars of the Plainview cases, including the reason for Dr. English's unavailability.

About twenty-five minutes after the hour, Pierce and Stevenson entered the room. Both had serious expressions on their faces.

Pierce took the lead: "He's not coming. He thinks you're going to tip Sheriff Dudley and Judge Lewis off to his whereabouts and he'll be arrested."

Davis felt no sympathy for English. He felt sure English either instigated or knew who instigated his beating. Either way, Davis refused to cut him any slack. As usual, English was wrong. Davis wanted English's deposition. Although he'd love to see the doctor arrested, betrayal wasn't on Davis's mind. It wouldn't be the right thing to do. "Your client is not a very trusting individual, is he?"

Pierce decided to hold her ace in the hole and force Davis to commit. "We can continue the deposition another day, but there's no guarantee he'll show up then. What about taking the deposition out of state? We have to be in Connors next month anyway for Adams's deposition. We can stay an extra day and get it done. Or how about Bowling Green, Kentucky? It's over the Tennessee line. That's only thirty minutes from Nashville."

"Why should I accommodate Dr. English? You haven't cut me any slack in where my depositions could be taken. I've had to travel to Plains County at least fifty times when it would have been more convenient for all four attorneys to take those depositions in Nashville, a four-minute walk for any of us. You've insisted that all of those depositions be taken in Plains County, despite any inconvenience to the witnesses. What about that quiet room? Could Stevenson have found any place more uncomfortable? Why should I be gracious now? Why shouldn't I just file a petition for civil contempt?"

Davis had given Amy her opening. "I'll tell you why. If you do, and English is held in contempt, his malpractice insurance company will deny him a defense in the Plainview cases. You'll proceed against Dr. English without any insurance coverage, and he doesn't have a pot to piss in. How do you think your clients would like that? I can tell you for certain that the other defendants would love it. Imagine an empty chair at trial. I can see it now. The hospital and Dr. Herman blaming English for killing poor Rosie Malone. Under those circumstances, the jury would award most, if not all, of the verdict against Dr. English, and with no insurance, it would be uncollectible."

Davis glanced over at Sammie and responded to Pierce, "I guess you'll be out of a job then?"

Pierce assured him that she wasn't kidding and that she had already spoken with representatives of the company, and they were willing to pull the plug.

Davis wasn't going to be intimidated. Although the insurance company's position was defendable, Davis couldn't let English ignore the subpoena. "Make sure you fax the petition for contempt to PIC. Don't waste time using the mail."

For the record, Davis made the subpoena Exhibit 1 and stated that it was ten o'clock and the witness failed to appear. Davis further stated for the record that Ms. Pierce had represented that Dr. English had refused to appear in Plains County or anywhere else in the state for fear of Judge Lewis's reprisal. Davis also put on the record Ms. Pierce's threat of the withdrawal of defense and coverage if Davis filed a petition for contempt.

Davis turned to Pierce. "Anything else you want stated for the record, Ms. Pierce?"

"Look, Dr. English is unstable and crazy. The affidavit of Mother Superior Nash and the fact you've got a restraining order prove that. Dr. English's insurer is not obligated to indemnify and pay out for someone who's not cooperating and who's capable of anything."

Davis glared back at Pierce. He was about to test her reaction. "PIC has to pay off if it knew or should have known he was unstable. Also, Plainview Community Hospital should have known of your client's incompetence and dishonesty. The hospital had the proof sitting in its pathology lab and did nothing. In fact, the hospital hid the proof."

Pierce gave Davis a funny look. He couldn't tell whether she knew about the gallbladder slides. If she didn't, she would find out soon enough in the Malone case. If she did know, she didn't take the bait.

The deposition was adjourned.

CHAPTER THIRTY

A RUDE AWAKENING

MONDAY, DECEMBER 13, 1993

After the meeting, Amy kept replaying their final conversation in her mind. Davis said that the hospital knew of her client's incompetency and dishonesty and that the proof was sitting in its pathology lab. She couldn't call her client. English was on the run, and she could speak to him only when he contacted her. She thought about confiding in Lowell Thomas but decided she better not since she didn't know the answer to the question. She decided to go straight to the source, the hospital, and call Grayson Stevenson.

"Grayson, something Davis said is nagging at me."

"You sound surprised. The man's purpose in life is to keep us off balance and chasing shadows."

"I'm serious. He claimed that the hospital's pathology lab knew that English was incompetent and dishonest. He implied that he had the evidence to prove it. I don't have a client to talk to, so I called you."

There was dead silence on Stevenson's end. After about thirty seconds, Amy asked, "Are you there?"

"Yeah, look, I don't want to discuss this on the phone. Call McCoy, and let's meet at my office at five."

"What about Barnes? He's Dr. Herman's co-counsel, Jack Barnes?"

"Forget him. He'd be trouble. We'll figure out how to deal with Barnes at the meeting."

"This sounds pretty serious."

"Unfortunately, it is."

For the next three hours, Amy speculated on the problem. With Dr. English as her client, she had to think outside the box. After his phone call to Mother Superior Nash, anything was possible. He was a real wild card.

Sean McCoy showed up wearing a black-and-white polka dot bow tie. When she invited him to the meeting, Amy told him only that the defense team needed to meet. After they sat down at Stevenson's conference room table, McCoy asked, "Where's Barnes?"

Stevenson responded, "He's not invited. Before we begin, I want to emphasize that this meeting and what's said here are protected by the co-defendant privilege, and we're bound to protect our clients from liability."

"Isn't the co-defendant privilege generally used in a criminal case?" Amy asked.

"Trust me, it's applicable here."

Amy looked over at McCoy, and he nodded.

Stevenson proceeded to explain that Custodian Johnston had lied in her deposition about the existence of the gallbladder slides and that immediately after the deposition, the slides from 1991 and 1992 had gone missing.

"Those slides prove that Dr. Herman made false diagnoses using his ultrasound, that Dr. English removed healthy gallbladders, and that the hospital's pathology department was a part of the conspiracy to perform unnecessary surgeries."

"That's what Davis alleges in his remaining nine lawsuits. He's got the slides," McCoy blurted out.

"Of course he's got the slides. They didn't walk out of the hospital on their own," Stevenson said angrily.

Amy said, "Okay, he's got them, but can he get them into evidence? They're stolen, aren't they?"

Stevenson had obviously given that question much thought. He'd assigned an associate to research the issue. "He can get them in. All he has to do is get one of our witnesses to lie and testify that the slides were destroyed, and he can introduce them to impeach the witness to prove that he or she is lying."

He handed Pierce and McCoy two different Tennessee Supreme Court decisions that supported this conclusion.

McCoy removed his bow tie and undid the top button of his shirt. "What the hell do we do?"

"I've spoken to the board, and if Davis has the slides and can use them, the board wants these cases settled cheaply."

They discussed how to negotiate the cheapest settlement. Everybody agreed that Davis didn't want to try the Jones case. It was scheduled first only because the defense won the flip of the coin. It wasn't a gall-bladder case, so the slides were definitely inadmissible.

Amy took the development of the defense strategy to the next level. "He's feeling pretty confident with those damn slides. We make an offer in Jones and the remaining eight cases but tie them to each other." Amy insisted that they make a take-it-or-leave-it offer. "Settle all nine, or try Jones. He'll have to communicate the offers, and that should get his clients fighting. Some will want to negotiate, while others won't."

Pierce was pretty proud of herself and could tell that she had impressed her co-counsel, McCoy, by his next comment.

"Great idea. Some of those cases aren't scheduled to be tried until 1996 or 1997. Those clients don't want to wait till then. They'll want money now."

Amy also shared her last conversation with Davis about PIC's withdrawal of English's defense. She could tell that neither attorney cared for the strategy because it reduced the number of sources of payment from three to two, but both conceded that the threat added pressure on Davis.

Amy asked her co-counsel under the privilege: "What do we do about Barnes?"

McCoy was quick to answer: "We share with him the settlement strategy, but we don't discuss the slides. He'd turn us in to the Disciplinary Board, for sure. I don't think he'd think he was bound by the co-defendant privilege; he'd rationalize reporting us as his ethical obligation."

Amy agreed. Jack Barnes was a straight arrow, and those slides proved the conspiracy between Dr. Herman, Dr. English, and the hospital.

When she got back to her office, a phone message was waiting from Dr. English: he would call her at eight. She made arrangements for her neighbor to pick up Carter after school. She grabbed a sandwich and worked in the office while waiting for English's call. At exactly eight, the phone rang.

The conversation didn't go well from the start. Amy tried to get Dr. English to return, face his contempt, and cooperate in his defense of the Plainview cases.

In response, he kept asking, "What's in it for *me*?"

Amy warned him that his insurance company, PIC, could pull the plug on his defense. He just didn't seem to get it. Either that, or he didn't care. When she mentioned the pathology slides, he went ballistic.

"Davis stole those slides. When did they go missing?"

Amy explained that the hospital discovered their disappearance about a week after the custodian's deposition and Steine's heart attack at the hospital.

"I bet there was no heart attack. Davis just used it as a diversion. He's a sneaky little prick."

Amy rejected that theory; she was there. Steine had a heart attack. There was objective evidence. But English was probably right that Davis obtained the slides during or right after Steine's hospitalization. "What difference does it make? He's got them and can prove that you removed healthy gallbladders."

"And I should come back why?"

"Because you'll be on the run for the rest of your life, and they'll eventually catch up with you."

"I'm not coming back until we get those slides."

"Well, I can't get them back."

"Maybe you should try a little harder!" he screamed at her. And with that English hung up.

CHAPTER THIRTY-ONE

COMPLICATED OFFERS

WEDNESDAY, DECEMBER 15, 1993

Davis preferred to open his mail rather than delegate the task to Sammie or Bella. Some days, like today, he was a day late. The third envelope he opened was from Amy Pierce. As he read the letter, he could feel his anger rising. He reread the letter and shook his head. Only Pierce had the ability to piss him off while making a settlement offer.

She wrote,

Dear Mr. Davis,

I've been designated and authorized by the defendants to make offers in each of the Plainview cases to settle all claims against all defendants. Please be advised that each offer is contingent on all of the plaintiffs in all cases accepting their offer. Please be advised that if one of the plaintiffs rejects this offer, all offers are withdrawn. The following offers are made:

Jones—$66,000
Malone—$120,000
Williams—$84,000
Boyers—$84,000
Andre—$89,000

Darsinos—$100,000
Mueller—$100,000
Lane—$126,000
Gerst—$170,000

These offers shall expire at 5:00 p.m. on Thursday, December 16, 1993.

Amy Pierce

Davis was furious. He grabbed the Code of Professional Responsibility, the ethical code for the practice of law. He quickly confirmed his suspicion that an attorney could not create a conflict of interest for another attorney. Davis slammed the book down so hard his hand vibrated. This offer placed all of his clients in conflict with one another because the acceptance of one offer was tied to all the others. *I just can't consider any of the offers because they are unethical,* he thought.

The Code of Professional Responsibility and his contracts required Davis to take all offers made to his clients for consideration. However, if Davis communicated the offers to his clients, thus creating a conflict, he would be willingly and knowingly buying in to the defendants' plan. They were trying to get him in conflict with his clients in the hopes of dividing and conquering them. That course of action would probably result in Davis's firing or withdrawal from one or more of the Plainview cases.

Littleton was a whole different problem. That asshole didn't care about the clients or the ethics. All he cared about was money, and these settlements meant a big payday for him. He hadn't done any of the work and wasn't planning on doing any.

Davis decided not to tell Littleton about the offers, but then he noticed that Pierce copied Littleton on the correspondence. She was a real piece of work. She refused to copy Littleton on dozens of correspondences and ignored him when he complained. The one correspondence that Davis didn't want Littleton to see, there was the "cc. Bradley Littleton." He needed to call Littleton before he read his mail and could get on the phone to their clients.

"Brad, have you opened your mail this morning?"

"No, what's up?"

It figured. He was a lazy bastard.

"There's a letter from Pierce. She's offering to settle the Plainview cases—"

Littleton cut him off. "That's great. Let me get it."

"Read it, but do nothing else. We'll meet later today to figure out how to respond. How's one o'clock? Don't call the clients. We need to talk this through first."

They agreed to meet at Davis's office at one. Davis was proud of himself. He didn't try to bully Littleton. He reasoned with him and put him off.

His next move was to call Pierce and demand that she withdraw the offers. If she refused, Davis would report her first to the Disciplinary Board and then to Judge Boxer. The defendants could make a collective lump sum offer as to all defendants in each case, but they couldn't ethically tie them to each other; that pitted one plaintiff against another.

Davis calculated in his head the attorney fees that he would earn if he presented these offers and all plaintiffs accepted. He would be able to recoup the $254,000 he had advanced in the Plainview cases. If he didn't settle, he would have to invest another $50,000 in the Jones case alone, and that case wasn't worth the investment, low damages.

Yet Davis blocked the idea of a settlement from his mind. He desperately wanted to settle, but ethically he couldn't consider these offers. He forced himself to finish opening the mail. He debated whether to call Morty, but he was a big boy and knew the answer to the question. He would tell Morty about the offers after he spoke with Pierce.

He got the firm's receptionist and asked for Ms. Pierce.

"Pierce here."

Davis didn't even like the way the bitch answered the phone. He controlled his voice as he said, "Hello, Amy, I got your letter and offers. Why would you mail it rather than fax it if you set a Thursday deadline? I just read your letter this morning."

Davis waited for a response, and after a long pause, Pierce replied, "I wanted to give you as little time as possible. You better get on the phone and communicate those offers to your clients, pronto."

"That may be the first honest thing you've ever said to me, Pierce. Well, your newfound honesty doesn't matter because you're withdrawing the offers."

More silence, then Pierce declared, "You're obligated to take those offers to your clients and then let the fighting begin. At least one of them will want the money. You created this conflict by taking all of these cases."

Davis leaned back in his chair and raised his voice significantly: "Look, asshole, your offers violate at least three disciplinary rules, and if you don't agree to withdraw these offers, I'll conference Boxer into this conversation and let him order you to. Oh, let's not forget the Disciplinary Board. I'll prepare a complaint against you and Tweedledee and Tweedledum. I'm one step ahead of you. You're not going to conflict me out of any of these cases, so forget it."

"Does Bradley Littleton agree with you?"

"I don't give a shit what that tub of lard thinks. He's just as unethical as you are. If he gives me a hard time, I'll bring his ass before the board too. Now withdraw your offers in writing and make new ones that stand on their own merits, or let's go to trial."

"Are you sure you want to try the Jones case?"

"I admit it's my weakest case, but eventually we'll get to a gallbladder case. That's when the fun begins."

Davis wasn't willing to admit that he had the slides, but they both knew what he was talking about.

Pierce didn't respond to his threat. She sheepishly said, "I'll have to talk to McCoy and Stevenson. I can't act on my own."

"You have one hour until I call Boxer and prepare my complaint to the board. You know how easy it is to file one of those."

Pierce hung up. Forty-five minutes later, she called back. "The offers stand, but they're not tied to each other."

Davis immediately responded: "Put that in writing and fax it over by one o'clock today, or I go to the judge and the board. Have a nice rest of your day."

At one o'clock, Littleton arrived at Davis's office and was ushered into the conference room by Bella. Davis, Morty, and Sammie joined him there. They discussed the dollar amounts of the offers and appropriate counteroffers. After a half hour, Bella interrupted and brought in copies of the fax from Pierce.

After Davis finished the letter, he turned to Littleton. "What do you think about the new offers?"

Littleton compared the new letter to the one he received earlier in the day. "The dollar amounts are identical. What's the difference?"

Davis mentally groaned, as he had to explain the ethical dilemma the first set of offers created.

Littleton shrugged. "I guess this is cleaner. Those other offers were complicated."

CHAPTER THIRTY-TWO

NECESSARY SETTLEMENT

MONDAY, DECEMBER 20, 1993

Davis was not looking forward to the meeting with David and Wendy Jones. He didn't want to compromise his principles, but the economics of the settlement made sense. The time and effort to get the Jones case ready for trial were not worthwhile investments. The damages to the Joneses were insignificant. She had unnecessary surgery, a permanent scar, and headaches that lasted months longer than they should have if properly treated. Davis was convinced that a jury would not award significant compensatory damages. That was why the defendants, after winning the coin toss, selected the Jones case as the first to be tried.

Davis never recovered the expenses he advanced in the Easter case after he was forced to withdraw. The dismissal of the Easter case reduced the number of his cases from ten to nine.

For the last fifteen months, the costs incurred by Davis were, for the most part, for the benefit of the nine remaining Plainview cases. For that reason, these expenses could be equally divided among all the cases with no one case bearing the excessive burden and risk. However, from this point forward the vast majority of the expense would be borne by the first case to be tried. The Jones case was a bad choice to shoulder that burden because the damages suffered were limited, and so was the dollar amount of anticipated recovery. That was the reason defense counsel chose Jones when they won the flip of the coin.

With only eight months left before that trial was scheduled to begin, Davis would have to devote most of his time and money preparing for a battle in the courtroom if the case didn't settle beforehand.

Davis had already spent $12,023.42 on specific expenses in the Jones case, and the Jones case share of the common expenses was $9,823.45. The $21,846.87 of expenses, as provided in the employment contract, would be deducted from the Joneses' portion of the settlement. Davis would take his one-third after the expenses had been deducted from the clients' share. The clients didn't get that money, so Davis knew the right thing to do was to take his cut after expenses. In the Malone case and others the specific expenses were greater than those for Jones, but each case had incurred $9,823.45 in common expenses.

David and Wendy Jones were newlyweds. He worked in a lumberyard, and she worked in Hewes City at the local bowling alley. They had gone to the library on a lark; they never thought that they would be filing a lawsuit. Before and after the surgery by Dr. English, Wendy suffered from severe headaches. They lasted for a total of six months after the surgery, and she was forced to take a three-month leave of absence to have the surgery and to allow the severe pain to subside. Eventually, her headaches were controlled by medication under the care of another doctor from Hewes City.

Davis assured the Joneses that Dr. Herman misdiagnosed Wendy's problem and that Dr. English performed an unnecessary surgery. He claimed that the hospital knew about it but ignored that it was unnecessary in order to make more money. Davis claimed that both English and Herman should have obtained a sedimentation rate, the gold standard, which was necessary to diagnose Wendy's problem. He knew the Joneses trusted him; he was their lawyer.

As soon as the Joneses arrived at Davis's office, Bella brought them back and offered them something to drink. Davis came out from behind his desk and joined them at the conference table. "Good news, I have another offer from the defendants. They've offered $80,000, up $14,000 from their first offer of $66,000."

David asked, "What does that mean to us, Mr. Davis? What do you recommend?"

He pulled out a settlement sheet that had the settlement broken down. It read:

Total Settlement: $80,000.00
Deductions:
Repayment of Medical Expenses to Medicare:
$6,423.00
Total Settlement for Distribution: $73,577.00
Specific Expenses: $12,023.42
Common Expenses: $9,823.45
Total Before Attorney Fee: $51,701.13
Attorney Fee (One-Third): $17,233.71
Payment to Clients: $34,427.42

Davis let the information sink in before he spoke. "I know that's a lot of money. How long does it take the two of you to earn that much?"

Based on what they told him, Davis figured that it would take them together more than a year and a half to earn $35,000.

Davis explained that if they did not settle, they would spend at least another $25,000 in expenses that would be deducted from their eventual share. He also reminded them that the trial, which was scheduled to begin July 5th, would last approximately two weeks and that they would have to take off work to attend.

That straw broke the camel's back. David looked at Wendy and said, "We'll take the deal, Mr. Davis. Thank you for all your hard work. Can we get our money by Christmas?"

"No, the money first needs to go in my escrow account, but you will have the money by the beginning of the new year. The insurance companies will want to get your case off their books before the end of the year."

"Well, it's going to be a good New Year's anyway," said David with a wide grin.

Davis was relieved with their choice.

Next Davis met with the children of Rosie Malone. There were eleven children in all and ten still living. Six showed up for the meeting; the others lived out of state. Thomas Malone and Lorraine Burke were the spokespersons.

"I begged Dr. Herman to transfer Momma to Nashville," Lorraine insisted. "It's not about the money. They need to explain themselves."

Davis explained that at first the defendants tied all of the offers to each other, but after some consideration they withdrew those offers and replaced them with new ones independent of each other. He reminded them that if they settled, the dollar amount would be sealed. They couldn't discuss it with anyone.

Thomas changed the subject. "What about the state charges, Mr. Davis?"

"I have no control over those. We believe the state case will be heard next year, before our July trial date, but I can't promise anything. I will tell you we've got strong evidence that Dr. English removed a healthy gallbladder from your mother and nicked her bowel while doing so.

"We were thinking of requesting mediation." Davis explained that mediation was a nonbinding hearing where the parties, in person, tried to negotiate a settlement of their case. If it failed, you gave up nothing, and the trial would proceed in July as scheduled.

Secretly, Davis wanted to go to mediation. At the negotiations he could rub the defense's noses in the slides and maximize the dollar amount of the settlement in the remaining eight Plainview cases. If it failed, he would use the slides in the Malone trial and take his chances with a jury.

The Malone family opted for mediation, and so did his seven other clients. They trusted Davis's confidence, even though they didn't know about the slides. The Davis team, with the knowledge of the existence of the slides, was even more confident of winning big.

The next day he sent a letter to defense counsel suggesting a mediation of all remaining Plainview cases, supervised by Judge Boxer, in January. He reminded them that the settlement of each case was independent of the others. His offer was accepted, and arrangements were made to use Plainview High School. The mediation was scheduled for the second Saturday in January.

CHAPTER THIRTY-THREE

MEDIATION

SATURDAY, JANUARY 8, 1994

Herman was anxious about the mediation. It took almost two weeks to set up. It involved coordinating the schedules of twelve people on the defendants' side and more than twenty-five people on the plaintiffs' side. Ultimately, a Saturday accommodated everyone's schedule. The high school was the only building with a sufficient number of rooms to separate all parties.

The participants signed a waiver agreeing that Judge Boxer could act as mediator and still preside as judge at the trials, should mediation fail.

Everyone started in the auditorium, and Barnes informed Herman that after the judge's instructions, they would move to their separate rooms. Barnes also explained that Boxer would move from room to room trying to pressure the parties to settle, pointing out each party's weaknesses.

He looked around the auditorium, which was almost a third full. Seven Malone children showed up, so Davis had twenty clients in the eight remaining cases. He would have to move from room to room, holding their hands and leading them through the process. Each defendant was assigned a classroom. McCoy, in a lemon yellow bow tie, Jack Barnes, Larry Pinsly from Tennessee Mutual, and Herman were assigned to classroom 35. Amy Pierce,

Lowell Thomas, and Davenport from PIC were assigned to classroom 39. English was still MIA, but McCoy, according to Pierce, informed Herman that English agreed to be standing by at a phone booth at the top of every hour, beginning at ten. Stevenson, Dr. Robert Kelly, and Woody Douglas were assigned to classroom 37.

Judge Boxer made it clear that although the defendants could continue to make lump sum offers in each particular case, rather than each making a separate offer, they could not tie the settlement of one case to another. Barnes advised Herman that because of the doctrine of comparative fault, Davis insisted that any case settled would require settlement with all defendants. Davis was unwilling to try a case only against the hospital or only against the doctors. According to Barnes, it was Davis's opinion that there was too much uncertainty in an empty chair trial, whereby the remaining defendants would take potshots at the settled defendant, trying to shift blame.

Judge Boxer's opening statement was short, and he concluded by saying, "Let's get these cases settled. Everyone needs to be reasonable. It's not in anyone's best interest to try all eight of these cases. Good luck."

In a serious tone and with the intent to motivate, Boxer told Dr. Herman, the only defendant physician present, "The ball's in the defendants' court to make the first offers. Isn't the Medical Licensing Board hearing set for next month? If the board finds recklessness, that finding will be admissible in the Malone case set in July. The doctor defendants might not want that to happen. You might be better off if there were no pending civil case at the time of the board's hearing. I suggest that your next increase be material as a sign of good faith.

The more you move forward, the more I'll expect them to meet you halfway."

Barnes told Herman that the settlement process was controlled by the hospital's board and the two insurance companies. Davenport of PIC and Pinsly of Tennessee Mutual called the shots for the doctors.

The defendants agreed in principle that the settlements would be structured forty percent paid by the hospital, thirty-five percent paid by English's insurer, PIC, and twenty-five percent paid by Herman's insurer, Tennessee Mutual. Those were the percentages paid in the Jones settlement, so there was at least reasonable basis for the division of liability and damages.

Pinsly explained to Herman that his coverage was a maximum of $1 million for 1991 and another $1 million for 1992. Neither annual dollar amount included the cost of defense and expenses. There was no dollar limit on defense costs. Tennessee Mutual paid $20,000 in the Jones settlement, which applied to the 1992 coverage.

Herman did the math: $980,000 left for that year. Four of the remaining cases occurred in 1992. He also understood that, since no payments had been made for any of the 1991 cases, he had the full $1 million coverage available for the four cases that occurred in 1991.

He was concerned about Boxer's last remark about the board hearing. He just wanted these Plainview cases to go away. He didn't care how much it cost Tennessee Mutual as long as it was within his coverage, and he didn't have to pay out of pocket. He knew that Pinsly wanted these cases over; they had cost his company a fortune in legal fees and expenses.

Tennessee Mutual, over less than two years, paid McCoy and Barnes, by Herman's estimation, more than

$750,000 along with more than $200,000 in expenses.

Herman was convinced that Pinsly of Tennessee Mutual didn't like him. At first, he was very supportive and encouraging. However, as Pinsly learned more about the Plainview cases and the board charges, he became more distant.

Once in classroom 35, Barnes turned to McCoy and Pinsly: "It's our turn to make an offer. The judge wants this to move quickly. We don't have to take his advice. It's your money, Larry, or at least it's your company's money."

Herman knew through Barnes that Pinsly was a veteran negotiator, and he was tired. He wanted to settle these Plainview cases.

Pinsly said, "Despite what Boxer says, all I care about and all my company cares about is the total amount we pay. We don't give a shit how it's divided among the plaintiffs. But the judge insists that these offers be made separate from each other, so let's see how much money we can save."

Barnes said, "Our share of the last offers was $250,000 of the $1 million. Let's increase it by ten percent. That should get the ball rolling." McCoy increased each offer by ten percent across the board.

Herman didn't think that $1,100,000 would settle the eight remaining cases. McCoy secured the agreement of Davenport, the other defendants agreed, and the offers were delivered to Davis.

Herman was surprised by how quickly Davis conferred with his eight clients. In less than thirty minutes, Davis returned and handed McCoy a piece of paper. Davis did not say a word.

McCoy read the note to himself and then out loud:

Defendants, their counsel, and insurers:

Let me start by demanding under Rule 54 of the Tennessee Rules of Civil Procedure that, based upon my affidavit filed in each of the remaining Plainview cases, the defendants pay costs of $284,636. These are expert witness fees, costs of deposition and hearing transcripts, copying costs, and other incidental expenses recoverable under the rule. The court, after jury verdict, would order these expenses paid if we tried these cases, and if tried, the dollar amount of costs would increase significantly.

Second, if we proceed to eight separate trials, your attorney fees and costs, independent of the dollar amounts awarded by the juries, will exceed $2.5 million.

Third, eventually, one of these juries will award punitive damages against one, but more likely all, of the defendants. I hope that the hospital shared with the other defendants and their insurance companies that it misplaced some important evidence, which I very fortunately found. I speculate that each doctor for the two years has at least $1 million in coverage. They'll need it.

I have been authorized to settle each of the Plainview cases, independent of each other, as follows:

Malone—$700,000
Williams—$440,000
Boyers—$700,000
Darsinos—$560,000
Mueller—$700,000

Andrews—$600,000

Lane—$700,000

Gerst—$600,000

These settlement offers are made in accordance with Rule 408 of the Tennessee Rules of Evidence, are confidential, and are not admissible in any proceeding, shall remain confidential, and may not be used for any purpose.

Benjamin Davis

Everyone in the room tried to do the math mentally. Pinsly pulled out his calculator from his briefcase and began punching numbers. After he finished his calculation, he announced: "That's a total of $5 million. Our share would be $1,250,000. He wants more than four times our last offer."

"That's within my coverage," said Herman. "I've got $1,980,000 left—"

Pinsly abruptly cut Herman off: "Read your contract. My company calls the shots of this negotiation. Don't interfere."

Herman felt helpless as Tennessee Mutual controlled his fate. No one pointed out that Dr. Herman was a shareholder, and technically Pinsly worked for him. It was all about the money in classroom 35, except for Jack Barnes, who was sitting in the corner; he was just watching the dog and pony show play out.

The bow-tied McCoy was certainly all about the money. He reminded Pinsly about the expenses under Rule 54.

Pinsly turned to him angrily: "I know there's

expenses, but let's just focus on the settlement. What evidence did the hospital lose?"

"You don't want to know," McCoy cut in.

Herman knew, but he could tell that Jack Barnes, who suddenly became alert in his corner, didn't know what the hell McCoy was talking about, and McCoy quickly closed the subject.

Feeling ignored, Herman decided that he needed to speak up: "I sure as hell want to settle these cases. Next month is my disciplinary hearing, and if I'm found guilty by the board, that's not going to sit too well with a future jury."

McCoy came to his aid. "Dr. Herman's right. If the board finds intentional or reckless conduct, those findings would be admissible in the Malone case and all the other cases. If a jury finds intentional or reckless conduct, there could be a substantial award of punitive damages. Lars, as I've told you, punitive damages are not covered under your policy."

Pinsly agreed, and Herman became nervous. After a long debate, the defendants countered with a take-it-or-leave-it set of offers totaling $1,500,000. Tennessee Mutual's share was $375,000 plus expenses. The other defendants agreed to the amount and the unconditional terms. It was more than a twenty percent increase over their last offer.

McCoy walked the offer over to Davis, Steine, and Littleton, who were in room 11 with Mr. and Mrs. Darsinos. Twenty minutes later, Davis returned with the plaintiffs' response.

Herman couldn't understand how Davis responded so quickly.

McCoy read the response out loud: "Nuts, we'll see you in court in July."

"What the hell is 'Nuts'?" Pinsly asked.

"It's what an American general told the Germans who had him surrounded at Bastogne during the Battle of the Bulge," Herman remarked. He was very familiar with the battles of World War II.

Barnes turned to Pinsly. "I think you started World War III."

It was four minutes to two when Herman entered the phone booth at the high school. He took a slip of paper from his wallet and dialed. "Hello, Charlie. It's over, and we didn't even get close. Davis wanted $5 million, and the suits offered him $1,500,000."

"Do those idiots from the insurance companies know what Davis is sitting on?" Charlie moaned.

"My guy doesn't. In his opening offer, Davis made reference to the slides, but my lawyer, McCoy, told the Tennessee Mutual guy, 'You don't want to know,' and he chose not to."

"I bet Pierce hasn't told my company either. You can bet that little weasel Douglas must have told upper management."

"Look, Charlie, two things need to happen. First, we need to get back those slides, and second, you need to come home and face these board charges, or you'll be on the run for the rest of your life."

"Call me tomorrow, same time and number, and we'll figure this out."

"We'd better, or I'll be joining you."

CHAPTER THIRTY-FOUR

WILDHORSE

SATURDAY, JANUARY 8, 1994

For the last twenty months, since she arrived in Nashville, Sammie lived in either the loft or the Davis home. Morty returned to work, and then the heart attack prompted the change in her living arrangements. She spent most waking hours either working with her uncle or being with his family. With free room and board, she saved almost $18,000 for law school. She loved getting to know her cousins Caroline and Jake. She had become particularly close to her aunt Liza, eleven years her senior, whom she had never known before moving to Nashville.

After Morty recovered enough from his heart attack, in June of last year, to return to live alone at the farm, she had moved back into the loft in September. She cherished her independence since leaving the Davis residence. After all, she was twenty-seven years old, had attended the University of Florida, a real party school, and she hadn't led a sheltered life in Miami. In the loft, she could have a social life.

Yet she didn't have many close friends because of her intensive and sometimes unpredictable work schedule. She sometimes met them in a restaurant or bar downtown, but when she wanted to be more on her own, she liked to go to the Wildhorse Saloon. The recently opened bar, occupying a historic warehouse, attracted tourists as well as locals. It had a great atmosphere, with often-famous bands or singers performing, scheduled and unscheduled. The dance floor was a bonus and almost always full.

She still had the taste of the failed mediation in her mouth and felt a little depressed. They had worked hard on Plainview up through the mediation and would have to work harder to get the Malone case ready for trial. She was also concerned by how extended the Plainview cases had become, exposing her uncle.

Tonight, she was putting Plainview behind her. It was her night to have fun. If Mr. Right presented himself, she might not put out all the way, but she would certainly give him the impression that she might. It had been more than ten months, and she was just plain horny. For Sammie, finding a sex partner had never been a problem. All she had to do was want it, and she got it.

For her seduction, she put on a very short denim skirt that showed off her extremely long legs. At one end were her red cowboy boots and at the other, her shapely ass. Her cowgirl red-checkered shirt, tied at the abdomen, was somewhat provocative. Her bra pushed her girls up, revealing more than two inches of cleavage. Since it was January, the cold air was sure to make her nipples erect. She wore very little makeup because she didn't need any. She would be hard to resist.

The Wildhorse was only two blocks away, but the minute she walked out the back door of Steine's Department Store, Sammie knew that she needed more than her black duster coat to keep from freezing her ass off.

As soon as she entered the saloon, the warm air hit her smack in the face. She could smell the seated crowd on the dance floor. The noise level, from both conversations and music, was at a much higher decibel than on the street. A DJ played the Allman Brothers' "Sweet Melissa," and several patrons were dancing. She strutted over to the fifteen-foot oak bar, with an equally long brass rail along the bottom, placed a red cowboy boot on the rail, and ordered a shot of Tequila Gold. The bartender responded immediately. Sammie usually didn't have to wait to be served. He brought a salt-shaker and a sliced lemon with the shot. She asked him to leave the bottle.

Two shots of tequila later, she got on the dance floor and began line dancing with about two dozen others. She figured her sensuous movements would soon attract an available male. She executed the move perfectly, and as she anticipated, a man by the name of Rex, no last name, appeared out of nowhere. One minute she was dancing without a partner; the next minute she was dancing next to him and smelling the heat of his body and his cheap cologne.

Sammie was over six feet with her boots. Rex, also in cowboy boots, was at least four inches taller. He had sandy colored hair and dark brown eyes. He was dressed in a denim shirt and extremely tight jeans. He seemed close to her age.

After they danced for thirty minutes, they returned to Sammie's bottle at the bar and downed a few shots together. A few minutes later, they were walking up the Alley toward the back entrance of her building and the loft. Sammie remembered a long embrace in the elevator, which ended with Rex ripping off her panties.

Once in the loft, they drank more tequila from his silver flask, and after that the details went completely blank.

She woke in her recliner, shirt and skirt still on, but no panties. Her head was splitting, and there was a bad taste in her mouth. She tried to place it but was too hung over to even think. She sat up slowly in the chair and regretted her sudden movement. The room was spinning, and she struggled to free herself from the recliner.

She moved as fast as she could to the bathroom. She barely made it to the toilet when she lost it. She slid to the floor and leaned against the bathtub, her head throbbing. She worked her way up to her knees, turned on the cold water, and splashed some on her face. It did very little good. *What the hell is that taste? It's overpowering, despite the fact that I threw up.*

She crawled to her bed, which hadn't been slept in, and spent all day there. How much tequila did she drink? What happened to Rex? Did they have sex? If they did, he must not have thought it was very good. He certainly didn't hang around for seconds or for breakfast. She couldn't remember him leaving or even saying good-bye. Maybe it was better that way, not knowing. She certainly wasn't proud of herself.

After resting all day, eating lightly, and going to sleep by nine, Sammie was ready to face the week, starting with Monday morning at seven. She wasn't the first to arrive at the office. Both Bella and her uncle were there. She greeted Bella in reception and went straight to her desk. On Friday, she ended her day in the middle of cataloguing the pathology slides against the surgical logs of Plainview Community Hospital. She left the slides in her unlocked briefcase on top of her desk.

When she opened the briefcase, she did a double take; the two boxes of slides were gone. Even though she knew exactly where she left them, she looked all around her office. No luck. Someone must have taken them, either her uncle or Bella.

Sammie stuck her head out of her office, which was almost painful in her condition, and confirmed that Bella hadn't moved them. Why would her uncle remove the slides this morning? It made no sense. He wouldn't.

Sammie felt another headache coming on. Who could have taken them? Who had access to her office since Friday night? The cleaning people hadn't come over the weekend. Who then?

And then it dawned on her: Rex. He was in her loft, which connected to the office by a stairwell. He didn't even have to use her keys to gain access to the office. He just had to walk down a flight of stairs.

She tried to remember his face and everything she could about him. Yesterday, she put Saturday night behind her and instead concentrated on her hangover and her recovery.

As she tried to focus on Saturday night, an image flashed through her mind that hadn't registered during her haze on Saturday. It was Rex's forearm, a tattoo, a T-rex with yellow eyes. She began to shake. She tried to get up but couldn't. She gripped the arms of her chair. That distinctive bad taste returned to her mouth, and she began to gag.

When she could get to her feet, using the wall as support she made her way to the bathroom. A moment later there was a knock at the door. It was Bella.

"You okay, honey? You didn't look so good."

Sammie began to cry.

Bella knocked again. "Sammie, let me in."

When she opened the door, Sammie fell into Bella's arms and was shaking so hard that both women shook. Bella held the younger woman so tightly that Sammie started having trouble breathing and broke away. In broken sentences, she explained what happened on Saturday night and her discovery of the missing slides that morning.

Sammie wasn't embarrassed that she had brought Rex back to the loft. She admitted that she had no idea whether they had sex. But she was humiliated that she had been victimized.

"When I got up Sunday morning, he was gone. I woke up sick as a dog. I'm pretty sure he drugged me. I can't remember what happened, but after I drank from his flask, he took his shirt off and I vaguely remember he had a tattoo, a dinosaur with big yellow eyes."

It had been four months since her uncle's beating, but the T-rex tattoo on one of the two reward artist renditions was burned into all of their memories. Bella was visibly upset by Sammie's story, which made Sammie even more uneasy.

She confided in Bella a few details she remembered before she drank from the flask, including Rex tearing off her underpants in the service elevator. Sammie questioned Bella about whether her panties were in the elevator when she arrived that morning. They concluded that Rex must have taken them as a souvenir.

"You've got to tell your uncle. If you want, I'll sit in, but he's got to be told immediately."

Sammie decided that it would be best for her to face her uncle on her own and man up to her mistake. Davis quietly listened and didn't interrupt as she told her story—the PG-13 version. Even that version was embarrassing enough.

Davis finally spoke: "The bastards have been watching us. I should have anticipated that they would try to get to one of us. We let our guard down. I'm sure they're watching even that idiot Littleton. I've got to warn everyone, including Sister Carson and the other experts."

Sammie hung her head and in a pitiful voice stuttered, "I've lost the slides. They're irreplaceable evidence. You rejected more than $1,500,000 because you thought a jury would get to see and hold them. Those slides were our ace in the hole, and I blew it."

"You couldn't have known. Maybe Morty and I should have seen this coming. We knew that they were getting desperate with the board hearing next month and the Malone case breathing down their necks." Despite his reassuring tone, Davis felt incredibly guilty that he hadn't taken precautions to prevent another attack on the family by T-rex.

Davis gave Sammie a hug and a kiss on both cheeks. "We'll get these bastards without the slides. These guys play dirty. You're not going to learn about these tactics in law school or in a book. These defendants want to win at any cost, and they don't care if they have to hurt or kill people to do so. Effective immediately, you are moving into our guest room until further notice."

CHAPTER THIRTY-FIVE

MEDICAL LICENSING BOARD

MONDAY, JANUARY 31, 1994

Sammie took her seat next to Bella, Davis, and Morty in the front row of hearing room 304 in the Andrew Jackson State Office Building. She would have preferred to sit a bit closer so she could breathe down English's and Herman's necks, but there was nothing closer.

The room filled up quickly, and by eight thirty it was at its capacity of two hundred. The audience was composed of people from Plains and Hewes Counties. Both print and television press were there, but Tennessee law didn't allow the cameras in the courtroom.

Through his Nashville connections, Morty secured coverage in advance of the hearing. The hospital kept the *Plainview Gazette* and the *Hewes City Express* silent.

Sammie still didn't feel like herself. At her uncle's insistence, she was seeing a psychiatrist to deal with her drugging. A rape test, performed the Monday afternoon after she discovered that the slides were missing, confirmed no semen was present, but that meant nothing. Whatever happened after the Wildhorse left her emotionally scarred. This hearing was the best medicine possible, and she wasn't going to miss any of it to sit on a couch and tell her problems to a stranger. Liza was her greatest comfort, and the rest of the Davis family did their best to help her too. The kids didn't know the details, but they knew that Sammie had gone through a traumatic event.

Within days of the disappearance of the slides, Dr. English reappeared. He walked into the Hewes County Courthouse with Amy Pierce and surrendered himself. Judge Lewis was both amazed and pleasantly surprised. He threw English into jail and told him that he would be serving his contempt sentence until his back alimony and child support were paid in full. A payment plan was never discussed. According to reports, English said nothing and had been a guest of Hewes County ever since.

Although English was dressed smartly in a gray suit, white shirt, and yellow tie, Sammie knew that he had awakened in the Hewes County jail, in an orange jumpsuit, serving his contempt sentence.

All four members of the Davis team were excited about the prospect of Dr. English's and Dr. Herman's medical licenses being suspended or revoked. If they were revoked, the bastards would never again practice medicine in Tennessee. If they were suspended, their licenses would be withheld by the state for a specific period of time and certain predetermined hurdles would be imposed when the state agreed to reinstate them.

Sean McCoy, sporting a teal bow tie, represented Dr. Herman at the hearing, and Amy Pierce represented Dr. English. The state prosecutor was a geek named Larry Dillingham. Davis tried to help Dillingham, but the prosecutor was hopeless. He was disorganized and inarticulate—a typical state employee. He had risen to his level of incompetency.

Morty explained that the state had a higher burden

of proof than the plaintiff did in the Malone case. He predicted, despite the overwhelming proof, that the state, due to incompetency, would fall flat on its face.

Sammie was also concerned. She had read Dillingham's pleadings, and she didn't think much of his writing ability.

From Morty's explanation, Sammie understood that the state, through the Medical Licensing Board, was authorized to issue and regulate medical licenses. The notice of charges accused the doctors of acts that did not involve the lawsuits filed by Davis. An administrative law judge would render rulings on procedure and evidence.

The finder of fact was a panel of physicians appointed by the governor. Tennessee Mutual insured Dr. Dean, an internist, and Dr. Peabody, a general surgeon. Sammie wondered why those panelists, who co-owned Tennessee Mutual with Herman, weren't conflicted out. The reason was simple; it wouldn't be easy to find a physician not insured by Tennessee Mutual to serve on the panel.

The remaining panelist, Dr. Bernard, a urologist, had recently begun practicing and teaching at Vanderbilt University, which was partially self-insured with the excess coverage with Lloyds of London.

The law required that their peers, other MDs, judge Dr. Herman and Dr. English. Sammie thought it was impossible to find three doctors as incompetent as Herman and English. She was convinced that Herman and English were criminals with medical licenses.

The judge called the hearing to order. McCoy, Pierce, and Dillingham agreed to waive the reading of the charges.

Davis whispered to Sammie: "That's Dillingham's first mistake. Those charges are so extensive and serious, reading them would have set the right stage and mood."

The first witness was an internist, Dr. Ernie Larson, from Columbia, Maury County, Tennessee. Dillingham reviewed Larson's background and the nature of his practice. Larson explained that there was a tremendous amount of overlap between the subspecialty of family medicine and internal medicine and that the two subspecialties performed the same services for their patients. He had privileges at two local hospitals. He confirmed that each of the tests and surgeries referenced in the charges were tests he had ordered or surgeries he had recommended with the consult of a general surgeon.

Larson proceeded to review each patient's chart referenced in the charges. He was careful not to mention the patient by name, referencing only initials. In each case, Larson testified how Dr. Herman's actions breached the standard of care of a family practitioner and/or an internist.

After three hours of testimony, the judge adjourned for lunch. Dr. Larson testified as to twenty-six patients by then, but his testimony was unremarkable.

After lunch, Larson testified about the remaining cases cited in the charges. By two o'clock, he reviewed the chart of R. M., a sixty-seven-year-old woman who died after an unnecessary laparoscopic gallbladder surgery.

Larson's direct testimony ended with Dillingham asking, "In each of those dozens of cases, are you of the professional opinion, with a reasonable degree of medical certainty, that Dr. Herman breached the standard of care and was negligent?"

"Yes, sir, I am of the opinion that Dr. Herman was negligent."

Dillingham smiled because he made his point. "Based upon your review of the patient charts identified in the charges, are you of the professional opinion, based on clear and convincing evidence, that Dr. Herman was engaged in a pattern of gross negligence and acted recklessly in the care and treatment of his patients?"

Larson didn't hesitate: "Dr. Herman was negligent in the care and treatment of each and every patient identified in the charges. There were dozens of acts of negligence. These were not isolated occurrences, and there was a definite pattern of gross negligence. Dr. Herman is also guilty by clear and convincing evidence of recklessness. He recommended to patients unnecessary tests and permitted Dr. English to perform unnecessary surgeries on his patients."

Dillingham closed his proof as to Dr. Herman, and the judge adjourned for the day.

The next day, Morty, Bella, Sammie, and Davis were in the front row. The entire day involved the cross-examination of Dr. Larson, first by McCoy and then by Pierce. Sammie didn't understand why Pierce got to cross-examine the witness since Larson's testimony was only directed at Dr. Herman. At the end of the day, the consensus among them was that Larson's testimony held up.

The morning of the third day began with Dillingham putting on the stand a general surgeon from Murfreesboro, Rutherford County, Tennessee: Dr. Kenneth Gayle. Davis whispered to Sammie that

Dillingham was rushing through the witness qualifications of general surgery.

Dr. Herman and Dr. English didn't have to take the witness stand, as in a criminal trial, because they had nothing to prove. However, in most cases the defending doctor did take the stand.

Dillingham completed his direct examination of Dr. Gayle by one o'clock. It was sloppy, even to Sammie's untrained eye, an abbreviated examination of Gayle's background and qualifications. Neither Pierce nor McCoy had questions for the witness. Dillingham looked dumbfounded. He closed his proof expecting both Herman and English to take the stand.

Pierce stood up and approached the podium. "May it please the court and the panel, the only proof introduced into evidence that Dr. English was negligent and/or engaged in a pattern of gross negligence was arguably the testimony of Dr. Gayle. Judge, I had the court reporter print out the portion of Dr. Gayle's testimony that dealt with his background and qualifications. It's pretty short, and with the court's permission, I would like the court reporter to read it back verbatim right now."

Dillingham objected, but Pierce argued that if the court permitted this, the hearing would be shorter by at least a day. Pierce convinced the court that it was worth a fifteen-minute investment.

The court reporter read that portion of Dr. Gayle's testimony.

When she finished, Pierce took over. "If Your Honor please, there is a fatal problem with Dr. Gayle's testimony. At no time during his testimony does he state that he's familiar with the standard of care in

Plains County or that the standard of care in Rutherford County is the same as in Plains County. Your Honor, Tennessee Code Annotated Title 62, section 17, requires such testimony be introduced into evidence as a prerequisite to a finding of negligence and/or a pattern of gross negligence. Mr. Dillingham has failed to prove that Dr. Gayle is a qualified witness to testify as to Dr. English's negligence."

Sammie glanced at Morty and her uncle, and they silently agreed. Dillingham committed a fatal mistake that disintegrated his case against English, and because he closed his proof and English elected not to put on any proof, no further evidence against English could be introduced.

Pierce went on: "I move for all charges against Dr. English to be dismissed with prejudice."

The judge turned to Dillingham and asked, "What do you say to that, Mr. Dillingham?"

Dillingham just stood there as if he had been hit upside the head with a brick. Regaining some sense of his duty, he responded, "Your Honor can take judicial notice that the borders of Plains County and Rutherford County are only twenty miles apart and that Plainview Community Hospital and the two hospitals where Dr. Gayle practices have about the same number of beds."

The judge gave Dillingham a look of disgust and stated, "Mr. Dillingham, those were facts that *you* should have introduced into evidence. This court cannot and will not take judicial notice of facts that you were required to introduce into evidence, but didn't. If you have nothing further, I will rule on Ms. Pierce's motion to dismiss."

Dillingham was obviously so embarrassed that he almost began to cry.

Sammie did begin to cry. Dillingham's extreme malpractice wouldn't help the Malone case or the other Plainview cases.

Dillingham finally said, "In light of Your Honor's remarks, nothing further, Your Honor."

The judge squirmed in his seat. He was clearly organizing his thoughts before he said, "Whether or not Dr. Gayle qualified as an expert witness in general surgery is a legal question for the court, not a factual determination for the panel. I am very familiar with the TCA section cited by Ms. Pierce and the case law that applies to that statute. Any attorney who asserts or defends against a claim of malpractice is. Apparently, Mr. Dillingham is not. That is most unfortunate for the citizens of this state. The state went to great expense to bring charges against Dr. English and to conduct this hearing. Because of the failure of Mr. Dillingham to introduce into evidence the required proof, the charges against Dr. English must be dismissed. Ms. Pierce, your motion is granted."

The audience, which included at least fifteen Plainview plaintiffs, became loud and angry. Even the three panel members looked upset by the judge's ruling.

After a good five minutes and threats to clear the room, the judge got control of the hearing room. He turned to McCoy. "Call your first witness, Mr. McCoy."

McCoy stood and made the same motion to dismiss as Ms. Pierce successfully made. He argued that Dillingham failed to prove that the standard of care was the same in Columbia, Maury County, and Plains County. He argued that Dr. Herman and Dr. Larson were of different subspecialties and that therefore, Dr. Larson couldn't pass judgment on Dr. Herman.

McCoy was eloquent, but the judge lost all patience. "Mr. McCoy, I distinctly remember Dr. Larson comparing Columbia to Plainview, and he did specifically testify that the standard of care in the two communities was the same. I also remember him testifying that internal medicine and family medicine overlap and that he had either ordered or recommended all of the tests and surgeries that are the subject of the charges. Your motion is denied. Now call your first witness."

McCoy didn't have an expert witness. Davis explained to Sammie that despite all of McCoy's efforts, no qualified doctor was willing to come to the state hearing and testify that Dr. Herman provided his patients treatment within the standard. McCoy advised the court that he had no proof and that Dr. Herman rested.

Dillingham's closing argument was short, just fifteen minutes. He was still shaken by the English dismissal. McCoy was equally brief.

The panel deliberated until six o'clock when it announced it reached a verdict. The panel reconvened in the hearing room, and Dr. Dean read the verdict: "We, the panel, find on each count of the charges that Dr. Lars Herman was guilty of negligence. We, the panel, find that Dr. Lars Herman did engage in a pattern of gross negligence by clear and convincing evidence. We, the panel, find that Dr. Lars Herman was guilty by clear and convincing evidence of recklessness in the care and treatment of patients R. M., H. H., T. P., F. K., B. D., D. C., K. O., R. U., T. D., and M. M. As to the other patients listed in the charges, we find negligence only."

That first set of initials stood for Rosie Malone. If Boxer was a man of his word, the jury in the Malone case would at least be told that the state of Tennessee had found by clear and convincing evidence that Dr. Herman was reckless in his care of Rosie Malone. Sammie wasn't sure what the jury would be told about Dr. English's care of Mrs. Malone or about the dismissal of the charges against him.

The judge asked Dr. Dean if the panel set a punishment for Dr. Herman.

Dean indicated that they had, and he began to read: "We, the panel, set the penalty and punishment of Dr. Lars Herman as (a) a fine of $85,000; (b) the suspension of his medical license for one year; (c) prior to reinstatement, the completion of a family medicine residency at a certified US medical school; and (d) that if Dr. Herman returns to the practice of medicine in this state after his suspension and completion of the residency program, he be proctored for his first year as to all tests and procedures he orders. This verdict is signed by each of the panel members."

Dr. Dean turned to the judge and asked if he could make a statement for the record. The judge said that as a panel member, it was appropriate.

McCoy and Pierce objected to the statement. Dillingham remained silent, not knowing what to do.

"I am a general surgeon who practices in Nashville. I have never been in Plains County, although I have briefly driven through on my way to Atlanta. I have never been to Plainview Community Hospital nor have I been to either of the two hospitals where Dr. Gayle maintains privileges. However, I know the standard of care for a general surgeon in Tennessee, and Dr. English's conduct fell well below that standard of care. I hope the appellate court reverses the travesty that has occurred here today."

The audience actually applauded, but Dr. Dean's speech was a waste of time. The appellate court would apply the law, and as set forth by the Tennessee legislature, Dr. English's dismissal would be upheld.

Outside the hearing room, several Plainview plaintiffs approached Davis. Peter Mueller, elected spokesman, asked, "What does today mean to our cases?"

"As to Dr. Herman, it's an admissible finding of recklessness. As to Dr. English, I'll do a much better job than the state."

Sammie was sure he would.

CHAPTER THIRTY-SIX

PARTNERSHIP

FRIDAY, FEBRUARY 11, 1994

Amy Pierce bought a new suit for the party to celebrate her promotion to partnership. She bought her son, Carter, a new suit as well. She had invited her aunt and two cousins to the party held at the elegant Hermitage Hotel, a gathering place for the rich, the powerful, and the influential.

Lowell Thomas sent around a memo to all partners, associates, and staff announcing her partnership. The memo complimented Amy's achievements and contributions to the firm. Everyone at the firm was aware of the Plainview cases and Amy's recent victory before the Medical Licensing Board.

The young woman was clearly on a high and on the rise. She had been aware of the partnership decision only a few days, yet she had already contacted Montgomery Bell Academy for Carter's fall semester, 1995, admission. She would now be able to afford the prep school, which would allow Carter to get the best possible education Nashville had to offer. It was the beginning of their new life together. Work would still be demanding, but the financial rewards would be worth it.

The firm invited most of its clients, including Jim Davenport of PIC, who was driving in from Memphis to attend. McCoy and Stevenson RSVP'd.

Jack Barnes sent his regrets in a personal note:

Dear Amy,

There's no question that you've worked hard on the Plainview cases and your defense before the Medical Licensing Board was an outstanding result, which will be upheld if appealed. But you played outside the rules. Dr. English, with your help, will simply move to another state and terrorize another community with his incompetence and dishonesty. I am disappointed in the system but not surprised. I will not be attending your partnership party.

I remain, Jack Barnes.

Amy was shocked by Barnes's note. Barnes was as experienced a litigator as there was. He represented murderers and the worst white-collar criminals. When she showed the note to Thomas, he just shook his head.

"Barnes has lost it. He's lost sight of our role in the system. If anyone failed in the process, it was Dillingham and the state. Your job was to represent your client. You did that brilliantly. I wouldn't give Barnes's note a second thought."

Yet she couldn't get that note out of her head. It tormented her. She couldn't shake Barnes's disappointment in the system and more particularly in her.

At 7:00 p.m. the party began with a short statement by Lowell Thomas, the managing partner: "Ladies and gentlemen, it is with the greatest pleasure that we at DMT have brought you here tonight to honor Ms. Amy Pierce Esquire, our newest and only female partner. Amy has worked hard and successfully to earn her partnership. She's determined and resourceful. Our clients have benefited from her legal skills and abilities. I am proud to call her partner. Thank you, Amy."

The crowd of about a hundred applauded loudly. Someone called for a speech, and then dozens of others followed suit.

Amy had waited eleven years, since she got out of law school, for this day. She cleared her throat and said, "I want to thank Lowell and the other partners for this beautiful reception. I'm sure Sid from accounting will deduct the cost as an operating expense."

Several people laughed, and Sid piped up: "You're damn right, Amy. Just make sure some of you lawyers talk to your clients tonight, so I can justify tonight as a business expense."

Now everyone in the room laughed, and Amy continued: "I want to thank my son, Carter, who's gone without a lot, including me. It has not been easy being an attorney and a single mother. I love you very much, Carter.

"The American judicial system is imperfect, but it's the best judicial system in the world. Our part, as attorneys, is to represent our clients to the best of our ability. That I've always done. It's the judge's job to determine the law. It's the jury's job to determine the facts and the dollar amount of damages, if any. That's how our system works, and I'm proud to be a part of it. Thank you."

The crowd broke into applause again. Several partners, associates, and clients came up to Amy to shake her hand. It was a great night for both her and DMT. But Amy could not stop thinking of Barnes's note.

CHAPTER THIRTY-SEVEN

A LONG-AWAITED DEPOSITION

MONDAY, FEBRUARY 14, 1994

Davis had been looking forward to this day for quite a long time. Judge Boxer was about to hold Dr. English in contempt in the Malone case. Dr. English's deposition had been set twice in December and twice more in January. On each occasion, English failed to appear. A solid record existed, and Boxer had the right to award a default judgment against English in the Malone case. It troubled Davis that he showed up only after the slides were stolen. He was convinced that the doctor's reappearance was tied to the return of the missing slides. According to Pierce, Dr. English materialized to defend his good name at the Medical Licensing Board hearing.

Dr. English was still a guest of the Hewes County jail, serving his contempt sentence in the proceeding brought by his ex-wife Susan. Davis first learned of English's surrender and availability when Pierce called him on Friday, January 28th, and informed him that Dr. English would be at the hearing before the Medical Licensing Board and that his deposition in the Malone case could be scheduled at the Plains County Courthouse after the hearing. Pierce also informed him that she had spoken to Judge Boxer, who selected the location and indicated he wanted to attend the deposition.

Although Morty and Sammie wanted to attend, they were busy with other matters. Davis had not prepared for this deposition because he could take it in his sleep. English had been on the run for almost five months, and Davis was dying to know where he had been, who had helped him, and who he'd been in contact with. This deposition would be more about English's life on the run than his care and treatment of poor Rosie Malone.

The Plainview Courthouse was an impressive building, with four large columns in the front, giving the building a Greek feel. Above the tops of the columns was a triangular-shaped stone cutting, which included a large dragon in the middle. Built in the center of the town square, the courthouse served as a central meeting place and as the building where justice was administered. Judge Boxer's courtroom, like the outside of the building, emanated a sense of power and justice. Davis felt comfortable in these surroundings.

Amy Pierce, Lowell Thomas, Sean McCoy, Jack Barnes, and Grayson Stevenson entered the courtroom together. To Davis, they appeared to be a united crew, as thick as thieves. How could they not be with the slides in their possession? He wondered which of them knew the details of how the slides were reacquired, and he clenched and unclenched his fists as he speculated.

Each one nodded to him, but nobody said hello. In the last two years a deep animosity had developed, and it was mutual, except with Jack Barnes. Morty always taught Davis to treat another attorney with respect and common courtesy, but even Morty ignored that golden rule when dealing with this bunch.

The court reporter was already set up to preserve the hearing. She had agreed to rush the transcript so Morty could read it. That would double the cost, but it was worth it.

A moment later, Judge Boxer took the bench. He greeted counsel with a warm smile. "Good morning, gentlemen and Ms. Pierce. This is a big day for the plaintiffs. Mr. Davis, you have been trying to get this deposition of this witness for quite some time, haven't you?"

Davis stood and responded to the court: "Yes, sir. I'm glad the court ordered this deposition to take place here in the courthouse. I anticipate the witness will be uncooperative and unresponsive."

Pierce jumped to her feet and almost screamed her objection. Davis was baiting Pierce, and it worked. Pierce argued that Dr. English surrendered himself and that he would respond to all appropriate questions under the Rules of Civil Procedure.

At that moment, Sheriff Buford Dudley of Hewes County led Dr. English into the courtroom. The handcuffed English was dressed in an orange jumpsuit with "Hewes County" written on the back.

Davis couldn't resist asking, "Is that your cooperative witness, Ms. Pierce?"

Everyone in the room knew Sheriff Dudley. He addressed Judge Boxer: "Morning, Your Honor. Judge Lewis sends his respects and asked me to tell you that the prisoner has to be back at the Hewes County jail by six. I would ask that I be permitted to leave your courtroom no later than five fifteen so I can comply with his order."

"Buford, that's a reasonable request, and we certainly don't want to upset Judge Lewis. I appreciate your cooperation in transferring your prisoner here today on such short notice. Mr. Davis, this deposition will end at no later than five fifteen. Do you understand, sir?"

"Yes, sir, but to accomplish that, may I request that we go over the ground rules to avoid unnecessary arguing and wasting of valuable time?"

"That's an excellent suggestion. Dr. English, you're to answer all of Mr. Davis's questions unless Ms. Pierce objects. Ms. Pierce, I suggest you sparingly use your right to object, not only because Rule 26 is broad and favors discovery but also because this witness has already been held in contempt for failing to appear at this deposition."

Davis stood and asked if he could ask a question of the court. Boxer nodded, and Davis said, "Your Honor, in light of your comment, it is my understanding that my questioning of Dr. English will not be limited to his care and treatment of Mrs. Malone but may also include Dr. English's whereabouts for the last year and why he refused to follow the orders of this court."

"Mr. Davis, there is a reasonable probability that the Malone case will go up on appeal to the Court of Appeals. One of the issues that will be presented is my order finding Dr. English in contempt. I still have not sentenced Dr. English for his contempt, and therefore his whereabouts and his decision to fail to appear are relevant to determine an appropriate punishment and for the Court of Appeals to review my ultimate ruling."

Boxer looked hard at Dr. English. "Doctor, how you conduct yourself during this deposition will affect my ruling on your contempt. Mr. Davis, have the court reporter swear the witness and let's begin. Buford, please remove Dr. English's restraints."

Davis opened: "Dr. English, the last time we were together was September 27th of last year, wasn't it?"

"I don't remember the date. If I recall correctly your arm was in an immobilizer, wasn't it?"

Davis held back his anger, but it wasn't easy. "While you were on the run, you provided your counsel with affidavits that were notarized in South Carolina and Pennsylvania. What were you doing in those states?"

"I was sightseeing."

"So you were living with the Amish. I'm sure you fit right in. Were you working as a medical doctor in either of those states?"

"Thanks to Judge Lewis and you, I've not practiced medicine anywhere in over six months."

"Have you worked in any capacity in the last year?"

"I did odd jobs for cash."

"Did your employers have your social security number?"

"No. Are you going to call the IRS and have me arrested for income tax evasion? I only made $1,000."

"You don't like me very much, Doctor, do you? Did you hire two thugs to come to my office and beat me up? Did you call my house on September 22nd at six thirty and speak with my wife? Did you call my office on that same date and hang up on me?"

Pierce objected: "Your Honor, Mr. Davis has just asked the witness four questions. He's not letting the witness answer."

Boxer sustained the objection and told Davis to repeat each question and wait for the answer.

Dr. English admitted that he didn't like Mr. Davis:

"You're just not one of my favorite people." He denied any knowledge of either the phone calls or Mr. Davis's "unfortunate beating."

"Doctor, do you have any personal knowledge of certain evidence in the Plainview cases that was stolen from my office?"

"Was it your property to steal?"

"Answer my question. Do you have knowledge of or did you participate in that break-in?"

"I don't know what the hell you're talking about."

For the next three hours, Davis thoroughly reviewed the Malone chart with Dr. English. English insisted that it was a complicated case and that the records did not even begin to reflect what was happening and how quickly the patient deteriorated.

Davis pointed out that Dr. English, Dr. Herman, and the staff of Plainview Community Hospital created those inadequate records and that the patient remained at Plainview five days postoperative before she was transferred on her death bed to Saint Thomas.

English correctly pointed out to Davis that he'd left the country the day after surgery and wasn't involved in Rosie Malone's postoperative care.

Judge Boxer had his clerk get Subway sandwiches for everyone so they wouldn't have to take a luncheon break.

"Doctor, have you read Dr. Adams's affidavit rendering his opinions as to your care and treatment of Rosie Malone?"

"I have, and for $300 an hour, he would say just about anything. You should know. You're the one pulling his strings."

"So, Dr. Adams is lying for money about your negligence and recklessness, is he?"

"He's your puppy dog."

Davis questioned English about whether reviewing the Malone chart and the deposition testimony took time. He pulled out Exhibit B to Dr. Adams's affidavit, which listed the documents and depositions Dr. Adams reviewed. It listed 204 separate documents.

"Isn't it true that many of these documents listed are more than a hundred pages long?"

"That's because you're verbose and like to hear yourself speak."

"That's a yes or no question."

"Yes."

"So, Dr. Adams reviewed more than twenty thousand pages of medical records before rendering his opinions. Don't you think he's entitled to be paid for the more than one hundred hours he spent away from his practice and family?"

"I don't know what he looked at. You drew up this list?"

"Doctor, you're here to answer my questions, not the other way around."

Davis continued: "Do you remember Mother Superior Paula Nash?"

"I know her voice. However, I better not swear I could identify it, or you'll be playing an audiotape."

"Have you read her affidavit, Doctor?"

"No, I haven't."

Davis threw the affidavit across the table for effect.

"Take a moment and read it, sir."

English spent a few minutes reading the two-page affidavit. He glanced at the handwritten notes that were attached. English was stalling, and Davis was growing impatient.

"Doctor, do you deny that you called Mother Superior Nash?"

"No."

"Do you deny anything that she alleges you said in that telephone conversation?"

"I don't think I said that I would contact the pope."

"Did you threaten to go to the bishop?"

"Yes, I told her if she didn't get Sister Carson off my back that I would go to a higher authority. I felt like Sister Carson had based her testimony on incomplete facts, your one-sided presentation of the facts."

"Did you reference in your conversation that you would pull out all guns?"

"That's just a figure of speech. I didn't mean literally using a gun."

"Are you aware that two days later, Judge Boxer issued a protective order preventing you from contacting either Sister Carson or Mother Superior Nash?"

"Ms. Pierce informed me, and I've had no further contact."

"How many times have you contacted Ms. Pierce since going on the run?"

Pierce objected on the grounds of attorney-client privilege. Judge Boxer sustained.

Judge Boxer looked at the clock and told Davis to wrap it up.

"Why did you come back, Dr. English, after being gone several months?"

"I didn't want you to win by default. I didn't want my license taken away. I didn't want eight judgments against me for malpractice. I wanted to defend myself against these bogus charges. I also wanted to see the look on your face when you figure out you're going to lose these cases, all your money, *and* your reputation."

With that answer, the deposition was adjourned. Sheriff Dudley placed the handcuffs on English, which Davis relished, and took him back to the Hewes County jail.

CHAPTER THIRTY-EIGHT

JURY SELECTION

MONDAY, AUGUST 8, 1994

Hewes City, although more than twice the size of Plainview, was still a sleepy little Tennessee town, where everybody knew just about everyone else. Jack Barnes was the exception; he actually knew everybody. That was apparent from the start of jury selection.

Hewes County was one of the three counties that Judge Robert E. Lee Boxer rode circuit over, and he lived there with his family. Boxer moved the Plainview cases to Hewes City upon Davis's motion out of fairness and for personal convenience. The courthouse was a two-minute walk to and from his home.

The trial was originally scheduled to commence on July 5th but was delayed until August 8th to accommodate the jury pool of Hewes County. On July 24th, a two-week criminal trial for arson was completed with a guilty verdict and a seven-year sentence. Hewes County understood swift justice.

Before jury selection began in the Malone case, Judge Boxer gathered all of the prospective jurors together into the courtroom and explained why the Malone case was being tried in Hewes County and not Plains County: "As the judge, it was my decision that to guarantee a fair and impartial trial, this case shouldn't be tried in Plains County, so I moved it here."

Boxer was concerned that they would try the Malone case, and then it would be overturned on appeal. The judge knew that his dozens of rulings would be challenged by at least one of the parties on appeal and would be scrutinized by the higher court.

"Let me assure you that Plains County will reimburse your county for most of the expenses incurred. I have also decided that the jury will be sequestered, which means that after each day of court, the jury's going to spend the night at a motel, with no access to television, newspapers, or magazines. We'll provide you with tapes of appropriate entertainment. I know this is a big inconvenience, but Plains County will owe those who serve a debt of gratitude."

Sequestering a jury for a civil case was unusual and costly, but Judge Boxer anticipated both print and TV media coverage. He didn't want his jury unduly influenced, adding complications to an already complicated legal case.

Without further fanfare, the process proceeded. In theory, the best juror was one with a clean slate, no predisposing attitude either for or against a party. In reality, each side wanted as many biased jurors to its side as possible. This prejudice was accomplished by excusing potential jurors who the lawyers felt leaned, for various perceived and unexplained reasons, to the other side. Jurors were excluded simply because the objecting party didn't like the way jurors looked. When possible, Davis tried to exclude jurors on the basis of cause. A challenge for cause was one where the juror was obviously biased, such as a relative or employee of one party.

A problem with jury selection in the Malone case

was how well connected Jack Barnes was in the community. Davis shouldn't have hesitated in hiring Barnes as his co-counsel. He should have insisted despite Littleton's refusal to share any portion of his fee. While Davis debated with that idiot Littleton, the defendants hired Barnes as their local counsel. Judge Boxer excluded any juror or spouse or child of a juror whom Barnes had represented, but the judge refused to exclude all jurors whose distant family member had been Barnes's client. If he did, there wouldn't have been a jury pool.

The judge ruled that there would be a jury of twelve with three alternates, but the alternates would not be identified until the jury began deliberation. This was done so that all of the jurors, including alternates, would pay attention during the incredibly long trial.

The next person up was a young lawyer, Jason Locke. Davis liked Jason on paper but was concerned that he would control the jury. Davis was absolutely confident that Jason would be the jury foreman if he permitted the young man to serve. The young lawyer made it through.

The next potential juror was Susan Connors, the daughter and granddaughter of doctors. She was far from an ideal juror. Davis's only hope was that she would compare Dr. Herman and Dr. English to her father and grandfather and conclude that they were blemishes on the profession. When she said that she believed the increased cost of health care was because doctors were afraid of being sued, Davis knew he had to get her off the jury, and he used his last challenge.

Boxer excused Mrs. Connors, and the jury selection went on. The defendants challenged two other jurors before an acceptable jury was empaneled.

After the jury selection was completed, Judge Boxer brought together all fifteen jurors and alternates and asked them to finish the day by selecting a foreman. He advised them that they would announce their selection in open court tomorrow before the trial began.

Davis was not happy with the jury. But he had done the best he could with what he had.

CHAPTER THIRTY-NINE

PRELIMINARY JURY INSTRUCTIONS

TUESDAY, AUGUST 9, 1994

The trial began on a hot, sultry Tuesday morning in August, and inside the courtroom, the air conditioning blew like an arctic wind. In the olden days, everyone would have been furiously fanning themselves, courtesy of the local funeral home. Davis scanned the faces of the fifteen jurors and tried not to look too anxious.

At nine o'clock sharp, Judge Boxer took the bench. He gave the jury preliminary instructions about how the case would proceed. He explained the purpose of opening statements. Then he told the attorneys that opening statements should not exceed an hour each.

Davis didn't even think that they would get to the first witness, but time management in a jury trial was very difficult to predict. Local witnesses who weren't allowed to watch the trial before they testified often waited in the hallway. However, if witnesses were from out of town, they would be put up in a motel room and await a call to walk over to the courthouse. It was often difficult to estimate when a witness would testify due to the unpredictability of testimony caused by objections and lengthy responses. A witness's testimony could be delayed as long as a day because of these circumstances. Other times, an attorney would come up dry, without a witness, because the case moved faster than expected.

The defendants had five lawyers at counsel table: Grayson Stevenson for the hospital, Amy Pierce and Lowell Thomas for Dr. English, and Jack Barnes and the red bow-tied Sean McCoy for Dr. Herman. The defense team decided to keep Barnes on during the trial rather than release him after jury selection, as originally planned. Davis, Steine, and Littleton were at the plaintiff's table.

What a waste of space Littleton is, Davis thought. Morty fought with Davis to convince him to let Littleton examine a witness. They agreed on the paramedic who treated Mrs. Malone in the ambulance from Plainview to Saint Thomas. Littleton insisted on questioning a witness on threat of going to the Malone family and causing trouble. Davis agreed so that he could focus on the trial rather than battle over the clients with Littleton.

Judge Boxer turned to the jury. "Have you selected a foreman?"

The young lawyer stood and responded, "Judge, I've been selected foreperson by my fellow jurors. It's an honor to serve."

"Very well. You will be the voice of the jury. You will contact me through my court officer or one of the sheriff deputies assigned to the case. Let's begin."

Boxer knew the preliminary instructions by heart. What he couldn't remember word for word, he was able to ad-lib. "Ladies and gentlemen of the jury, you've been approved by the parties to decide all factual questions in dispute in the Estate of Rosie Malone vs. Plainview Community Hospital, Dr. Charles English, and Dr. Lars Herman."

Boxer introduced all the attorneys and the parties, even though the jury already knew each of them.

"You've been selected to determine the facts of this case. As the judge, I'm the finder of the law. Fortunately, this isn't my first rodeo, so I should get that part right. Another part of my job is to control what goes on in the courtroom. I will not let two people talk at the same time. I will try to be respectful to the attorneys, their clients, and the witnesses, but so there's no misunderstanding, I'm in charge of this courtroom and this trial. I may have to assert myself during this trial. Don't think that the increased level of my voice indicates any preference for either party's position. I'm an equal opportunity yeller."

He explained that it was the jury's job to weigh the evidence, the testimony from the stand, and the documents entered into evidence. He also instructed them that they could believe all, part, or none of a witness's testimony.

Judge Boxer explained bias; the parties were biased because they had a financial interest in the outcome, but he made it clear that other witnesses could be biased as well.

Davis mused, *All witnesses who testify are biased to some extent, but usually they aren't blatant liars. They have at least convinced themselves that their testimony is true.*

The judge continued, "Expert witnesses are hired because of their knowledge in a particular field. In a medical malpractice case, the plaintiff must prove liability through expert testimony because the defendants are doctors or hospitals. You don't practice medicine, so you're not familiar with what constitutes the standard of care. You don't know what constitutes a breach of that standard. The law requires expert testimony because you are not a doctor. You should not completely discard an expert's testimony because he or she is paid to read documents, give an affidavit, give a deposition, or testify at trial.

"Expert witnesses render opinions as to liability, negligence, and breach of the standard of care and do so after the fact, based upon documents, scientific journals, and accepted standards within their field of study. Expert witnesses are paid so they do at least have the bias of compensation."

The hospital retained two experts, but neither Dr. English nor Dr. Herman could convince another physician to testify on his behalf. Davis retained Sister Carson, Dr. Adams, and Dr. Swanson as the plaintiff's experts.

"The witness's job, both fact and expert, is to swear an oath and tell the truth. If you, the jury, find that a witness has been untruthful on one subject matter, then you are free to disregard the testimony as to other matters. You decide what proof introduced into evidence is accurate and truthful."

Davis was prepared to hear plenty of lies from the witness stand during this trial.

Boxer explained that the attorney's job was to ethically represent the client and present the evidence in the best possible light. He predicted that there would be many objections by both sides. "If I agree with the objecting party, I sustain the objection. If I disagree with the objecting party, I overrule the objection.

"From time to time, the lawyers and I will have bench conferences following an objection. We're not trying to keep a secret from you. What the lawyers say is not evidence. Remember, nothing said in the opening and closing statements is evidence. Only the witnesses' testimony and documents let into evidence should be used by you to determine liability, and if you find liability, then damages."

Davis thought, *Boxer's instructions about the procedure of a lawsuit were clear and straightforward. He's a good judge, but he's also a politician.*

He then instructed them about the law: "The burden of proof is on the plaintiff, Mrs. Malone. Thomas Malone represents the estate of his mother, Rosie Malone. She can't testify. According to the plaintiff, she died in 1992 because of the negligence and recklessness of the hospital and the doctors present."

Boxer ruled in a pretrial motion that if the state found either doctor liable for recklessness, that finding would be admitted into evidence in the Malone case. He still hadn't ruled on how he would explain the dismissal of the charges against English. Anything Boxer did would become an issue on appeal. Davis, defense counsel, and Boxer knew that.

"Mr. Malone, on behalf of his mother, is alleging that first the doctors provided medical care below the standard of care of a doctor providing similar medical services in the same or a similar community.

"Second, Mr. Malone is asserting that the hospital, through its employees, provided substandard care and that it failed to properly monitor the doctors in their care and treatment of the patient.

"Mr. Malone must prove negligence or substandard treatment against each defendant, separately, by a preponderance of the evidence. He must tip the scales of justice just slightly, more than fifty percent.

"The plaintiff has alleged comparative fault. In determining what percentage of liability is collectible by the plaintiff, if you find liability, negligence, or recklessness, then you must assign a percentage liability to each of the defendants and, if appropriate, to the plaintiff. Think of the liability of the lawsuit as a pie. Each party can be assigned his or her piece of the pie and is responsible for only that piece of the pie. For example, if you award one dollar in damages, the whole pie is one dollar, and you must divide that award of one dollar among the parties. If you find that the plaintiff is more than fifty percent liable, more than half, then there is no recovery.

"In a professional negligence case, the plaintiff must prove a breach of the standard of care or negligence by expert testimony. In the case of a doctor, that testimony must come from a doctor of the same medical subspecialty from the same or a similar community. That expert must testify that the defendant doctor was below the standard of care. In the case of the hospital, the plaintiff must prove that the hospital failed, through its employees and doctors, to provide reasonable care and treatment within the standard of care. If the care and treatment were below the standard, then you can find that the hospital is liable for a percentage of the comparative fault."

The judge informed the jury that the plaintiff alleged not only negligence but also recklessness. He explained that recklessness was when a defendant disregarded the consequences of his actions to the detriment and safety of others. He emphasized that recklessness must be proven by clear and convincing evidence, not a mere preponderance, more than fifty percent. If recklessness was proven, the jury could award punitive damages.

"Compensatory damages are to compensate, while

punitive damages are to punish the defendants. If you find recklessness, you may consider an award of punitive damages. Remember, you will not consider any amount of damages unless you find negligence. If you find recklessness, then I will instruct you on punitive damages."

Davis had heard preliminary jury instructions more than fifty times, but the comparative fault instruction was new. The Tennessee Supreme Court decision in 1992 significantly changed the law and what juries were told at the beginning of a trial. Davis thought that Judge Boxer had done a very good job in explaining the law to the jury.

"After the parties close their proof, the court will give closing jury instructions. Those words of wisdom will be the last information provided to you prior to your deliberation."

Davis was excited. Morty had heard Davis's opening statement before. Davis wouldn't rely on notes; instead, he would watch the jury and, based on their reactions, modify his presentation. Davis learned from the master.

CHAPTER FORTY

PLAINTIFF'S OPENING STATEMENT

TUESDAY, AUGUST 9, 1994

After the preliminary instructions, Judge Boxer broke for an early lunch. It was only ten thirty, but it wouldn't be fair to interrupt an attorney during the opening statements.

The Davis team exited the courthouse, went to their car, and retrieved sandwiches and soft drinks from an iced-down cooler in the trunk. The restaurants meant contact with reporters, jurors, defense counsel, insurance company representatives, or defendants, except Dr. English, who would be eating lunch in his jail cell. They needed their privacy to talk freely. Despite their efforts, the press was persistent, and Davis had to chase away two reporters.

Davis wasn't usually nervous in court, but Plainview wasn't like most cases. He didn't trust the defense team not to interfere with his opening statement.

Opening statements were protected from interruption and objection as a professional courtesy under normal circumstances. If a lawyer went too far outside the evidence, then his misstatements would be shoved down his throat by the other side during closing. Boxer was taking no chances. He warned counsel not to object during another party's opening statement unless there was an obvious abuse by counsel or a perceived reversible error being committed.

"Mr. Davis, plaintiff's opening statement, please."

Davis stood, jerked his shirt cuffs straight, revealing his monogrammed BAD gold cuff links, and glanced one last time at his notes, which would remain on the table. Most attorneys needed the security of their notes, but Davis learned from Steine that the purpose of an opening statement was to tell the jurors a story. The one your side wanted them to believe.

He deliberately relaxed his face, neither too serious nor too friendly, a neutral expression. He wanted to build a relationship with the jurors, so he moved slowly toward the jury box. He needed to look them directly in the eyes. His were a piercing, convincing blue.

Prior to trial, Davis clarified with the judge that he was not tethered to the podium but could wander around the courtroom as long as he remained a "respectful distance" from the jury. Mobility brought Davis both physically and emotionally closer to the jury.

"Ladies and gentlemen of the jury, my name is Benjamin Davis, and I represent the estate of Rosie Malone. Rosie Malone couldn't be here today because she died as a result of the negligent and reckless conduct of the defendants. If the defendants had just acted reasonably, within the standard of care, we wouldn't be here today."

Davis walked behind Dr. Herman and Dr. English and raised his right hand, as if to take an oath. "These men, as doctors, took the Hippocratic Oath, and Rosie Malone trusted these men. They repaid her by killing her through their neglect and reckless conduct."

Without warning, English stood, quickly turned, and looked hard at Davis. There was murder in his eyes.

Boxer yelled for English to sit down. He complied, and Davis walked away from the defense table.

"Mr. Davis, I want you to keep a respectful distance from the defendants, or there will be a one-foot rule from the podium. Am I understood?"

Davis moved behind his client, a safe place to stand. He was testing the judge; no damage was done.

"Thomas Malone has been named the administrator of his mother's estate. He represents the Malone family, not just his own interests."

Davis felt like he was connecting with the jury; he was building their trust. He promised them that each lawyer's opening statement was being preserved by the court reporter and that during closing arguments, at the end of the proof, he intended to read portions from each lawyer's opening, including his own. He assured the jury that what the defense lawyers claimed in their opening statements just wouldn't be proven by the evidence. He'd later poke holes in the promises made during their opening.

As he spoke, Davis watched the jury's facial expressions; he was looking for a tell, something that indicated which way each juror was leaning. He thought the first row, with the exception of juror number four, was paying close attention. He decided to focus on juror number four in the hope of winning him over and securing the front row.

Davis told the Rosie Malone story. How she worked hard at the local bakery and raised eleven kids. He helped the jury identify with the deceased. He apologized that they'd never get to meet Rosie Malone because the defendants killed her.

He showed the jury a poster-sized photograph of a much younger Rosie Malone in her bakery uniform and a hairnet. She was not an attractive woman, tired looking, even a little worn out, but she was just like any of the jurors. It was important for the jury to have a face to go with a name and to understand that she was one of them.

He described in detail her medical history through 1991. It was not a pretty picture. She was a smoker almost all of her life and unsuccessfully tried to stop many times.

"Rosie Malone, in 1991, began suffering from severe stomach pain and went to see her family doctor, Dr. Herman, to figure out what was wrong. Dr. Herman owned an expensive piece of equipment called an ultrasound machine, which was able to take pictures of his patients' internal organs."

Davis showed the jury a poster-sized photograph of Herman's ultrasound machine. "This machine cost a pretty penny, almost $200,000. How many years would you have to work to purchase this machine? Dr. Herman was able to pay it off in about seven months. After that, the fees paid by the insurance companies were pure gravy."

He could tell that the cost of the machine and how quickly Herman paid for it concerned the jury. He pointed at the photo.

"Looks complicated, doesn't it? A radiologist, a doctor who specializes in reading X-rays and ultrasounds to help diagnose patients, is required after four years of medical school to study three more years to learn how to use an ultrasound. Not Dr. Herman, though. He trained only three days on the ultrasound machine before, in his office, he began using it to test his patients, such as Rosie Malone. He charged almost $2,000 a test. He did so many that Blue Star of Tennessee is investigating him and refusing to pay for any more tests done in his office."

He explained that in the last two weeks of her life, Dr. Herman ordered three ultrasounds of Rosie Malone, two at his office and one at the hospital.

Next, Davis identified his three experts: "Dr. Swanson will testify that Dr. Herman failed to perform an available test that would have discovered Rosie Malone suffered from irritable bowel syndrome, which should have been treated by medication, not surgery.

"Dr. Gerald, the hospital's radiologist, reported no problem with the gallbladder, yet the hospital booked Dr. English a surgical suite to remove Mrs. Malone's gallbladder. Why would the hospital allow such an unnecessary surgery?"

Davis explained how Dr. English performed Mrs. Malone's gallbladder surgery laparoscopically. He showed a picture of a laparoscope and described how the laser and camera were used. He could tell the jury was surprised that the recovery time was two days rather than two weeks after an open procedure.

"In 1992, Dr. English was the only surgeon performing laparoscopic gallbladder surgery at Plainview Community Hospital. There was no other doctor to verify that he was competent to perform the procedure. All Dr. English did was attend a three-day course in Atlanta, and away he went."

Davis argued that the hospital had an obligation to make sure Dr. English was competent to perform that particular surgery by having another surgeon proctor him and observe him perform several surgeries.

"This didn't happen. There was no one on the staff qualified to proctor him. Dr. Adams will testify that Dr. English was not competent and that he nicked Mrs. Malone's bowel."

Davis now turned his attention to the hospital. The jury learned that the hospital, under its own Utilization Review Plan, failed to examine Mrs. Malone at twenty-four hours, forty-eight hours, and seventy-two hours after her admission to the hospital.

"Why didn't Nurse Perry, who worked for the hospital, ask why Dr. English was performing surgery on a gallbladder with no stones or apparent gallbladder disease?"

The faces of the jurors told Davis that he had gotten their attention.

"In a medical malpractice case, the plaintiff, through expert testimony, must establish not only the standard of care but also a breach of that standard of care. As to Dr. Herman and Dr. English, the plaintiff is relying on the live testimony of Dr. Swanson and Dr. Adams. Their testimony establishes the standard of care and the defendant doctors' breach of that standard. Dr. Adams and Dr. Swanson will also testify that Dr. Herman and Dr. English were reckless in their care of Rosie Malone."

The jury next learned about the plaintiff's third expert witness, Sister Carson. She wasn't there to testify about the Catholic Church. She was a registered nurse and the president and chief executive officer at Saint Francis Hospital in Saint Paul, Minnesota. She served on each of the medical committees at Saint Francis and knew the standard of care required of a hospital to properly credential, proctor, and monitor their doctors.

She'd read Plainview Community Hospital's own rules and requirements and was familiar with the rules promulgated by the Joint Commission on Accreditation of Healthcare Organizations. Davis described JCAHO as an organization that licenses hospitals and regulates what goes on at those hospitals.

"Sister Carson will testify that Plainview Community Hospital was not only negligent in its care and treatment of Rosie Malone but also reckless."

He had tied all three defendants to Rosie Malone's death and identified for the jury which of his experts implicated which of the defendants.

Davis described in detail Rosie Malone's February 1992 hospitalization and how her temperature rose and how her condition deteriorated. Davis insisted that she needed to be transferred to a better-equipped hospital, with a cardiologist, a pulmonologist, and an infectious disease specialist.

Davis argued that Mrs. Malone wasn't transferred until February 5th at 6:00 p.m., only after her daughter insisted that she be transferred.

"It was too little and too late. If it weren't for Lorraine Burke, Mrs. Malone's daughter, the defendants never would have transferred Mrs. Malone. They didn't want outside physicians to discover their negligent care. The failure to transfer Mrs. Malone was reckless.

"All of the plaintiff's experts will testify that the deteriorating medical condition of Mrs. Malone and the need to transfer her were apparent from the medical records, written by the defendants. Those records, which in the case of Dr. Herman must be translated, prove their negligence and recklessness."

Davis took a breath. His allotted time was about up.

He pointed out that neither Dr. Herman nor Dr. English could find an expert to testify on his behalf. The defendants were their own experts. He assured the jury that this failure to secure experts proved that their conduct was negligent and reckless.

The judge gave Davis a stern look. He was out of time.

Davis quickly closed his opening statement. He thanked the jury, not only on behalf of the Malone family, but also for the citizens of Plains County. He expressed his confidence that after hearing all the evidence, they would find for the plaintiff and do the right thing. He nodded, turned, and walked back to his seat.

As he approached his co-counsel, Davis saw the pride on Morty's face. But when Littleton mumbled, "Good job," Davis thought, *I don't give a rat's ass about what you think.*

Davis was satisfied. He challenged the defense counsel and told them that if they strayed from the truth in their openings, their clients would be held accountable for their misrepresentations. He thought what he said made good sense, and he hoped the jury would agree.

"Thank you, Mr. Davis. Ladies and gentlemen, we're going to take a fifteen-minute comfort break, and then we're going to hear from the defendants."

Davis guessed that McCoy would go first, then Pierce, and then Grayson for the hospital. Morty agreed. Littleton offered no opinion.

CHAPTER FORTY-ONE

DEFENDANTS' OPENING STATEMENTS

TUESDAY, AUGUST 9, 1994

Back in the courtroom, Jack Barnes, the local attorney, was standing at the podium to make Herman's opening statement. Morty looked at Davis and just shook his head ever so slightly, but Davis recognized that it made sense. Barnes knew these people. He spoke their language. Neither Davis nor Morty thought of this possibility because their egos, unlike McCoy's, wouldn't have allowed them to miss giving the opening statement. He was the defense's logical place to start.

"Ladies and gentlemen, my name is Jack Barnes, and together with Mr. McCoy, I represent Dr. Herman. I won't be as long-winded as Mr. Davis. Remember, what the lawyers say isn't evidence. I think we are better served if we just get to the evidence.

"As Judge Boxer told you, the plaintiff goes first, and that's a big advantage. Please do not make up your minds until you hear all the proof. That's what the law requires, and I'm confident that's what you'll do. Remember, the burden of proof is on the plaintiff, not the defendants. Dr. Herman doesn't have to prove anything."

Barnes assured the jury that the facts surrounding the death of Mrs. Malone were not as black and white as Mr. Davis had misled them to believe. She was a complicated patient, with a long medical history. He informed the jury that in June 1991, at Lorraine Burke's insistence, Mrs. Malone began seeing a gastro-enterologist, Dr. Randall Sizemore. Barnes emphasized that Dr. Sizemore treated Mrs. Malone for almost five months, and he didn't solve her problems but rather made them worse.

"He prescribed various medications and performed various tests, and he couldn't find out why Mrs. Malone was experiencing abdominal pain. Mr. Davis didn't mention Dr. Sizemore and his failure to correctly diagnose Mrs. Malone, did he?

"Another thing that Mr. Davis didn't mention was that Mrs. Malone was a drug seeker. Dr. Herman knew this. It's apparent that Dr. Sizemore did not."

Davis had to give Barnes high marks. He was placing Sizemore on trial, even though he had not seen the patient since October 1991, months before her death.

Barnes attacked Sizemore for overprescribing narcotics and not understanding that the patient had a low tolerance for pain. He insisted that Dr. Herman knew the patient and prescribed placebos, such as sterile saline, because most of the pain was psychological, not physical.

"The plaintiff's experts from Atlanta weren't there in February 1992; they never met Mrs. Malone. As Mr. Davis says, all they have to look at are medical records. They didn't talk to the patient. They didn't examine the patient."

Barnes walked over to the defense table and drank from his glass of water. When he resumed, he was standing very close to the jury. Davis thought he was violating their space, but that was Boxer's call. Davis secretly wished he dared to get that close to them.

Barnes convincingly argued that Dr. Herman inherited from Dr. Sizemore a very sick and drug-dependent patient. He assured the jury that Dr. Herman did the best he could, but that Mrs. Malone was an uncooperative patient, who refused to follow her prescribed diet and who continued to smoke two packs a day.

Davis was concerned that Barnes was so effective that the jury might award damages against Dr. Sizemore rather than Dr. Herman.

"With due respect to your intelligence, your job as the jury boils down to listening to the proof and the jury instructions, given by the judge, and determining if the standard of care was met. Dr. Herman will testify that he did his best and that he provided care and treatment within the standard of care. These claims of recklessness by Mr. Davis have absolutely no merit and have no basis in the facts. Thank you for your attention."

The judge thanked Barnes for his opening statement, and Grayson Stevenson III rose and walked to the podium. His navy suit and white hair were immaculate. He had on his traditional red power tie. Even at a distance, Davis could see his reflection in the man's shoes. Neither Davis nor Morty liked Stevenson either before or during the Plainview cases. He was pretentious and a part of the Nashville elite.

Stevenson spoke as he moved toward the jury box: "Ladies and gentlemen, I represent the hospital, and unlike Mr. Davis, I'm not going to tell you what the proof will be. I'll leave that to your good judgment."

Stevenson had chosen to attack Davis himself in his opening. Not an uncommon tactic.

"Mr. Davis didn't explain the hospital's committee system and how it acts as checks and balances to protect the patients. What Mr. Davis didn't tell you in his opening statement, but that the law requires, is that the minutes of the committees must be kept confidential. The Tennessee legislature passed a statute that requires confidentiality. Sister Carson has no idea what the hospital did because by law, she was not permitted to read those minutes."

Davis thought Stevenson might have just made a terrible mistake. The minutes, prior to trial, had not been discoverable because of the law. The judge might reverse his ruling based on Stevenson's opening.

"It is also important for you to remember what the judge said about biased witnesses. Several nurses who will testify are former employees of the hospital and have sued the hospital. Mr. Littleton, who is seated at Mr. Davis's table, represents them. It is the hospital's position that they have an axe to grind and may not testify accurately."

So Littleton's first contribution to the case has been as a prop for Stevenson. Davis wished that Littleton would simply disappear. He was tired of defense counsel attacking him, but it would break the golden rule to interrupt Stevenson.

"The hospital's expert, Dr. Leonard Sparks, will testify that the hospital did nothing wrong and that its employees acted within the standard of care. The hospital must let its doctors make medical decisions as to the care of their patients. The reference by Mr. Davis to the utilization review nurse is misleading. Utilization review has to do with hospital costs, not care. Mrs. Malone was a Medicare patient. The hospital lost money during Mrs. Malone's February 1992 hospitalization."

Stevenson emphasized that Dr. Herman was paid for the two ultrasounds and that the hospital was paid a very minimum dollar amount for the eight days Mrs. Malone stayed at Plainview Community Hospital. "The moment Mrs. Malone was transferred to Saint Thomas Hospital was the moment that Plainview Community Hospital stopped losing money. It was Dr. Herman who delayed transfer; he was her treating physician, responsible for her postoperative care.

"The fact that Mrs. Malone died is a tragedy. But tragedies happen in life, and that doesn't mean anyone was negligent. It certainly doesn't mean anyone was reckless. We all feel sympathy for the Malone family. But as Judge Boxer will instruct you, sympathy is not to be considered. The plaintiff must carry the burden of proof. If the plaintiff fails, you must not award any amount of money because of sympathy. Thank you."

When Stevenson sat down, he smiled at Davis, which Davis found very annoying.

Judge Boxer asked Pierce, "Should we take a break? It's four thirty-seven."

"No need, Your Honor. I would like the court to explain to the jury the defendant English's right to reserve opening argument."

Judge Boxer explained that a defendant could give an opening argument at the beginning of the plaintiff's proof or at the beginning of the defendant's proof.

"Dr. English's counsel has elected to wait until the plaintiff closes its proof and to give her opening later in the trial."

Davis couldn't tell whether Morty was as surprised as he was. An effective defense was to keep the plaintiff off balance. Passing on her opening statement threw Davis for a bit of a loop.

Judge Boxer reminded the jury that they were sequestered and were not to discuss the case with their families, their fellow jurors, or anyone else. He told them to be back in the jury room by eight forty-five the next morning.

CHAPTER FORTY-TWO

PLANNED CONTEMPT

WEDNESDAY, AUGUST 10, 1994

Sammie was actually enjoying watching the Malone trial. Almost all of her work was done. Her research was finished, and the motions and briefs were written. She helped outline the direct and cross-examination questions for each of the anticipated witnesses and worked on the proposed jury instructions. At this point her job was to watch the jury's reaction to the proof. The case was now up to her uncle and Morty.

Morty called the first witness: Celia Perry, the utilization review nurse. Boxer agreed that she was an adverse witness and that Steine could ask leading questions. Morty had Ms. Perry explain her background; the jury was probably surprised that she only had a GED. She read into the record her job description. Morty also discussed with the witness the Utilization Review Plan of Plainview Community Hospital, which was already an exhibit in evidence.

Morty then specifically reviewed the January 29th hospitalization of Rosie Malone with the witness. Morty asked, "It was your job to look at Dr. Herman's office record to determine if hospitalization was appropriate?"

"Yes, sir."

Morty handed the witness Dr. Herman's office record. "What aspect of that record prompted you to allow the admission of this patient?"

"I can't read the record."

No one could read it.

"So, on what medical basis did you recommend admission to the hospital?"

"A conversation I had with Dr. Herman. He told me that he had done three ultrasounds and that he suspected gallbladder disease. He wanted to admit the patient to have a third ultra-sound to be read by the radiologist, Dr. Gerald, and to perform other investigative tests."

"Ms. Perry, the patient didn't have to be admitted to have an ultrasound read by Dr. Gerald, did she?"

"No, sir."

"Wasn't it your job to admit the patient only if the admission were necessary?"

Perry insisted that Dr. Herman was the patient's treating physician for years, and she was just a nurse, not even an RN. She testified she wasn't in a position to question him.

Morty reviewed with Ms. Perry the Malone chart from admission on January 29th until right before her surgery. "You were required under the Utilization Review Plan to assess the patient forty-eight hours after admission, right?"

"Yes, sir."

Perry admitted that she could not read the history, the physical, the physician orders, or the progress notes written by Dr. Herman. Morty asked on what medical basis she recommended that Mrs. Malone undergo surgery.

"I had another conversation with Dr. Herman. He assured me that the patient required the surgery and that Dr. English confirmed the need for the surgery. They were the patient's doctors, so I concurred."

"Ms. Perry, do you realize that you gave up your role as utilization review nurse to Dr. Herman? You did not do an independent review."

"I guess I didn't, but he was her doctor."

Morty reviewed Mrs. Malone's chart through admission till the 5th and how her temperature rose and how her condition deteriorated. "You were required to do a seventy-two-hour review of the status of the patient under the Utilization Review Plan?"

"Yes, sir."

"Did you discuss with either Dr. Herman or Dr. English the transfer of the patient to Nashville after your seventy-two-hour review?"

"No. They were responsible for the patient and were tending to her."

Morty concluded with the witness.

Then Stevenson asked fifteen minutes of questions. They established that Rosie Malone was Dr. Herman's patient and that as her treating physician, it was his call as to whether she needed to be hospitalized and what tests he needed to obtain a diagnosis.

Neither McCoy nor Pierce had questions. Boxer called a fifteen-minute recess.

When they returned from the break, Judge Boxer asked Morty to call his next witness, and Morty announced Karol Hyde. She testified that she had worked at Plainview Community Hospital from February 1989 through the date of her resignation on July 7th, 1992. She testified that she knew Rosie Malone because she had been admitted several times at Plainview, including January 29th, 1992. Ms. Hyde, an RN, had been the charge nurse for seven shifts during Rosie Malone's January-February 1992 hospitalization.

Morty reviewed the chart with her. When they got to February 4th, he directly asked Nurse Hyde if she discussed Mrs. Malone's deteriorating condition and need to transfer to Nashville with anyone. She became agitated and pointed to Dr. Herman and loudly said his name.

"I told him that I thought the patient had become septic and should be transferred to Saint Thomas or Vanderbilt. He indicated that they were considering that possibility."

"Mrs. Malone wasn't transferred until the evening of February 5th, correct?"

"Yes, sir."

"You resigned your position at Plainview Community Hospital. Why?"

"I was concerned for my license. I had made complaints about both Dr. English and Dr. Herman to my supervisor and directly to Mr. Douglas, the hospital administrator. I'd written up six incident reports—"

Stevenson rose and objected. He argued that the committee process and the incident reports were confidential. Boxer sustained the objection and instructed the jury to ignore that last answer. It was not admissible.

"Did Dr. English and Dr. Herman continue to have privileges after you complained?"

"Nothing was done to them."

Stevenson objected.

Boxer sustained the objection and chastised Morty: "Ladies and gentlemen, what the Plainview Community Hospital's committees may or may not have done is confidential. Move on, Mr. Steine. If you continue with this line of questioning, I'll hold you in contempt of court."

Sammie thought that the judge was being a little hard on Morty, but she was biased in favor of the old man. She recalled what he had told her many times: a judge can reprimand, but the jury can never completely erase either a question or an answer from their minds.

"Who did you give your resignation to?"

"I handed my resignation to Mr. Douglas. I apologized for not giving two weeks' notice, but after witnessing all the negligence, I was afraid of getting sued because my name was in the charts."

Stevenson jumped up and turned to Morty. "You're in contempt of court—"

Boxer looked like he was going to blow a gasket. He stood and, in a much louder voice than he had used so far, yelled at Stevenson: "That's *my* determination, not yours, sir. Mr. Steine, I hold you in contempt. That will be $500. I again instruct the jury to ignore that last answer from the witness. It is not admissible evidence and cannot be considered by you in your deliberations."

Sammie wasn't concerned. Both her uncle and Morty warned her that they would be pushing the judge and that he might just push back. They specifically discussed the possibility that somebody might be held in contempt. The negative implications of finding Morty in contempt in front of the jury certainly created an issue for appeal. They even agreed that it would be better if the culprit was Morty, not Davis, because the judge and jury were more likely to forgive him than Davis.

Morty then asked if the witness had filed a lawsuit against Plainview Community Hospital. Morty knew that Stevenson would bring up the lawsuit on cross-examination to prove bias. Morty established that Bradley Littleton was her attorney and that she had sued the hospital for breach of contract and for forcing her to resign to protect her license.

After Morty finished with the witness, Boxer broke for lunch.

When court resumed at two o'clock, Stevenson began with the witness: "You've sued the hospital?"

"Yes, sir."

"But you quit?"

"I was forced to quit."

"Who held the gun to your head?"

"I had to quit; it wasn't a safe place. My license was in jeopardy every day."

"You believe that if this jury awards a verdict to the plaintiff in this lawsuit, it will benefit you in your lawsuit?"

"I haven't thought about it, but I guess you're right."

The witness confirmed that she was represented by Littleton. Stevenson quickly established that Nurse Hyde in less than a month of her resignation got a better job, paying a dollar more per hour. Stevenson did the math right in front of the jury, and Nurse Hyde made $4,250 more working her new job than working at Plainview Community Hospital.

"And you and Mr. Littleton have sued the hospital for $1 million?"

"Yes, sir."

Stevenson paused and then said, "And you're telling this jury that you're not here for money?"

Karol Hyde didn't know what to say.

Stevenson sat down. McCoy and Pierce had no questions.

Morty thought, *The defense really wanted to end on that note, very smooth*. Morty planned on calling two more nurses who had sued the hospital and were represented by Littleton. But he asked for, and Boxer permitted, a recess.

During the break, Morty explained to Davis, Sammie, and Littleton that in his opinion, Karol Hyde came off as a biased witness and lost her credibility with the jury. Her suit for $1 million, given her limited damages, made her look like a money-grubber. Littleton tried to defend his lawsuit and the amount of the suit. Davis ended the discussion by concluding, why repeat the same mistake? Hyde's association with Littleton was probably the most damaging aspect of her testimony. They decided not to put on the stand any of the other nurses that Littleton represented because of the obvious bias.

Davis shook his head, trying to remember why he ever had anything to do with the idiot Littleton and why they were still joined at the hip. *Oh, yeah, Littleton's name is next to mine on the client contracts. Can't escape that.*

CHAPTER FORTY-THREE

THE BUFFOON

WEDNESDAY, AUGUST 10, 1994

Davis looked over at the jury. They were still paying close attention, and he mentally tried to assess who was leaning in his direction. Davis was confident that the young lawyer-foreman understood that the hospital had violated its Utilization Review Plan, but he was less certain of the less-educated jurors. Davis remembered something Morty taught him: a jury is as smart as its smartest member and as stubborn as the last juror who needed convincing. He hoped the foreman learned how to be persuasive in law school.

They elected to call next Nurse Carole Black, who was still employed at Plainview Community Hospital. Nurse Black, under Davis's direct examination, testified about Rosie Malone's last three days at the hospital. Davis concluded by asking her who was responsible for determining when or if Mrs. Malone should have been transferred to Nashville.

"Dr. Herman was her treating physician, and he was monitoring her condition closely."

"Did he wait too long?"

Stevenson objected on the basis that Nurse Black was not a medical doctor and not able to testify as to the standard of care.

Boxer sustained the objection but then asked, "Ms.

Black, as a registered nurse, is it your professional opinion that Mrs. Malone should have been transferred sooner?"

"Yes, sir. Her temperature had been over one hundred and four, almost one hundred and five, for several days. She should have been transferred as soon as it hit one hundred and four and the antibiotics couldn't lower it."

Boxer looked over at Davis. "Anything further, Mr. Davis?"

"No, sir."

Davis sat down, and Stevenson tried to undo how Boxer finished the witness. He made little progress, except she emphasized that Dr. Herman was in charge of the patient's care and that she and the other hospital employees were following his orders. Pierce got up and in a few questions established that English had left town following the surgery and was not at the hospital for Mrs. Malone's postoperative care. McCoy didn't ask a single question. No good would have come from it.

Davis next called the hospital custodian of records, Ms. Johnston. Davis knew she would lie, but it needed to be on the record.

"What happened to the gallbladder pathology slides from 1991 and 1992?"

"They were destroyed in the regular course of business the next year."

Davis pulled out the Joint Commission Rule 301, which required the slides be kept five years.

"We changed that policy after my deposition, after you pointed out that rule to us."

"So the hospital hasn't destroyed any slides since your deposition?"

"No, sir."

You lying bitch, Davis thought. *What about the slides that scumbag stole from my office and drugged my poor niece to get?* If he still had the slides, he would have impeached Johnston at this point. But she was going to get away with her perjury.

It was late in the day, and the jury was getting tired. Morty suggested to Davis that they let Littleton question the paramedic as their next witness. Davis shrugged in agreement and whispered to Littleton to call the next witness.

Littleton moved to the podium: "Your Honor, Bradley Littleton, for the plaintiff."

Boxer looked at Littleton strangely. "Yes, we've met before."

A few jurors smiled. The barber, Josh Paulson, showed all of his teeth, and the mailman, Ray Breyer, smirked.

"Who is your next witness, Mr. Littleton?"

"The plaintiff calls Tommy Nelson."

A young man in a blue uniform went up to the witness stand. He took the oath and sat down. Littleton established that Mr. Nelson was the paramedic who on February 5th transferred Rosie Malone from Plainview Community Hospital to Saint Thomas Hospital. Littleton seemed nervous, but at least the testimony was coming through.

"Isn't it true that you were in the back of the ambulance—"

McCoy jumped up and objected: "Leading question, Your Honor."

"Sustained. Please rephrase that question, Mr. Littleton."

"Weren't you in the back of the ambulance—"

Pierce jumped up this time: "Objection, leading question."

"Sustained. Please rephrase the question."

"Didn't Rosie Malone—"

With a smile, Stevenson rose and stated, "Objection, leading question."

"Sustained. Mr. Littleton, please refrain from asking leading questions. Ladies and gentlemen, a leading question implies the answer, such as, 'Isn't it true?' Mr. Littleton needs to ask open-ended questions so the witness, rather than Mr. Littleton, can testify."

Littleton stood there, his head nodding. He looked like one of those baseball bobble-head dolls. Morty thought that Littleton might lose it. But a moment later, Littleton seemed to regain his composure and stated in a higher voice than before: "My intent is to establish that Mr. Nelson was the paramedic who rode with Rosie Malone to Saint Thomas."

Boxer looked crossly at Littleton and said, "Just ask him, sir."

Some jurors found this amusing. Breyer the mailman, who was seated in the front row, openly laughed at Littleton. So did the bookkeeper, Mabel Donner. Davis thought, *Littleton is losing the jury that Morty and I worked so hard to win over*. The laughter was contagious. Betsy Blue, the waitress who was seated next to Ms. Donner, giggled. Even a few spectators joined in.

Littleton became even more anxious and, in an even higher voice, said, "Your Honor, I ask that you declare the witness an adverse witness so that I may ask leading questions."

Boxer looked at Morty and Davis and seemed annoyed with them for even allowing Littleton to call a witness. Obviously, in retrospect, it was a bad idea.

Boxer said, "Mr. Littleton, why don't you ask the witness where he was on February 5th and what he remembers of that date?"

Littleton repeated Judge Boxer's question, and the witness gave a five-minute answer.

After the witness paused, Littleton asked, "Didn't Rosie Malone—"

McCoy stood and almost laughingly blurted out, "Objection, leading question."

Breyer could no longer contain himself. He started uncontrollably laughing in the front row of the juror box. Steve Paine, the assistant manager of Kroger, was laughing so hard that tears came to his eyes. Mabel Donner kept poking Betsy Blue and giggling. The second row of the jury box had better self-control but was close to breaking down.

McCoy, Pierce, and Stevenson snickered. Dr. Herman remained silent. Dr. English found Littleton's painful situation so funny, he almost fell out of his chair, he was laughing so hard.

Littleton looked around the room. He was getting angry. His face was as red as a beet, and he started waving his arms up and down. His body language made the situation that much funnier. At least seventy-five percent of the courtroom was laughing *at*, not *with*, Littleton. It was an embarrassing moment, and Davis felt sorry for the man.

Finally, through all the laughter, Littleton yelled, "Your Honor, I ask that you admonish Dr. English for his unprofessional conduct. He's laughing during my examination of the witness. This is no laughing matter."

Pierce stood and, in an even louder voice, pointed out, "Your Honor, if you admonish Dr. English, I insist that the court also admonish Mr. Davis, who has been laughing openly at Mr. Littleton since the fourth question of the examination. You've got to admit, Your Honor, Mr. Littleton's examination has been entertaining."

Judge Boxer did not address the comment and broke for the day after determining that none of the parties had any further questions for the paramedic.

CHAPTER FORTY-FOUR

ADVERSE WITNESS

THURSDAY, AUGUST 11, 1994

Judge Boxer began at nine o'clock sharp. His job was difficult, but at least he was prompt. Some judges let their court and jury function on their own time schedule rather than by the clock.

Davis also appreciated that Boxer made decisions; right or wrong, he wasn't indecisive. Davis admired that quality, particularly since everyone knew that, in all probability, there would be an appeal.

Boxer also inherited what Davis called the "English factor"—one of the defendants was a fugitive from justice. Dr. English's disappearance made for interesting drama and complicated the Plainview cases. Even with the surrender of Dr. English, the Malone trial was not a typical malpractice case.

Every morning Sheriff Dudley, who was forced to sit through the trial all day, delivered Dr. English from his Hewes County jail cell to the courtroom.

Judge Lewis was taking no chances with his prisoner. It took five months for Lewis to get his hands on Dr. English, and he wasn't letting him go until he cured that contempt.

After the parties and the jury were settled in, Judge Boxer addressed Davis: "Call your first witness."

"Your Honor, the plaintiff calls Dr. Charles English to the stand."

English walked slowly to the witness stand and was sworn in by the judge's clerk.

Davis asked the judge to give the jury the adverse or hostile witness instruction.

Boxer said, "Ladies and gentlemen, when a party calls a witness, usually that witness is at least neutral to that side. When a party calls a friendly or neutral witness, the attorney may not ask leading questions. However, if you call the opposing party or a witness that the court deems hostile or adverse, the attorney may ask leading questions."

Davis had been thinking about getting to question English before a jury for more than two years. He loved his job because of such moments.

"Please state your full name."

"Dr. Charles English."

"Do you go by any aliases?"

"I have a nickname. My friends call me Charlie, but you can call me Dr. English."

Several jurors laughed, and Davis just smiled back at English. Davis went through English's background. When he asked if Dr. English's two children lived with him, Judge Boxer gave Davis a stern look. The last thing that Boxer wanted the jury to know about was Dr. English's alimony and child support problems and where he was staying at night and why.

Davis asked about English's education, including his medical training at Peterson University. He established that English graduated in 1982, and that in 1984, Peterson University's accreditation was suspended for issuing false medical licenses.

"I have no information about that, Mr. Davis."

Davis offered into evidence the findings of the accreditation body and the order of suspension of Peterson University as the next exhibit.

Boxer allowed the documents into evidence under Rule 9.02. Davis figured he had no choice after the exchange. But Davis knew Boxer would be keeping a closer eye on him.

Davis asked English about his medical subspecialty of general surgery, including the types of surgeries he performed at Plainview Community Hospital. What about the credentialing process and how the hospital approved the types of surgical procedures he performed there?

"Did anyone at Plainview Community Hospital ever ask you about Peterson University?"

"No, sir."

"I guess the Credentialing Committee didn't look too deeply into your background?"

"I wouldn't know."

Davis established that the hospital granted English privileges for every surgical procedure he applied for and then moved on to English's contract with the hospital. He established that Dr. Herman was his landlord and that the hospital paid his rent for six months and guaranteed his lease. The hospital also guaranteed an income of at least $10,000 per month.

English started to get out of the witness chair. "What the hell are you driving at?"

"My point is that the hospital invested a pretty penny in bringing you to Plainview, and you needed to order tests and perform surgeries for the hospital to get its money back."

Pierce objected on the grounds of relevancy.

"What's the relevancy, Mr. Davis?" asked Boxer.

"Your Honor, the financial relationship between Dr. English and Dr. Herman is relevant. If Dr. English's practice flourished and he performed a lot of surgeries, the hospital didn't have to pay him $10,000 because he would earn his $10,000 minimum."

"Objection overruled. Let's move this along, please."

Davis moved into the Malone case. He asked English if Dr. Herman was an important referral source to Dr. English, providing most of his income.

Pierce objected, but Boxer overruled, holding that the business relationship between the two doctors was relevant.

Davis pulled the credentialing document he introduced into evidence. "When you were originally credentialed at Plainview Community Hospital, you were not authorized to do laparoscopic gallbladder surgery, were you?"

"No, I was trained in 1991 and began performing that particular procedure in October 1991 at Plainview."

"Your training consisted of a two-day course in Atlanta, Georgia, at the Southern Laparoscopic Institute?"

"It was a three-day course."

English, for the second time, rose from his chair. He was obviously getting agitated with Davis, which was exactly what Davis wanted. He loved pushing English's buttons and having him upset in front of the jury.

Davis knew it was three days, but English would not look any more competent with a three-day course than a two-day course. The defensive correction made English look guilty. Davis was just getting warmed up.

"You didn't operate on human beings when you trained in Atlanta, did you?"

"No."

"They were pigs, right?"

"Yes, but pigs are very close to humans in anatomy and are used all the time in training."

"Doctor, you're not telling this jury that there is no difference between one of your patients and a pig, are you?"

Several jurors laughed out loud. Judge Boxer was obviously amused.

English didn't know what to say.

Pierce jumped up. "Objection! What is the relevancy of that question? Mr. Davis is wasting our time."

"Your Honor, how similar a pig is to a human being is pretty darn relevant since Dr. English's training consisted of doing laparoscopic gallbladder surgery on a pig only."

"Objection overruled."

"Your first laparoscopic gallbladder surgery on a non-pig was at Plainview Community Hospital on October 18th, 1991?"

"That sounds about right."

"You performed fifty-one laparoscopic gallbladder surgeries between October 1991 and January 31st, 1992, the day you performed one on Rosie Malone?"

Pierce stood and loudly yelled her objection: "Objection! I request permission to approach the bench!"

As soon as she reached the bench, Pierce could hardly contain herself: "The court has ruled that no evidence of a pattern of negligence may be introduced."

Davis was ready for that: "Your Honor has ruled

that the logs are admissible into evidence to prove the number of surgeries. Therefore, the number of surgeries between two dates is admissible. I intend to prove that Dr. English preferred the laparoscopic procedure to an open one and that beginning in October 1991, he regularly performed the procedure at Plainview Community Hospital." Tying the proof to Rosie Malone would convince Boxer to admit the evidence.

The judge thought a moment. "Objection overruled. Let's return to our spots and give the court reporter an opportunity to set back up."

Davis waited for the reporter to set up. "That was a correct number, fifty-one, in less than a four-month period, about every other day?"

English was quiet. Davis loved the silence, his question hanging in the air.

"Isn't that a lot of gallbladder surgeries in just four months in a town the size of Plainview?"

Boxer quickly woke up. "Ask your next question, Mr. Davis."

Davis regrouped. "In an open procedure, a large incision is made, and the surgeon physically removes the gallbladder, right?"

"Yes."

"In a laparoscopic procedure, three little holes are made and a camera and laser are used?"

English spent the next fifteen minutes describing the procedure and how the laser burns away the gallbladder. English also described an open procedure. He explained why the laparoscopic procedure was better for the patient. There was a much quicker recovery time: back at work or back to your family sooner.

Davis let English talk. He believed that English was

delusional enough to think that he was connecting with the jury. Davis was sure that Pierce had told English to keep his answers short. English had, for the most part, listened until now.

Davis waited for English to catch his breath. "How many open procedures did you do after October 1991 through January 31st, 1992?"

"I don't know, but it wasn't many. Nobody wanted the open, the pain, the scar, and the longer recovery time."

"The answer is none, Doctor. Remember, I have the surgical logs."

Davis was glad he had those surgical logs; he wished he still had the pathology slides so he could prove that most of the fifty-one gallbladders removed by English were healthy. Unfortunately, the jury would never know the truth.

Davis decided not to pull out the surgical logs. The jury believed him.

"You botched the surgery, didn't you?"

"That's your opinion, and you're not a surgeon." English led with his chin.

"Well, I may not be a surgeon, but my expert Dr. Adams is a general surgeon with twenty-five years of experience, and he claims that the surgery was unnecessary and that your conduct was reckless."

"He would say anything you asked him to say. He's on your payroll."

"So you're telling this jury that you weren't the cause of Rosie Malone getting septic and then dying?"

"I don't know why she became septic, but that's a well-recognized risk of laparoscopic gallbladder surgery."

"It could have been an open procedure, right?"

"She didn't want a scar. She was very vain."

"You're telling this jury that Rosie Malone, age sixty-seven, insisted on a laparoscopic procedure rather than an open one because she didn't want her scar to show when she wore her bikini to the beach?"

English turned red in face, he was so angry. That's what Davis wanted.

He asked the next question: "You say she didn't want a scar, but was that worth risking her life? You did nick her bowel with the laser, didn't you?"

"I don't know. That's a possibility."

Davis was wearing English down. He was sweating, and he was about to explode.

"What other explanation is there?"

"Spontaneous combustion!"

Davis let that answer hang in the air. The smart-ass answer wouldn't sit well with the jury. Davis suggested to the court that it was a good time to break for lunch. The judge agreed.

When they came back from lunch, Davis went through the Malone chart with English. It was a little boring, but it was essential. Morty taught him that before you put your experts on the stand, the patient's medical records, which were what your experts relied upon, had to be in evidence.

Davis reviewed the only two progress notes that Dr. English made. "Why did you only make two progress notes, and there's no indication in the records that you saw her after the first day postoperation?"

"You know I went on vacation with my family the day after the surgery to Nassau, in the Bahamas."

"Did you tell Mrs. Malone before her surgery that

you wouldn't be around to help with her postoperative care?"

"I don't think so."

"So she thought her surgeon would be around if there were complications?"

"She was Dr. Herman's patient. He had treated her for years."

Davis got English to admit that Mrs. Malone was a complicated patient with a long medical history. He also admitted that Dr. Herman's office records reflected that history and those problems. Davis handed English Dr. Herman's records and asked him to read from the first page. He couldn't. Davis then handed him Dr. Herman's admission note for the January 1992 hospitalization of Rosie Malone. He couldn't read that note either.

"Doctor, if you can't read Dr. Herman's handwriting, how did you communicate about the care of your patients, such as Rosie Malone?"

"By telephone or in person."

"Doesn't that defeat the purpose of medical records?"

Davis didn't get an answer to that question, and the lack of response suited him just fine.

They used the transcribed version of the medical records, since no one could read Dr. Herman's handwriting, not even Dr. Herman. Davis kept asking English why Mrs. Malone wasn't transferred to Nashville in light of her persistent fever over 104. English kept insisting that he wasn't there and that Dr. Herman was in the best position to make that call. After much badgering, Davis got him to admit that maybe Herman should have transferred her sooner.

"Rosie Malone died because of your recklessness and the recklessness of Dr. Herman, didn't she?"

"Dr. Herman was trying to figure out the problem. You weren't there. Your paid experts weren't there."

"All we have is your and Dr. Herman's version of what happened, right? Rosie Malone is dead?"

"Yes, she's dead."

"Wait! We do have the medical records, including your operative report, which you, Dr. Herman, and the nursing staff of the hospital created?"

"Yes."

"That's the best evidence of what happened, the written record, right?"

English didn't respond.

"That's what the plaintiff's experts are relying upon. No further questions."

Boxer ordered a fifteen-minute break and left the bench.

CHAPTER FORTY-FIVE

SUBSEQUENT TREATING PHYSICIAN

FRIDAY, AUGUST 12, 1994

The hard rain on this Friday morning cooled the courtroom by at least ten degrees. August in Middle Tennessee was usually brutal and the humidity unbearable.

The courthouse square of Hewes City opened early, about six. Davis refused to eat out of his car, as they did on the first two days of the trial. Today the four (they had to include Littleton) dined at Mother's, a greasy spoon on the square.

Davis was feeling pretty confident. He wasn't afraid of the jury, and they were no longer wary of him. The problem really was that he was no Jack Barnes. Davis quickly made friends with the jury; Barnes was a lifelong friend, who'd helped family members and friends out of serious problems and jams. Davis knew the defense's saving grace, as disreputable as the defendants were; Jack Barnes sat at their table. Barnes was connected to both Plainview and Hewes City: he maintained a one-room office in Plainview and had his main office on the court square of Hewes City.

Davis sat at the table at Mother's, trying to finish proofreading his proposed closing jury instructions. Each side was required to submit to the court what it purported the law was. Sometimes, the answer was clear, and what both sides submitted on a particular issue was identical. Other times, the answer was unclear, subject to interpretation or by conflicting precedent from past cases.

Frequently, Tennessee law didn't have the answer, and both parties cited law from other jurisdictions. Morty taught Davis to avoid citing California law. You were better off citing the law of Mars in a Tennessee court. Interestingly, New York or Delaware law, particularly in business cases, carried extra weight.

The big problem was the doctrine of comparative fault and the new law on recklessness and punitive damages because there were no clear answers. Davis inserted his interpretation of the two cases in his proposed jury instructions. He admitted to himself that Boxer would have an even more difficult job of choosing whose interpretation to follow. He might even go in his own direction. Davis struggled with the proposed instructions for days, but he had to meet the deadline at the close of court today so the judge could read them over the weekend.

Davis was worn out. He had stayed up till one every night, either preparing for trial the next day or dealing with office problems that Bella brought to him. For all intents and purposes, Bella was running the office and practicing law. At best, she would steal Davis's attention for thirty minutes every day. He stood at her desk at seven each night and signed letters and pleadings that she prepared (often asking for an extension of time) and reviewed telephone messages. Bella called the client or adversary counsel the next day to convey information or extend an apology. Davis knew how amazing Bella was, and he appreciated everything she did. She was keeping his law practice afloat singlehandedly.

After breakfast, Davis and his group walked over to the courthouse and settled in for the day. The jury, led by the judge's clerk, came into the courtroom.

Boxer entered the courtroom and was all business: "Call your first witness, Mr. Davis."

"The plaintiff calls Dr. Randall Sizemore."

Dr. Sizemore had gone to the University of Tennessee on a football scholarship and then on to medical school at Davis's alma mater, Vanderbilt. Davis examined him thoroughly to establish his credentials. He wasn't about to have a Dillingham fiasco.

Sizemore explained that he was a gastroenterologist, a medical subspecialty that dealt with ailments of the stomach. They established that he had treated Rosie Malone on three occasions and that his diagnosis was irritable bowel syndrome. Sizemore confirmed that in each of his three office notes he documented that she was suffering from irritable bowel syndrome and that the proper course was medication.

"So, if Dr. Herman in October 1991 had simply looked at your office records for Mrs. Malone, he would have seen that you were treating her for irritable bowel syndrome?"

"Yes, it was clearly reflected in my records. Dr. Herman never requested them."

"Is that a breach of the standard of care, Doctor?"

"It's my practice, and it's good medicine. I don't think it's required by the standard of care, but information helps you better diagnose and treat your patients."

"What is the treatment for irritable bowel syndrome?"

"I would recommend a restricted diet and medication."

"Was that your treatment of Miss Rosie?"

"Yes, she was placed on a bland diet. I prescribed nicotine patches so she could address her nicotine addiction. Cigarettes were a serious health issue because of her history. Her smoking was causing respiratory, heart, and stomach problems."

Dr. Sizemore conceded that Mrs. Malone had a low tolerance for pain and used narcotics daily.

"Was Mrs. Malone's pain psychological or physiological?"

"Both. It was physiological, but it also had a psychological component. She exaggerated the pain in her mind. To her, the pain was unbearable."

"Doctor, have you ever given a patient sterile saline and misrepresented that it was pain medicine?"

"Absolutely not. That would be unethical. The only time that would be appropriate would be a drug study."

When Davis first learned that Dr. Herman provided sterile saline to address Rosie Malone's pain, Davis was amazed. It seemed dishonest to him, even if Herman's motives were allegedly good. Davis strongly believed that a professional, either medical or legal, should never intentionally deceive his patient or client.

"Have you reviewed Mrs. Malone's hospital record from February 1992 and Dr. Herman's office record?"

"Yes, I have."

"Did you ever do an ultrasound of Mrs. Malone's abdomen to make your diagnosis?"

"Yes, sir, on June 15th, 1991, I did an ultrasound in my office and determined that Mrs. Malone's gall-bladder was functioning fine and that she had no gallstones. I also reviewed the sixteen medications that she was on and decided to discontinue five of them. This lady was on a tremendous number of medications, many of which contradicted the others in cause and effect. There is no way to know how each of those drugs impacted the other fifteen. The first thing I did, in June, was to start weaning her off certain drugs that I thought were contradicting. When I reviewed Herman's office records in October, he put her back on four of the medications that I had deleted and added three more."

Dr. Sizemore confirmed that he reviewed Mrs. Malone's February 1992 hospital records. He testified that the admission to the hospital was unnecessary and that rather than surgery, Mrs. Malone should have been treated with medication, a bland diet, and nicotine patches to help her stop smoking.

"Doctor, you are a gastroenterologist, specializing in the stomach. Have you reviewed Mrs. Malone's ultrasound done in Dr. Herman's office and at the hospital taken before her 1992 surgery?"

"Yes, I have reviewed all three and Dr. Gerald's report. There were no significant gallbladder disease, no gallstones, and no reason for the surgery performed by Dr. English. I can't imagine why English did the surgery and Herman allowed it. She was Herman's patient. He had an obligation to protect his patient."

"Was the surgery a breach of the standard of care?"

"Absolutely. It was negligence of the worst kind."

Davis read the legal definition of *recklessness* to Sizemore and asked, "Doctor, in your professional opinion was the surgery reckless?"

"Mr. Davis, any medical student who reviews Mrs. Malone's chart would not allow that patient to have undergone that surgery. The most basic training and understanding of medicine are all that was necessary to question the surgery. These doctors knew better. They did disregard the medical information and, in a gross deviation from the standard of care, went forward with that surgery. It was reckless."

Davis waited for the testimony to sink in before continuing; the silence was deafening, particularly for the defendants. Dr. Sizemore, without looking at the chart, discussed the specific details of Mrs. Malone's final days at the hospital. He indicated that it was apparent that Dr. English nicked the patient's bowel during her surgery. Sizemore insisted that the antibiotics weren't working, and her temperature remained over 104 after the 2nd.

"She was septic. Bile was flowing through her bloodstream, literally poisoning her from within."

Davis discussed with Sizemore the failure to transfer Mrs. Malone from the hospital to Nashville until February 5th. The doctor cited several reasons why transfer no later than the 3rd was required under the standard of care. He indicated that by the time the patient was transferred, she had a less than ten percent chance of survival because she was too far gone.

Davis asked, "Was it recklessness to wait until the 5th to transfer the patient?"

Sizemore didn't answer right away. He was choosing his words carefully and said, "This patient should have been transferred on the 2nd, no later than the morning of the 3rd. Their decision to keep her at Plainview was a conscious decision. The utilization review nurse also looked at the chart on the 2nd. There had to be a discussion about transfer on the 2nd or 3rd.

The patient's temp was 104.7. That discussion is not reflected in the hospital record. They all failed to document that discussion. The decision not to document the reasons for keeping the patient was also a conscious decision. The failure to transfer under these circumstances, with no pulmonologist, no cardiologist, and limited facilities, was a gross deviation from the standard of care. It was reckless conduct on the part of Dr. Herman and the hospital; Dr. English had left the country."

Davis sat down, and Boxer took a break.

When court reconvened, McCoy was at the podium. He was wearing a royal blue bow tie with a beige suit. His hair was salt and pepper, which gave him an air of experience and respectability. McCoy was ready to cross-examine the witness.

As soon as the jury was seated, Boxer nodded to McCoy, and he went after Dr. Sizemore. He got the witness to concede that he treated Mrs. Malone for irritable bowel syndrome for four months and was unable to improve her condition.

"Mrs. Malone didn't stop smoking, did she?"

"No, sir, she didn't."

"She didn't stick to that bland diet, did she?"

"She was not compliant."

Dr. Sizemore admitted that Mrs. Malone was a difficult and complicated patient, who was on too many drugs, and that it was impossible to understand the interaction of so many drugs.

"If you had cured Mrs. Malone's problem in October, she never would have seen Dr. Herman in January?"

"I can't say that."

"Mrs. Malone stopped seeing you in October because she didn't get better under your care?"

"I don't know why she stopped seeing me. She decided to go back to Dr. Herman."

"You spent three office visits with Mrs. Malone, right?"

"Yes, sir."

"Maybe you treated her for a total of forty-five minutes?"

"That sounds about right."

"Who do you think knew this patient better, you, who spent less than an hour with her, or Dr. Herman, who treated her for years and saw her more than twenty times?"

"Dr. Herman."

Dr. Sizemore was excused, and Judge Boxer broke for lunch.

In the afternoon, Davis called two nurses who still worked at the hospital. Both described in detail how Rosie Malone deteriorated during her last days at Plainview Community Hospital. Davis turned and saw Thomas Malone's swollen eyes. He hoped the jury saw them as well.

Stevenson returned to his old theme: the doctors, not the nurses, practiced medicine. It reminded Davis of the defense of the Nazis at Nuremberg: "We were just following orders."

At the end of the day as Davis was leaving the courthouse to take a well-deserved Saturday off from Plainview, Lorraine Burke and one of her sisters approached him. "How do you think it's going, Mr. Davis?"

"So far, no major surprises, but it's far from over. Remember, they haven't gotten their turn yet. I know you're ready to testify. Sammie gave you very high marks."

"What a sweetheart she is. She's very patient. She's been working with both Thomas and me to get us ready."

"Lorraine, all you need to do is tell the truth. You saw firsthand how these so-called doctors dragged your mother through an unnecessary surgery, then couldn't figure out what went wrong and let her die to cover up their incompetence."

"I just hope I don't get too nervous."

"The members of the jury are just like you. They expect you to be a little nervous because they would be. Go have a nice weekend with your family. You'll probably testify on Tuesday or Wednesday."

On the ride home, Davis shared his conversation with Lorraine Burke with Morty and Sammie.

Sammie commented, "She'll be fine. She's a teacher. She talks in front of thirty students every day."

Davis reminded her that it wasn't the same. "She's the authority figure in the classroom, but in the courtroom, Judge Boxer's in charge."

They all agreed that they would take Saturday off and work all day Sunday. Dr. Adams and Dr. Swanson were driving in from Connors, Georgia, and were scheduled to testify on Monday.

After dropping Morty off at his farm, where he'd been living since the day after Davis's beating, Sammie asked if she would be welcome to have a home-cooked meal and to spend the night. Davis put the top down and drove them home to his loving family. Liza was still upset about the mounting bills and the trial's effect on her husband, but she mentally declared a truce so that he could concentrate and do his best to end the nightmare. The sooner the trial ended, the sooner the family could regain a sense of normalcy.

CHAPTER FORTY-SIX

EXPERT TESTIMONY

MONDAY, AUGUST 15, 1994

Davis spent a relaxing Saturday with his children, his wife, and Sammie. They went to the Cumberland Science Museum, a favorite place of both children, and took a short walk at Radnor Lake on the way home. Sammie left around nine after a gourmet dinner of shrimp scampi over pasta. Davis ate almost the entire loaf of bread by himself. The bread and butter worked just like Valium; they helped calm his nerves.

Sunday morning, the Davis team, except Morty, met Dr. Adams and Dr. Swanson at the office. Morty took the entire weekend off. He was worn out and desperately needed the rest. Bella brought an eggplant Parmesan casserole for lunch. Davis, Sammie, Bella, and the doctors spent most of the day preparing their direct testimony and discussing possible cross. Each expert's testimony outlined his statement that had been given to the defense more than a year ago, and both doctors had been deposed for several hours by McCoy and Pierce. Davis was pretty sure that there wouldn't be any surprises.

On Monday morning, Boxer called the court to order and asked Davis to call his next witness.

"Dr. Harlan Swanson," Davis said proudly.

Dr. Swanson described his background to the jury: undergraduate work at Vanderbilt University, medical school at the University of Georgia, and a fellowship in family medicine at Johns Hopkins. He had practiced family medicine in Connors, Georgia, just north of Atlanta, for the last ten years. Dr. Swanson described his office practice and how Connors was a similar medical community to that of Plainview. Davis wasn't going to make the same mistake that Dillingham had at the board hearing.

Davis reviewed with Swanson all of the documents and depositions he had reviewed in preparation for his testimony.

Swanson confirmed that he was paid $200 an hour and that he'd been paid a total of $18,000 in the Malone case, for ninety hours of work.

"Have you ever acted as an expert witness before?"

"No, sir, I generally support my fellow physicians. I believe that anyone is capable of making a mistake. Medicine is not perfect. Bad results occur. However, the care and treatment of Mrs. Malone were so far below the standard of care that I felt compelled to testify. This travesty has to be addressed and brought to light."

Davis needed to bring up the doctor's fee rather than wait for Pierce or McCoy to do so. All experts charged for their time, but how it was presented to the jury could impact how they viewed the witness's credibility.

Davis moved on to Mrs. Malone's office records written by Dr. Herman. Swanson testified that Herman's handwriting was illegible and defeated the purpose of medical records to communicate between health care professionals. He refused to confirm such handwriting was a breach of the standard of care.

Using the transcribed copy of Dr. Herman's office record, Davis reviewed Rosie Malone's chart with Dr.

Swanson. After thirty minutes, he asked, "Do you have a professional opinion on what was causing Mrs. Malone's stomach pain?"

Swanson testified that based upon the records, the patient was suffering from irritable bowel syndrome, and that he would have treated with medication, certainly not with saline.

Davis reviewed the Malone hospital chart with Swanson for an hour. Davis used the overhead projector and flashed several exhibits on a screen while Swanson explained each one's importance.

"Doctor, in your professional opinion, should Dr. Herman have transferred Mrs. Malone to Nashville before the 5th?"

"By the morning of the 3rd, there's no question she should have been transferred to Nashville. This patient was obviously septic, with a temperature of almost 105 for two days. She had a cardiac and pulmonary history, and there was no cardiologist, pulmonologist, or infectious disease specialist on staff at Plainview."

"In your professional opinion, was it reckless for Dr. Herman to wait until 6:00 p.m. on the 5th to transfer Mrs. Malone?"

"It was an obvious move. I can't understand why he waited so long. I've read his deposition three times, trying to figure out what he was thinking. His explanation makes no medical sense. I'm of the professional opinion that he didn't want the Nashville doctors to examine the patient, discover he had ordered an unnecessary surgery, provided grossly negligent postoperative care, and let her get septic. I've read the definition of *recklessness* several times. In fact, if you'd like, I can quote it to you. Dr. Herman's care and treatment of Mrs. Malone were inexcusable, and his failure to transfer was reckless."

Davis sat down, and McCoy jumped up. He practically ran to the podium. He was chomping at the bit to get to Swanson.

"Have you ever been sued, Doctor?"

"Yes, sir."

The lawsuit was no surprise to Davis or his team. It was disclosed in discovery, and Dr. Swanson had been questioned about it in his deposition.

McCoy established that Dr. Swanson was sued for failure to diagnose cancer in his patient.

"Were you reckless in your care of that patient?"

"Absolutely not. When she came in, I ordered the appropriate tests and made the correct diagnosis. It wasn't detected early enough."

"You settled that case, didn't you?"

"My insurance company insisted."

McCoy requested an immediate bench conference. He requested that the jury be instructed to ignore Dr. Swanson's last answer because, under Rule 409 of the Tennessee Rules of Evidence, the existence of insurance is not admissible. Davis argued that McCoy had opened the door by asking the question. Boxer decided that McCoy should move on to the next question rather than try to correct the testimony.

"You've made mistakes as a doctor?"

"Everybody makes mistakes. That's human. I'm not perfect, and neither are you."

"The fact that you've made mistakes doesn't mean you've been reckless, does it?"

"I've never been reckless because I've never disregarded the safety of one of my patients, like Dr.

Herman did with Rosie Malone."

Davis mentally chuckled as he heard Swanson shove the definition of recklessness, which he had memorized, right down McCoy's throat.

After lunch, Davis put Dr. Ralph Adams, the general surgeon, on the stand. Dr. Adams's testimony was directed at Dr. English's negligence and recklessness. He did a solid job, but after Swanson's finish, Davis found the testimony less dramatic.

Pierce did the cross. Davis admitted that, despite her limited experience compared to the other lawyers, she was quite effective. Dr. Adams looked a little ragged by the end of her examination.

"You testified on direct, by Mr. Davis, that you thought Dr. English was reckless in his care of Mrs. Malone?"

"I'm certain he was. The surgery never should have been performed. The fact that he nicked her bowel wasn't negligent. It was a known risk, but the unnecessary surgery was reckless."

"Doctor, isn't it true that the Medical Licensing Board dismissed all charges against Dr. English in his care of Rosie Malone?"

"On a technicality, he got off."

"Let me show you the order. Please read it to the jury."

"The alleged negligent and reckless claims against Dr. English for his care and treatment of Rosie Malone are dismissed."

"Isn't it true that the same panel found Dr. Herman negligent and reckless in his care of Rosie Malone?"

"Yes, ma'am."

McCoy and Barnes certainly wanted to object, but Boxer ruled that both panel findings could be admitted. Pierce's questions exposed the ruling prematurely. Davis intended to ask Dr. Herman about the finding, but Pierce got there first. She maximized Dillingham's big mistake to the best interest of her client. She ended on that high note.

CHAPTER FORTY-SEVEN

MEDICINE IS AN ART, NOT A SCIENCE

TUESDAY, AUGUST 16, 1994

Dr. Herman had been dreading this day since a sheriff's deputy served him with the first Plainview complaint in October 1992. It had been an exhausting twenty-two months. He had been sued ten times, and the board brought charges. Herman swore to himself that, at the bottom of it all, was that bastard Davis. Herman dreamed of Davis, and they were not pleasant dreams. He wanted Davis, Steine, and their clients to disappear from the face of the earth.

Herman sat in the courtroom reflecting on how drastically his life changed. His once busy office and hospital practice was gone. His gross revenue was more than $1.5 million per year. Not too shabby for a sleepy little town like Plainview. After Davis, by January 1994, he had been forced to resign his appointment at the hospital, and his office practice had dried up almost completely. He still had a few loyal patients who, despite the lawsuits and other problems, stuck by him, to their credit and for the drugs.

Last week, Charlie English did a terrible job and was not prepared. Throughout the entire examination, Davis made him look like a fool. Herman knew the Malone chart inside and out. His attorneys, Barnes and McCoy, drilled him on the issues they knew Davis would raise.

He was ready, but he was nervous. D-day was less than fifteen minutes away.

The courtroom was filling up. It was a public hearing that anyone could attend, first come and first serve. Most days it was standing room only. Davis's clients were usually there. The representatives of both insurance companies were in constant attendance. They were footing the bill for the doctors' defense. Tennessee Mutual and PIC had each invested more than $600,000 in Plainview, and there was a lot more to spend. The insurance companies had a real vested interest in the outcome of the Malone case because seven other cases were behind it.

The hospital had a lot riding on the Malone case. Not only was its reputation in the community on the line, but it had paid Stevenson's firm more than $500,000. Woody Douglas was in and out; he still had a hospital to run, but Dr. Kelly remained. Kelly was the hospital's company representative.

Davis and his team arrived only minutes before nine. Several Malone children were with them. *Each one of the ten spawn wants a piece of the golden ring,* thought Herman. *I tried to help their mother. She was a very difficult patient to assess.* He kept telling himself that he had done his best and tried to help her, wishing he could believe it.

Davis called his first witness: "The plaintiff calls as an adverse witness, Dr. Lars Herman."

Herman thought, *Davis, you don't know how adverse I actually am. But you'll appreciate how adverse by the end of the day.* Barnes and McCoy schooled him not to be led by Davis. Pierce told English to give short answers, but Barnes and McCoy told Herman to expound on the medical questions. Obviously, the short answers hadn't worked for English.

Davis wasted no time. After establishing Herman's background and the fact that he was born in Germany, after World War II, and had grown up in Argentina, Davis went into his education. He made the doctor's résumé an exhibit and asked, "Doctor, I notice a gap in your résumé from 1982 through 1986. What were you doing those four years?"

"I was studying."

"You had already graduated from medical school. What were you studying?"

Herman knew that was coming. That fucking test would haunt him for the rest of his life. He just didn't test well. That didn't mean he wasn't a good doctor. "I was studying for the FLEX exam."

"That's the test that foreign-trained doctors must pass in order to practice medicine in the United States, right?"

"Yes."

Herman knew he was falling into a trap by giving one-word answers, but there really wasn't any good explanation.

Davis continued, "The FLEX exam only establishes minimum competency, right?"

Herman grunted a "yes."

Davis then painfully established that Herman had failed the exam eight times. He went slowly; it was brutal.

"Now, on the sixth time you took the exam, you were disqualified. Someone had stolen the exam, isn't that true?"

"The exam was stolen, so they threw out the exam."

"But they didn't throw out everyone's exam, only some, right?"

"I don't know."

"Let me read to you from the deposition of Dr. Allen Foster, who was the president of the division of the American Medical Association that monitors and issues the scores for the FLEX exam. Attached as an exhibit are the results of the fall 1984 FLEX exam, which show that fourteen candidates were disqualified."

Barnes jumped to his feet. "Objection! The defendant renews his objection to the testimony of Dr. Foster on the grounds of Rule 26. This testimony is not relevant to these proceedings."

Davis was ready for the objection. "Your Honor, Dr. Herman's unusual difficulty in passing the FLEX exam is very relevant. Dr. Herman and Dr. English are being offered as the defendant doctors' only expert witnesses. Dr. Herman's repeated failures to pass the FLEX exam go directly against his qualifications as an expert witness."

"Stop right there. I've ruled on this before trial. The testimony of Dr. Foster and the exhibit are admissible evidence. Objection overruled."

Davis established that Dr. Herman couldn't practice medicine until he passed the FLEX exam and that he was in limbo for more than five years because he kept failing the test.

Davis went back to Herman's background. He established when Herman came to Plainview. Another topic of questioning was the ownership of his office building and the fact that Dr. English was his tenant. Davis went through his contract with the hospital and his credentialing.

Davis then asked, "So, the hospital is paying Dr. English's rent to you? Has been since 1991 and has continued to pay his rent since October 1993 when English took a leave of absence?"

"Yes."

"So, the hospital has stood behind Dr. English?"

Before he could answer, Stevenson ran to the podium, objecting as he went. "Objection, Your Honor, improper question. The hospital simply honored its legal commitment. The hospital isn't—" Stevenson stopped midsentence and waited for Boxer to rule.

"Objection sustained. The hospital simply honored its contract with Dr. Herman, nothing more."

Davis plowed on: "Are you familiar with the Hippocratic Oath, Doctor?"

McCoy stood and argued, "The Hippocratic Oath is not relevant. The standard of care is the measure of liability."

Davis's quick response indicated he expected the objection. "Your Honor, the Hippocratic Oath is at the heart of the standard of care. I guarantee the court that if I asked ten doctors of different subspecialties what the common denominator of the standard of care was for each of those subspecialties, it would be the Oath. It's the most basic principle of medicine. The court cannot exclude its overall vision from this trial. These doctors, if they did nothing else, were required to live by its words. It is the Ten Commandments of medicine."

Even Herman thought that Davis was compelling. The judge directed Herman to read the Hippocratic Oath. Herman tried to read the long text with enthusiasm, but it was not an easy read, particularly because he was forced to do so.

Davis reviewed with Herman Mrs. Malone's medical history. In 1990, she had a heart attack and was treated by Dr. Herman at Plainview Community Hospital. She was a chronic smoker, and Herman had prescribed nicotine patches. Davis reviewed with him the sixteen medications that Mrs. Malone was on right before her January 1992 hospitalization, and he asked, "Isn't it true that every medication has side effects, Doctor?"

"Yes, but the benefits outweighed those side effects."

It took Davis twenty minutes, using the *Physicians' Desk Reference* (*PDR*), to review the sixteen medications that Dr. Herman prescribed to Rosie Malone and their side effects. "Doctor, there's no way on God's green earth that you could begin to fathom all the interactions of those side effects, right?"

Herman hesitated and then admitted that it would be difficult. He was committed to regaining points with the jury.

"Mrs. Malone was your patient from January 1990 through June 1991, and then she returned to your care in October 1991, correct?"

Herman took this as his opportunity to turn the tables. "The patient personally told me that one of her daughters made her go to a doctor in Nashville. To the best of my recollection, she told me that she did not want to but that she was forced to. According to her family, he was a GI specialist."

Herman confirmed that he never requested or reviewed Dr. Sizemore's records when he resumed treatment of Rosie Malone in October 1991.

"I didn't need his records. This was a chronically ill patient with almost no tolerance for pain. I would give her placebos, sterile saline, so she would feel like her complaints were being addressed. I tried to wean her off narcotics. When I replaced them with a placebo, she did just as well. I certainly didn't need Sizemore's records to deal with the patient. I had a trusting relationship with her. She would call my office, sometimes three and four times a day."

Herman claimed that, unlike Rosie Malone's family, he was supportive and comforting, and he tried to help her deal with her pain. "She was a chronically ill person, a hypochondriac with real problems. That's why she was so difficult to assess. Many of her symptoms were psychological while others were real. She told me that her family members didn't come to see her. She told me that they didn't understand and had abandoned her."

Morty rose and said four words: "Objection, Dead Man's Statute."

In Tennessee, the Dead Man's Statute prevented a witness from testifying about a conversation with a dead person because the deceased could not refute it.

Judge Boxer looked at McCoy and Barnes. They did not say anything, so Boxer sustained the objection.

The judge broke for lunch. It was past twelve, and they hadn't had a morning break.

When they returned, Davis reviewed the Malone chart with Herman. Herman knew the chart, but he did a poor job of explaining why the patient wasn't transferred when her condition deteriorated. He admitted that there was no pulmonologist, cardiologist, or infectious disease specialist at Plainview and that the patient needed those medical subspecialties.

Davis had him spinning by the end of the examination. It was almost four o'clock when he asked his last question on direct: "Doctor, you filled out Rosie

Malone's death certificate, correct?"

Herman squirmed in his seat. "Yes."

Davis continued, "But you were not the attending physician at the time of Miss Rosie's death in Nashville. The law and medical ethics require that the attending physician fill out the death certificate. Why did you violate the law and your ethics?"

Barnes objected, stating that the question called for a legal conclusion. The judge overruled the objection. Davis repeated the question.

Herman hesitated and then said, "Because it was mailed to me, and I didn't know the law."

Davis responded, "Doctor, everybody knows that ignorance of the law is no excuse."

Davis handed Dr. Herman the Medical Licensing Board finding that he was negligent and reckless in his care of Rosie Malone. Dr. Herman cringed because he knew what was coming.

"The board that found you reckless in your care of Mrs. Malone consisted of three doctors?"

"Yes, sir."

"And the state had its own expert that asserted you were reckless, right?"

"Yes, sir."

"And the state's expert testified basically the same as Dr. Sizemore and Dr. Swanson?"

"I've not compared their testimonies."

"They've each testified that the surgery was unnecessary and that it was reckless not to transfer before the 5th?"

"I guess so."

Davis sat down, convinced that the jury saw Herman for what he was.

Pierce asked only one question: "The same panel that found you reckless dismissed all claims against Dr. English for his care of Rosie Malone?"

Herman choked out, "Yes."

Herman's face filled with fury. He wasn't sure who he hated more, Benjamin Davis or Amy Pierce.

Judge Boxer broke for the day.

CHAPTER FORTY-EIGHT

THE HOSPITAL'S LIABILITY

WEDNESDAY, AUGUST 17, 1994

Sister Carson and Dr. Laura Patel spent Tuesday night at the Davis home preparing the Sister's testimony. She was to take the stand the next day. She felt stressed, but Laura sat with her, and Davis guided them through the depositions, the plaintiffs' strategy, and the hospital's liability as well as the liability of the doctors.

From their conversations, Laura knew that Sister Carson had already read her own deposition six times, though in good conscience, she had charged for only three. She explained to Laura that she had been questioned thoroughly at her deposition in January by the defense team: first by Stevenson, then by McCoy, and finally by Pierce. Davis hadn't asked her any questions, so the deposition was taken from the defendants' perspective. Davis explained that there was no need to question her because Sister Carson agreed to testify live at trial.

Although she no longer lived in the house, Sammie stayed the night working on the Plainview cases and drove Laura and Sister Carson to the Hewes County Courthouse. Davis had to go to the office to read and sign documents in an unrelated case before leaving for court.

Laura, Sister Carson, and Sammie were seated in the first row when the lawyers began to arrive. Laura recognized McCoy, Stevenson, Barnes, and Pierce. She couldn't forget Stevenson, who pulled out the recorder the day she was suspended from the hospital. She knew Sister Carson's testimony was damaging to all the defendants, but it was most critical of the hospital.

The courtroom filled up quickly. It must have been very close to nine when Davis and Morty entered the courtroom.

Dr. Herman came in and sat between Barnes and McCoy. As Laura was staring at Dr. Herman, an officer and Dr. English entered the courtroom.

The trial began almost immediately after the judge entered the courtroom. The judge's clerk swore in Sister Carson, and Morty began with the Sister's background. She had been a nurse in Vietnam and joined the order in 1965. She held various positions and worked in the Congo. Sister described her rise in the ranks at Saint Francis and her move from nursing into administration. She detailed her duties as president and CEO of Saint Francis, including her dealings with the board and the various medical committees. She was a member of the American College of Hospital Executives, and she was the keynote speaker for the group in 1993.

Laura was proud of her mentor, an amazing woman whose life focused on medicine and God.

Sister Carson then described in detail the role of the Joint Commission on Accreditation of Healthcare Organizations, JCAHO. She made it clear that there were different levels of hospitals, but within each level the standard of care was the same throughout the country. She confirmed that both Plainview and Saint Francis were about the same size, 225 beds, and were at the same level within JCAHO. The Sister testified that the standard of care at both hospitals was, or should have been, the same.

Morty announced that he offered Sister Carson as an expert witness.

Sister Carson, through Morty's questioning, described the standard of care at a community hospital such as Plainview and the hospital's responsibilities in credentialing its medical staff.

She took up the responsibilities of the medical committees and the Executive Committee of the hospital. She emphasized the difficulty of the hospital administrator's job because the administrator had to be an advocate for the patients, the nursing staff, and the medical staff while also protecting the administration.

Morty asked her to look at her affidavit; it was her résumé. He made that ten-page document the next exhibit. He then asked her to look at the next exhibit, the list of materials she reviewed. The first document was the complaint in the Malone case, which was more than an inch thick. He laid the document on the table where Thomas Malone and the plaintiff's counsel sat. He identified the next document on the list, asked if the Sister reviewed it, and then placed it on top of the other document. He spent the next ten minutes repeating the process and creating a pile. Within no time, the stack of documents was as thick as two telephone books.

Based on their expressions, Laura could tell that the jurors were intrigued and were paying close attention to Morty's theatrics.

Stevenson broke in with an objection, arguing repetition.

Morty was prepared for the objection: "May I please address the objection, sir?"

"Of course, Mr. Steine."

Boxer respected Steine, despite his earlier finding of contempt, and afforded him great deference. He was the type of person who commanded every room he entered. Morty had not taken the lead in the Plainview cases, but his presence was always there. Boxer also obviously recognized his contribution.

Stevenson argued that Mr. Steine had already introduced the list of documents and that he was wasting valuable time reviewing each document with the witness: "It's highly prejudicial, and any good from identifying these documents is outweighed by the prejudice. It should be excluded in accordance with Rule 4.03."

Morty countered with the obvious: "In order for the jury to weigh Sister Carson's testimony, they need to know how extensive her investigation of the records was."

Boxer agreed and allowed Morty to continue to build his pile. By the time he finished, it was four feet high, and the jury was watching it carefully to see if it would topple over. Morty was quite a showman; he held the jury's complete attention.

"You're pretty busy running Saint Francis Hospital. Is that a forty-hour-a-week job?"

"No, sir. I'm on call twenty-four, seven, and I work about sixty hours a week."

"So, when did you read all this material?"

"Well, these documents have been sent to me over an almost two-year period. As depositions were taken, Mr. Davis would send me a copy. I worked at night and during my free time."

"Have you been paid for your time?"

"Yes, I have been paid $100 an hour for my time, but I did not charge for every hour."

"What do you mean?"

"Well, for example, I've read my deposition at least six times. I think I charged for only three. That is true of many documents."

"How much have you been paid in total?"

"I've received $11,400, but I donated every cent I was paid to the church. I didn't agree to testify because of the money."

"Why did you testify?"

"Because it was the right thing to do."

The judge decided it was a good time to stop for lunch. Within an hour and fifteen minutes, the Sister was back on the witness stand.

Sister Carson testified that a hospital owed certain obligations to its community and patients, according to the JCAHO manual. For instance, JCAHO required that the hospital secure an informed consent for all tests and surgeries performed at the facility.

"JCAHO requires that the hospital only issue medical privileges to their medical staff for which they are competent, and the hospital must maintain an adequate Quality Assurance Plan to protect the patients.

"I am of the professional opinion that the governing boards of Plainview Community Hospital, its Board of Directors, Board of Trustees, Executive Committee, and the various other committees, breached the standard of care and breached their obligations to patients, including Rosie Malone."

There was fire in Sister Carson's eyes as she spoke: "I am of the opinion that Plainview Community Hospital permitted members of its medical staff, Dr.

Herman and Dr. English, to provide substandard medical care as described in the testimony of Dr. Adams and Dr. Swanson. Plainview Hospital did not establish and enforce an adequate quality assurance of its patients."

Sister Carson testified that she reviewed the credentials of both Dr. Herman and Dr. English and that Plainview Hospital had not followed the standard of care in its credentialing of those physicians.

Sister Carson was critical of Dr. English's training in laparoscopic surgery: "He only performed surgery on a pig." She testified, "There was no proctorship. The hospital just let him loose to perform surgery; it was a breach by the hospital of the standard of care."

The Sister quoted specific sections of the JCAHO manual that the hospital violated. She also quoted specific sections of the hospital's own bylaws that it violated. She concluded her direct testimony: "I have carefully reviewed all the testimony, and I am of the professional opinion that the hospital's, Dr. Herman's, and Dr. English's treatment of several of their patients was in reckless disregard of the safety of their patients' lives. If the hospital acted within the standard of care, both Dr. English and Dr. Herman would have been suspended long before poor Rosie Malone was admitted to Plainview Community Hospital on January 29th, 1992."

Morty sat down, and Grayson Stevenson walked to the podium.

Laura didn't dislike many people, but everyone she hated was in this courtroom, and Stevenson was among them.

"Sister, does your order know that you're giving expert testimony in this case?"

"Absolutely, my Mother Superior notarized my expert statement, and as you well know, Dr. English threatened her."

Pierce was on her feet within two seconds.

Laura knew exactly what happened. Stevenson figured that English's threat toward the Mother Superior increased Dr. English's portion of the liability pie, thereby reducing the liability of the hospital.

Stevenson tried to get the witness to testify that her nurses at Saint Francis didn't practice medicine and followed the doctors' care plan. The Sister fought back hard and didn't let Stevenson put words in her mouth.

"I expect my nurses to bring to my attention anything a doctor does that they seriously question. If the treatment is below the standard of care, they're required to bring it to the doctor first, and if he's ignoring them, then to me."

"But these nurses aren't doctors. They're not familiar with the appropriate standards."

"Says who? The standard of care is what a reasonable doctor would do under similar circumstances. They watch doctors treat patients every day. They know what to expect, and if they see substandard care, they better speak up. In fact, Nurse Perry's job as utilization nurse was to question whether or not the orders of the doctors were appropriate."

Stevenson shut up and sat down. The witness had gotten the better of him.

Pierce got up next. "You've testified that all three defendants were negligent and reckless in their care of Rosie Malone?"

"Yes."

"You're not a medical doctor or a surgeon?

"That's right. I'm a registered nurse and certified hospital administrator."

"Are you aware that a medical panel of three doctors dismissed all claims against Dr. English for his care and treatment of Rosie Malone?"

"I read the hearing. They did, but they didn't want to."

"Move to strike that answer."

"Stricken," Boxer proclaimed.

"I need a yes or no?"

Sammie thought that Pierce was being unfair and trying to mislead the jury. *Why am I surprised? Maybe the jury will see through her deception.*

CHAPTER FORTY-NINE

THE CHILDREN ARE HEARD

THURSDAY, AUGUST 18, 1994

Sammie spent days preparing two of the Malones to testify: Thomas and Lorraine. They were the oldest. Thomas was the court-appointed administrator of the estate, and Lorraine insisted on the transfer. Sammie told her uncle that Lorraine was the stronger witness, so he called Thomas first.

Davis quickly established how Thomas was related to Rosie Malone and how he had been elected administrator as the oldest living child. He testified that after his daddy died, his momma raised them the best she could. He talked about her work at the bakery and the deterioration of her health that forced her to retire.

Plainview was a small town, and most of the residents knew most of the Malone clan. But this was Hewes City, so Thomas's testimony was new to the jurors.

Sammie went shopping with Thomas and helped him pick out his blue blazer. But Davis and Morty agreed: no tie. Thomas would have looked out of place with a tie.

He was a mechanic and had to take off a lot of work to be the administrator, including two weeks for this trial. "Someone in the family had to step up. I'm the oldest. It was my responsibility to do it."

Davis went through all of Rosie Malone's medical problems up to February 1992.

"I thought she was in good hands with Dr. Herman. It was my sister, Lorraine, who made Momma go to see the specialist in Nashville."

"Dr. Sizemore?"

"Yes, sir, he was a stomach doctor."

"Was your mother addicted to narcotics?"

"I don't know if she was addicted, but she liked her pills. She was in a lot of pain, and they made her feel better."

"In February, did you visit your mother at Plainview Community Hospital when she had her gallbladder out?"

"Not until after the surgery, when her temperature was high. Lorraine called me and told me the surgery didn't go well and that Momma was real sick."

"Did you talk to either Dr. English or Dr. Herman after her surgery?"

"I've never met Dr. English. I was standing there when Lorraine begged Dr. Herman to transfer Momma to Nashville. Dr. Herman told her that he had everything under control and that Momma shouldn't be moved."

"Did you believe him?"

"Yes, sir. I'm no doctor. If you need someone to work on your Chevy truck, I'm your man. But I don't know anything about medicine. He'd been her doctor for years. I know Momma trusted him."

"If the jury awards your family money, what will you do with it?"

"We'd split it into two parts. The first part we'd divide up eleven ways. Momma had eleven kids, but

Melvin's dead. We'd give his share to his two kids, Bubba and Kimberly. The other half we'd put in some kind of trust for the education of all the grandkids and great-grandkids. Momma would've liked them to get educated."

"What would you do with your share?"

"First thing I'd do is put an angel headstone on Momma's grave. Depending how much there was, second, I might put a down payment on a house in Plainview with a few acres."

Sammie thought that he gave a good, honest answer. A juror could identify with it. The education trust was Lorraine's idea, and it was a good use of the money.

McCoy crossed first. "You say that your mother trusted Dr. Herman. If she had lived, do you think she would have sued him?"

"Momma didn't believe in lawsuits—"

"But you obviously believe in them, right?" McCoy interrupted.

"It was a family decision. Lorraine convinced my brothers and sisters that it was the right—"

"So Lorraine Burke, your sister, is behind this lawsuit?"

Sammie didn't think McCoy was giving Thomas time to answer, and she wished her uncle would object.

"She's a teacher. She understands more than the rest of us about—"

Davis rose and said, "He's not letting the witness answer the questions."

"Stop cutting off his answers, Mr. McCoy."

McCoy straightened his lavender bow tie and moved on. "Your mother was a smoker for forty years, right?"

"Yes, sir."

"She was prescribed narcotics for pain?"

"Yes, sir."

"She was so addicted that Dr. Herman gave her fake drugs, placebos, some of the time?"

"I learned that during the trial. I didn't know that."

"You didn't know your mother was a drug addict, did you?"

"Momma wasn't a drug addict!" Thomas was about to lose it.

McCoy could smell blood in the water. "What do you call someone who takes narcotics twice a day?"

"I'm no doctor."

"You're not much of a son either. You didn't visit your mother in the hospital until you thought she was dying?"

Davis jumped up and yelled, "Argumentative!"

Thomas got up and started for McCoy.

Sherriff Dudley rushed forward and placed himself between Thomas and McCoy. Davis also rushed forward.

McCoy in a low voice said snidely, "I have no further questions for this witness."

Pierce and Stevenson passed because they couldn't achieve a better stopping point. Her uncle also passed. Thomas was too upset to continue.

Sammie thought, *Thomas was a good witness until his outburst. He lost control, and that won't sit well with the jury.*

After lunch, Davis called Lorraine to the stand. She was dressed in her Sunday best, and she didn't appear nervous at all. She had taught American history to tenth graders for the last twenty-two years. She was the only Malone child with a college degree.

She talked about her mother's health and the fact that she tried to get her to stop smoking. She blamed Dr. Herman for her drug use. "She had never used anything stronger than an aspirin until he came to town."

Sammie grinned at that answer.

Lorraine testified that in the summer of 1991, she convinced her mother to see Dr. Sizemore, a specialist in Nashville. It wasn't that she didn't trust Dr. Herman. She just thought a specialist should see her mother.

"But Momma was very loyal to Dr. Herman, so after only three visits to Dr. Sizemore, she insisted on being treated by Dr. Herman."

Davis went through the Malone records until he got to the January 31st gallbladder surgery.

"Dr. Herman showed me the ultrasound and where the stones were. He lied to me. He lied to my mother. He wanted her to have the surgery so he could make money."

McCoy objected, "Calls for speculation. She couldn't possibly know what Dr. Herman was thinking."

Boxer sustained the objection, so Davis asked, "You know the board found that the surgery was unnecessary?"

"Yes, that's the same surgery that killed her."

McCoy objected, "Calls for a medical conclusion."

"Overruled, there's been no other explanation, other than Dr. English's suggestion of spontaneous combustion."

McCoy tried the same tactic with Lorraine, but she wouldn't lose her cool. "You're about the money, aren't you?"

"We've sued for money, but I want your client put out of business. I don't want him hurting or killing anybody else."

"So you're about money *and* revenge?"

"Dr. Herman deserves whatever this jury dishes out to him. I'll be happy with their verdict. I'm confident they'll be fair."

Sammie was very pleased with Lorraine's last answer and her testimony as a whole. Obviously so was her uncle. After McCoy sat down, Davis closed his proof.

Boxer said, "Let's quit a little early today. Tomorrow, the defendants will begin their proof."

He addressed the jury: "Remember, the defendants haven't yet had their turn, so don't predetermine the case. Go back to the motel and have a good dinner, and we'll see what the defendants have to say in the morning."

CHAPTER FIFTY

THE DEFENSE STEPS UP

FRIDAY, AUGUST 19, 1994

The plaintiff's proof lasted eight full trial days. All of the proof was damaging to Dr. English, Dr. Herman, or the hospital. Pierce appreciated that a lawsuit was like a boxing match. It lasted ten rounds, and throughout the fight, each boxer threw punches, some of which landed while others missed. At the end of each round, the judges determined the round's winner. Whichever fighter won more rounds won the fight, unless there was a knockout. The key was to be standing at the end of the trial. Dr. Herman and Dr. English were standing, but just barely, and they lost every round but one.

Every lawsuit was divided into two distinct parts: liability and damages. The plaintiff proved negligence by more than the required preponderance of the evidence. Pierce anticipated that compensatory damages would be awarded; the purpose of her opening statement was to limit that amount. The unanswered question remained: Had Davis and Steine proved recklessness by clear and convincing evidence? Boxer, through his rulings, placed serious obstacles in their path. Pierce believed that they failed and that no punitive damages would be awarded.

Pierce was the only defense attorney who saved her opening statement until after the plaintiff's proof. She stood, walked to the podium, and started, "Ladies and gentlemen, this is my opportunity as Dr. English's attorney to tell you what the proof will show in this case. I elected to wait until after the plaintiff closed his proof so that I could deliver my opening statement, which reflects on the proof rather than on speculation, as Mr. Davis did at the beginning of this trial."

She paused to let the concept sink in. She continued, "It is a fact that Rosie Malone, prior to any treatment by my client Dr. English, was a sick woman. Before February 1992, she was hospitalized at Plainview Hospital three times for life-threatening health issues. She had a heart attack, COPD, and several other debilitating health problems. She had to retire from the bakery. At the time of her death, she had no income and was on Medicare. The plaintiff has not proved significant damages in this case, only minimal out-of-pocket expenses. Any compensatory damage award is a windfall to the Malone family."

She was about to attack Rosie Malone's character. It was easier because Mrs. Malone wasn't present to defend herself. An attack on an injured person, sitting between Davis and Steine, would have been more difficult.

"Rosie Malone was self-destructive. She smoked two packs of Camels each day for more than forty years. She wasn't even trying to cut back or even use a filtered cigarette. She even smoked after Dr. Herman insisted she quit smoking by prescribing nicotine patches. She used the patches and continued to smoke. Do you realize how dangerous it is to smoke and wear those patches? The combined use multiplies the dose of nicotine and exponentially increases the risks of stroke and heart attack."

Pierce was aware that three jurors were smokers. That question had been asked during jury selection. She needed to distinguish those jurors from her criticism of Mrs. Malone: "Smoking is a life-threatening addiction. We are all human, and to forgive is divine. But Rosie Malone had an even deeper secret that I am confident you will recognize as a part of her destructive behavior. She was a drug seeker and drug abuser. She had no tolerance for pain and a high tolerance for painkillers. Her pain was more in her mind than actual physical pain and suffering. Drugs made her feel better. Dr. Herman recognized her addiction and gave her fake narcotics, placebos, and they worked. She took the fake drugs and felt better.

"We're here about liability and damages. Mrs. Malone and the Malone family haven't suffered significant damages because of the negligence of the defendants. I further submit that mistakes were made. The most significant and egregious mistake occurred when Mrs. Malone was not transferred before the 5th to a better-equipped hospital. May I remind the jury that my client was not in town when these decisions should have been made? Mrs. Malone's postoperative care was the sole responsibility of Dr. Herman. Remember, the Medical Licensing Board dismissed all charges against Dr. English.

"Mrs. Malone's abusing her body for more than forty years caused the damage. I submit that there has been no proof of recklessness to warrant an award of punitive damages.

"I remind you that you have heard the plaintiff's

entire case, and the defendants are only about to begin to present theirs. Please be fair and listen to our proof. The law and justice require that of you. Thank you for your time and attention."

She sat down and felt good about her opening. She decided she couldn't put English back on the stand. She had no other witnesses. Her last chance to convince the jury would be her closing argument. She was now relegated to watching the hospital put on its proof. She would be helpless as Stevenson attacked her client and Dr. Herman.

CHAPTER FIFTY-ONE

STABBED IN THE BACK

FRIDAY, AUGUST 19, 1994

Davis was satisfied with the plaintiff's proof. In his mind, there was no question that he had proved that Herman and English had been negligent and, more important, reckless in their care and treatment of Rosie Malone. Based on the evidence admitted, the jury knew that they were incompetent and motivated by greed. The proof clearly established that Rosie Malone's admission and surgery were unnecessary and that the hospital knew exactly what was going on.

Today was the hospital's opportunity to provide its proof. Davis figured that Stevenson had two choices: he could claim innocence, or he could convince the jury that the doctors were in charge of the patient's care and much more comparatively at fault. It was true, the greater the comparative fault of the doctors, the smaller the hospital's piece of the liability pie. Davis was absolutely convinced that the two-year alliance of the defense was about to crumble. A strategy of every man for himself was in the plaintiff's best interest.

The hospital's first witness was Dr. Leonard Sparks, the medical director of Davenport County Hospital, located south of Hewes City near the Alabama border. The hospital was offering the good doctor as an expert on how a community hospital conducts utilization reviews of the patients. As the medical director of a community hospital, Sparks served on several medical committees, including serving as chairman of the Davenport County Hospital Utilization Review Committee. He was also a family practitioner, like Dr. Herman.

At first, Davis couldn't figure out why the hospital offered Sparks as an expert witness. Sparks's expert witness statement was only three pages long; he had reviewed only the hospital's Utilization Review Plan and none of the depositions taken in the case. He was an expert for a very limited purpose. In contrast, Sister Carson's expert witness statement on the hospital's liability was fourteen pages long.

At his deposition, Sparks emphasized that the process of utilization review had nothing to do with patient care but was intended to protect the hospital from financial loss. The hospital, under its own rules and regulations, at periodic intervals had a nurse review each chart to confirm that the patient should remain in the hospital. Sparks's deposition testimony was that Plainview Community Hospital lost money on the Malone case because of inadequate utilization review but that the injury was to the hospital because it never got paid for those services.

At the deposition, Davis took a chance and asked Sparks questions that were outside the content of his expert witness statement about the specific care and treatment of Rosie Malone. Sparks's answers were damaging to both doctors. At the time, Davis thought he was brilliant, but in retrospect he knew he had been set up.

After the deposition, Davis and Morty realized

Stevenson's real purpose of offering Sparks as an expert. It was to shift as much of the liability, under comparative fault, to Herman and English as possible. Every percentage point assigned to Herman and English was a percent not assigned to the hospital. When the verdict was awarded, those percentage points would turn into real dollars.

Barnes and McCoy, in a pretrial motion, objected to Davis's cross-examination, but Boxer ruled the testimony was admissible. He held even though the hospital offered Dr. Sparks's testimony for the limited purpose of utilization review, he was a family doctor, qualified in the subject matters that Davis questioned him about, and therefore, the testimony was admissible.

That was exactly what Stevenson hoped for. Sparks's testimony on utilization review supported the hospital, but more important, Sparks's other testimony damaged Herman and English. Stevenson was using Davis to do his dirty work and lower the hospital's percentage of liability.

Stevenson called Sparks to the stand and began questioning him about his background. In addition to his other qualifications, Sparks chaired the Utilization Review Committee. Stevenson offered Sparks as an expert witness, though he intentionally did not specify Sparks's area of expertise.

Davis thought, *Stevenson is baiting either Barnes or McCoy to argue Sparks's qualifications in front of the jury.*

The crack in the defense was opened. For two years there had been a unified front. The brick wall was crumbling. Davis proved the doctors' negligent and reckless conduct, and the hospital could no longer ignore it, or it would go down, right alongside them.

Davis rose and sheepishly acknowledged that the witness was qualified, also intentionally not specifying in what. McCoy asked if the attorneys could approach the bench. Boxer turned off his microphone, and the defense counsel and Davis moved closely around the judge's bench. Morty and Littleton stayed seated. Davis wanted the jury to know that this was a fight between the defendants.

After the court reporter was set up, McCoy said, "Your Honor, neither Mr. Stevenson nor Mr. Davis has advised the jury what Dr. Sparks is being offered as an expert for."

Boxer leaned forward, tapped his fingers together, and smiled. He seemed to enjoy McCoy's predicament. "Mr. McCoy, we all know what's about to happen. I ruled on this pretrial. The hospital is offering Dr. Sparks as an expert in utilization review. Mr. Davis is going to cross-examine the hospital's expert on how the hospital committee system works and then finally his professional opinions about the care and treatment of Mrs. Malone. I have already ruled that Dr. Sparks is qualified to give those opinions."

McCoy was making a record for the appeal. "With all due respect, Your Honor is committing reversible error."

Boxer did not like McCoy's last remark and retorted, "I don't think you're right, Mr. McCoy. But if you are, we'll be doing this all over again, won't we?"

"That's what I'm trying to avoid, sir."

Boxer waved for everybody to return to his or her seat; he was losing his patience.

Stevenson asked the witness about the purpose of utilization review, and Dr. Sparks began: "I reviewed the Utilization Review Plan of Plainview Community Hospital. It's almost identical to the plan of Davenport County Hospital. Mrs. Malone was a Medicare patient; under the plan, prior to admission, her chart required review. At that time, all the information was in Dr. Herman's office record."

Sparks explained in no uncertain terms that utilization review was for the hospital's protection, not the patients'. "Hospitals generally lose money on Medicare patients because Medicare discounts its payments for many procedures. I have reviewed the chart of Mrs. Malone and the hospital bill for the charges. Medicare paid less than twenty percent of the actual charges. Plainview Community Hospital lost more than $40,000 in its care and treatment of this patient. Mrs. Malone was not a money maker for the hospital."

Sparks's testimony surprised the jury. It was clearly written on their faces.

"The purpose of utilization review is to prevent doctors from over-utilizing the hospital and to prevent the hospital from incurring expenses that do not get paid. The plan establishes certain deadlines for review. As I said, the first review, with a Medicare patient, is prior to admission. The second review is forty-eight hours after admission. Thereafter there is a required review at least every seventy-two hours."

Sparks described the role of the utilization review nurse, who was a hospital employee. He testified that Nurse Perry failed horribly to do her job. He insisted, however, that her poor performance caused no damage to Rosie Malone, but she did financially injure the hospital. Stevenson next discussed with Sparks the fact that the hospital guaranteed Dr. English's lease with Dr.

Herman and guaranteed Dr. English a minimum income of $10,000 per month. Sparks assured the jury that Plainview Community Hospital did nothing improper and that Davenport Community Hospital made similar guarantees, because he was the one who signed the contracts. Stevenson ended his examination of Dr. Sparks and turned the witness over to Davis.

Davis quickly established that he'd taken the witness's deposition in April. "You have reviewed Dr. Herman's office record. That was the only information that you had about Rosie Malone before her admission to Plainview Community Hospital on January 29th, 1992?"

"Yes, sir."

Dr. Sparks testified that Mrs. Malone's symptoms were abdominal pain and black stools. He admitted that a rectal should have been done but wasn't. He also admitted that he had reviewed Mrs. Malone's entire chart for her February hospitalization but could read neither Dr. Herman's office records nor his notations in the hospital records.

Dr. Sparks testified that the patient should not have been admitted into the hospital. Prior to her surgery, a forty-eight-hour review was required by the Plainview plan. He stated that the patient should have been discharged before the surgery.

Sparks acknowledged that he was of the same medical subspecialty as Dr. Herman. He testified that in his professional opinion, the ultrasounds done at Herman's office and at the hospital did not indicate surgery. He would not have recommended surgery to this patient.

Davis reviewed the balance of the chart with Sparks

and established how sick the patient became on the 4th. Sparks admitted that Herman should have discovered that Mrs. Malone had become septic. The obvious cause of the septicemia was the surgery performed by Dr. English by injuring the bowel. Dr. Sparks admitted that the patient should have been transferred to Nashville no later than the morning of the 4th.

"So, it was Dr. Herman's negligence that resulted in this patient undergoing unnecessary surgery?"

"She never should have been admitted, and she never should have had the surgery."

"Dr. English nicked her bowel during the surgery?"

"That's the most likely cause."

"Can you think of another, Doctor?"

"No, sir."

"Was the utilization review nurse negligent in not insisting that the patient be discharged prior to the surgery?"

"She didn't do a very good job. The hospital lost a lot of money on this patient."

"As the chairman of the Davenport County Hospital Utilization Review Committee, what action would you take if your utilization review nurse had done such a poor job?"

"I would fire her."

"It was that bad a job?"

"Yes, sir."

"If the Plainview utilization review nurse, a hospital employee, had done her job, Rosie Malone would be alive today?"

"I don't know."

Davis sat down after announcing no further questions. The defense lawyers representing the doctors collectively decided not to dig the hole any deeper by asking questions. It was better to get Sparks off the witness stand.

The hospital also put on the witness stand its head nurse, who explained that her nursing staff had followed the doctor's orders and that it was near impossible for a nurse to challenge a physician.

On cross, Davis asked, "If one of your nurses was of the professional opinion that a patient, under a doctor's current treatment plan, was going to die, and if an alternate treatment was available that would save the patient's life, what should she do?"

"Talk to the treating physician about the alternatives."

"What if the doctor rejected the alternatives available and continued under the same plan toward the patient's death?"

"She could talk to me; Woody Douglas, the hospital administrator; or Dr. Kelly, the medical director; or make a formal complaint to be reviewed by the appropriate committee."

"Did any of your nurses question Dr. Herman's care and treatment of Rosie Malone?"

"No, sir."

"Did anyone?"

"Dr. Laura Patel made a formal complaint."

Stevenson jumped up and objected on the grounds that the committee system and its findings were confidential. Boxer sustained the objection.

She admitted that Dr. Herman didn't transfer the patient until the evening of the 5th, despite the fact that Mrs. Malone's temperature was almost 105 for days.

"All of the nurses who treated her during those shifts did nothing?"

"They followed Dr. Herman's orders and treatment plan. The only person who complained was Dr. Patel."

"No further question."

There was no cross from the defense table. Davis hoped that Stevenson would make the tactical mistake of putting either Woody Douglas or the hospital's medical director on the stand. He would eat their lunch on cross. Unfortunately, Stevenson was too smart for that move and rested the hospital's case.

If Davis still had the pathology slides, he probably would have used them now in rebuttal to prove Ms. Johnston a liar. He hoped that he had proved the recklessness of all three defendants. He announced, "No rebuttal," and the proof closed.

Judge Boxer turned to the jury: "It is important the closing arguments be presented on the same day and not be broken up. I will give the jury the choice to either take the weekend off and start on Monday, or work through the weekend, even on Sunday, if the jury is willing. Let's take a half hour, and through your foreman, you can tell me your preference."

When they returned, Judge Boxer nodded at the foreman, and he stood. "We'd like to start tomorrow morning at nine, work through the weekend, and get our job done. We need to get back to our lives and our families."

"Court is adjourned till tomorrow at nine."

CHAPTER FIFTY-TWO

CLOSING ARGUMENTS

SATURDAY, AUGUST 20, 1994

Despite his desire to give the closing argument, Davis asked Morty to do so as a gesture of appreciation and respect. The old man earned his dollar, and he deserved it.

Boxer called his court to order, warned the jury "what the lawyers say is not evidence," and gestured for Davis to approach the podium.

"With the court's permission, Mr. Steine will be making the plaintiff's closing argument."

Morty rose and moved slowly in front of the jury. He had no notes, just more than forty years of experience.

"Ladies and gentlemen of the jury, I am an old man who's seen human nature at its best and at its worst. Medicine is a calling and it's also a business, but it's not a place for greed. We have a right to expect our doctors to place their patients' best interest and health ahead of their wallets.

"Dr. Herman, Dr. English, and the hospital administration of Plainview Community Hospital let the dollar, not the Hippocratic Oath, control their decision making. They recommended tests, procedures, and surgeries motivated by profit and not what was in the best interest of their patient, Rosie Malone. These defendants disregarded the most basic aspect of the standard of care, first do no harm."

Davis hoped that Sammie was not only listening but also watching Morty. His body language was so graceful, he almost danced around the courtroom. He resembled a lion, proud, powerful, and ready to pounce. His words were mesmerizing. The jurors couldn't take their eyes off him.

"Ladies and gentlemen, negligence, as Judge Boxer will explain, does not require that the plaintiff prove bad intent on the part of the defendants. To find negligence, all you have to conclude is that it is more likely than not that the defendants breached the standard of care. If, based upon the proof, being the testimony and documents introduced into evidence, the scales of justice tip in favor of the plaintiff, then the defendants were negligent, and you should award compensatory damages."

Davis expected a modest award of compensatory damages. Rosie Malone was neither a brain surgeon with a big income nor a young mother with a husband and three or four dependent children.

Morty spent the next forty-five minutes recounting the testimony of Dr. Swanson, Dr. Sizemore, Dr. Adams, and Sister Carson. He recited each breach of the standard of care to which each expert witness had testified. Using an overhead projector, courtesy of Sammie, Morty displayed about two dozen exhibits that proved the defendants' negligence.

At one point in his closing, Morty walked over to the defense table and stood behind Dr. Herman and Dr. English so the jury would stare at them for a long minute.

Davis could see on Morty's face that the adrenaline was coursing through him, but he needed to wrap things up.

"As the judge will tell you, the plaintiff gives the first closing and the last closing because the burden of proof is on the plaintiff. So, I will get the honor to speak to you later today, hopefully not tonight, because all three defendants get to speak before I return.

"Remember, Mr. Davis made you a promise at the beginning of this trial and told you that he would transcribe all the opening statements, even his own. Here they are."

Morty walked over to Davis, who handed him the four opening statements. Morty read to the jury highlights from Barnes's opening statement. Morty pointed out several incorrect statements made by Mr. Barnes, including his comment that Rosie Malone was a "drug seeker."

He next read portions of Stevenson's opening: "Mr. Stevenson's version of the facts is not correct. With all due respect to Mr. Stevenson, the hospital knew exactly what was going on and let it continue so it could make more money. I submit that not only should the hospital have known that these doctors were ordering unnecessary tests and performing unnecessary procedures but also that through several employees, including Woody Douglas, the hospital administrator, it did know."

Morty held up Pierce's opening statement and read sections to the jury. Then he said, "You've met Dr. English. You heard about the care he gave poor Rosie Malone. Was Ms. Pierce accurate in her opening statement? Not even close. Dr. English should never have performed surgery. He doesn't deserve to be called a doctor.

"The last opening statement that I'm holding in my hand is Mr. Davis's. He promised you what he believed the proof would show. Rather than read from this opening statement, which is over one hundred pages long, I'm going to challenge any member of the defense counsel to find a material statement in this opening statement that was not proved.

"I know that I've been long-winded, but I submit that the proof was long and that my presentation has been accurate. I have spent all of this time talking about the proof and the defendants' wrongful conduct.

"I need to say a word about Rosie Malone. You never got to hear from her, and you never will. Neither Mr. Davis nor I met her because these defendants cut her life short. She was a retired baker. She spent forty-one years baking and feeding Plains County. She was not a rich woman, but she had a worthwhile life and made a difference. The defendants will focus on the fact that she lost no income and that she was on Medicare at the time of her death. She had worked hard and was entitled to those benefits. The proof is clear. These defendants, through their negligence and recklessness, took her life away from her."

Morty slowly walked back to the table where Davis, Littleton, and Thomas Malone were seated. Malone grabbed Morty's hand and emotionally thanked him on behalf of his family.

After speaking for more than an hour, Morty was exhausted. He hadn't looked at one note. He spoke from the heart, and he surely touched the jury. He sat down, and Judge Boxer called for the morning break.

When they returned to the courtroom, Barnes was standing at the podium. Morty would be a tough act to follow, but Barnes couldn't change the fact that he represented Dr. Herman.

"I first want to thank each one of you for the time, patience, and attention you have afforded these parties. With all due respect, not only was Mr. Steine a little long-winded, as he admitted, but the entire plaintiff's case was drawn out unnecessarily. I submit that your time has been wasted. Mr. Davis and Mr. Steine, at great expense, brought in their expert witnesses. Those witnesses were paid more than $75,000 for their testimony. Sister Carson admitted that she was the dear friend of Dr. Patel, who was let go from the hospital staff because of a confrontation with Dr. Herman and Dr. English. Sister Carson is the definition of a biased witness."

Barnes stopped for effect. He looked at Dr. Herman and then back at the jury. "You heard Dr. Herman's testimony. Mrs. Malone was a very difficult patient to assess. She had a very low tolerance for pain and often was treated with a placebo, sterile saline. I know it is not popular to say, but she was a drug seeker. Dr. Herman knew that, and he treated her accordingly. Remember, Dr. Sizemore treated her for five months and couldn't solve Mrs. Malone's problems. She was her own worst enemy. She smoked and took pain pills because she couldn't tolerate any pain."

Barnes told the jury to listen carefully to Judge Boxer's jury instructions, particularly to the fact that they were not to consider damages unless they found liability. Barnes discussed the fact that each defendant was separate and that Dr. Herman was not liable for the actions of Dr. English and the hospital.

He reminded them that everyone, including Dr. Herman, was sorry that Mrs. Malone was dead, but that sympathy had nothing to do with their job as jurors.

He reminded them that Dr. Herman testified that he had befriended Mrs. Malone and that he had known her much better than Mr. Davis, Mr. Steine, or any of the paid expert witnesses.

Barnes concluded his closing statement: "Mrs. Malone is gone. Nothing anybody does or says will bring her back. If it was within Dr. Herman's powers to do that, he gladly would. This is about money. Mrs. Malone's children, represented by Thomas Malone, are hoping for a big payday. That's what this lawsuit's about, money.

"I mention recklessness and punitive damages, not out of concern, but as Mr. Steine told you, this is my only opportunity to talk with you. Listen to the judge's instructions on recklessness. First, it must be proved by a much higher burden than negligence by clear and convincing evidence. Second, this is a professional negligence case. There was no disregard for the safety of the patient. Dr. Herman did the best he could under difficult circumstances. These hired guns have a lot of nerve claiming that Dr. Herman was reckless. They weren't there. All they did was read pieces of paper years after the fact. I know there will be no finding of recklessness by the people of Hewes County."

Trying a lawsuit was a young man's job. Barnes moved slowly back to the defense table and placed his palms flatly on the table for support as he eased himself down. He had done an excellent job, considering that his client was a scumbag.

Judge Boxer told everyone to be back at two o'clock. Morty couldn't wait to give his final closing argument.

When Davis and Morty returned, Stevenson was standing at the podium. Grayson Stevenson was a year older than Morty but lived in a different world of Nashville's social elite. He was a member of Belle Meade Country Club; he went hunting with the governor and both United States senators from Tennessee. His grandfather was the founder of his firm in 1907, and his father and two uncles managed it through the Depression and World War II. Grayson was at the end of his career, and Davis knew Stevenson wanted to let this closing argument count.

"Ladies and gentlemen, I represent Plainview Community Hospital. My closing argument is simple. The doctors, not the hospital, practice medicine.

"It was Dr. Herman who performed the three ultrasounds and made the diagnosis that Mrs. Malone had gallbladder disease and gallstones. Remember, Dr. Gerald's report said that there were no stones and no apparent gallbladder disease. Dr. Gerald worked for the hospital.

"It was Dr. English, with Dr. Herman's approval, who performed the surgery, and it was English who nicked her bowel. It was Herman and English who initially managed Mrs. Malone's postoperative care, and it was Dr. Herman who decided when to transfer the patient. Remember the concept of comparative fault; each defendant is liable for only his percentage of the negligence that proximately caused damage to Mrs. Malone, not what some other defendant may have caused.

"The only alleged claims against the hospital are that

it negligently credentialed Dr. Herman and Dr. English and that the hospital was negligent in its utilization review of Rosie Malone. You heard the testimony of Dr. Sparks; utilization review is for the protection of the hospital, not the patient. Its purpose is to make sure that the hospital uses its resources wisely and does not waste those resources.

"In the case of Mrs. Malone, she stayed at Plainview Community Hospital from January 29th until February 5th. She ran up a hospital bill of $53,000, and Medicare paid $9,000. Plainview Community Hospital lost $44,000 in its care and treatment of this patient. The utilization review process failed miserably. The utilization review nurse was negligent, and the party that was harmed was the hospital. Judge Boxer will explain that a defendant is liable only for damages that it proximately causes. The hospital's negligence in its utilization review did not proximately damage Mrs. Malone, and therefore, her estate cannot recover from that negligence.

"Dr. Sparks also testified that the hospital's relationship with Dr. Herman and Dr. English is identical to the relationship of Davenport County Hospital and its physicians. There was no breach of the standard of care as to that relationship.

"In retrospect, Dr. Herman and Dr. English made some errors in judgment, but they didn't have a crystal ball or the benefit of hindsight like the plaintiff's experts. These were medical decisions made by Dr. Herman and Dr. English, not the staff of Plainview Community Hospital. The hospital is not liable for these medical decisions. Thank you."

Amy Pierce marched toward the jury. It was evident that she was furious at Stevenson for dumping on her client. Whatever common strategy the defendants might have once had now lay in pieces and was abandoned.

Pierce explained that Rosie Malone had been Dr. Herman's patient for several years. Dr. Herman did three ultrasounds before her admission on January 29th, and it was his diagnosis of gallstones and gallbladder disease. Herman recommended surgery based upon the ultrasounds he performed and interpreted.

"Dr. English met Mrs. Malone on the 30th and performed surgery on the 31st. The injury during surgery was a known risk disclosed on the consent form. Surgery is an art, not an exact science," she said.

She reminded them that after the surgery, Dr. English left town on a scheduled vacation. She argued that he left the patient in the care of Dr. Herman and the hospital staff. He was available only the first day after surgery and made only two notations in the patient's chart. Dr. English was outside the loop when Mrs. Malone's temperature spiked and her condition deteriorated.

"He left the patient's postoperative care in the hands of Dr. Herman, who was faced with a sick and deteriorating patient. It was Dr. Herman who decided when to transfer the patient, and by then it was too late.

"It is only natural for you to feel sympathy for Mrs. Malone. She had many health issues long before she met Dr. English. She had heart problems, breathing problems, digestion problems, and drug problems. She was in pain both emotionally and physically. But she was not a victim. These health issues had developed over more than forty years of her abusing her body. The surgery performed by Dr. English was a mere moment in a lifetime of abuse. Thank you for your time and attention."

Pierce sat down and the courtroom grew silent. Boxer ordered a short break.

In the hall, Davis told Morty, Sammie, and Littleton, "I can't believe that the defendants turned on each other in closing arguments. They held it together for years, and at the last moment, their common defense crumbled." Davis whispered to Morty that he needed to take advantage of this turn of events. They agreed that the focus should be on recklessness and assume they had won the issue of negligence. Littleton, who overheard the conversation, insisted that Morty urge that the jury throw caution to the wind and sting the defendants until it hurt.

Back in the courtroom as Morty got up from counsel table, Davis squeezed his elbow. In that split second, there was an exchange between the two men of love, friendship, respect, and Davis's complete confidence in the old man—who had no shortage of confidence in himself.

Morty thanked the jury for their service and attention. He then walked too close to the defense table, violating Boxer's rule, as Boxer let him know.

"Members of the jury, this lawsuit was filed in October 1992. These defendants, in at least two dozen pleadings and in at least a dozen depositions, have denied liability. We just spent almost two weeks together in trial, and at the beginning of these proceedings, these defendants denied liability. Just minutes ago I heard each defendant, like rats leaving a sinking ship, blame the other for liability.

"You heard them concede negligence, but it was the other guy's fault. They've made my job a lot easier. All I have to do is talk about recklessness. I will not lecture you on compensatory damages. Collectively, you the jury must decide the amount. How much is a human life worth? It's a difficult question, but I am confident you will be fair and just.

"Under the law, a defendant acts recklessly when he disregards the consequences of his actions and places others at significant risk. The plaintiff has proved recklessness by clear and convincing evidence. In a nutshell, it was reckless for Dr. Herman to recommend surgery when Dr. Gerald's report stated no gallstones or gallbladder disease existed. It was reckless for Dr. English to perform a totally unnecessary surgery. It was reckless for Dr. Herman to fail to transfer the patient to Nashville when there was no pulmonologist, cardiologist, or infectious disease specialist at the hospital. These were not negligent acts below the standard of care. They were *reckless* acts.

"The hospital was also reckless. It granted these two doctors privileges that never should have been granted. Dr. English was not properly trained, proctored, or competent to perform the surgery that killed Rosie Malone. The hospital, through its recklessness, made that possible.

"I anticipate a finding of recklessness against all three defendants. Those damages are to punish, not to compensate. That award is to send a message to these defendants and to others that conduct such as this will not be tolerated.

"On behalf of Mr. Davis, Mr. Littleton, Mr. Malone, and myself, thank you for your time and attention."

CHAPTER FIFTY-THREE

THE COURT'S FINAL INSTRUCTIONS

SATURDAY, AUGUST 20, 1994

A long day of closing arguments was winding down, and Davis was tired, even though he said nothing in the proceedings. Morty carried the ball, and Davis reluctantly sat on the sidelines. It was now all up to the judge, who would instruct the jury on the law. Davis and the defense fought hard over exactly what Boxer would tell the jury. Boxer would actually read it to them, and Davis and the other lawyers would follow along as he read.

The Malone verdict was important not only to the Malone family; it would also affect the outcome of all the other Plainview cases. It was most likely that Judge Boxer would be consistent in his rulings throughout all the cases. Over the last two years, Judge Boxer had ruled on various motions. Several of them were procedural in nature, while others determined the scope of the law and its application to the facts of the Plainview cases.

Boxer had made several decisions that had shaped the Plainview cases. The ruling, in the Malone case, that no pattern of negligence or recklessness could be argued was a devastating blow to the plaintiff's proof.

On several occasions, Boxer had refused to rule, taking the motion under advisement to be considered at a later date. This allowed him to apply the law to the specific testimony or document presented. The law was unclear. The Tennessee Supreme Court in 1992 changed critical aspects of the law, and now, eighteen months later, a trial judge, such as Boxer, was no closer to knowing what he should instruct a jury.

For the last three days, the attorneys, after the day's proceeding, stayed past eight o'clock arguing what Boxer should charge the jury in regard to the law. Each side, in writing, filed briefs objecting to several aspects of the charge. Both sides, through their actions and positions, created appealable issues.

Davis looked at the faces of the members of the jury. Male, female, black, white, young, or old, they had one thing in common: they were tired. Almost two weeks together, confined in the courtroom, in the jury room, or at the motel, away from family and friends, they wanted the trial to be over. Davis was confident that they paid attention and would do their duty. He hoped that they were convinced that the defendants deserved to be punished and that they had the guts to do so.

The last thing the jury would hear before it began its deliberations was the jury charge. For that reason and because it came from the judge, the jury instructions were important—and possibly pivotal.

Boxer said, "I want to thank you on behalf of the citizens of Plains County. The alleged wrongful conduct occurred there, at Plainview Community Hospital. The case was moved to Hewes County so that the parties could receive a fair and impartial trial. That did occur. As citizens of Hewes County, you should be proud that you were instrumental in guaranteeing that our system of justice diligently worked to afford an unbiased trial.

"As we discussed in the preliminary instructions, we all have our jobs to do in this trial. The attorneys have finished their part. They have presented the proof and given their closing statements. Remember, what the lawyers say is not evidence. The evidence is the testimony from the witness stand or the depositions read into evidence and the documents introduced into evidence as exhibits. There were one hundred sixty-eight documents introduced into evidence as exhibits. Those documents will be available for your review and discussion during your deliberation.

"You are the judges of the facts. Based on the evidence presented, you must determine the truth of what happened. My job is to tell you what the law is. I am not the one who determines what happened. That is solely your job based on the relevant evidence."

Judge Boxer gave them the definition of *relevant evidence*: anything that would make a fact more or less likely. He also discussed how during the trial, each of the parties objected to certain testimony or exhibits. The judge reminded the jury that if he sustained an objection, the jury was to disregard not only the answer but also the question.

The judge discussed the credibility of witnesses. He provided the jury with a list of factors to consider in evaluating witnesses' credibility:

> Was the witness able to see, hear, or be aware of the matter to which he or she testified about?
>
> How well was the witness able to recall and describe the facts he or she asserted?

How long was the witness watching and listening?
Was the witness distracted in any way?
Did the witness have a good memory?
How did the witness look and act during testimony?
Did the witness evade questions?
Did the witness have any interest in the outcome?
Did the witness have any motive, prejudice, or bias that would influence his or her testimony?
Was the witness's testimony reasonable in light of the other evidence?
Was the witness's testimony contradicted by other testimony?
What is the witness's reputation for truth and veracity in the community?

He explained that if the jury found discrepancies in a witness's testimony, they could disregard that witness's entire testimony. He also emphasized that if the jury believed that a witness had lied under oath, the jury could accept or reject any part of that witness's testimony.

Judge Boxer made it clear that the burden of proof was on the plaintiff to prove by a preponderance of the evidence liability of the defendants. If the plaintiff failed to meet that burden, the jurors' job would stop there, and they should award a defendants' verdict. If they found the defendants more liable, then and only then would they consider damages.

He discussed the importance of expert testimony in the case. Because this was a medical malpractice case, the plaintiff had to prove a breach of the standard of care through expert testimony. Judge Boxer identified the expert witnesses who testified, including Dr. English and Dr. Herman.

He then turned to the newly adopted concept of comparative fault. This part of the jury instruction, he read verbatim: "Ladies and gentlemen, I want you to picture a hot apple pie. That entire apple pie represents the total liability of this case. If you believe that the plaintiff Rosie Malone contributed to her death, you must assign a portion or a slice of that pie to her. If Mrs. Malone did nothing wrong, the pie, or the liability, must be divided among the defendants. The more liable a defendant, the bigger piece of the pie you assign to them. It may be that only one defendant breached the standard of care; if so, then that defendant gets assigned the whole pie and all the liability. As a jury, you must collectively decide how to divide up the pie. After the pie is divided, the jury must collectively decide how much the pie is worth. If you assign any liability to the plaintiff, the damage award will be reduced by that percentage of liability. For example, if you were to award one dollar in damages and determined that Mrs. Malone was twenty percent responsible, the compensatory damages would be eighty cents, reduced by the twenty percent comparative fault of the plaintiff. The remaining eighty cents would be divided by the percentage of liability you assigned to each of the defendants."

While the judge explained various aspects of the law, the jurors listened intently. Most of them took notes. Boxer, in a pre-trial motion filed by the plaintiff, issued notebooks at the beginning of the trial.

Boxer finally got to compensatory damages. He described how compensatory damages were to compensate the plaintiff or, in this case, the plaintiff's family.

Davis thought, *It would have been much better to have tried a case where the plaintiff was in the courtroom rather than some middle-aged son. The jury is far less likely to compensate a family member than the victim herself. That was the luck of the flip of the coin. There is nothing I can do about it now.*

The judge explained that the plaintiff had alleged that the defendants had been reckless in their care and treatment of Mrs. Malone. Then he defined *recklessness:* "A person acts recklessly when the person is aware of, but consciously disregards, a substantial and unjustifiable risk of such a nature that its disregard constitutes a gross deviation from the standard of care that an ordinary person would exercise under all of the circumstances."

Judge Boxer continued, "In order to find that any of the defendants have acted recklessly, you must do so by a higher burden of proof. Liability is determined by a preponderance of the evidence. In order to find recklessness, you, the jury, must find such recklessness by clear and convincing evidence. Clear and convincing evidence requires the plaintiff to prove that there is no serious or substantial doubt about the conclusion the party is attempting to prove. It is a much higher burden of proof than preponderance, but not as a high as in a criminal case, which is beyond a reasonable doubt.

"If you find that any of the defendants acted recklessly, by clear and convincing evidence, then you may award punitive damages to punish one or more of these defendants and to send a message to others to refrain from similar reckless conduct."

Judge Boxer handed out to the jurors the questionnaires that they would be using to determine liability and damages. The first four questions on the questionnaire asked:

> Do you find, by a preponderance of the evidence, that the plaintiff Rosie Malone breached the standard of care and was negligent?
>
> Do you find, by a preponderance of the evidence, that the defendant Dr. Lars Herman breached the standard of care and was negligent?
>
> Do you find, by a preponderance of the evidence, that the defendant Dr. Charles English breached the standard of care and was negligent?
>
> Do you find, by a preponderance of the evidence, that Plainview Community Hospital breached the standard of care and was negligent?

The questionnaire proceeded:

> Please assign to each party a percentage of comparative fault from zero to one hundred percent. The total of the comparative fault must equal one hundred percent.
>
> Rosie Malone _______________%
> Dr. Lars Herman _____________%
> Dr. Charles English ___________%

Plainview Hospital __________ %
Total Comparative Fault: 100%

IF YOU ASSIGNED MORE THAN FIFTY PERCENT TO ROSIE MALONE, THEN STOP NOW. YOU HAVE COMPLETED THE VERDICT FORM. IF YOU HAVE ASSIGNED MORE THAN FIFTY PERCENT OF THE COMPARATIVE FAULT TO THE DEFENDANTS, THEN ANSWER THE NEXT QUESTION.

What dollar amount of compensatory damages do you award to the plaintiff Rosie Malone?

$______________________

Do you find that any of the defendants acted recklessly, by clear and convincing evidence?

If so, which defendants?

Dr. Herman YES____ NO_____
Dr. English YES____ NO_____
Hospital YES____ NO_____

PLEASE STOP HERE!

Judge Boxer was almost finished. All he had left was to give the concluding instructions.

Davis was generally pleased with the jury instructions. His defeat occurred when Boxer excluded the pattern of gross negligence on the part of the defendants.

Boxer concluded, "Your attitude and conduct at the beginning of your deliberations are very important. It is rarely productive for a juror to immediately announce a determination to hold firm for a certain verdict before any deliberation or discussion has taken place. Taking that position might make it difficult for you to consider the opinions of your fellow jurors or to change your mind after you review the evidence. Please remember that you are not advocates for either party. You are the judges of the facts, and you must apply the law that I have instructed you."

Boxer reminded the jury: "You are a collective body. You must, in the end, speak with one voice. You must come to a unanimous decision as to liability and, if necessary, to appropriate damages. It is your duty to consult with one another. You should listen carefully and respect the opinions of others. In the course of your deliberations, do not hesitate to reexamine your own views and to change your opinions. However, do not surrender your honest conviction as to the weight of the evidence solely because of the opinions of your fellow jurors or for the mere purpose of returning a verdict. On behalf of the people of Plains County, Hewes County, the parties, their attorneys, and this court, I wish you Godspeed in your deliberations and good luck."

With that said, Boxer dismissed the jury to deliberate.

Davis turned to Morty: "Now the hardest part begins. We wait."

CHAPTER FIFTY-FOUR

THE VERDICT

SATURDAY–MONDAY, AUGUST 20–22, 1994

As Davis watched the jurors leave to begin their deliberations, his heart skipped a beat. This was the most important trial of his life. He knew that, and the defense knew it. Despite his game face, the math and his tired blue eyes couldn't lie.

A lot was riding on the verdict. He didn't know how much more his marriage could take. It wasn't only the fact that he had gone into debt. It was the time and commitment that Plainview required of him. He missed his family. His kids were growing up without him, and he desperately needed to be there for his wife, who had sacrificed in so many ways.

The problem was that even if the jury returned a large verdict of both compensatory and punitive damages, there would still be an appeal and seven more cases to try. Logic dictated that he first had to win the Malone trial, avoid an appeal, and negotiate a settlement of the remaining cases. He had quite a difficult task ahead.

The defense team had the luxury of waiting in Barnes's office across the street from the courthouse, right there on the square. It had air conditioning and access to a kitchen and soft drinks while the defense team waited in comfort.

Boxer took pity on the Davis team, who had no place to go, and gave them a small office in the courthouse to wait. Although he was clearly an outsider, Littleton was included as a common courtesy. Davis, Morty, Sammie, and Littleton easily over-crowded the very small room.

There was no room for the clients. The Malone family was everywhere. All ten living children were in the courtroom, as were more than a dozen grand-children. With spouses, the group added up to more than thirty people.

Davis and Sammie took turns leaving their cramped retreat to visit with the family in the courtroom. Out of respect, Morty was given a deferment, and out of the abundance of caution, Davis kept idiot Littleton away from the clients. Davis and Sammie could only repeat to the family, "It is in the hands of the jury," so many times.

Morty took out a deck of cards and challenged Davis to gin rummy. The old man loved the game and never lost. Over the last nineteen years, Davis figured the two of them had spent more than two hundred hours playing while waiting on juries. Morty knocked with two, and Davis was caught with eighteen points.

At five o'clock, the judge sent the jury back to the motel so they could get a fresh start in the morning. The clerk told Davis's team to go home and called Barnes's office and sent the defense home.

Sunday morning opened with the judge reminding the jury, "You've taken an oath to find the facts of this case, determine liability and, if necessary, award appropriate damages. Good luck and Godspeed."

The defendants, with the exception of Dr. English, left the courtroom for the sanctuary of Barnes's office, and Davis and his team settled in to wait. Sheriff Dudley returned Dr. English to his cell on Judge Lewis's orders.

Davis took his turn with the Malone family and approached Lorraine Burke, sitting with three of her sisters. Davis wasn't sure who was who. He just started talking, "Hello, ladies, we're close to the end of a long road."

Lorraine smiled and held out her hand to Davis. He grabbed it, and she squeezed so hard, it almost hurt.

"That's quite a grip. I wouldn't expect that from a history teacher."

"All of us kids worked the farm while Momma worked the bakery. Thomas was the foreman at fourteen. He had his own private army."

"It must have been hard with no adult."

"We didn't know any better, and between the bakery and the farm we had enough to eat. It wasn't too bad. I was the only one of the eleven who got to go to community college."

Lorraine and Davis discussed the tension in Plainview. People were picking sides. Either they or their relatives worked at the hospital, and the lawsuit was affecting business and morale. Some patients believed and supported Dr. Herman, despite the finding of the Medical Licensing Board.

"You can feel the tension in the air. Our community is being torn apart by these lawsuits," said Lorraine.

"Are you feeling secure with your job at the high school?"

"The principal is a good friend of Woody Douglas, but the parents of my students will protect me if Douglas tries to get me fired. I'm too good a teacher, and I've been there over twenty years."

Davis hoped she was right.

Three hours later, just before lunch, the judge's clerk came into the courtroom and told Davis that the jury had a question. He needed to get his people. They even brought Littleton. The clerk had already called Barnes's office, and the defense was on the way over.

When everyone was in the assigned places, the judge took the bench, and the jury was brought in. From experience, Davis knew that a jury's question could be very telling about how the jurors were leaning.

The young foreman stood and looked straight at Judge Boxer.

"What's the jury's question, Mr. Foreman?"

"It has to do with the obligation of the hospital when it credentialed Dr. English. Did the standard of care require the hospital to verify his competency to perform laparoscopic gallbladder surgery if he was the first at the hospital to perform that procedure?"

Boxer paused a moment and then answered, "The hospital, under the standard of care, shouldn't have allowed any surgery, unless with a reasonable degree of medical certainty it knew that surgery would be performed with a reasonable degree of safety to the patient."

Davis liked the question, and he loved Boxer's answer. The jury was seriously considering the liability of the hospital, which meant that it had probably already found the doctors liable.

The jury remained out for the rest of the day. At 6:00 p.m. the judge sent them back to the motel and told them that they would start again at nine the next morning.

Davis believed the lengthy deliberation was a good sign. The jury was taking its time reviewing the evidence. After all, there were 168 exhibits, and they heard testimony from fifteen witnesses. And there were several complicated issues to consider: comparative fault, how much blame to place on each defendant, and whether to find recklessness and award punitive damages. Davis wished he could be a fly on the wall and learn from the process.

The next day, Monday, the defense team hunkered down at Barnes's office all day. The Malone family had now overflowed to outside the courthouse. Morty kept winning at rummy, first against Littleton, then Davis, and then Sammie. He chewed on cigars the whole time. Eventually he switched his cigar out when the end got too disgusting. At five there was a knock at the door of their small office. It was Thomas Malone.

"Mr. Davis, the jury's been talking about twenty hours. Is that normal?"

Davis's tie was loosened. He was getting as nervous as the Malone family, but he knew he couldn't show it.

"There is no such thing as normal when it comes to a jury, Thomas. It's a weird and wild animal. I'm only guessing, but I bet they're fighting over whether to find the defendants reckless and whether to award punitive damages. Our burden is much higher at clear and convincing evidence. They're divided over something, and eventually it will get worked out."

"Could you talk to the family?"

Davis agreed to go to the courtroom. Morty, Sammie, and Littleton followed. Davis was shocked to see more than a hundred people in the courtroom. The Malone family constituted about a third, about another third were his clients from the other Plainview cases, and there were at least forty others. Dr. Laura Patel and the six nurses represented by Littleton and more than twenty other interested persons had driven from Plainview to Hewes City for the verdict.

Davis knew he had to say something. These people had a vested interest in the Malone case, and they were looking to him for encouragement.

"I'm stunned by your support and overwhelmed by the importance of the outcome of this case, not only to the Malone family and myself, but to a community. Plainview hasn't been a safe place to get sick the last few years. The hospital and these doctors took advantage of the most vulnerable members of your community, and I hope the jury appreciates that breach of trust and sends a message: no more. Even if we win, these cases are not over. There could be an appeal, and seven other cases are pending. I promise that my team and I will see it through to the end."

As the words left his mouth, Davis thought, *I might have just made the biggest mistake of my life.*

Fifteen minutes later, right in the middle of a hand of gin rummy, after twenty-one hours of deliberation, the court clerk announced that the jury had reached a verdict.

They all assembled in the courtroom. The defense side, including lawyers, defendants, and insurance representatives, totaled more than a dozen additional persons.

Boxer took the bench and called for the jury. They walked in single file, led by their foreman. The jurors were trying not to make eye contact with any of the parties. That was a dead giveaway.

Davis stared hard at the jurors, looking for a smile or a twinkle in their eyes. Betsy Blue gave him what he wanted, and his stomach finally stopped doing flips.

Judge Boxer became very serious and in a ceremonial tone asked: "Has the jury reached a verdict?"

The young foreman responded: "Yes, we have, Your Honor. We, the jury, in the case of Malone vs. Plainview Community Hospital, Dr. Lars Herman, and Dr. Charles English, find that all three of the defendants were negligent."

"What is the amount of compensatory damages awarded?"

"We award $250,000."

Davis never expected a large award of compensatory damages. Rosie Malone was sixty-seven years old and in ill health, regardless of any negligence of the defendants, and without any lost income because she had retired.

"How do you divide the fault among the parties?"

"We find that Rosie Malone had no contributory fault; Plainview Community Hospital is forty percent at fault; Dr. English thirty-five percent; and Dr. Herman twenty-five percent comparatively at fault."

Davis noted that the percentages assigned against each defendant were the same as the Jones settlement. *Jury's got to the right place, even through all the bullshit thrown at them.* The next question was critical, and Davis actually held his breath.

"Do you find any of the defendants by clear and convincing evidence reckless?"

There was a hush in the courtroom. The foreman looked at Davis, and a big smile broke out across his face. Davis relaxed for the first time in two years.

"Yes, we find that all three defendants were reckless."

"Do you award punitive damages, and if so, in what amount?"

"We award the plaintiff $2 million in punitive damages, for a total verdict of $2,250,000."

It was bedlam in the courtroom. The Plainview plaintiffs and their families were shouting and jumping, hugging, or crying for joy.

There was a completely different reaction from the other side of the room, however. The defense lawyers didn't appear very upset. They would make more money with an appeal and seven trials, but Herman and English were visibly shaken.

Although Boxer tried to get control of his courtroom, it was almost impossible to hear either him or his gavel.

Herman began to cry, his body heaving as he did.

English had a crazed look on his face, and Davis vindictively gave him a victory smile. Without warning, English flipped the defense table over, causing a deafening noise. He balled his fists and tried to run across the room to attack Davis. Several people, including the foreman of the jury, forcefully tackled English to the floor. Sheriff Dudley, who had been close by, slapped the handcuffs on the distraught physician.

At that point, Boxer took control of his courtroom and shouted at the top of his lungs: "Everybody get in a seat right now! Anyone standing in ten seconds is the loser of my game of musical chairs and will spend the next twenty-four hours in the Hewes County jail."

Davis believed him, and apparently so did everybody else. Within seven seconds, no one was standing.

"Tomorrow morning at nine o'clock, I want all of the plaintiffs and their lawyers, the defendants and their lawyers, and their insurance representatives to meet me at Plainview High School to discuss the status of these cases. Attendance is mandatory, no exceptions. Now everyone, except Dr. English, leave this courtroom, and unless you live here in Hewes County, get out of the city limits of Hewes City. You've got thirty minutes to leave, or you'll be a guest of our jail. Dr. English, you're in contempt of court. Sheriff Dudley, take him to a cell."

Most people in the courtroom didn't know that Dr. English was going to his jail cell anyway, regardless of how well he took the verdict. English was now being held in contempt by two judges, and his prospect of seeing daylight was increasingly unlikely.

As Davis walked out the courtroom door, the jury foreman grabbed him by the elbow. "Mr. Davis, I just want you to know what a learning experience watching you and Mr. Steine has been. I know it's been a once-in-a-lifetime experience to participate in these jury deliberations. I'll be a better lawyer for it. Thank you for keeping me on the jury."

Davis wished the young lawyer good luck. He was waiting on his Bar results taken in July.

Morty, Davis, and Sammie made their way past a pushy TV news reporter from Nashville and the newspaper reporters from Plainview County standing just beyond the courthouse steps. They figured that Boxer's gag order was still in effect, offering no comment as they went. There were reporters taking notes in the courtroom, so Davis knew that Dr. English's antics would be mentioned in the press, despite any gag order.

The Davis team headed straight for Davis's convertible and out of town. In the safety of the car Sammie asked, "What do you think Boxer has up his sleeve?"

Davis laughed and said one word, "Settlement."

CHAPTER FIFTY-FIVE

THE JUDGE TAKES CONTROL

TUESDAY, AUGUST 23, 1994

Davis learned from Lorraine Burke that Judge Boxer called the high school principal and commandeered the facility for the entire day. School didn't start until next Monday, but the staff was supposed to be there, preparing for the new school year. Instead, the staff was given the day off. Boxer refused to inconvenience Hewes County's high school. Plainview needed to clean up its own mess.

Plainview was just as hot, and the humidity just as unbearable, as Hewes City. It was so bad that Morty wouldn't let Davis drive with the top down.

As everyone assembled in the high school's auditorium, Davis spotted Stevenson.

Wearing a perfectly pressed blue pinstriped suit and with his white hair styled immaculately, Stevenson looked like a television attorney. He addressed the judge, and Davis could tell that he regretted the decision the moment he opened his mouth.

"Well, we're back here at the high school. It feels like déjà vu, doesn't it, Judge?"

"Not quite, Mr. Stevenson. The Medical Licensing Board has found Dr. Herman reckless, and the jury found all three defendants reckless in the Malone case. Or have you forgotten?"

Stevenson turned the same shade of green as McCoy's bow tie.

"Look, gentlemen and Ms. Pierce, I want these cases settled," said Boxer. "It's in the best interests of all the parties, and more important it's in the best interests of two communities. These lawsuits are tearing Plainview apart. The community is taking sides, and many people have lost faith in the hospital. The town needs a hospital. I'm also concerned about Hewes County. Its resources and citizens will be exhausted by these cases."

Davis had to agree. An appeal and seven more trials would destroy not only both communities but also his law practice and marriage.

"I want all counsel, the defendants, and their insurance people in classroom 11 in five minutes. The plaintiffs will wait in the auditorium. It's the only room big enough to hold the plaintiffs from all eight cases. Mr. Davis or one of his team will be providing you with updates as these negotiations progress."

Classroom 11 was a tight squeeze with more than fifteen people in the room. Boxer came in and suggested that the men take off their jackets and roll up their sleeves if they thought it would help.

"Look, there's no court reporter present. That's no accident. We're going to have a frank discussion off the record."

No one dared challenge the judge. He held substantial discretionary power under the law.

"I'll decide what record is made after this hearing if this case goes to the Court of Appeals. I meant what I said in there. We've got to get these cases settled."

Stevenson spoke up again. Davis gave him credit for guts. "It has to be fair—"

Boxer cut him off. "A jury's found your hospital guilty of recklessly credentialing these two doctors and allowing them to perform unnecessary surgeries to make more money. You might want to listen rather than talk. I'm reversing my ruling about whether the plaintiffs can introduce evidence of a pattern of reckless care. This jury verdict supports that decision. Mr. Davis, you draw the order."

Morty cleared his throat and asked the judge if he would take a question.

"Go ahead, Mr. Steine."

"Can you tell us if each defendant is liable for the $2 million punitive damage award, or is that award divided between the parties based upon the percentages assigned by the jury? There's a pretrial motion pending that the court took under advisement."

"Good question. I elected to hold off ruling on that one; I have no guidance because our Supreme Court didn't answer the issue. If the Supreme Court meant to apply comparative fault to punitive damages, it could have held so. I'm holding each of the defendants liable for the entire $2 million, just like in the old days, joint and several liabilities. Mr. Davis, you can go after any of the defendants, or one of the defendants to collect your $2 million in punitive damages. The defendants can file a lawsuit against each other to figure out if the $2 million should be divided based on percentage. That should cost them each at least another $200,000 in legal fees."

Boxer was letting the two insurance companies and the Board of Directors of the hospital know that they would be spending a fortune in legal fees to resolve all these issues and that they were better off using those same funds to settle Plainview.

Davis thought that he would add fuel to the fire: "Just for everybody's information, the plaintiff will be seeking collection of the award of punitive damages from the hospital, not the doctor defendants, since I suspect their policies might not cover punitive damages. That could be another lawsuit between the defendants."

Boxer turned to Pinsly of Tennessee Mutual and Davenport of PIC and demanded, "What's the dollar limit of your policies, and are punitive damages covered?"

Both remained quiet, and McCoy broke in: "Judge, this isn't federal court where insurance limits are discoverable. Under Rule 408 of the Tennessee Rules of Evidence, those dollar amounts are not admissible or even discoverable under Rule 26 of the Rules of Civil Procedure—"

"Damnit, McCoy, I'm not the plaintiff, and I'm not trying to introduce the dollar amounts of coverage into evidence. How much does each of your companies have?"

Pinsly reported that $1,980,000 was left, and Davenport, English's insurer, had a few dollars less because of the Jones settlement.

"You're both kicking in $2.5 million each to get these cases settled," said the judge firmly.

Pinsly protested, "That's more than our coverage."

"You would have spent more than $2 million each on legal fees if you were to appeal and try all cases. I'm doing you a favor. Let me remind everyone, I'm the presiding judge on the other cases in which there will probably be more than a hundred motions filed. If the defendants aren't reasonable and get these cases settled, I predict they might not win any of those motions."

Davis thought, *Boxer made a good point. A smart lawyer knows when to keep his mouth shut.*

"The jury found that the doctors were sixty percent comparatively at fault, so the hospital's going to match the payment of the two insurance companies and pay another $5 million, for a total settlement of $10 million. I'm saving the hospital legal fees as well. That's a nice, round, even number. Does that work for you and your clients, Mr. Davis?"

"I'd like to confer with my team and my clients, but I think I can make that work, Your Honor. How would the settlement funds be divided?"

"That will be my decision. You'll submit a damage sheet on each case, and I will divide the total settlement among the eight cases. Everyone will agree to be bound by my decision as a condition of settlement. This method doesn't place Mr. Davis in a conflict of interest between his clients. He won't be in the uncomfortable position of dividing the pie among them."

Pierce got the judge's attention: "Mr. McCoy and I have to make a phone call before we can agree to the terms of any settlement."

"There are three pay phones in the lobby. Call whoever you want, but come back here in one hour with a settlement."

Davis, Morty, Littleton, and Sammie joined their clients in the auditorium and got their permission to take the deal. They spoke in vague terms without disclosing the total settlement of $10 million. His clients trusted Davis and gave him the authority to settle their cases. Davis wondered whether the defense would succumb to Boxer's blackmail and pay the $10 million.

An hour later, they were all back in classroom 11, and they had a deal.

All of the attorneys and Sammie went to the typing classroom, and Sammie was designated official typist of the settlement agreement. It was a short document, which provided that the total settlement amount and the individual settlement amounts would remain confidential. It provided that Davis's clients, the plaintiffs, would be told only the amount of their own settlement and that all parties were bound to keep the settlements confidential from any third party. All that could be revealed to the press was that all of the cases had been settled. Nothing more could be said. The defense insisted upon that term. It provided that Judge Boxer had complete authority to divide the settlement among the Plainview cases.

The document was circulated, and every party signed it. There were almost twenty signatures. A copy was made for Davis, Stevenson, Pierce, and McCoy. The judge kept the original. No other copies would be made.

Boxer emphasized the need for confidentiality: "I want each of you to explain to your clients the importance of confidentiality. I don't want anyone talking to the press. Limit your remarks to 'the cases have settled. No further comment.' Period. Don't let me find any of you in contempt. As a gesture of goodwill, I release both Mr. Steine and Dr. English from their contempt findings."

Boxer could release Dr. English only from his contempt finding. English would be returning to his cell under Judge Lewis's contempt finding.

Davis went into the auditorium to address his clients: "This has been a long fight. We've worked hard together, and we've won an important victory. We will collect money, but Plainview is the true winner. Remember, you must keep the dollar amount of your settlement confidential. You can't discuss it, not even among yourselves. Judge Boxer was very clear on that point. After the judge decides how to divide the settlement, I'll be meeting with you individually to go over expenses and arrange payment through my escrow account. You should all be proud of the part you played in these cases. I know I am.

"A wise old man once taught me," Davis looked over at Morty, so the clients would know his source, "that as a lawyer, all I could get my injured clients were money and justice. Good health was beyond my means. I hope today that you all believe I secured you both good settlements and justice. If you feel that way, then I've done my job."

All of the parties left the high school and were just standing around on the steps when a tall man in a blue suit walked up to Littleton and Davis.

"Mr. Littleton, Mr. Davis, I'm John Rothschild. I'm a United States marshal. I have a notice of lien to serve on both of you on behalf of the Internal Revenue Service for taxes owed by Mr. Littleton."

Littleton was shocked. Davis felt a heavy weight on his shoulders and felt sick to his stomach. He looked over at the defendants, and English was giggling like a little girl. Those bastards were behind this. Davis knew that an IRS lien would cause a long delay of payment to the clients and of repayment of his expenses and his fee.

Davis was furious at Littleton and let him have it: "Brad, you're a useless piece of shit. You did nothing to earn your fee, and now your IRS problems will delay our clients getting their settlements. You're a disgrace to the profession and to human beings."

Davis and the others strode away, leaving Littleton alone on the steps of the high school.

CHAPTER FIFTY-SIX

A LITTLE GLIMMER OF JUSTICE

MONDAY, NOVEMBER 14, 1994

The last ten weeks had been hellish. Davis lost whole nights of sleep; he'd stay up and eat. Not snack, but have a second continuous supper. He'd gained more than fifteen pounds. Littleton's IRS lien prevented payment of any portion of the $10 million of settlement proceeds. Morty filed a lawsuit in federal court to get the funds released so they could at least be paid to the clients. All of the Plainview clients had called at least twice about the status of their funds. Several called twice a week. All Davis could tell them was that there was a hearing scheduled in front of Judge Henry Wise on November 14th and that he was sure that the clients' portion of the settlement would be released—at least he hoped so.

The bastard Littleton was in hiding, not answering the telephone or responding to hate mail. Littleton wasn't a likable guy, but now he was downright hated.

Today was the big day of the hearing before United States District Court Judge Henry Wise, scheduled at one o'clock. Davis had appeared before Judge Wise at least thirty times, but Morty would argue the motions. The judge was a personal friend of Morty, who helped Wise get to the bench during the Kennedy administration. They played poker together every third

Thursday of every month. Davis was confident that he would be treated fairly because of Morty's relationship. Besides, right was still right.

Littleton and the IRS attorney, Barton Lee, shared the defense table. Davis enjoyed watching Littleton squirm, sitting next to the IRS attorney. Littleton was forced to hire his own lawyer, Robert Yates. Littleton was a fool but not fool enough to act as his own lawyer. Yet Yates was marginal at best.

Morty filed a federal lawsuit on behalf of Davis and the Plainview clients alleging that they were entitled to the Plainview settlement proceeds. It claimed that the court, in its discretion, should determine the portion to which Mr. Littleton was entitled under the contract and the Code of Professional Responsibility and that the IRS should be paid that amount and the balance released. The lawsuit named both Littleton and the IRS as defendants. Judge Wise expedited the hearing so the matter could be heard in weeks rather than a year. The judge understood that people were waiting on this money.

Every Plainview client was seated in the audience, as were other interested friends and family. Pierce, McCoy, Stevenson, and their clients, Pinsly and Davenport, made an appearance. They were there for the show.

It was a large courtroom, but with all the players it was crowded. Bella was seated in the first row, saving Sammie a seat. Sammie was circulating among the clients, trying to calm them down. Davis assured them that after this hearing, their funds should be released.

Davis was glaring at Pierce when Dr. English and Dr. Herman entered the courtroom. English waved hello to Davis and Morty. Davis turned to Morty and indicated that he would like to give English the finger but decorum stopped him. *It might be worth it, though,* he thought.

Judge Wise walked into the room, and his clerk announced, "Benjamin Davis et al. vs. the Internal Revenue Service and Bradley Littleton."

Judge Wise sat as everyone else stood. He smiled at Morty. "Mr. Steine, are you ready to proceed?"

"Yes, sir."

"Are the defendants ready to proceed?"

Both Yates and Lee of the IRS responded affirmatively.

Morty walked over to the podium and began, "It was my distinct honor to act as second chair to Mr. Davis in the Plainview lawsuits. Prior to the settlement of eight cases in late August, the parties settled one case and tried another to judgment.

"Mr. Littleton played a very minor role in the Plainview cases. He did not take any of the 146 depositions. Mr. Littleton breached his contract and failed to advance any portion of the $284,000 of expenses. At the two-week-long Malone trial, Mr. Littleton presented one witness, the paramedic."

Morty asked if he could hand the court Littleton's direct examination. Wise took five minutes to read the examination. At one point, Davis thought that Wise was smiling.

Wise asked Morty to continue.

"In fairness to Mr. Littleton, he did attend the meeting where Mr. Davis initially signed up the clients. After that, he was more of a problem than a solution. I would like to mark Mr. Littleton's direct examination of the paramedic at the Malone trial as Exhibit 1. I would also like to mark the contracts with the Plainview clients as collective Exhibit 2."

Each contract was only two pages.

The judge broke in, "Mr. Steine, are all the contracts with the clients identical?"

"Yes, sir, the attorneys are required to advance expenses. Littleton failed to advance his share of more than $70,000. I submit as collective Exhibit 3 four letters from Mr. Davis demanding payment of Littleton's share of expenses."

The judge took several minutes to review the documents. "Does your firm have any time records?"

"Yes, Mr. Davis had 2,420 hours from July 1992 to date. I have spent 1,879 hours. Sammie Davis, our paralegal, spent 1,823, and Bella Rosario, our legal secretary, spent 567 hours. A total of about 6,700 hours over a 31-month period."

Morty handed Wise a document with the supporting hours of each member of the Davis team listed on a monthly basis. There was a monthly total, an annual total, and a total number of hours from July 1992 till November 14th, 1994.

Judge Wise was looking at the document and asked, "What do you base these summary numbers on, Mr. Steine?"

Morty pulled a box from underneath the table. "These are the daily time tickets maintained by the firm over the last 31 months. Each time ticket reflects who did the work, what was done, and how long that task took. They total 6,689 hours."

The judge made the summary sheets collective Exhibit 4, but told Morty to put the box back under the table. He took his word on the details.

"Mr. Davis took all of the risk in these contingency cases. Despite Mr. Littleton's obligation to advance more than $70,000, he failed to do so. Mr. Davis advanced the full $284,000. Despite his ethical obligation to perform one-third of the work, Mr. Littleton did almost nothing. Littleton did less than one percent. Mr. Davis gave him every opportunity to perform, but I submit that Littleton was incompetent and lazy. Even after his obligation was reduced from one-third to twenty-five percent, he continued to fail to perform.

"I propose to this court that the court enter an order that does the following:

"Release to the Plainview clients their portion of the proceeds in accordance with the settlement sheets filed with the court;

Reimburse Benjamin Davis the $284,000 he advanced in the Plainview cases;

Judicially amend the contract between Davis and Littleton and divide the legal fees earned in the Plainview cases ninety-five percent to Mr. Davis and five percent to Mr. Littleton. Such a division would be consistent with the rules of our Code of Professional Responsibility;

Order that Mr. Littleton's reduced portion of the legal fees in the Plainview cases be paid to the IRS and that the IRS lien on the Plainview settlement proceeds be dissolved."

Morty sat down, and Mr. Lee of the IRS took the podium.

Before Lee could begin, Judge Wise asked, "Mr. Lee, how did the IRS learn about the Plainview settlements, and how did the IRS happen to be waiting for Mr. Littleton at the high school to serve him?"

"Your Honor, Mr. McCoy and Ms. Pierce contacted my office and made me aware that a settlement conference was taking place at Plainview High School. I had been monitoring the Plainview cases and was aware of the Malone verdict because I knew that Mr. Littleton, who owed the government $250,000, would eventually earn a fee. I dispatched Marshal Rothschild to serve Mr. Littleton and Mr. Davis."

Lee explained that he contacted McCoy and Pierce and requested their help in collecting Littleton's fee for the government. "They seemed very patriotic, wanting to help their government."

Davis muttered to Morty: "I bet they were."

"Ms. Pierce faxed me the style of each case and the date, time, and location of the settlement conference. With that information, the IRS could be waiting for Mr. Littleton at the high school after the settlement was consummated. I spoke twice, once with Mr. McCoy and Ms. Pierce, during the settlement conference, getting progress reports as to the status of the settlement. At some point, Mr. McCoy called me and told me it was a done deal. They were working on the paperwork, and Mr. Littleton would be leaving the high school within the hour."

Judge Wise asked McCoy and Pierce to approach the bench. McCoy turned the same shade of red as his bow tie, and Pierce looked weak in the knees.

"Mr. McCoy and Ms. Pierce, has Mr. Lee correctly described your dealings with the IRS as they relate to the notice of lien and the Plainview settlements?"

Neither of them responded.

"I'll ask you one more time. Is what has been described on the record accurate?"

McCoy said weakly, "For the most part."

"What parts are not accurate, or do you want to add something else that you consider relevant?"

"We thought we were helping our government collect tax dollars owed."

"Excuse me? Do I need to put you under oath? You and Ms. Pierce did this to get revenge and to tie up the Plainview settlements. You're both officers of this court and the Plains County court. You misled Mr. Davis, Mr. Steine, and Mr. Littleton into believing that you were negotiating in good faith. Under Rule 408 of both the Tennessee Rules of Evidence and the Federal Rules and the settlement agreement, you were obligated to keep your negotiations confidential. You kept the IRS abreast of your negotiations. In fact, immediately after your clients signed the settlement agreements with the Plainview plaintiffs, you turned around and disclosed those settlements to the IRS. Did Mr. Stevenson or Mr. Barnes have anything to do with your dealings with the IRS?"

Stevenson jumped up and almost ran to the podium to protest, "I had no knowledge of any of this. I am ignorant of these communications with the IRS."

"Lucky for you, Grayson. Mr. McCoy, was Mr. Barnes involved?"

"No, sir."

"Mr. McCoy and Ms. Pierce, please be advised that I am bringing both of you up on disciplinary charges before the Board of Professional Responsibility for your mishandling of the Plainview settlement and your communications with the IRS. I will copy all counsel of record and Judge Boxer of my letter of complaint to the board.

"Mr. Yates, does your client have any time records evidencing his time expended in the Plainview cases?"

"No, sir."

"Does he dispute that there were 146 depositions and that he didn't take any of the depositions?"

Yates consulted with Littleton and responded: "That sounds about right."

"How many of those depositions did your client attend?"

Yates consulted again. "About twenty."

Morty stood up and advised the court that the correct number based upon the record was seven. Littleton squirmed in his seat at being confronted with his exaggeration.

"I will be issuing a written opinion in the next day or so. But I am following Mr. Steine's recommendations. The funds will be released to the Plainview plaintiffs. Mr. Davis will be reimbursed his advanced expenses. Mr. Littleton's fee is reduced from the amended twenty-five percent to five percent and is awarded to the IRS, and the IRS lien is removed. This order will be effective upon signing, and if appealed by the IRS, an injunction will be denied and the funds will be released."

The noise level in the courtroom rose dramatically as the spectators reacted. Judge Wise banged his gavel so hard that it broke and the top portion flew into the middle of the courtroom.

"One last matter. I received in the mail the affidavit of Ms. Johnston, the custodian of records of the Plainview Community Hospital, recanting her deposition and trial testimony in the Malone case. She now claims that between her two testimonies, the slides were destroyed by the hospital. I've turned this matter over to the US attorney's office for federal prosecution. Let the chips fall where they may."

With that said, Wise left the bench.

Davis turned to Morty: "I didn't see that one coming, did you?"

"Remember our motto, 'Always try to do the right thing.'"

"Well, we share that philosophy with a country lawyer from Hewes City, who has the same sense of right and wrong."

Jack Barnes was standing in the back of the courtroom, not at the defense table. He had secured Ms. Johnston's affidavit admitting her perjury and revealed the conspiracy to destroy evidence to Judge Wise. Justice would eventually be served.

EPILOGUE

FRIDAY, JULY 16, 2010

(MORE THAN 15 YEARS LATER)

Davis enjoyed riding with the top down. He had owned many convertibles over the years, but his 2006 black Bentley was by far his favorite. Although it was four years old, the engine purred, and the car was in pristine condition. Davis's longish gray hair blew in the wind as he drove. It was overcast so he did not have to wear a baseball cap to avoid burning the top of his head where his hair was more than beginning to thin.

Davis slowed the car and took the next exit because Sammie needed a restroom. After she left the car, Davis went to the drive-through at Starbucks and got each of them a double espresso for the seventy-five-minute drive to the Davenport County Courthouse.

This would be Sammie's hearing. Davis promised her, and she insisted, that he would keep his big mouth shut. In a strange way, Davis felt calm and confident. Sammie, no question, was a dynamic trial attorney. She was bright and hardworking with a commanding presence in the courtroom.

When she arrived in Nashville as a twenty-four-year-old, she was beautiful, but now she had matured and grown into her looks. She had no problem keeping a jury's attention.

Davis did for Sammie what Morty had done for him.

It was Morty, though, who put her through Vanderbilt Law School after Plainview. She worked summers at the firm and worked her way up to Davis's partner.

At eighty-nine, Morty lived on his farm with a thirty-year-younger female companion. Davis tried to visit every other Sunday, and in good weather, the old friends went fishing.

Davis, who had been daydreaming about the old man, swerved.

Sammie yelled, "Where are you? I need you to focus. You may have to take the stand and testify. A motion for sanctions is no joking matter. As you have told me at least a hundred times, 'Don't underestimate your adversary.'"

Annoyed, Davis thought, *There is nothing worse than having yourself quoted to yourself.*

"I'm ready. This motion for Rule 11 is bullshit. The motion doesn't even cite any case law to support the disciplinary action sought against me. My only concern is that I don't know the judge, and more important, he doesn't know me. That's the real problem."

Sammie acknowledged that Davis was right. Davis had brought a legal malpractice lawsuit against a prominent Nashville attorney who was a partner in a prestigious law firm. Davis alleged that the attorney had not only been negligent but also lied under oath and committed fraud on the client.

Davis even took the attorney's deposition, prior to filing suit, to afford the attorney an opportunity to explain any possible misunderstanding. Instead, the lawyer outright lied in his deposition and went so far as to misrepresent that he never represented Davis's client. Davis, during the deposition, confronted the lawyer-witness with five transactions in which the attorney had either represented Davis's client or a company owned by his client. He didn't file suit until he was convinced that the attorney was a liar.

The lawsuit alleged that the attorney, Ronald Defoe, had represented all four businessmen in the same transaction. The complaint alleged that the joint representation was an ethical violation and was negligent, that the attorney acted for the benefit of one client to the detriment of another, and that the attorney participated in a scheme to defraud one of his clients.

They were serious charges against a member of the Bar, but Davis was convinced that the allegations were true. The closing statement revealed that the legal fees paid to the attorney's law firm, Goodman, Defoe, and Smith, were charged to the defrauded client only.

The answer filed by Defoe and his firm alleged that Davis filed a false pleading and that under Rule 11, Davis should be disciplined. Davis, by that time, had practiced law for more than thirty years. It was only the second time he was accused of unethical conduct and a violation of Rule 11. Twice in thirty-one years was not a bad record. The first time he was charged, the court dismissed the motion as frivolous. Now Davis was once again wrongly accused of filing a false pleading. The defendants were trying to turn the tables on Davis and put him on the defensive.

Unfortunately, Goodman, Defoe, and Smith was the third largest law firm in Nashville, with more than ninety lawyers, and its members regularly appeared before all of the judges in Nashville and the surrounding counties. No local court could hear the case. So Davis, by motion, asked the Tennessee Supreme

Court to appoint an unrelated and unbiased judge to hear the case. This appropriate and reasonable request was granted. However, the defendant law firm was very powerful in the state and had friends everywhere. Davis was well known for his ability but never bothered to play the political games that were necessary in Tennessee.

The Supreme Court appointed Judge J. B. Locke of Davenport County as special judge. Sammie made some phone calls and determined that Judge Locke had been on the bench for three years, he was a Republican, and he represented small rural banks, mostly doing transactional work and simple litigation. He was said to be bright and diligently read what was filed with the court.

Both Sammie and Davis thought Locke was a good selection since the documents filed with the court clearly showed that Davis, by taking the deposition of Defoe, did a good faith investigation before filing the complaint. If the judge actually read the three-hundred-page deposition and looked at the twelve exhibits, he would exonerate Davis and eventually rule that Defoe and his law firm breached the standard of care by representing multiple parties—an obvious conflict of interest.

Davis pulled the Bentley convertible into a parking space in the courthouse square. Sammie checked in with the court clerk to confirm that no additional pleadings were filed in the last two days. She also confirmed that her case was first on the docket. This was a courtesy because all of the attorneys were from out of town.

The courtroom was on the third floor of the two-hundred-year-old courthouse. When they entered the courtroom, Davis was impressed with the oak furnishings and its historical presence. Behind the bench were both the Stars and Stripes and the Tennessee state flag.

Two motions were scheduled to be heard: the motion for sanctions against Davis and a motion for summary judgment to dismiss the case against Defoe and his firm. Sammie would handle both motions.

The bailiff came in and announced in open court: "Oyez, oyez, the Circuit Court of Davenport County is open to conduct business. Stand ready to plead your case. The Honorable J. B. Locke presiding. Please rise and you will be heard."

Everyone in the courtroom rose, and Judge Locke entered the room from behind the bench. He was younger than Davis expected, probably in his early forties. The bailiff called the first case, and Sammie and Davis moved to counsel's table while John Peters, another Nashville attorney who was representing the defendants, moved to the other.

Defoe took his seat next to Peters. Several attorneys from the defendant law firm were in the audience. After the attorneys got settled in at their respective tables, Judge Locke took control of his courtroom.

"Ms. Davis and gentlemen, before we begin this hearing, I have an important disclosure I must make. I don't think it will require my recusal, but I feel compelled to make this disclosure. Mr. Davis may not recall, but he and I have worked closely together before."

Davis was perplexed. *I have no recollection of working either as co-counsel with or as adversary counsel against Judge Locke when he was a member of the Bar.*

Sammie whispered to Davis, "What's he talking about? I hope you treated him well. We don't need him taking revenge on you today."

Davis was dumbfounded. He didn't remember the judge, even as a lawyer. But Davis knew if they had dealings, he tried to do the right thing.

The judge could read confusion on their faces, so he said, "I'm hurt you do not remember me. I certainly remember both of you."

Now both Sammie and Davis were nervous. Neither of them could place prior dealings with the judge. Davis looked over at Peters, who was relishing the fact that both Davises were uncomfortable.

The judge waited for a response, and when neither Davis spoke, he continued, "Almost twenty years ago, as a young lawyer, I sat on a jury in which Mr. Davis was one of the attorneys."

The judge smiled, and Davis and Sammie relaxed.

Davis rose and addressed the court: "Your Honor, in my more than thirty years practicing law, I have only allowed one attorney to sit on my juries, and that was the Plainview malpractice cases. Your first name is Jason, isn't it?"

The judge smiled again. "I had taken the Bar exam but not gotten the results. If I remember correctly, that trial lasted about two weeks. I learned more watching you in that trial than I did in my three years of law school. Sitting on that jury and being part of those deliberations were some of the more educational experiences of my legal career. Even today, as a judge, I don't get the same insight of how a jury operates as I did as foreman of that jury."

Davis also remembered the Plainview cases but not as fondly as Judge Locke did. He would never forget the beating, the threats, the fights with Liza, and his near bankruptcy. His shoulder, depending on the weather, still gave him fits sometimes.

He readily admitted that he met some snakes and some wonderful people during that period of his life. The Medical Licensing Board's punishment of Dr. Herman had been a fine and a one-year suspension, with his license reinstated after a US residency. Once qualified to practice, he managed to find a position in a tiny town in northwest Tennessee with an older doctor nearing retirement. The older doctor served as his proctor according to the terms of his suspension. If he did well under the doctor's watchful eye, it would be possible for Herman to eventually buy the doctor's practice.

But Herman couldn't change his ways and stay out of trouble. In 2001, his license was again suspended for a year for gross misconduct. The Medical Licensing Board, after Herman met certain conditions, returned his license. He was currently serving a three-year suspension for overprescribing narcotics to drug-seeking patients. Davis wondered whether the Medical Licensing Board at Herman's next hearing would wake up and refuse to let him loose on the unsuspecting public. He doubted it.

Davis knew that Herman was no longer a threat. He felt the same way about the other defendants, but T-rex was still out there. Davis figured he was a hired gun and probably didn't have a vendetta, but he never stopped looking over his shoulder.

As for English, he had faded from sight, most likely moving from state to state, practicing where he could find a gullible hospital administration, and staying one step ahead of each state's board.

Then there was Dr. Patel, the woman who blew the whistle. Given his level of ineptitude, it was no surprise that Brad Littleton lost her case and the cases of the nurses formerly of Plainview Hospital. Laura, Maggie, and their daughters moved to Nashville shortly afterward. Laura often mailed photos of the girls to Bella and occasionally called her to say hello.

Back in the courtroom with Judge Locke, Peters realized that the judge was not going to award sanctions against Davis, whom he held in high esteem. The motion for sanctions was strategically dismissed by Peters, rather than let the judge deny it. Sammie and Peters argued the motion for summary judgment.

In his memorandum opinion issued two days after the hearing, the judge in a footnote compared the attorney's deposition testimony to that of the affidavit testimony of Davis's client and concluded that the testimonies were so diametrically opposite that someone had to be lying.

The next day, Davis settled the lawsuit for an even $1 million. The money was nice but secondary. Davis learned from Morty that success was measured not by dollars but by a sense of accomplishment. It was more important to stay true to Morty's motto, "Always try to do the right thing."

Davis was proud that he always tried.

ABOUT THE AUTHOR

A. Turk was born in 1954, in Brooklyn, New York, and he grew up on Long Island. He earned a BA from George Washington University, an MBA from the Vanderbilt Owen Graduate School of Business, and a JD from Vanderbilt School of Law. He was licensed to practice law in Tennessee in 1980. In 1983 he also was licensed, but never practiced, in New York because of a promise he made to his mother.

A. Turk for more than thirty years was a prominent Nashville attorney and a veteran of fighting courtroom battles. He garnered national media attention in 1994 when he won a unanimous US Supreme Court decision, which held that 2 Live Crew's parody of Roy Orbison's song "Pretty Woman" did not require a copyright license. With the support of NBC, HBO, Time Warner, *Mad Magazine,* and others, A. Turk won this landmark case preserving the right of commercial parody under the Fair Use Doctrine.

A. Turk recently retired to begin his second career as an author of courtroom dramas based upon his personal experiences. *First Do No Harm* is A. Turk's debut novel, where he introduces his fictitious alter ego, Benjamin Davis. The Benjamin Davis Book Series will explore and address the same legal issues and moral dilemmas that A. Turk faced during his legal career.

A. Turk has been married to his wife, Lisa, for thirty-three years, and they have two adult children, Jessica and Ben, as well as three pugs. A. Turk currently splits his time between Nashville, Aspen, and Highland Beach.

ACKNOWLEDGEMENTS

As a first-time author, I found the writing of *First Do No Harm* a rewarding and exciting experience, which I planned for almost twenty years. I approached the writing of the first draft of this manuscript with the same dedication and tenacity as I did preparing a case for trial. The process began the day after my retirement when I sat down to review the sixteen banker boxes that inspired *First Do No Harm.* I completed the first draft in three months, and it was very rough, to say the least. I knew that I needed help and the perspective of others. Fortunately, I found friends and strangers who came to my aid.

Over the next year, I held three separate focus groups of individuals who read the manuscript and then met with me at my home and discussed the strengths and weaknesses of my work, providing valuable feedback and insight. With each rewrite the manuscript improved. I would like to thank these focus group participants: Denise Alper, Amy Anderson, Robert Anderson, Gayle Brinkley, Brandon Bubis, Martin Bubis, Anita Dowdle, Doug Dowdle, Sharon Duncan, Amy Flynn, Charles Patrick Flynn, BJ Givens, Karen Goldsmith, Steve Goldsmith, Elliot Greenberg, David Kipp, Sharon Kipp, Jay Lefkovitz, Steve Lefkovitz, DeeAnn Melton, Paula Milam, Tom Milam, Scott Newman, Amy O'Hoyt, Wes Perry, Kristin Rosario, David Tiner, and Janina Tiner.

As a practicing attorney I appreciated the need to rely on experts to help me try my cases and convey my clients' stories. It was only reasonable that I'd do the same as an author. I would like to thank Mary Buckner, Barry Goldsmith, and especially Dimples Kellogg for their editorial review and assistance.

The writing of *First Do No Harm* was not a solo project. My daughter, Jessica Turk, was my collaborator throughout the process. I love her and thank her for her contribution.

First Do No Harm is only the beginning of the Benjamin Davis Series. I intend to share other fictionalized accounts of my thirty years of experiences as a practicing attorney.

A. Turk